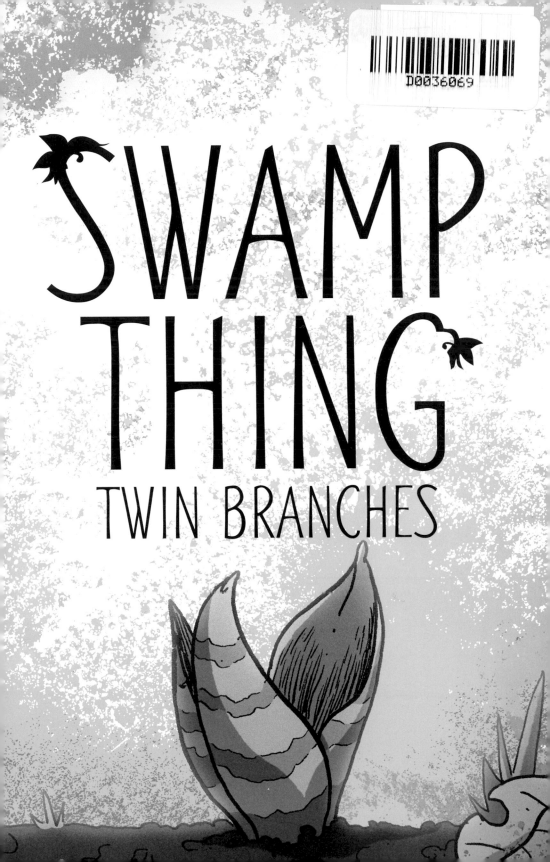

SWAMP THING
TWIN BRANCHES

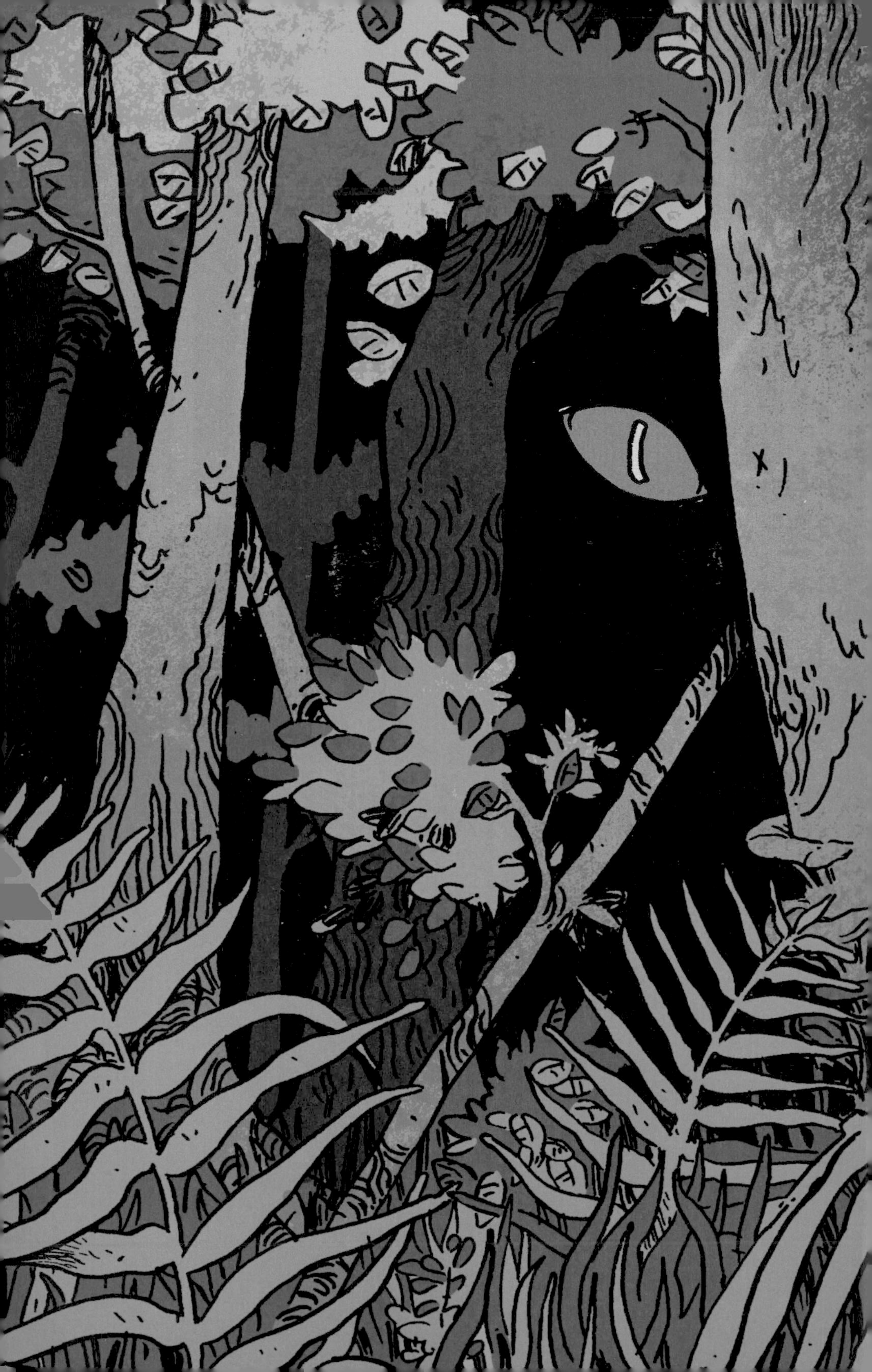

SWAMP THING

TWIN BRANCHES

Written by
Maggie Stiefvater

Illustrated by
Morgan Beem

Letters by
Ariana Maher

Swamp Thing created by
Len Wein and Bernie Wrightson

Alex R. Carr Editor
Diego Lopez Associate Editor
Steve Cook Design Director – Books
Louis Prandi Publication Design

Bob Harras Senior VP – Editor-in-Chief, DC Comics
Michele R. Wells VP & Executive Editor, Young Reader

Jim Lee Publisher & Chief Creative Officer
Bobbie Chase VP – Global Publishing Initiatives & Digital Strategy
Don Falletti VP – Manufacturing Operations & Workflow Management
Lawrence Ganem VP – Talent Services
Alison Gill Senior VP – Manufacturing & Operations
Hank Kanalz Senior VP – Publishing Strategy & Support Services
Dan Miron VP – Publishing Operations
Nick J. Napolitano VP – Manufacturing Administration & Design
Nancy Spears VP – Sales
Jonah Weiland VP – Marketing & Creative Services

SWAMP THING: TWIN BRANCHES

DC Comics, 2900 West Alameda Ave., Burbank, CA 91505. Printed by LSC Communications, Crawfordsville, IN, USA. 9/4/20. First Printing. ISBN: 978-1-4012-9323-9.

Library of Congress Cataloging-in-Publication Data

Names: Stiefvater, Maggie, 1981- writer. | Beem, Morgan, illustrator. | Lawson, Jeremy (Cartoonist), colourist. | Maher, Ariana, letterer.
Title: Swamp thing : twin branches / written by Maggie Stiefvater ; illustrated by Morgan Beem ; colors by Jeremy Lawson ; letters by Ariana Maher.
Description: Burbank, CA : DC Comics, [2020] | "Swamp Thing created by Len Wein and Bernie Wrightson" | Audience: Ages 15+ | Audience: Grades 10-12 | Summary: "Twins Alec and Walker Holland have a reputation around town. One is quiet and the other is the life of any party, but the two are inseparable. For their last summer before college, Alec and Walker leave the city to live with their rural cousins, where they find that the swamp holds far darker depths than they could have imagined. While Walker carves their names into the new social scene, Alec recedes into a summer-school laboratory, slowly losing himself to a deep, dark experiment. This season, both brothers must confront truths, ancient and familial, and as their lives diverge, tensions increase and dormant memories claw to the surface"-- Provided by publisher.
Identifiers: LCCN 2020022146 (print) | LCCN 2020022147 (ebook) | ISBN 9781401293239 (paperback) | ISBN 9781779506399 (ebook)
Subjects: LCSH: Graphic novels. | Graphic novels. | CYAC: Science--Experiments--Fiction. | Twins--Fiction. | Memory--Fiction. | Science fiction.
Classification: LCC PZ7.7.S7496 Sw 2020 (print) | LCC PZ7.7.S7496 (ebook) | DDC 741.5/973--dc23
LC record available at https://lccn.loc.gov/2020022146
LC ebook record available at https://lccn.loc.gov/2020022147

PEFC Certified
This product is from sustainably managed forests and controlled sources
PEFC
PEFC/29-31-337
www.pefc.org

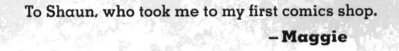

To Shaun, who took me to my first comics shop.

– Maggie

To my parents, Cliff and Kristi, without whom I
would have no roots to hold me up. And to Jorge,
for being the light I need to grow tall.

– Morgan

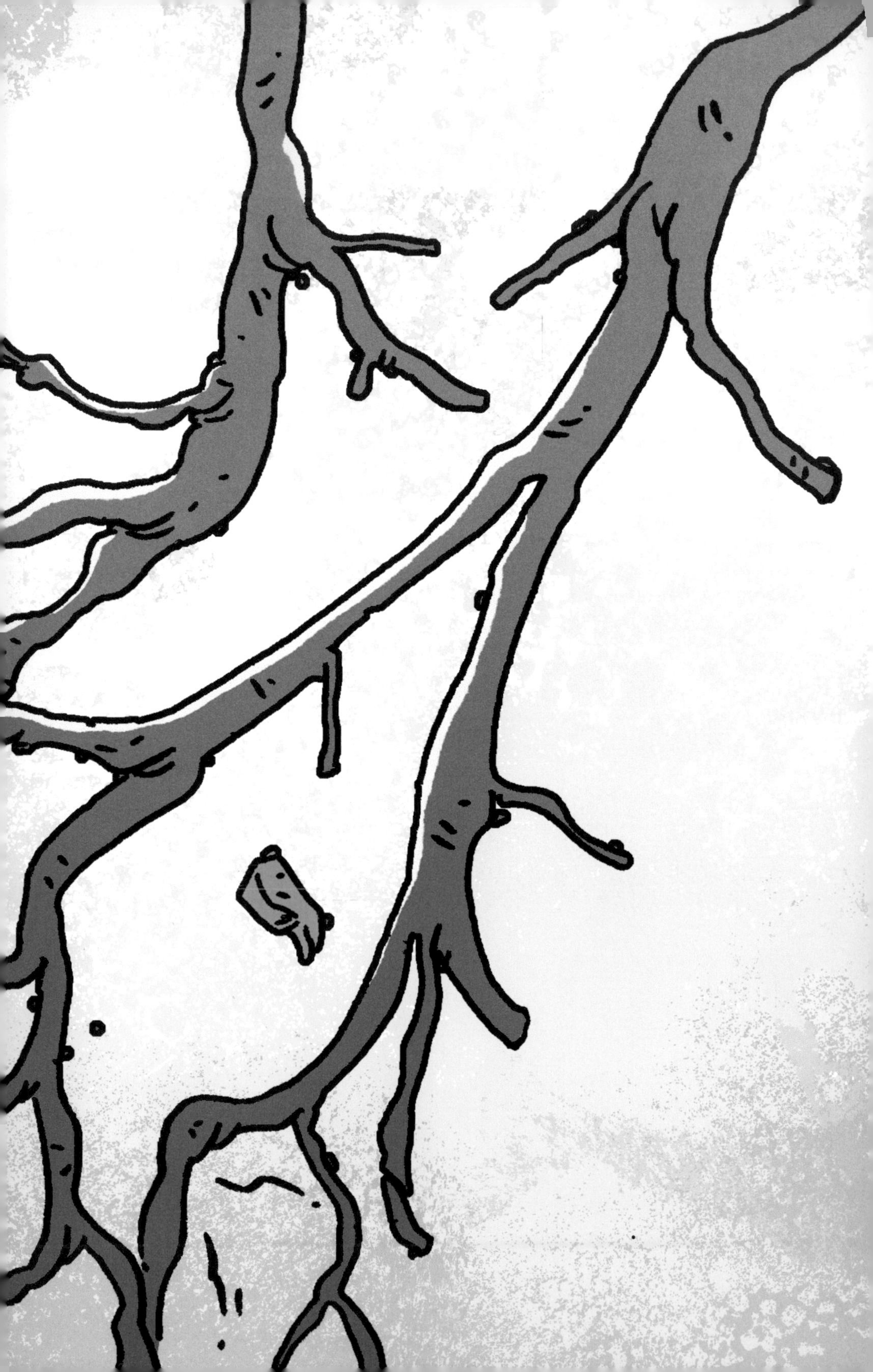

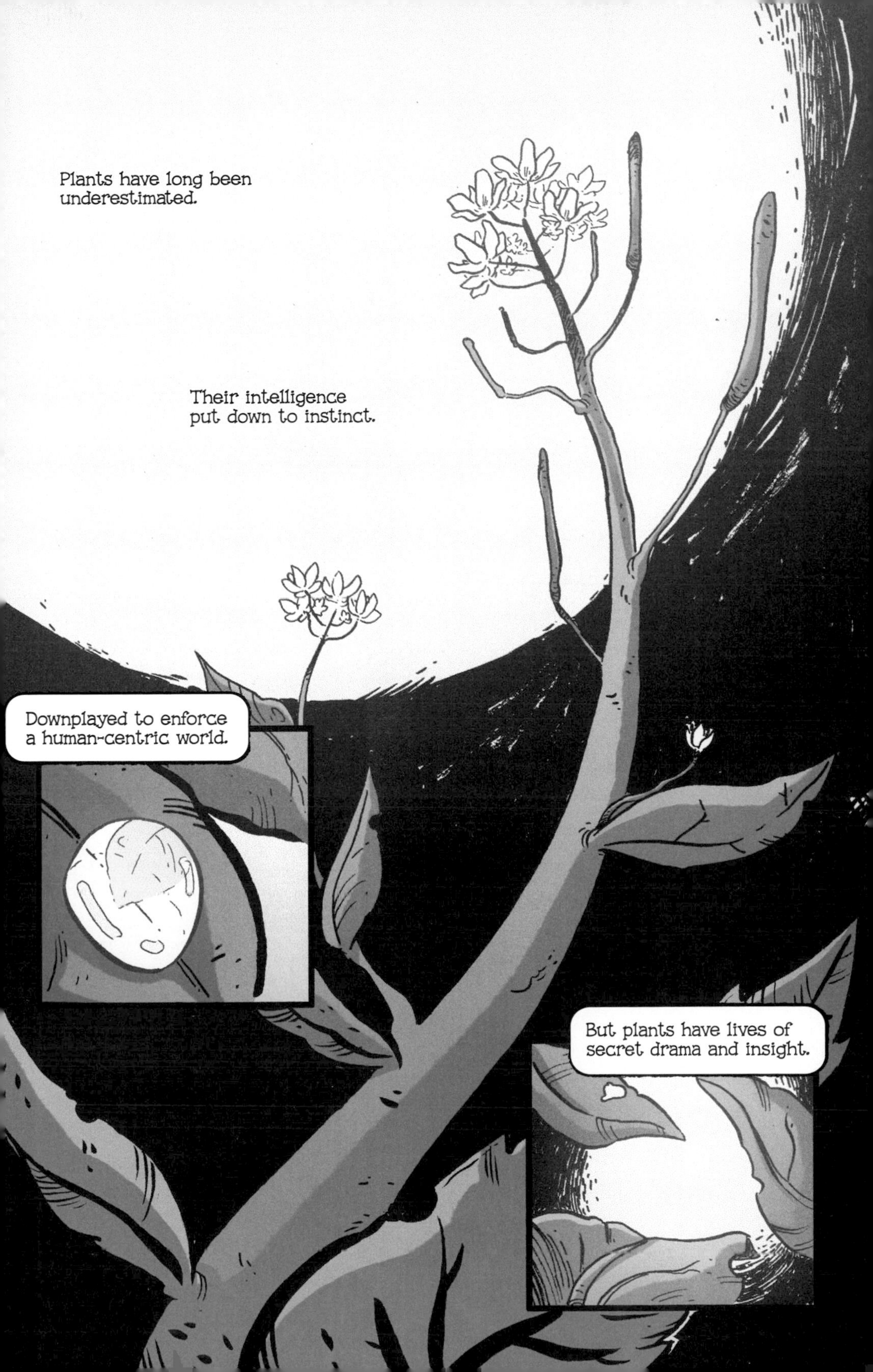
Plants have long been underestimated.
Their intelligence put down to instinct.
Downplayed to enforce a human-centric world.
But plants have lives of secret drama and insight.

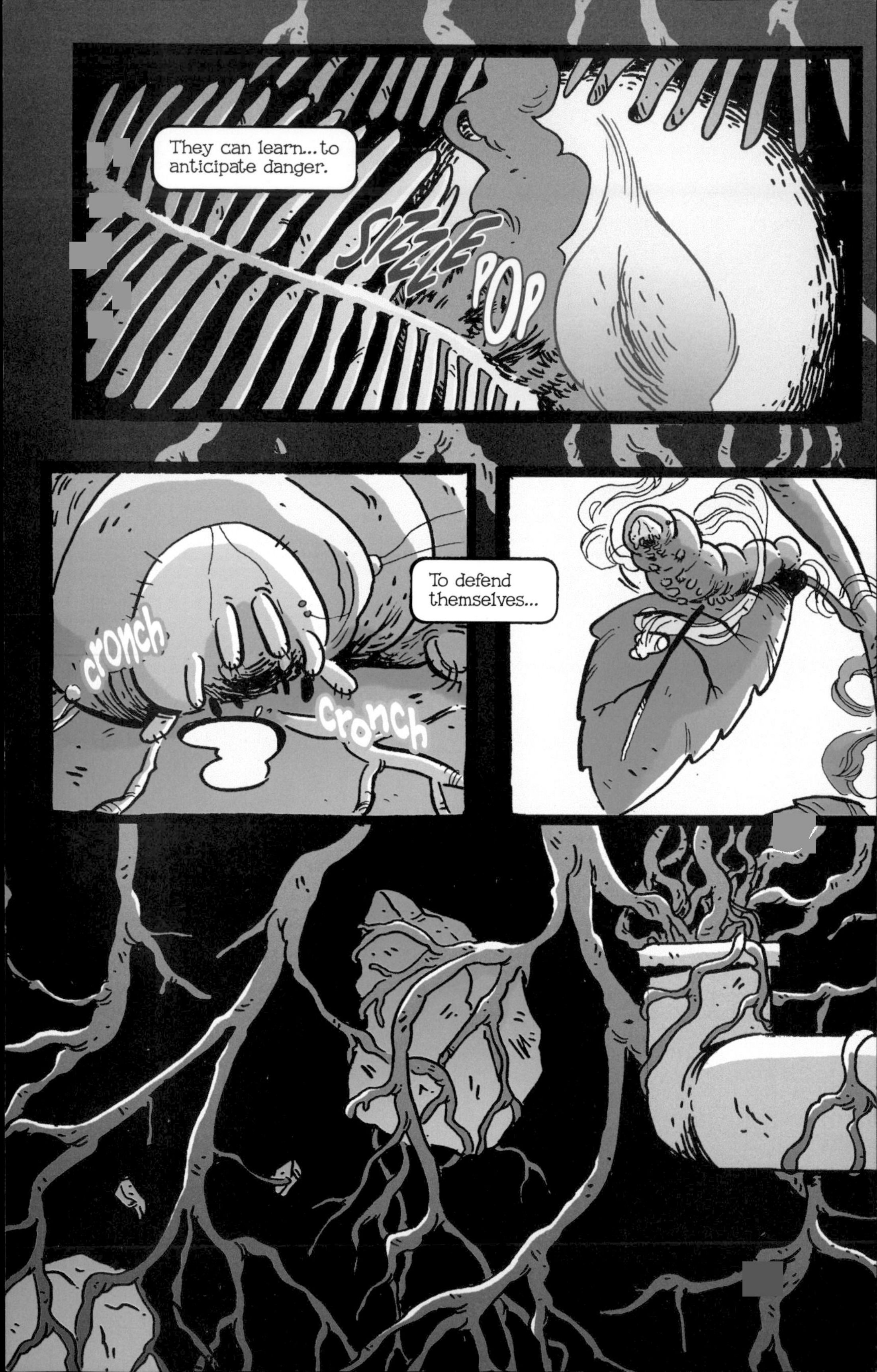
They can learn... to anticipate danger.
SIZZLE
POP
cronch
cronch
To defend themselves...

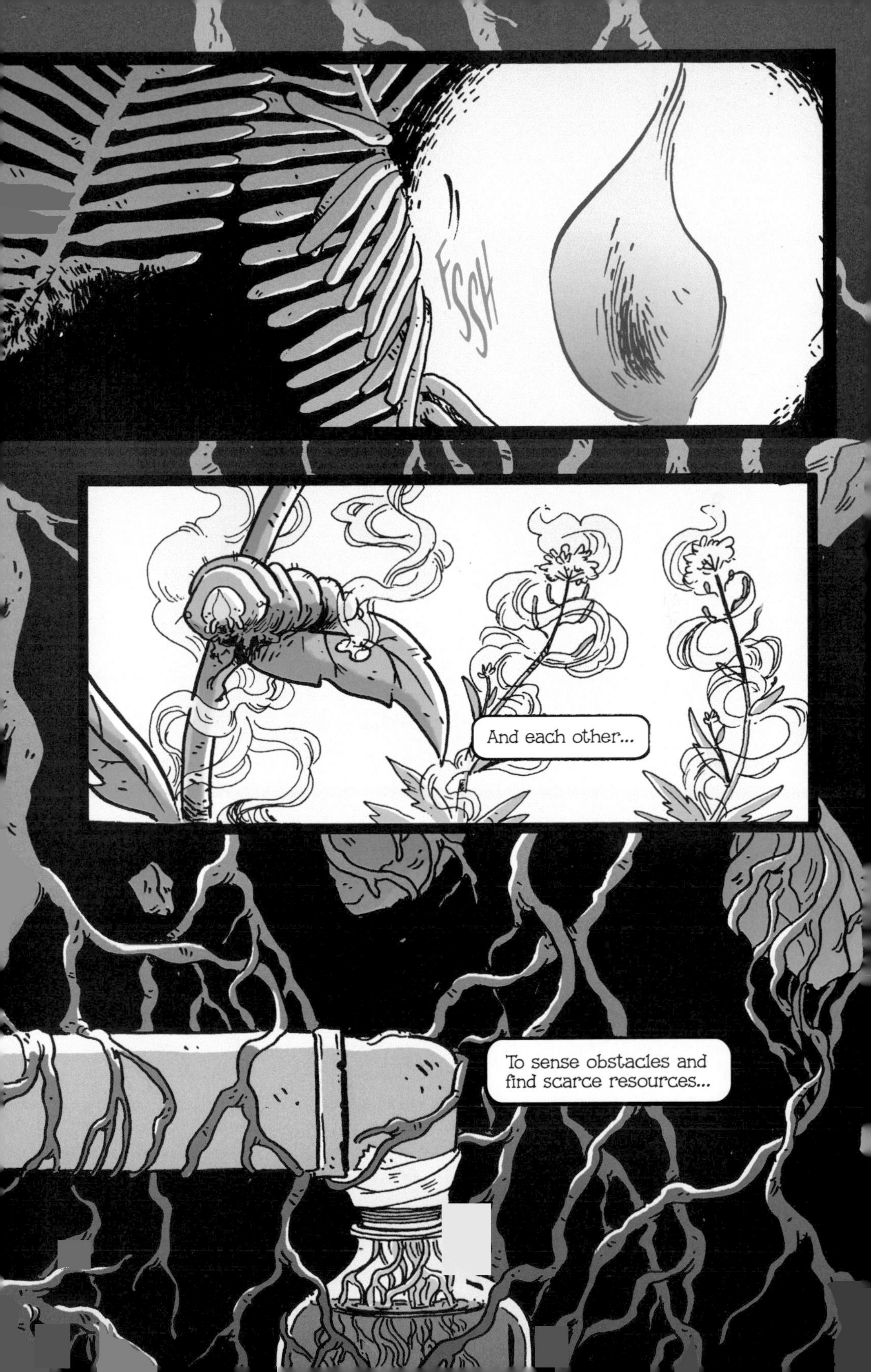
FSSH
And each other...
To sense obstacles and find scarce resources...

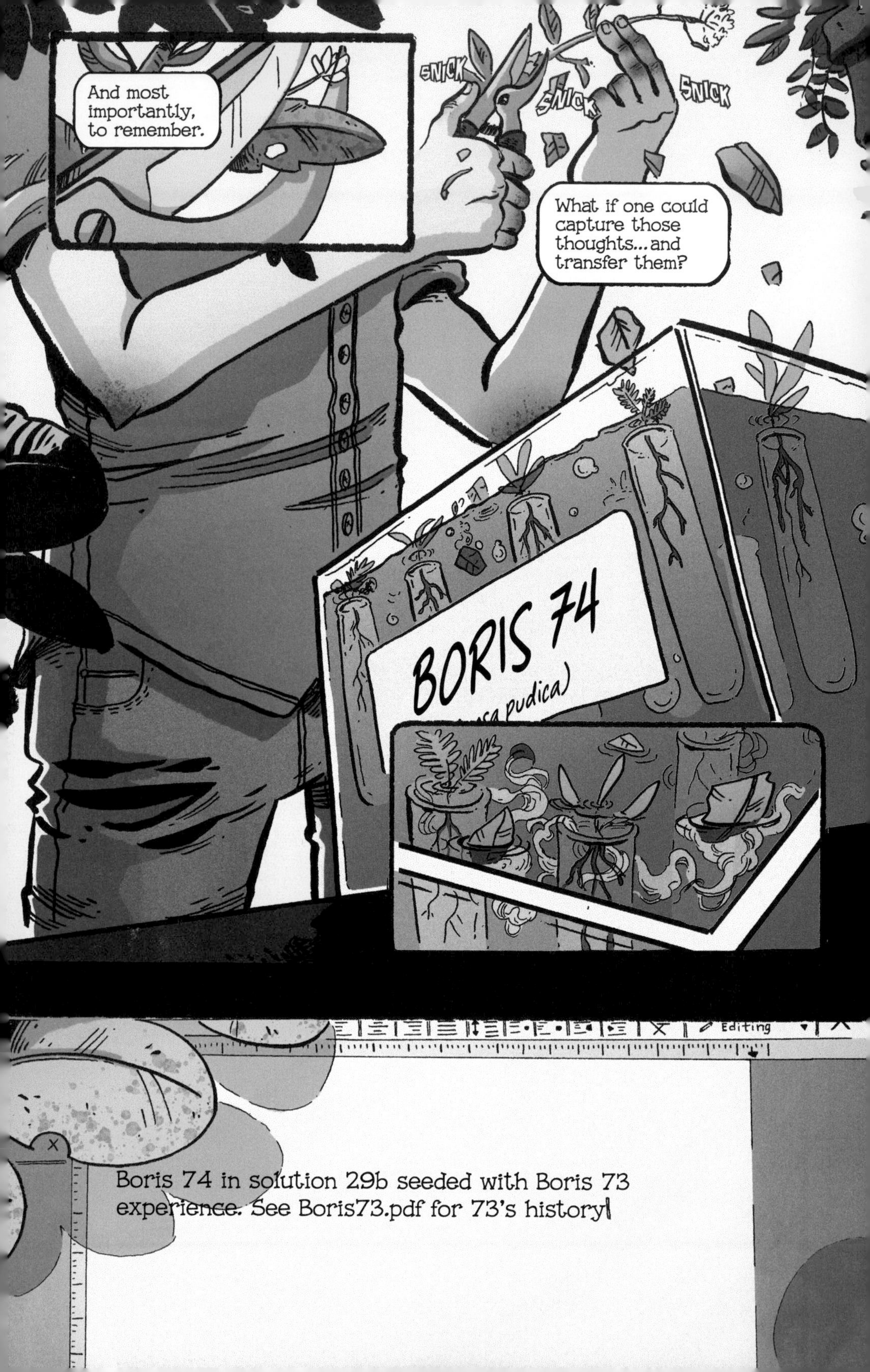
And most importantly, to remember.
SNICK
SNICK
SNICK
What if one could capture those thoughts...and transfer them?
BORIS 74
pudica)
Editing
Boris 74 in solution 29b seeded with Boris 73 experience. See Boris73.pdf for 73's history

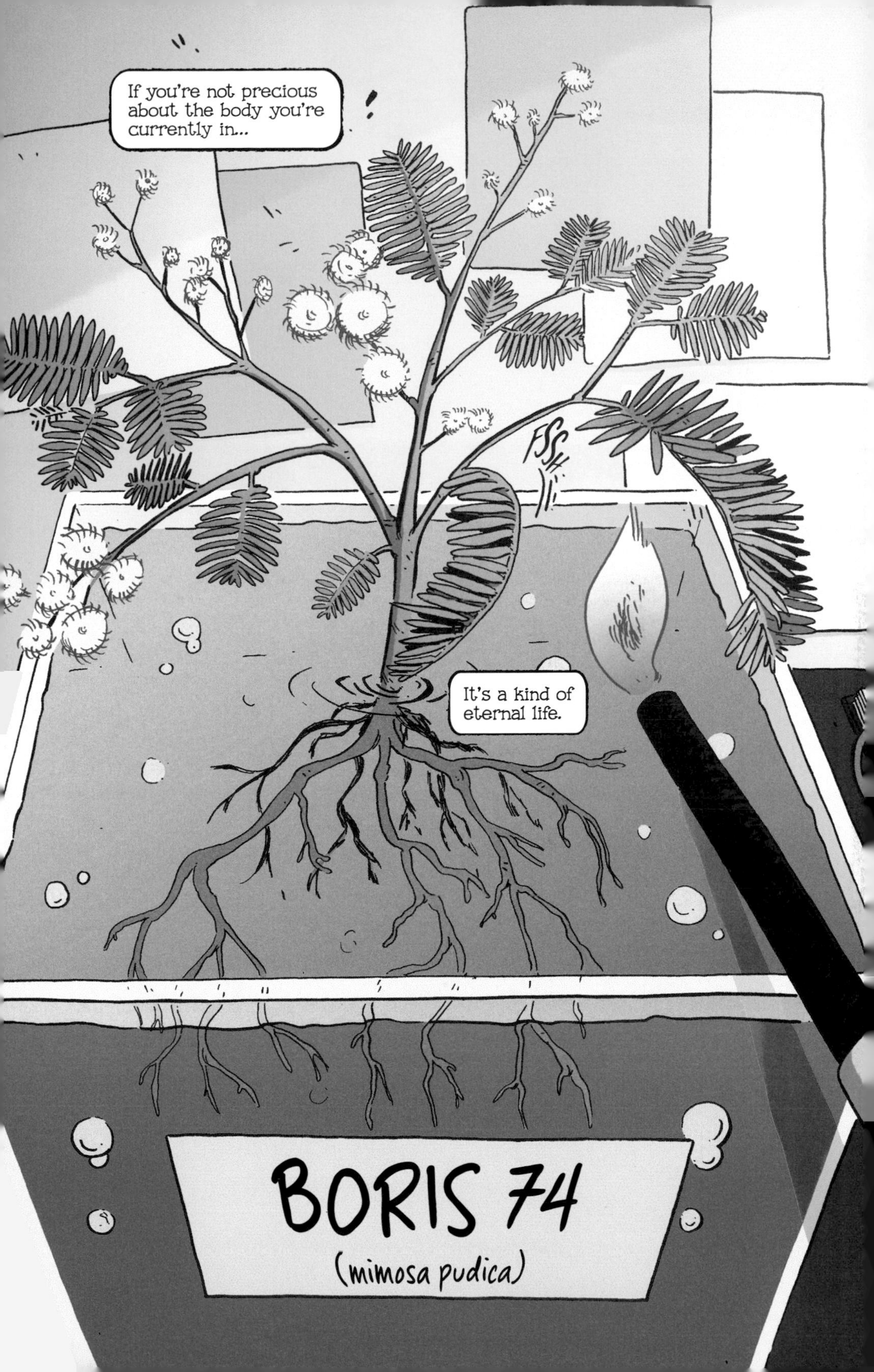
If you're not precious about the body you're currently in...
FSSH
It's a kind of eternal life.
BORIS 74
(mimosa pudica)

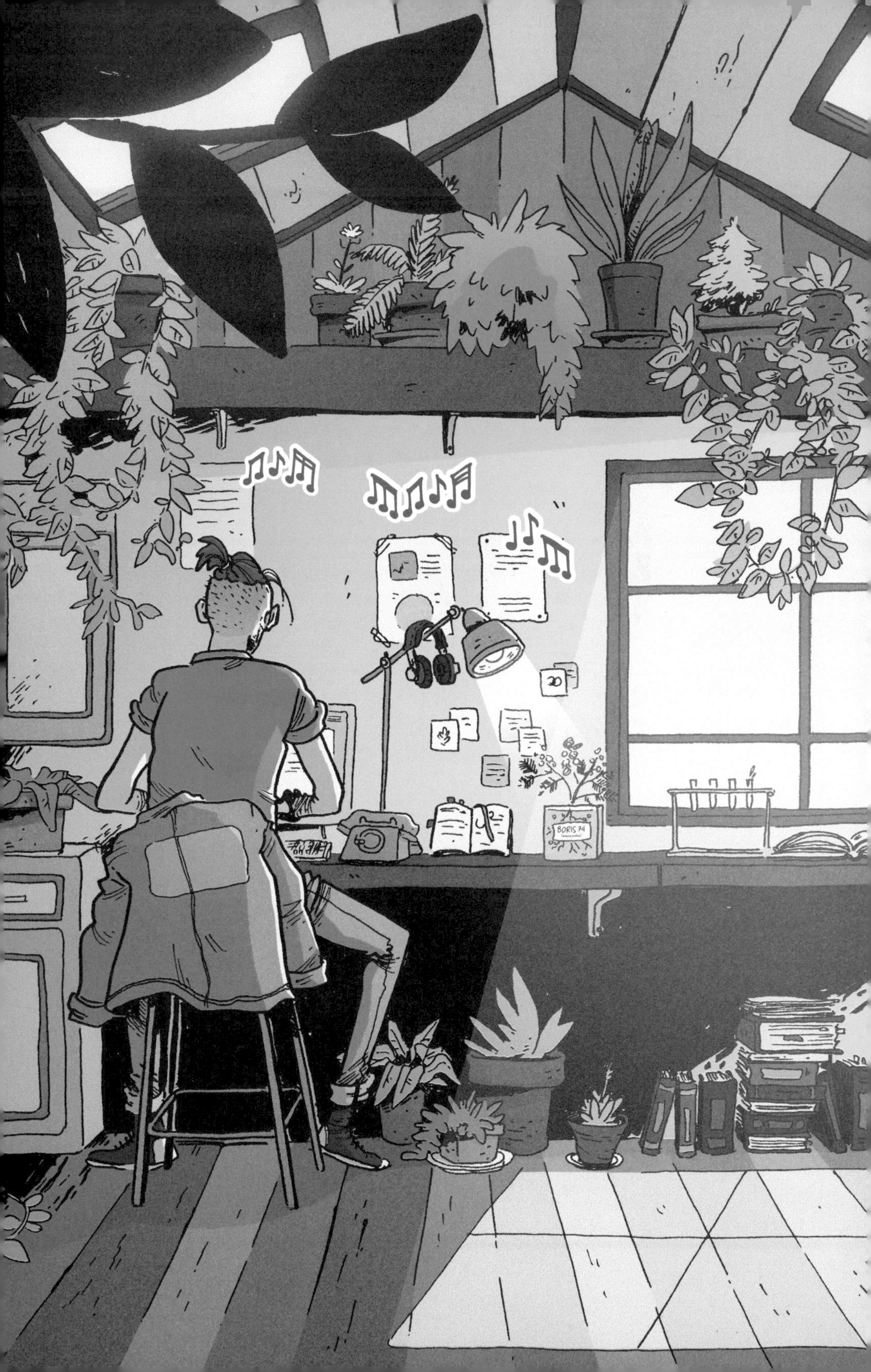
BORIS 74

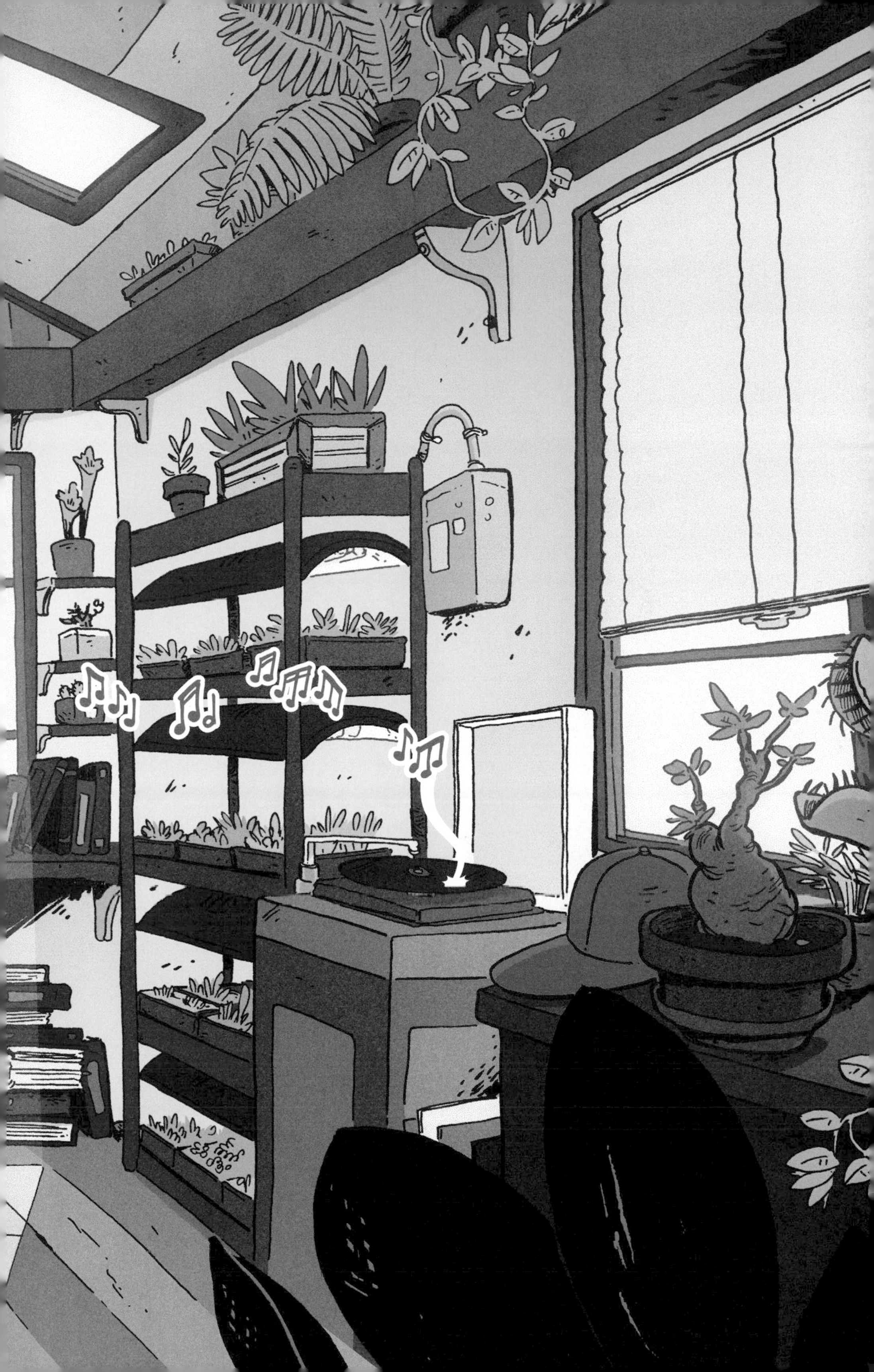

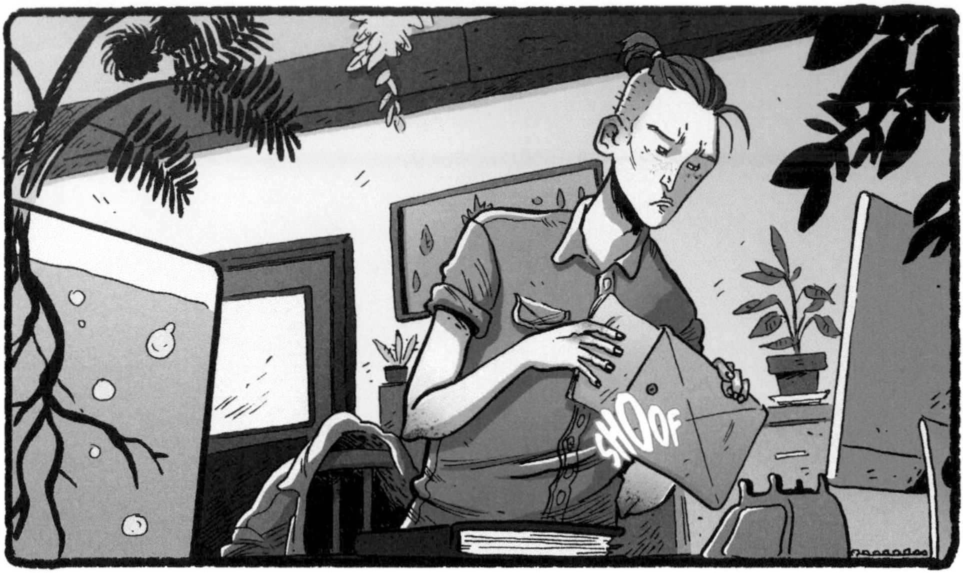
SHOOF

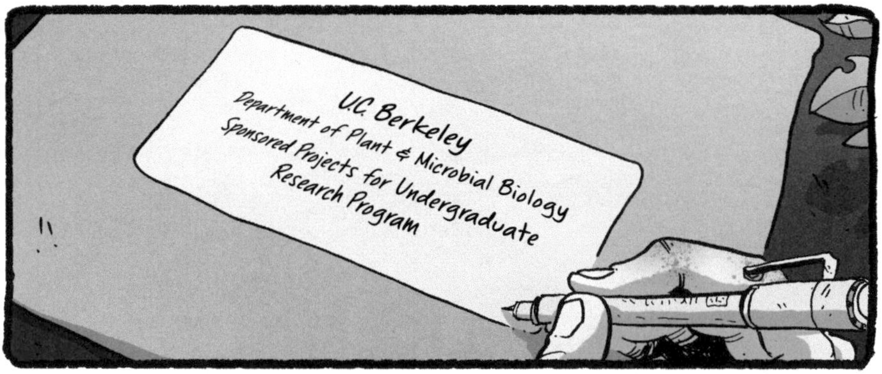
U.C. Berkeley
Department of Plant & Microbial Biology
Sponsored Projects for Undergraduate
Research Program

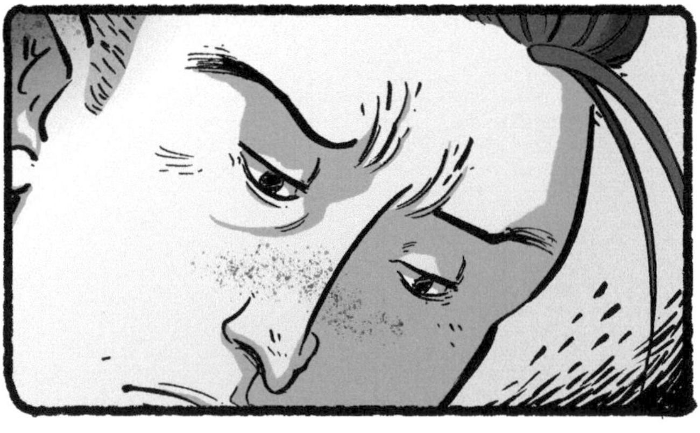

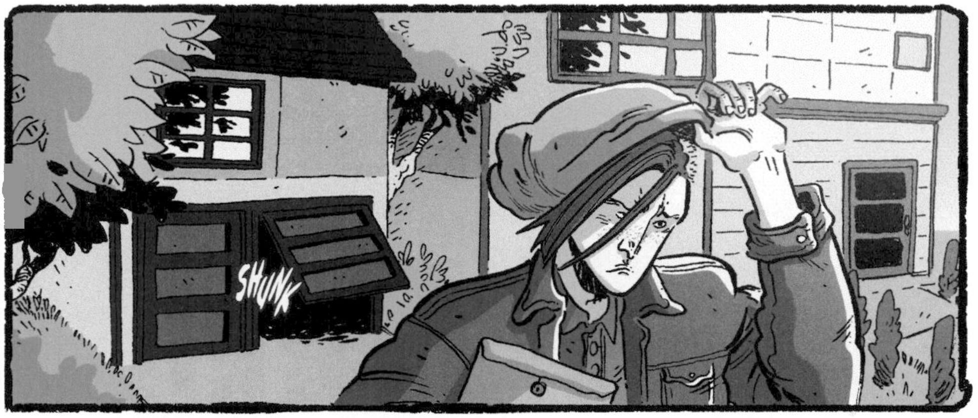
SHUNK

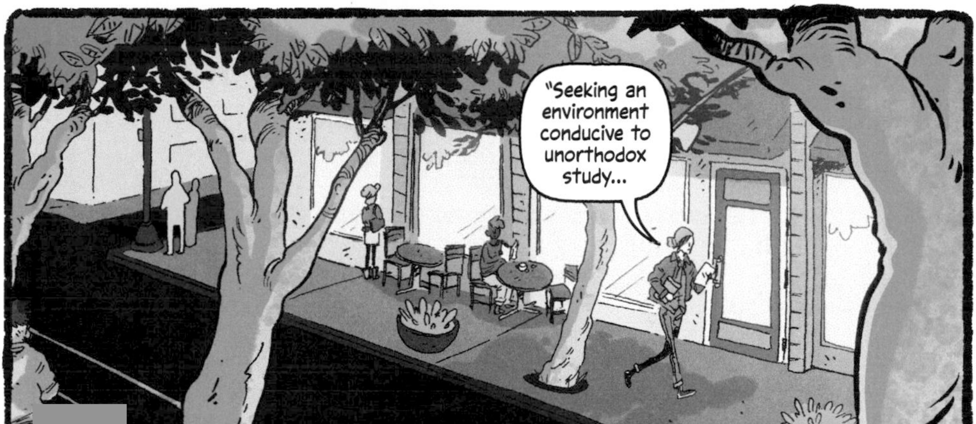
"Seeking an environment conducive to unorthodox study...
Coffee

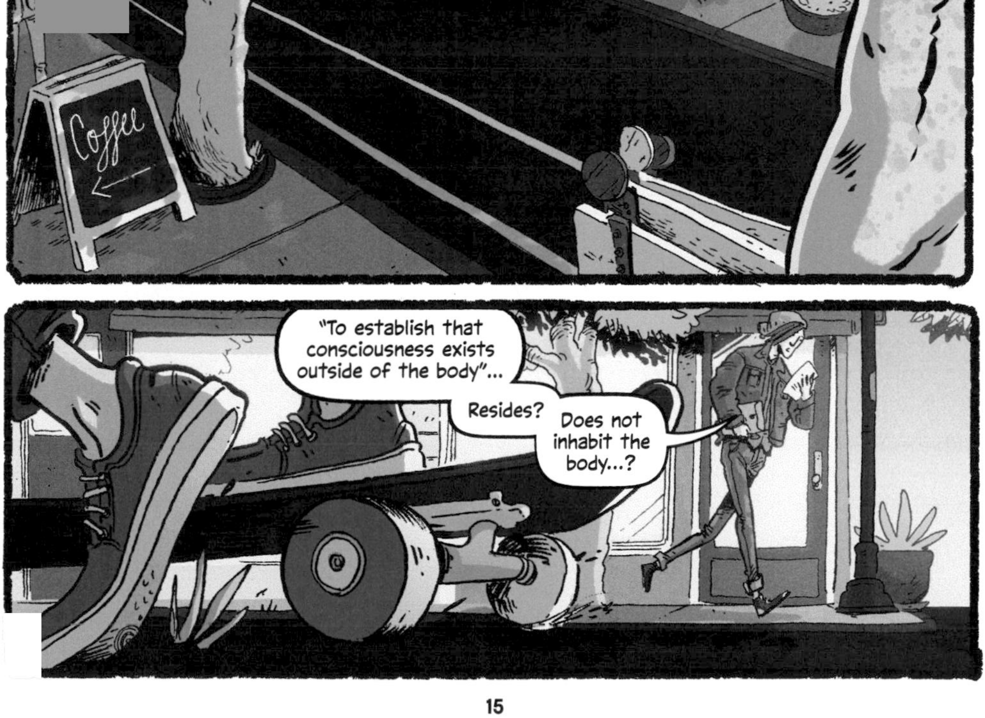
"To establish that consciousness exists outside of the body"...
Resides?
Does not inhabit the body...?

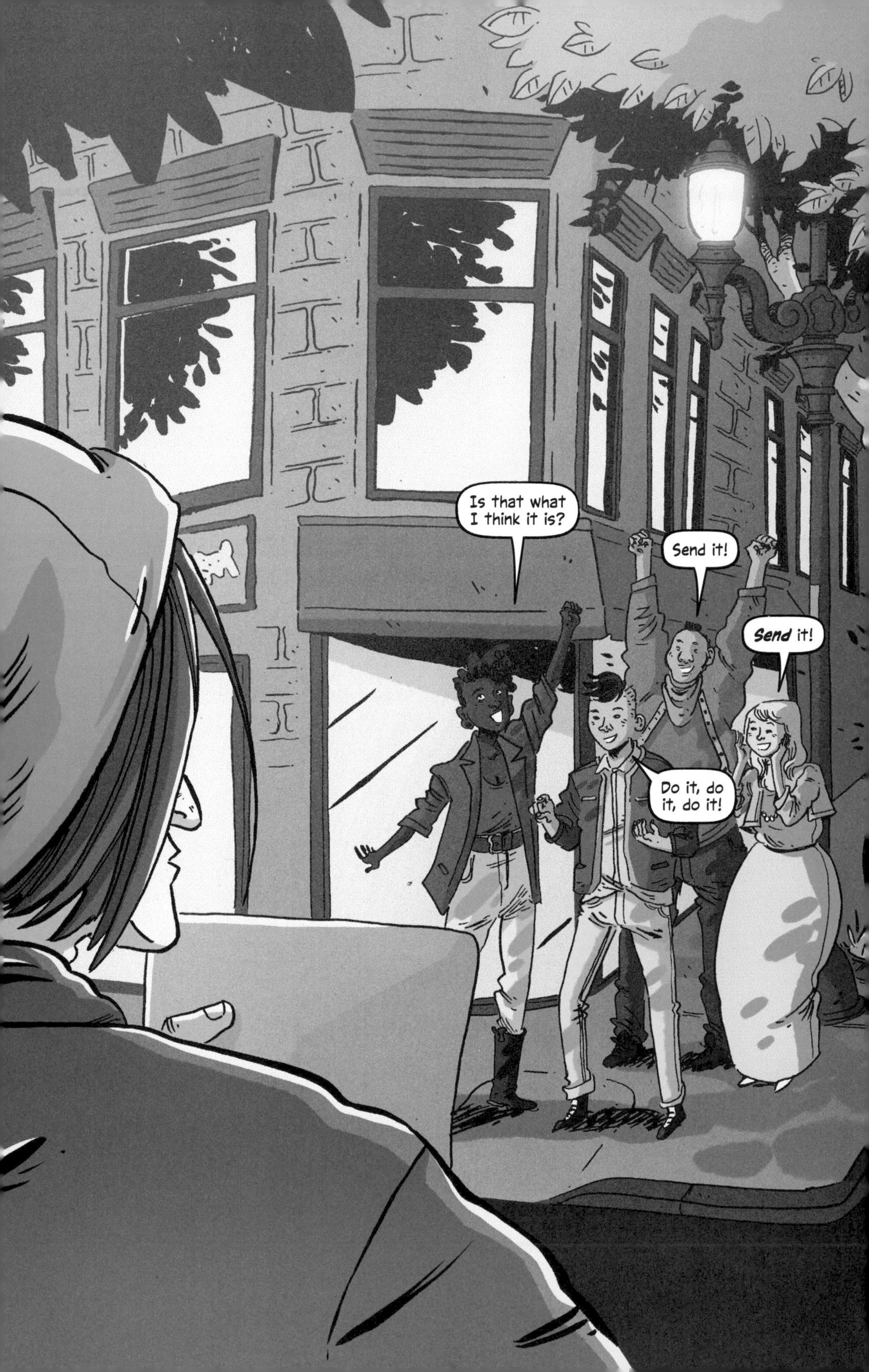
Is that what I think it is?
Send it!
Send it!
Do it, do it, do it!

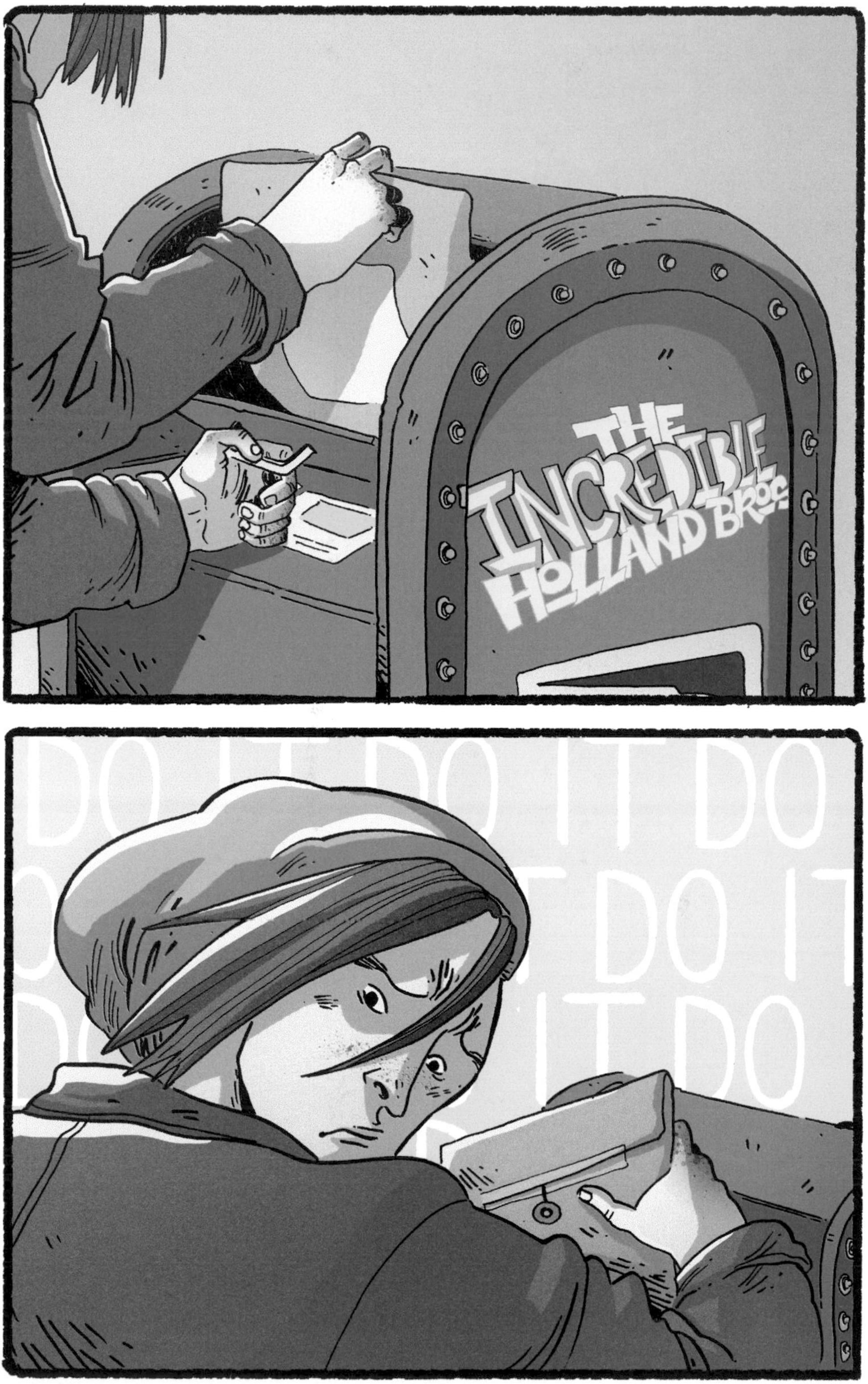
THE INCREDIBLE HOLLAND BROS
DO IT DO IT DO
DO IT DO IT
DO IT DO

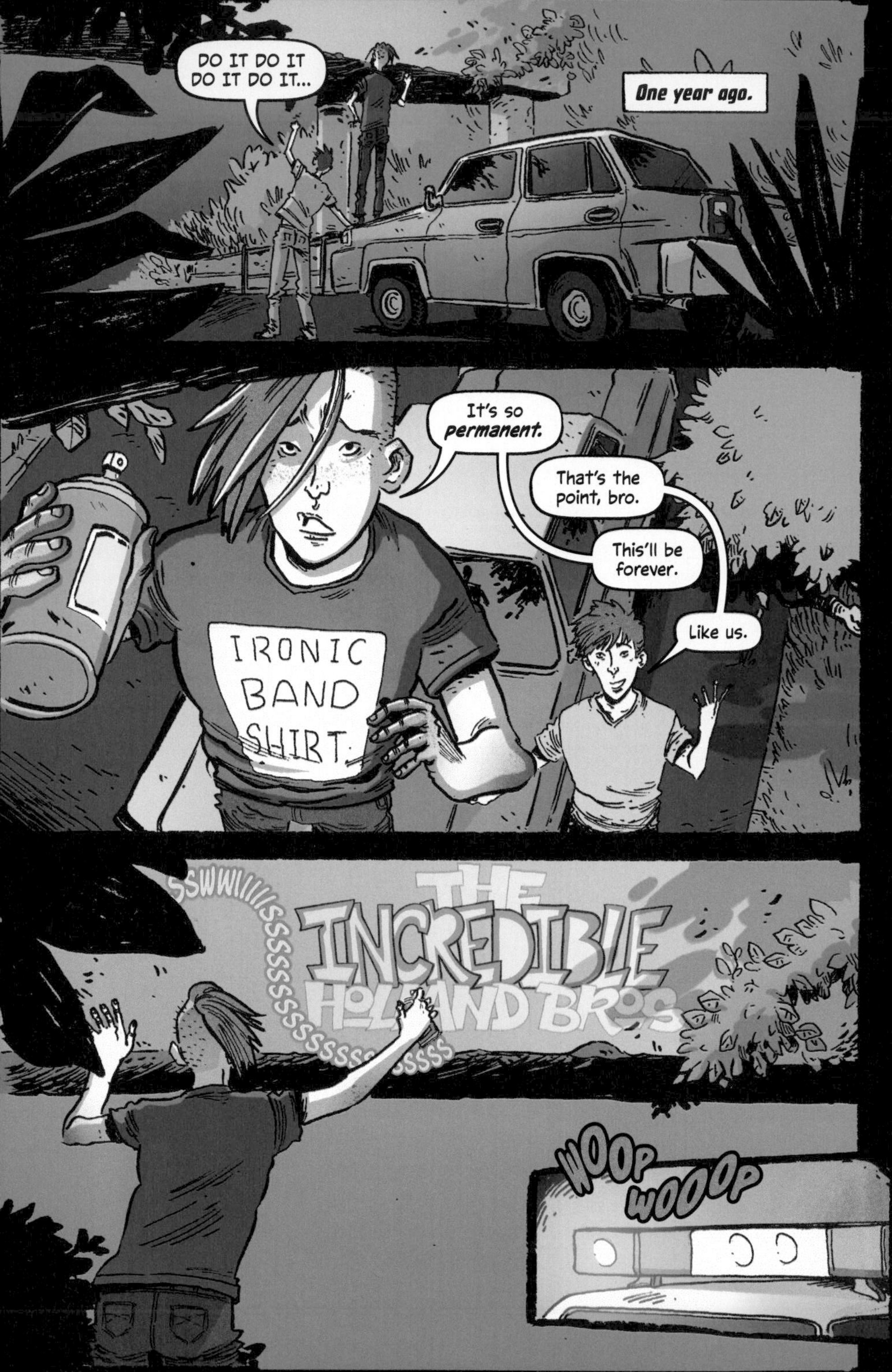
DO IT DO IT
DO IT DO IT...
One year ago.
IRONIC BAND SHIRT
It's so *permanent.*
That's the point, bro.
This'll be forever.
Like us.
SSWWIIIIIISSSSSSSSSSSSSSSSSSSSSS
THE INCREDIBLE HOLLAND BROS
WOOP WOOOP

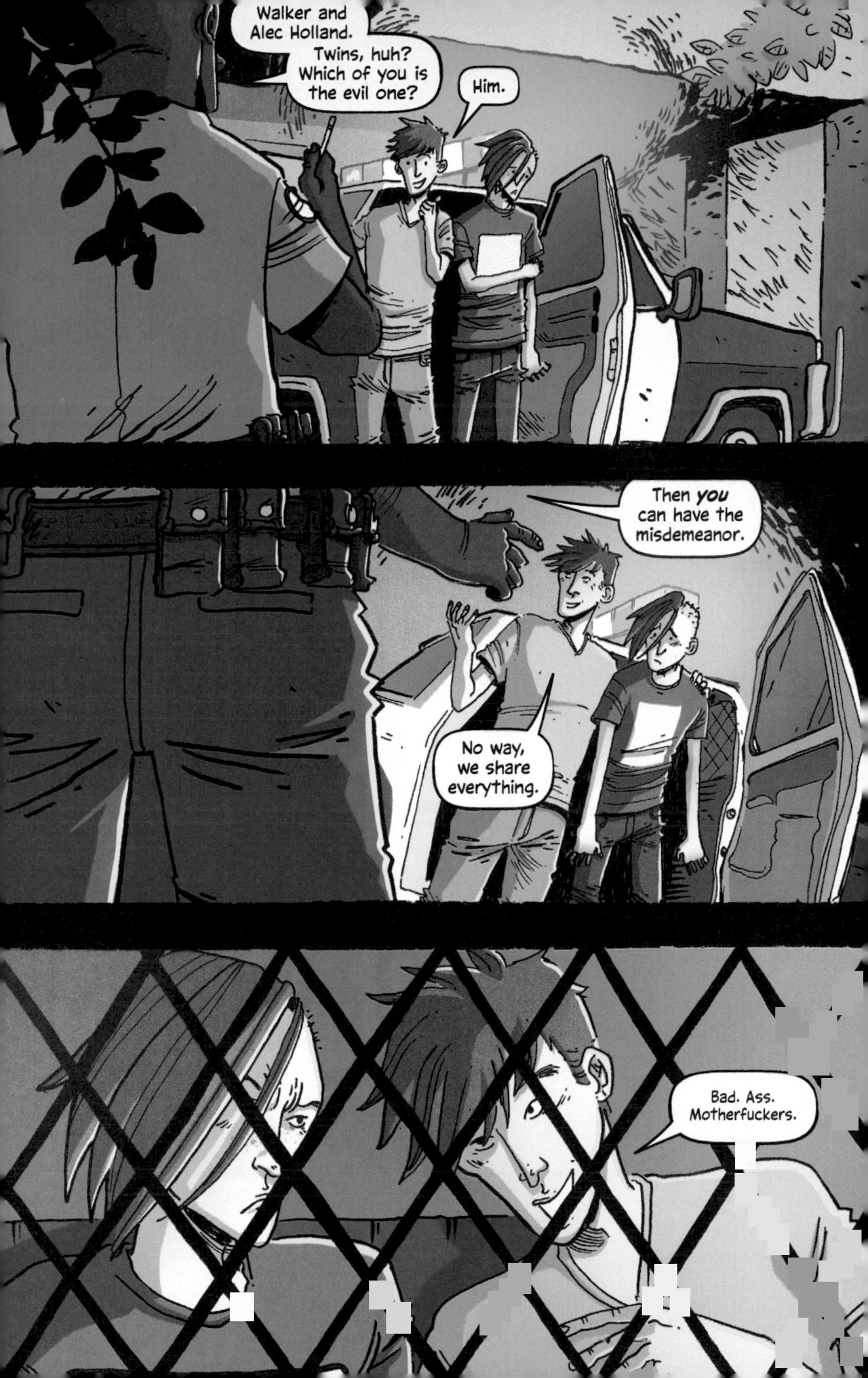
Walker and Alec Holland.
Twins, huh? Which of you is the evil one?
Him.
Then *you* can have the misdemeanor.
No way, we share everything.
Bad. Ass. Motherfuckers.

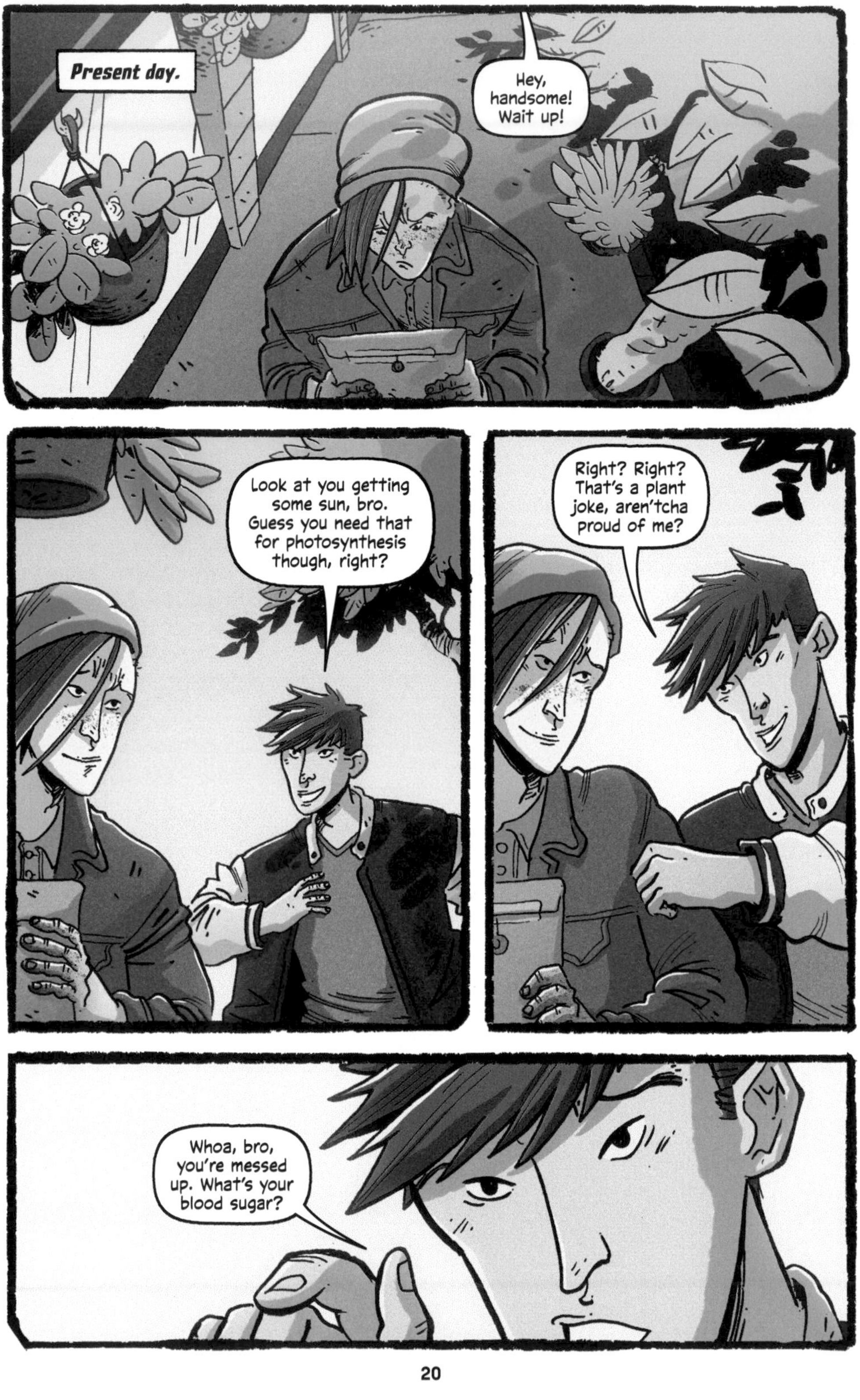
Present day.
Hey, handsome! Wait up!
Look at you getting some sun, bro. Guess you need that for photosynthesis though, right?
Right? Right? That's a plant joke, aren'tcha proud of me?
Whoa, bro, you're messed up. What's your blood sugar?

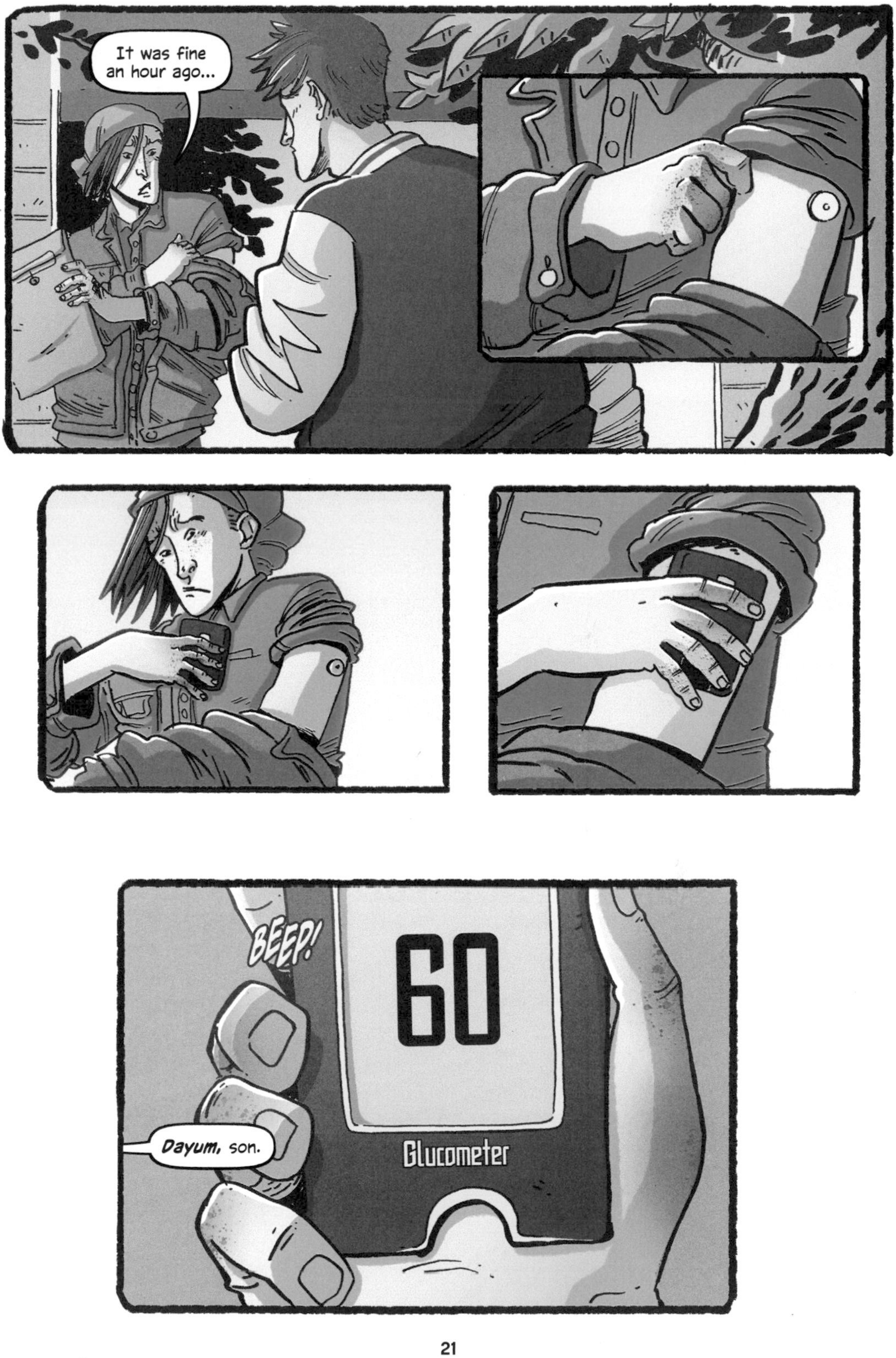
It was fine an hour ago...
BEEP!
60
Glucometer
Dayum, son.

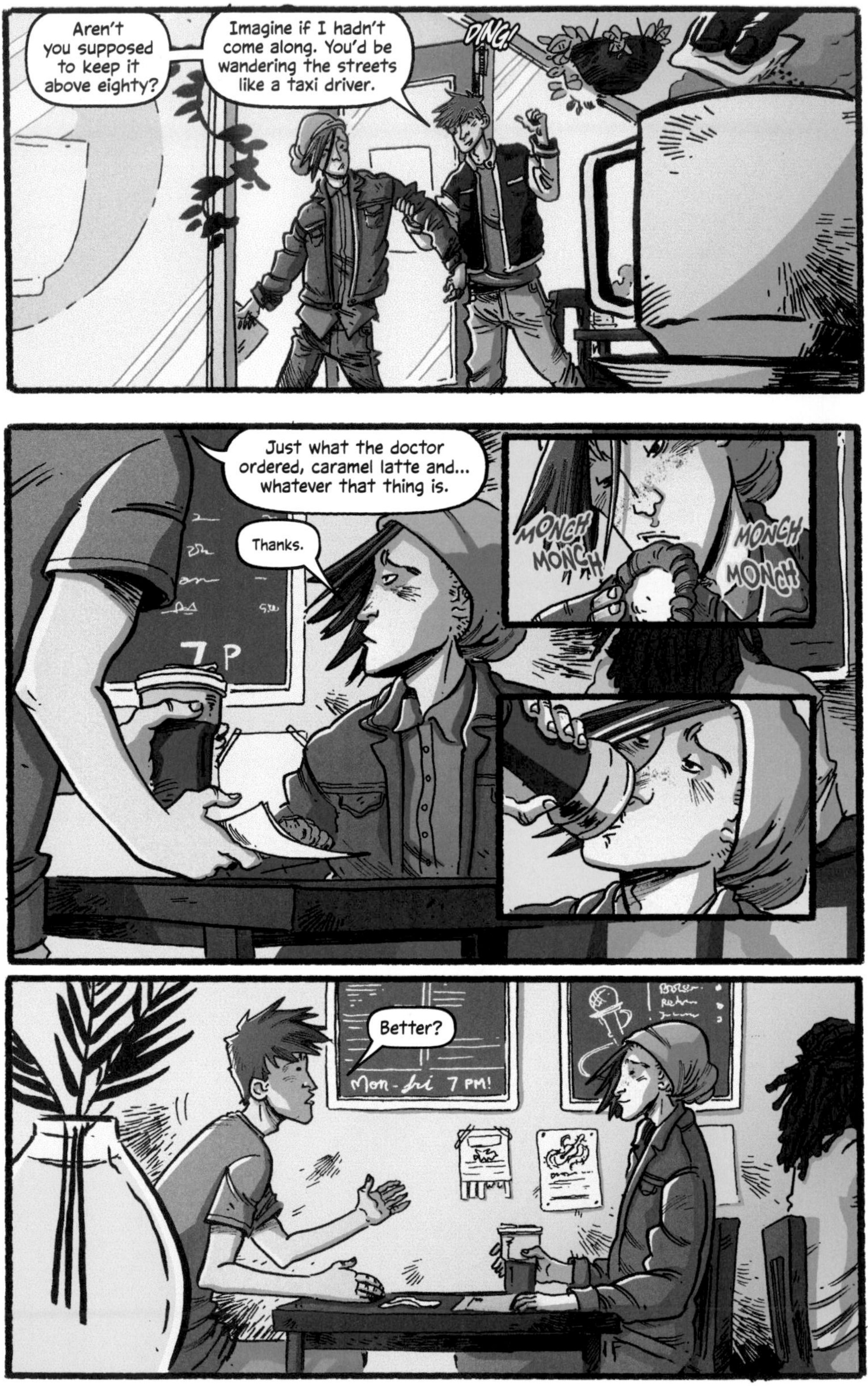
Aren't you supposed to keep it above eighty?
Imagine if I hadn't come along. You'd be wandering the streets like a taxi driver.
DING!
Just what the doctor ordered, caramel latte and... whatever that thing is.
Thanks.
MONCH MONCH
MONCH MONCH
Better?
Mon-fri 7 PM!

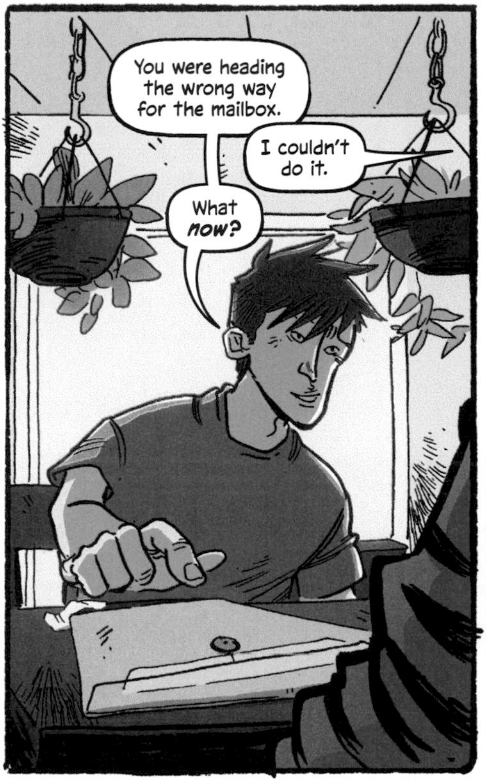
You were heading the wrong way for the mailbox.
What now?
I couldn't do it.

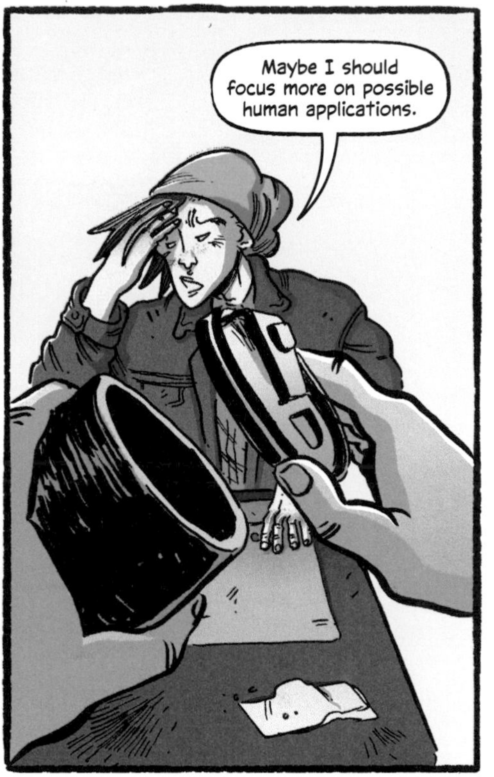
Maybe I should focus more on possible human applications.

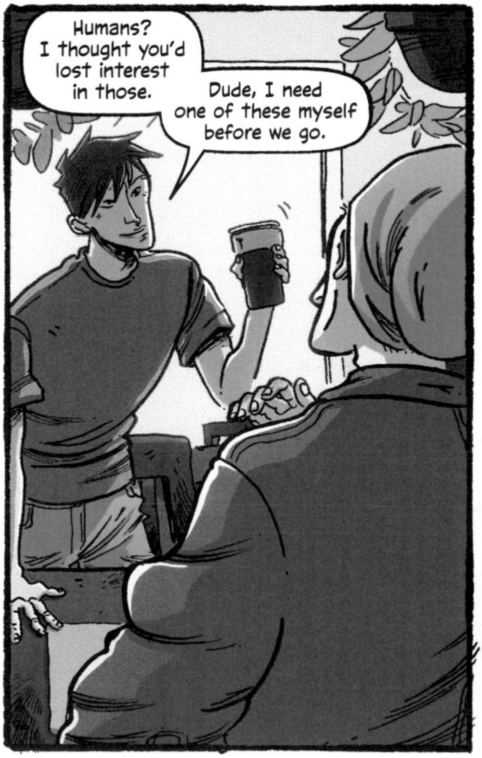
Humans? I thought you'd lost interest in those.
Dude, I need one of these myself before we go.

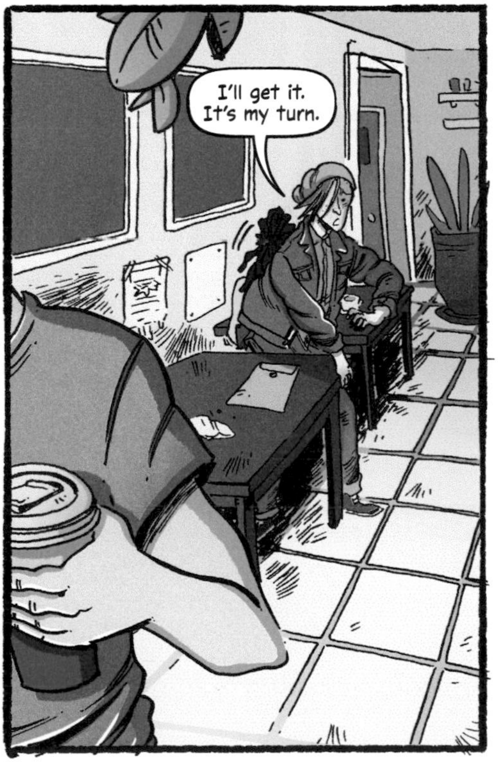
I'll get it. It's my turn.

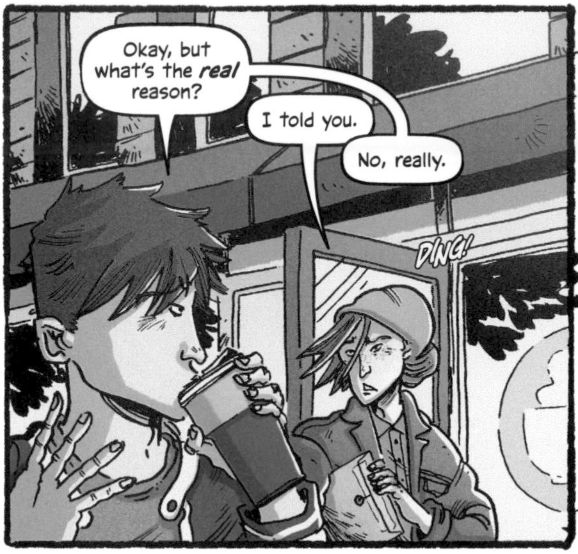
Okay, but what's the *real* reason?
I told you.
No, really.
DING!

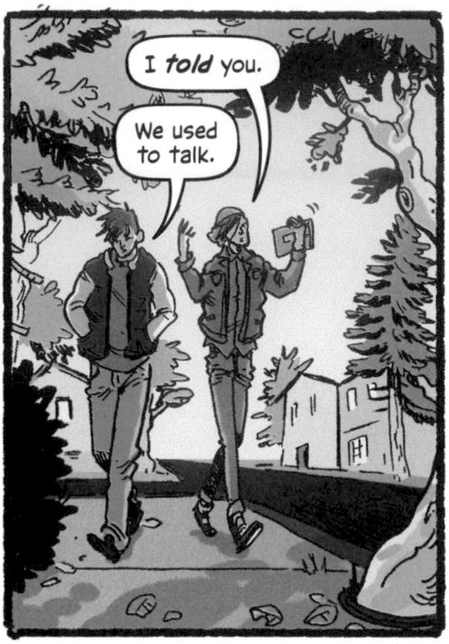
I *told* you.
We used to talk.

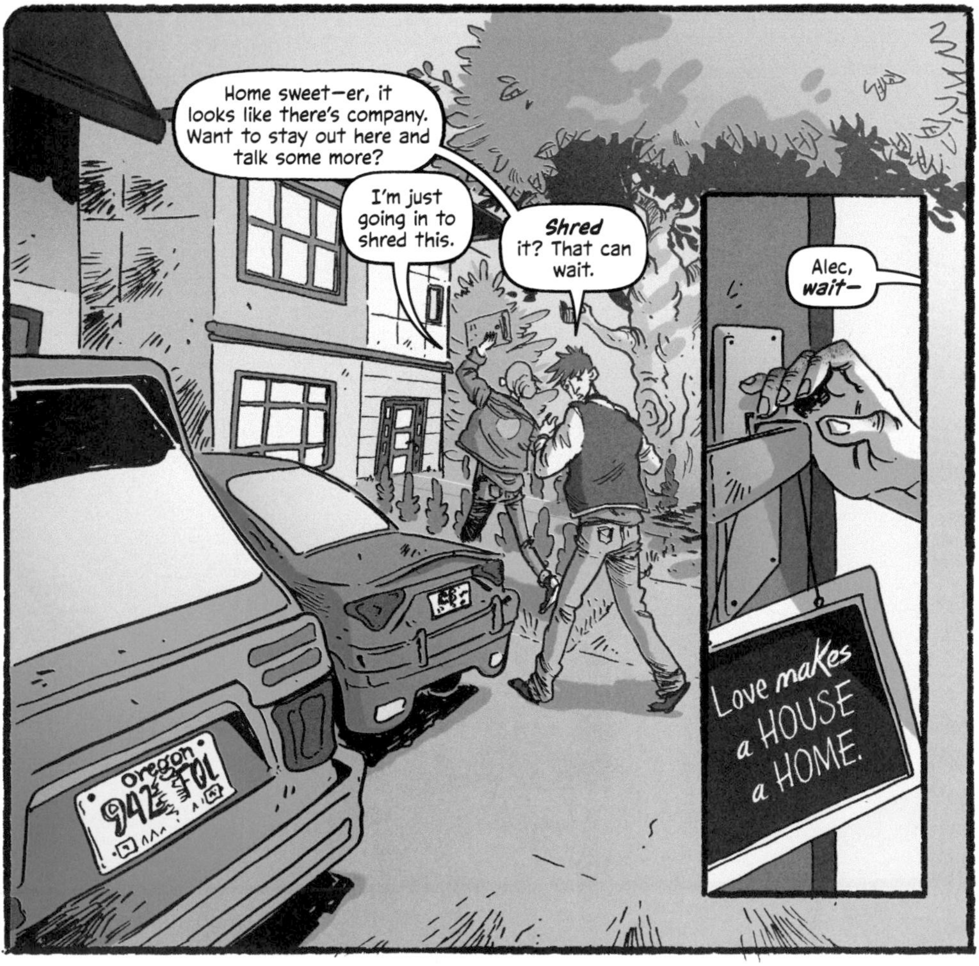
Home sweet—er, it looks like there's company. Want to stay out here and talk some more?
I'm just going in to shred this.
Shred it? That can wait.
Alec, *wait—*
Love maKes a HOUSE a HOME.
Oregon

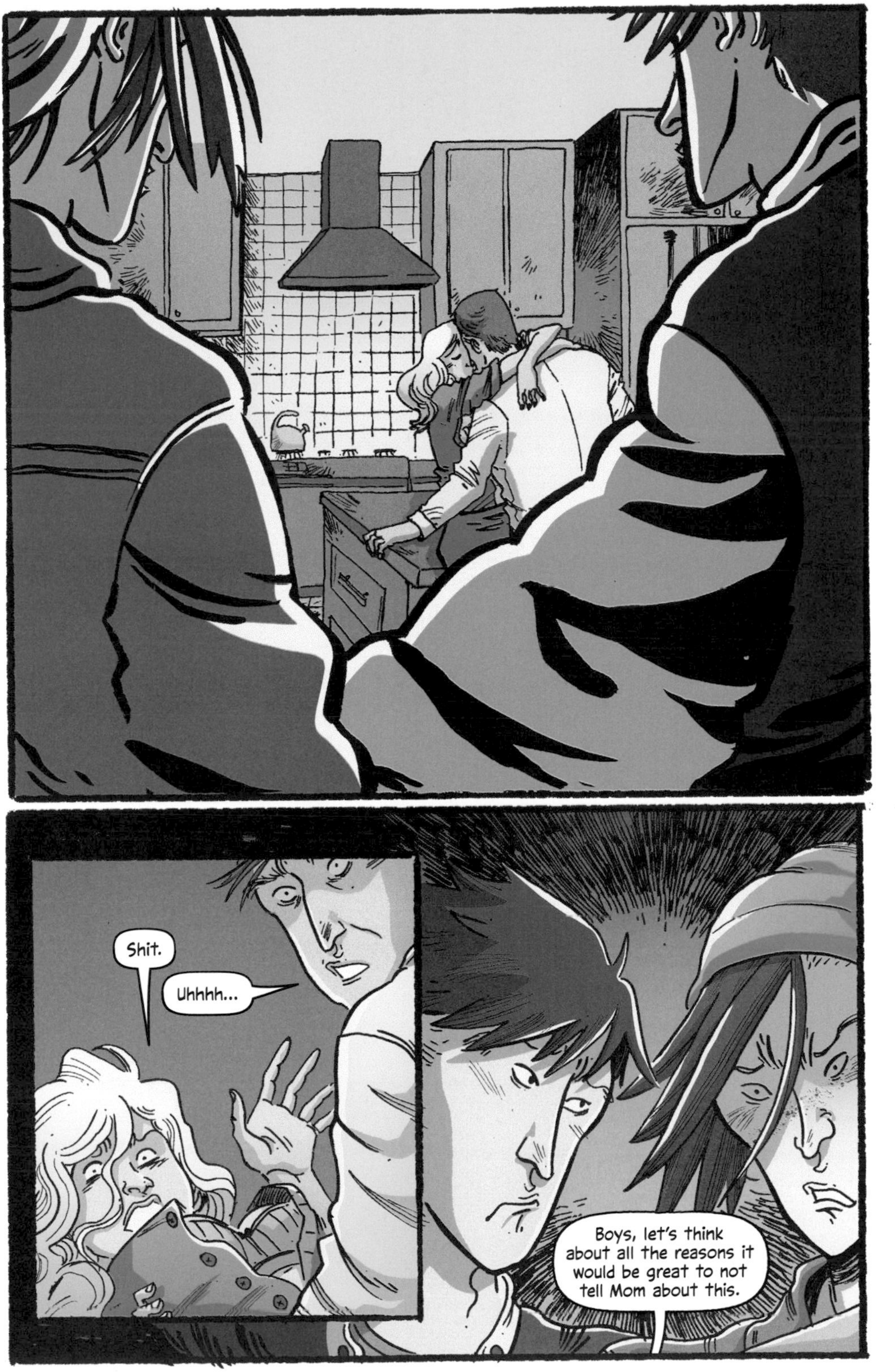
Shit.
Uhhhh...
Boys, let's think about all the reasons it would be great to not tell Mom about this.

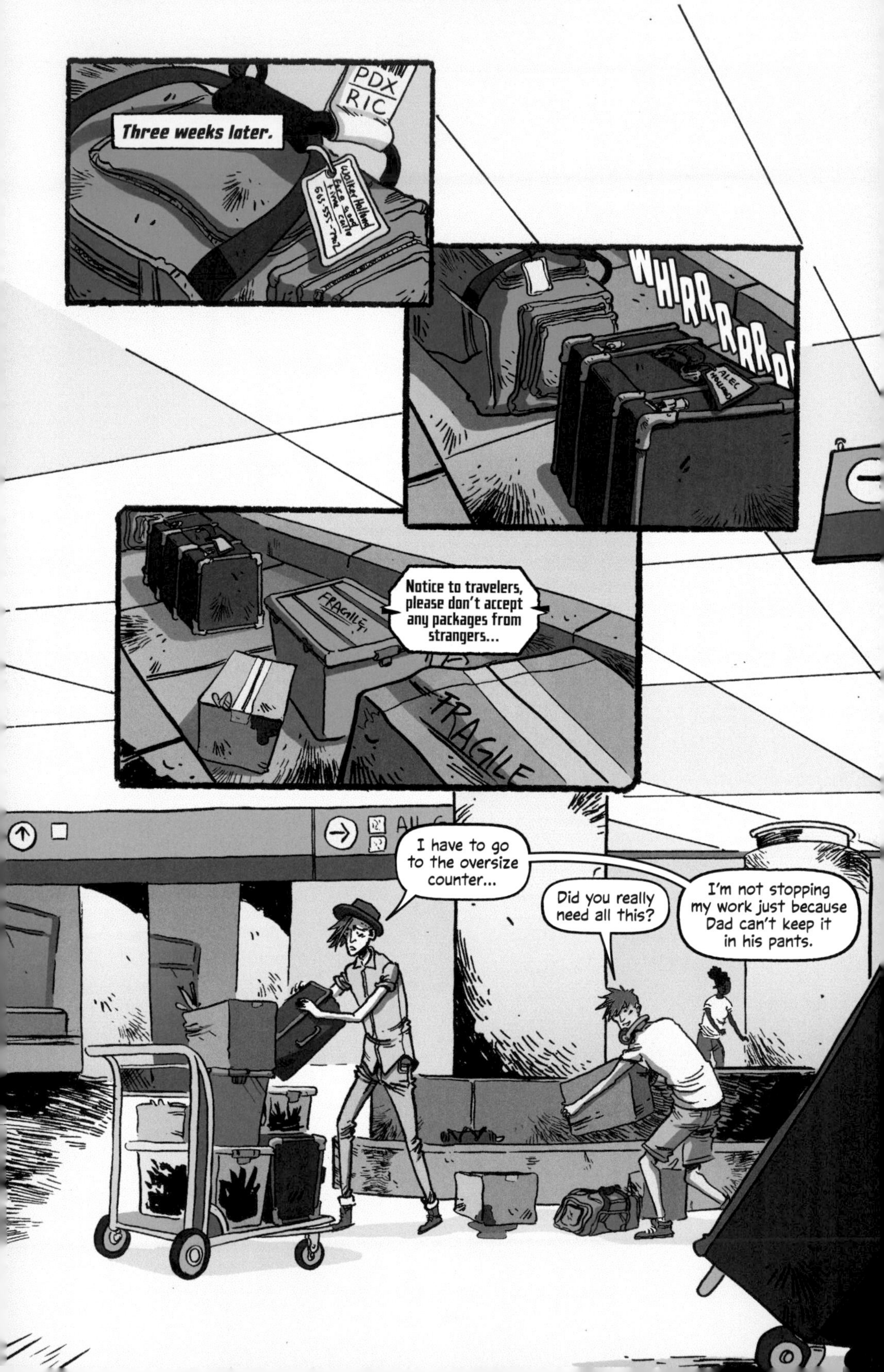
Three weeks later.
PDX
RIC
WHIRRRRRRR
ALEC HOLLAND
Notice to travelers, please don't accept any packages from strangers...
FRAGILE
FRAGILE
I have to go to the oversize counter...
Did you really need all this?
I'm not stopping my work just because Dad can't keep it in his pants.

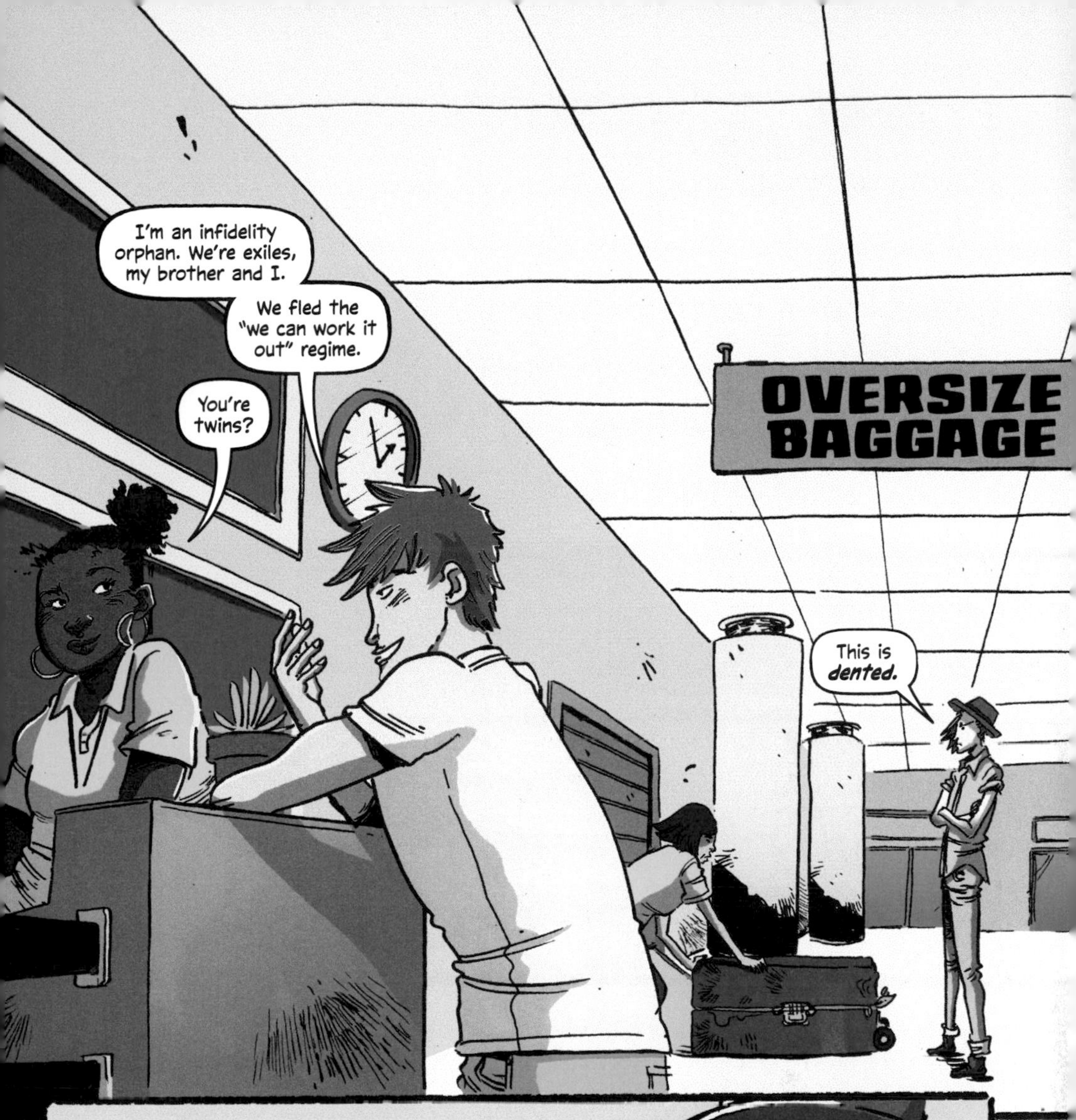
!
I'm an infidelity orphan. We're exiles, my brother and I.
We fled the "we can work it out" regime.
You're twins?
OVERSIZE BAGGAGE
This is *dented.*

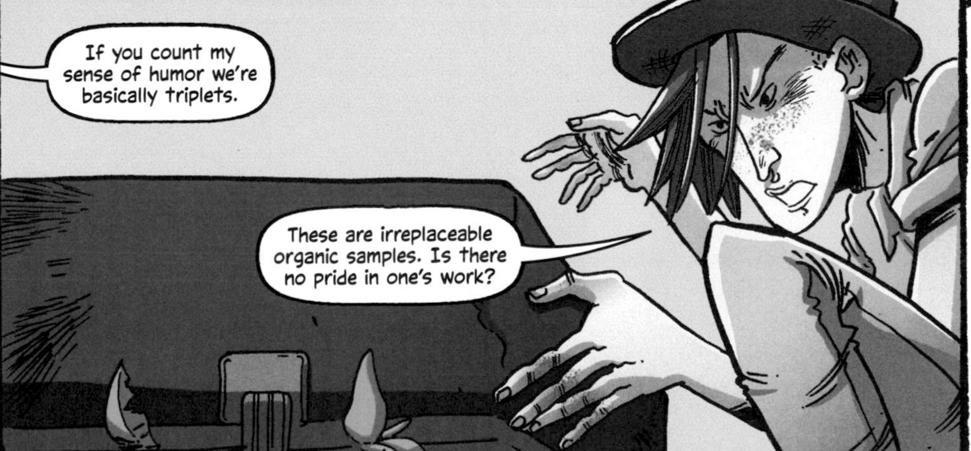
If you count my sense of humor we're basically triplets.
These are irreplaceable organic samples. Is there no pride in one's work?

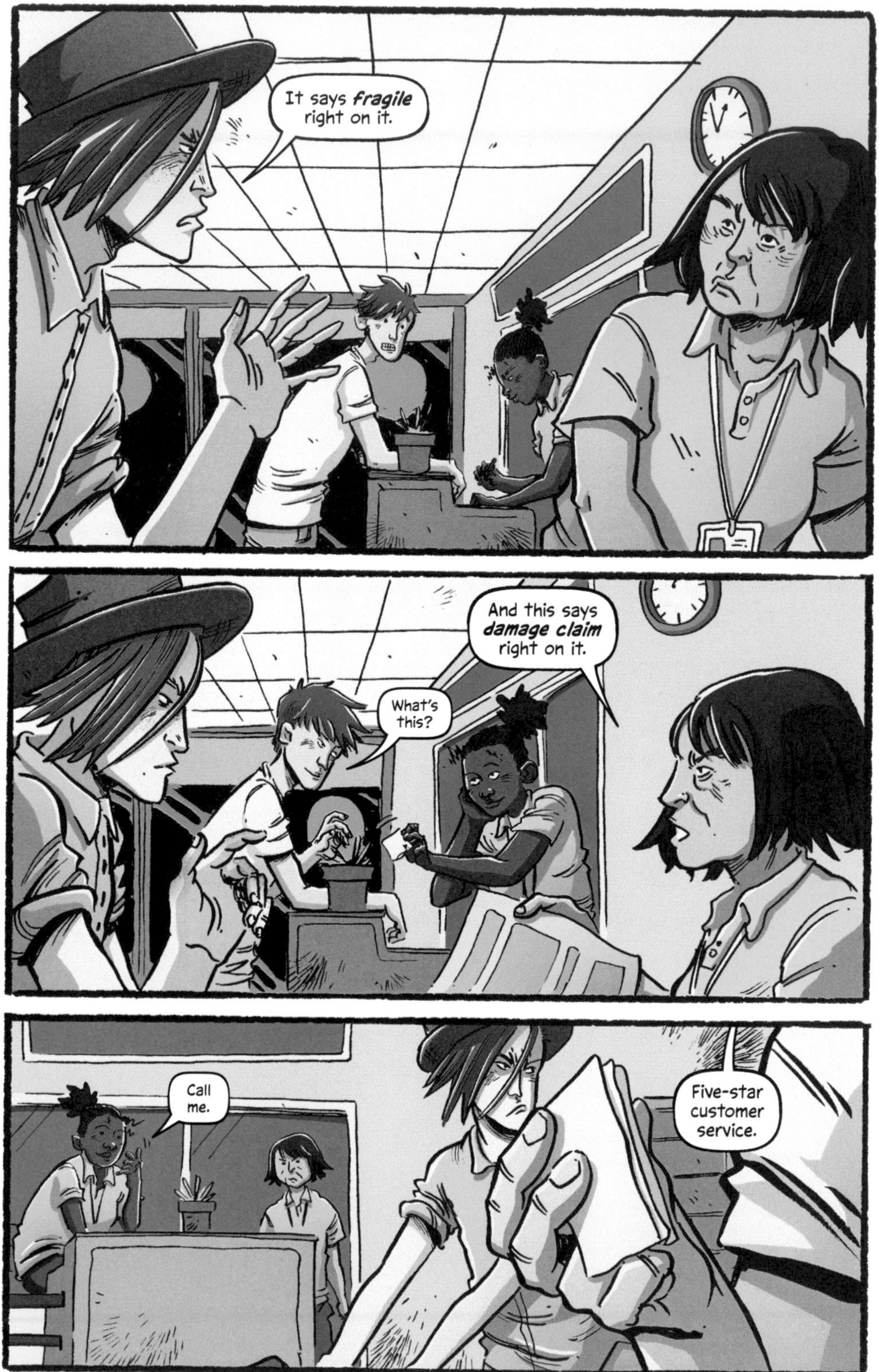
It says *fragile* right on it.
And this says *damage claim* right on it.
What's this?
Call me.
Five-star customer service.

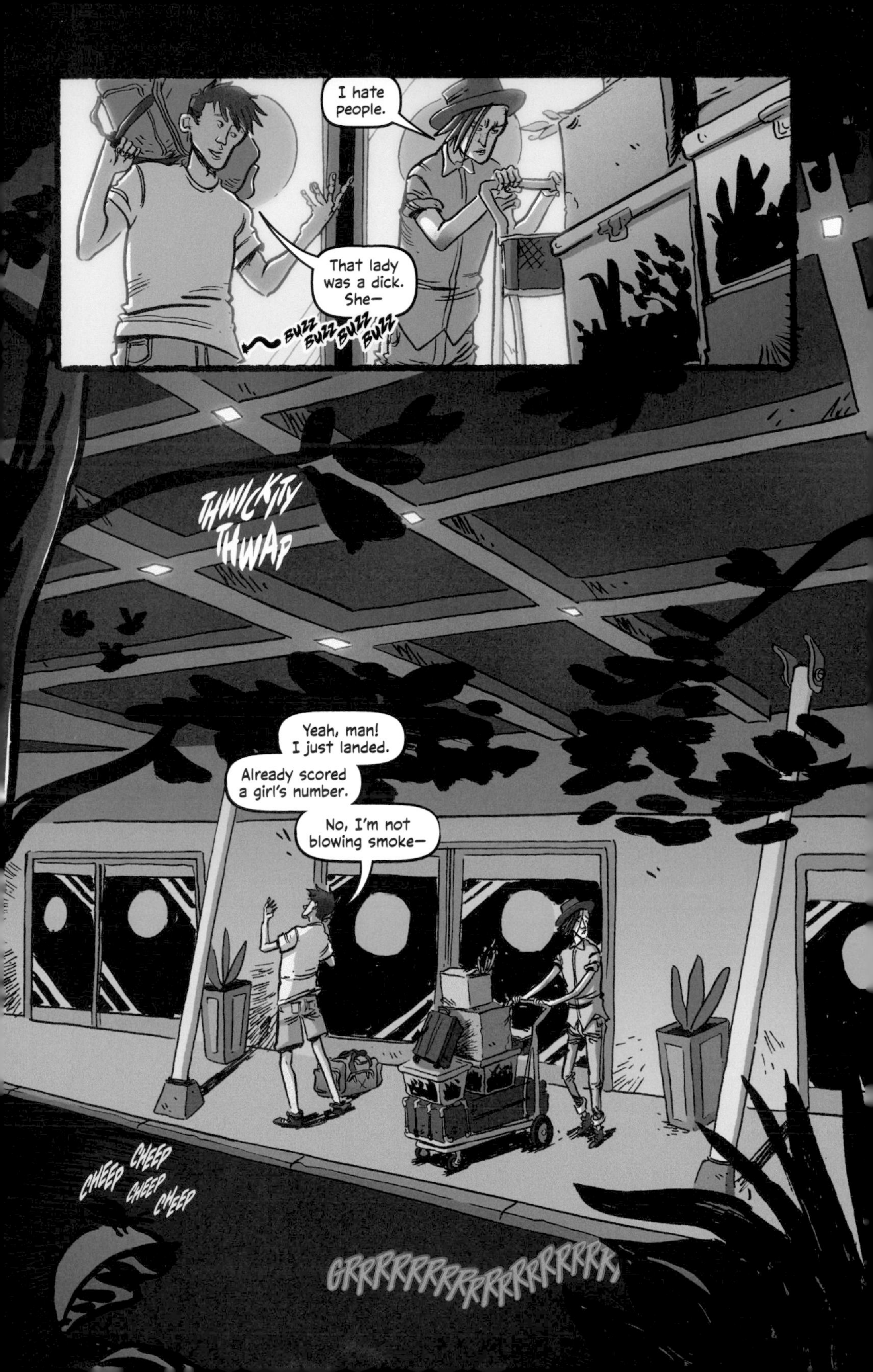
I hate people.
That lady was a dick. She—
BUZZ BUZZ BUZZ BUZZ
THWICKITY THWAP
Yeah, man! I just landed.
Already scored a girl's number.
No, I'm not blowing smoke—
CHEEP CHEEP CHEEP CHEEP
GRRRRRRRRRRRRRRRRRR

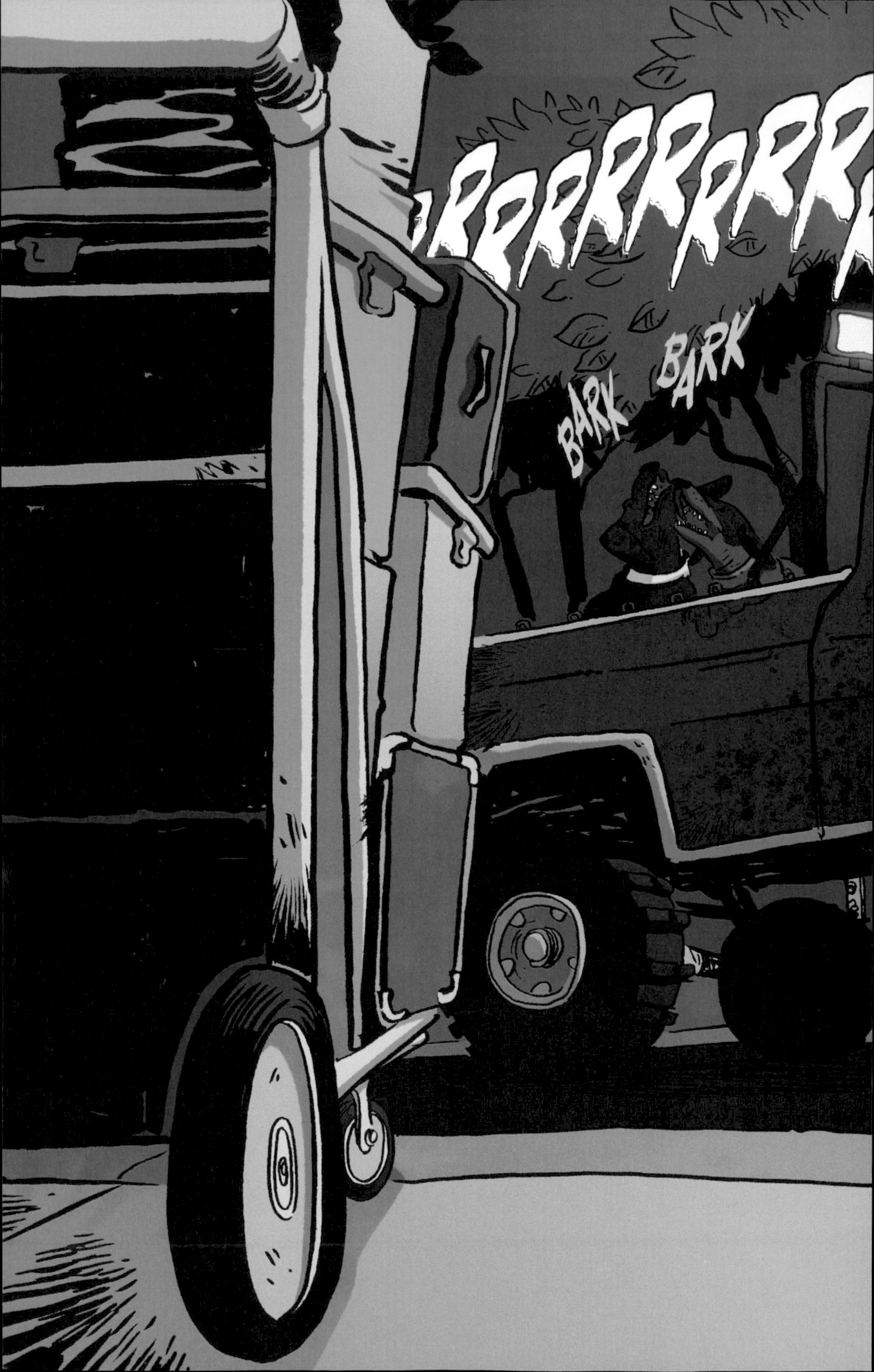

RRRRRRRRR
BARK BARK

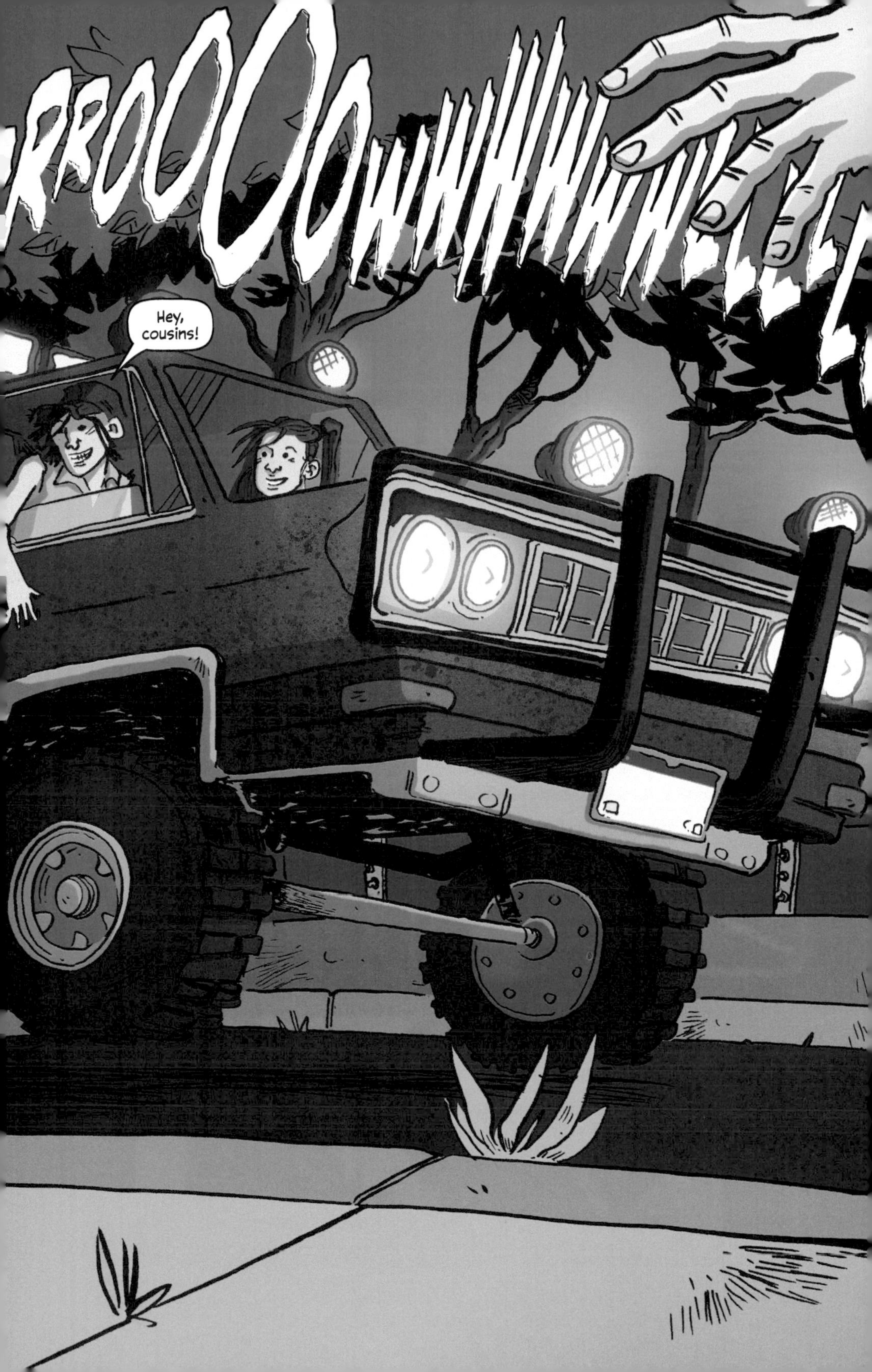
RROOOOWWWHHHWWWWWRRRRR
Hey, cousins!

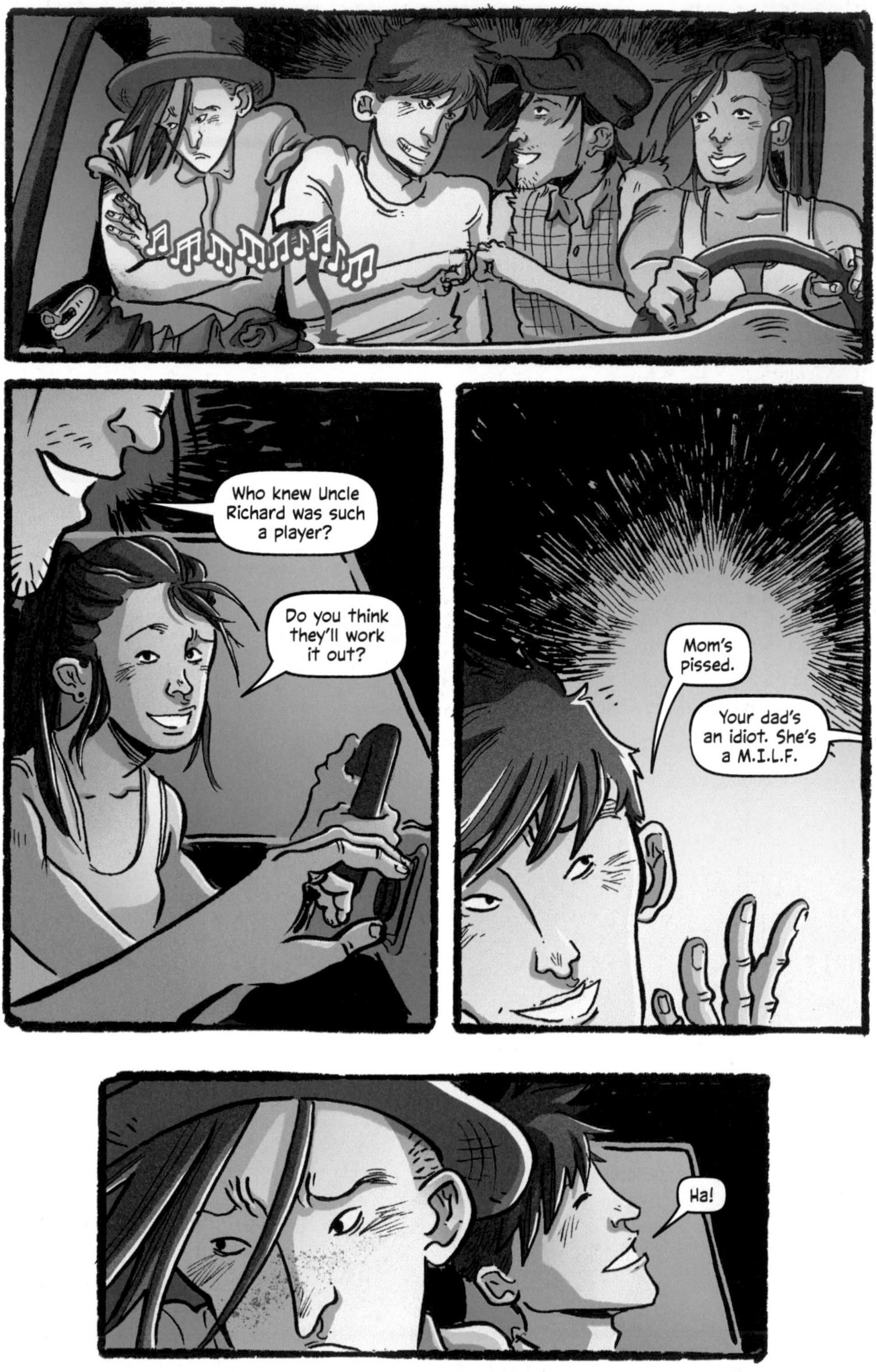
Who knew Uncle Richard was such a player?
Do you think they'll work it out?
Mom's pissed.
Your dad's an idiot. She's a M.I.L.F.
Ha!

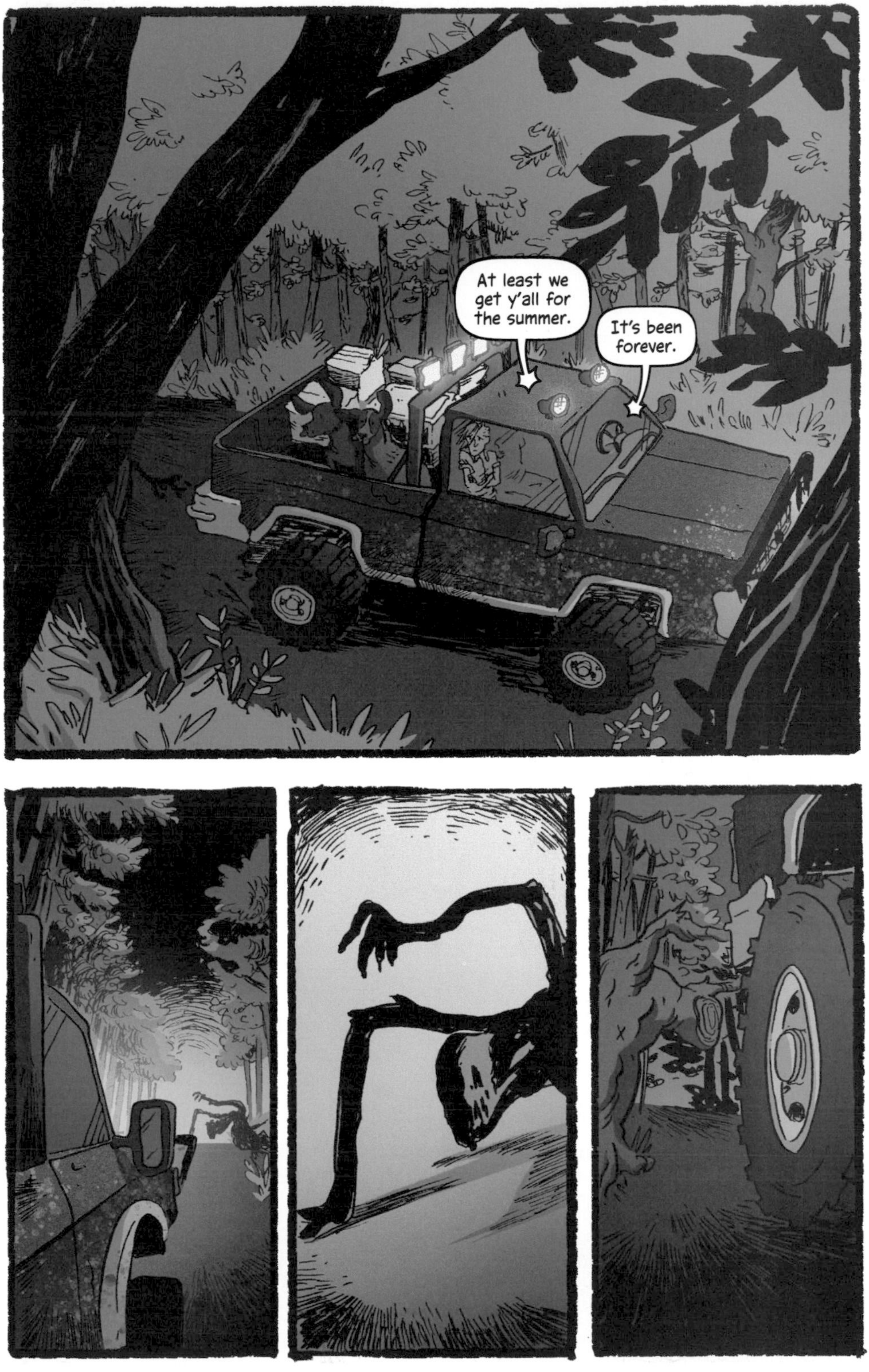
At least we get y'all for the summer.
It's been forever.

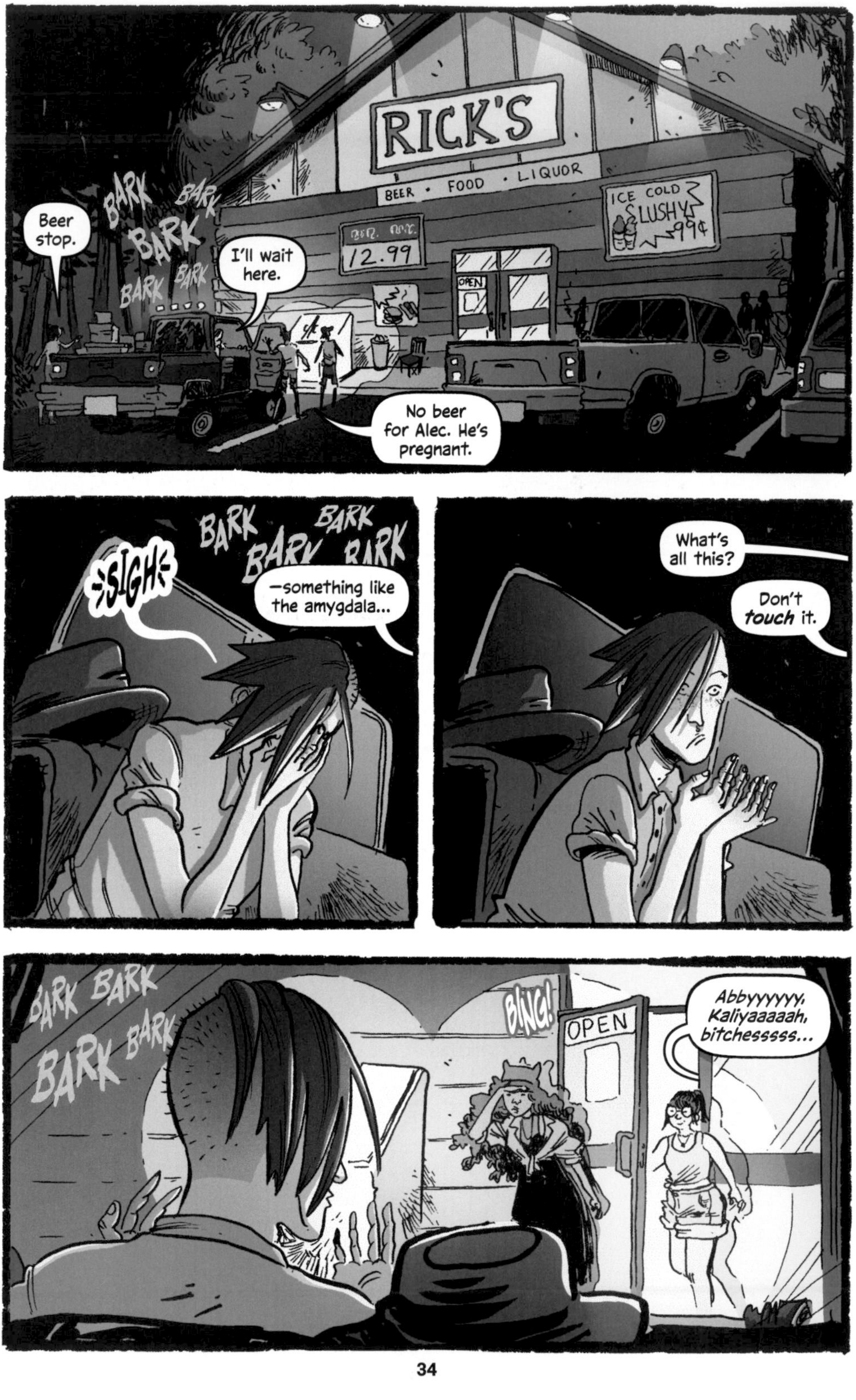
RICK'S
BEER · FOOD · LIQUOR
ICE COLD SLUSHY 99¢
12.99
OPEN
BARK BARK BARK BARK BARK
Beer stop.
I'll wait here.
No beer for Alec. He's pregnant.
BARK BARK BARK BARK
SIGH
—something like the amygdala...
What's all this?
Don't *touch* it.
BARK BARK BARK BARK
BING!
OPEN
Abbyyyyyy, Kaliyaaaaah, bitchessssss...

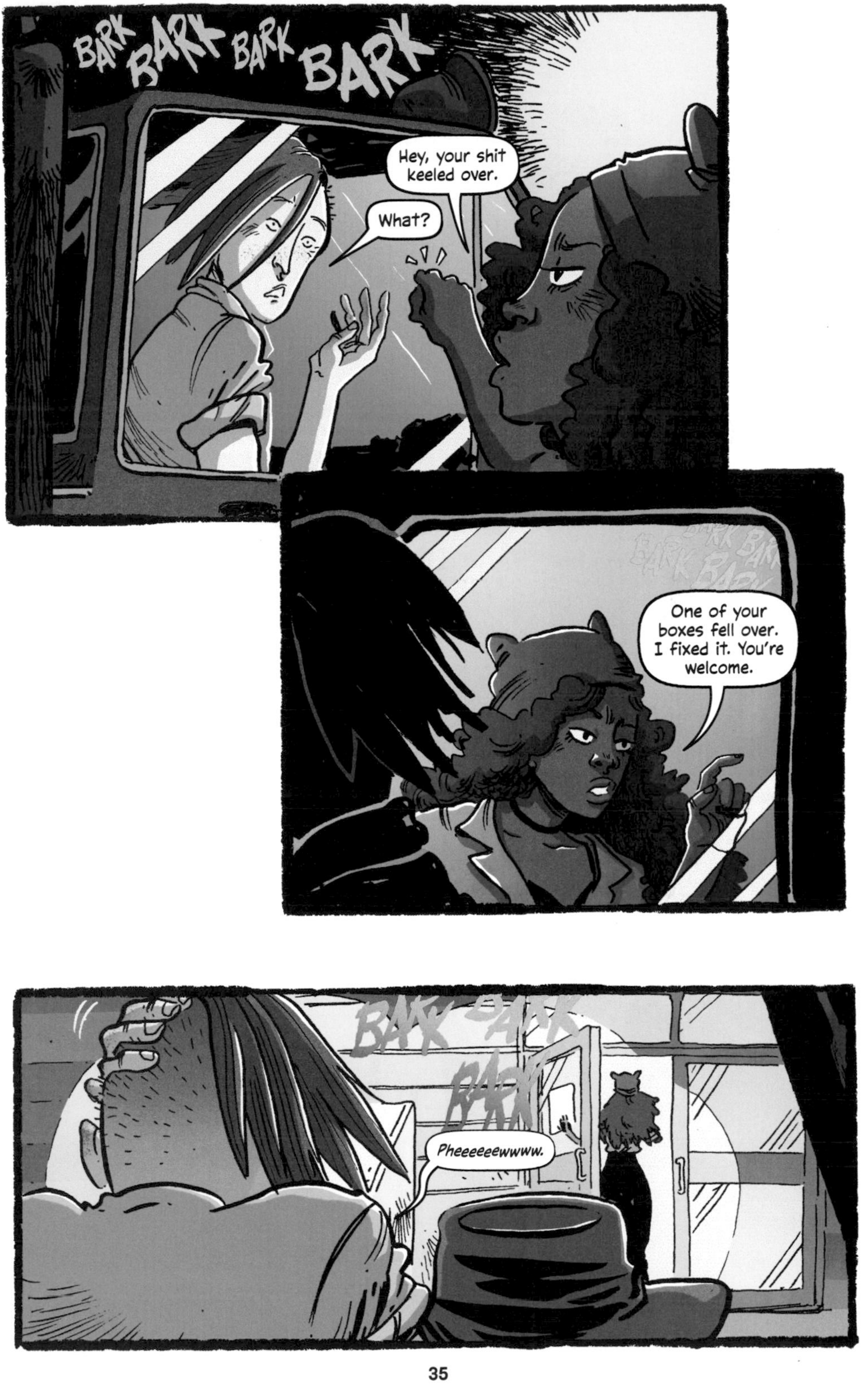
BARK BARK BARK BARK
Hey, your shit keeled over.
What?
One of your boxes fell over. I fixed it. You're welcome.
Pheeeeeewwww.

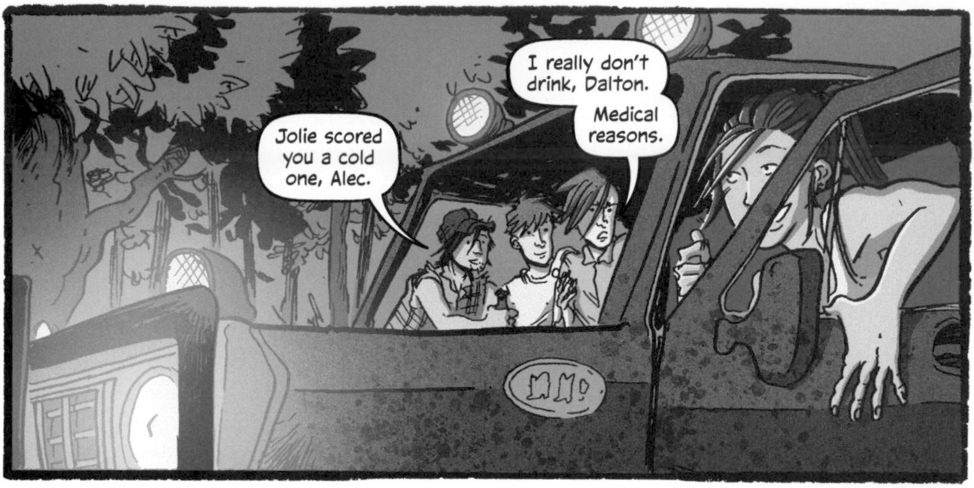
Jolie scored you a cold one, Alec.
I really don't drink, Dalton.
Medical reasons.

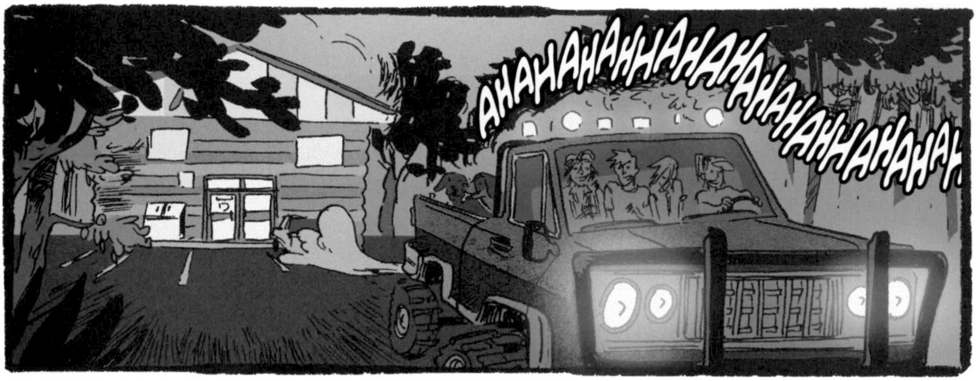
AHAHAHAHHAHAHAHAHAHAHAHHAHAHAH

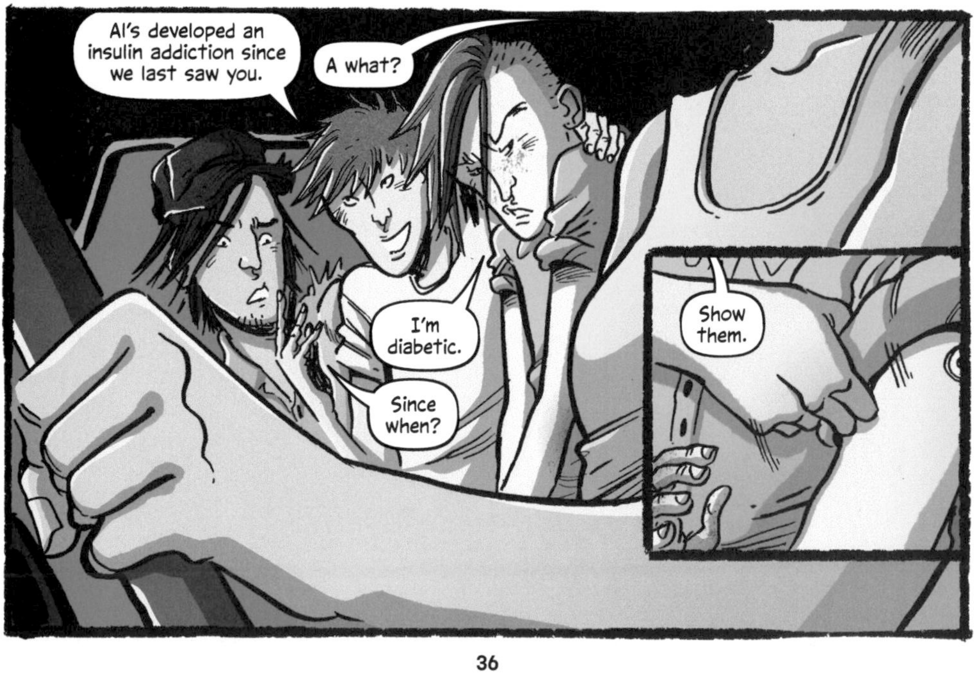
Al's developed an insulin addiction since we last saw you.
A what?
I'm diabetic.
Since when?
Show them.

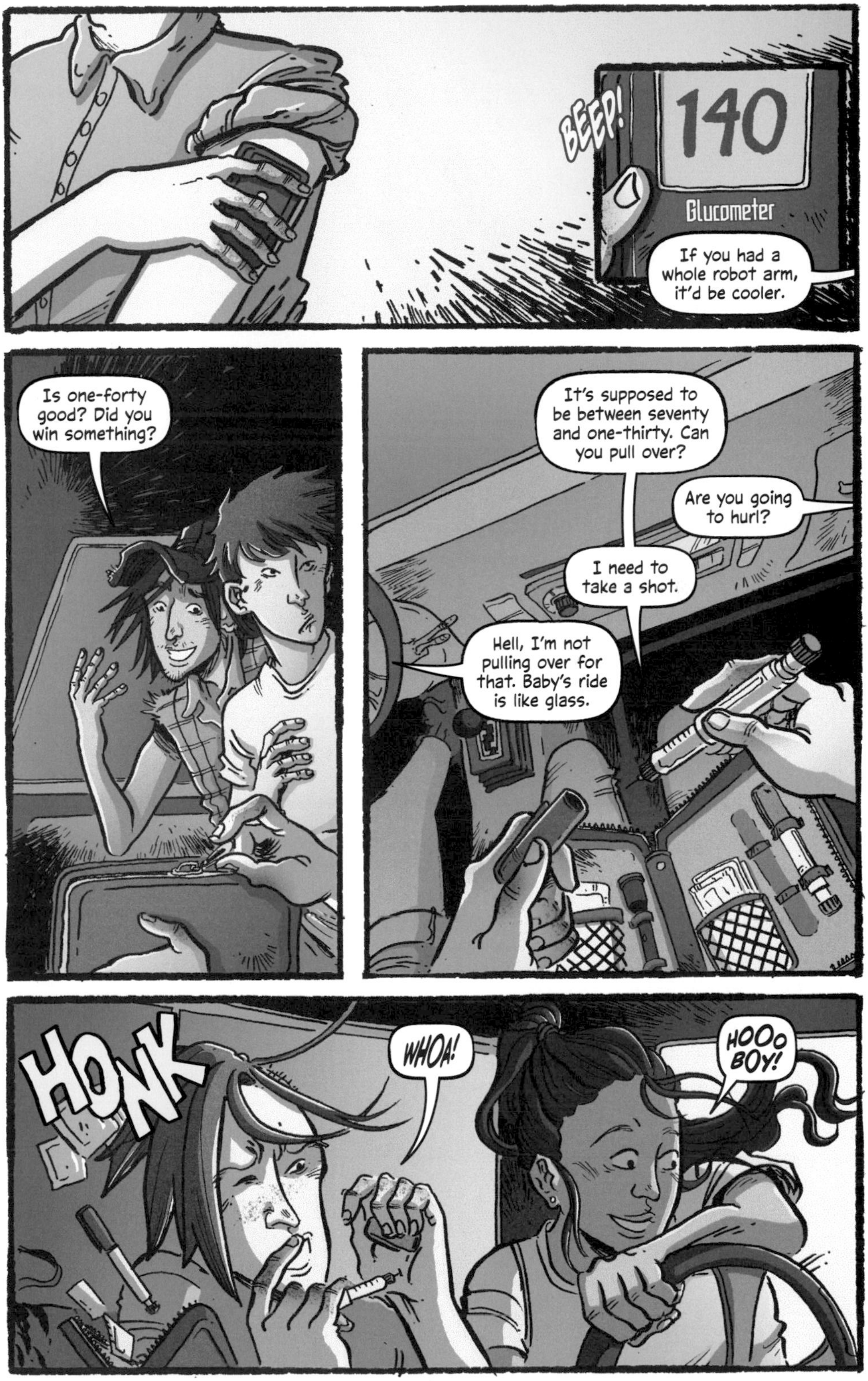
BEEP!
140
Glucometer
If you had a whole robot arm, it'd be cooler.
Is one-forty good? Did you win something?
It's supposed to be between seventy and one-thirty. Can you pull over?
Are you going to hurl?
I need to take a shot.
Hell, I'm not pulling over for that. Baby's ride is like glass.
HONK
WHOA!
HOOo BOY!

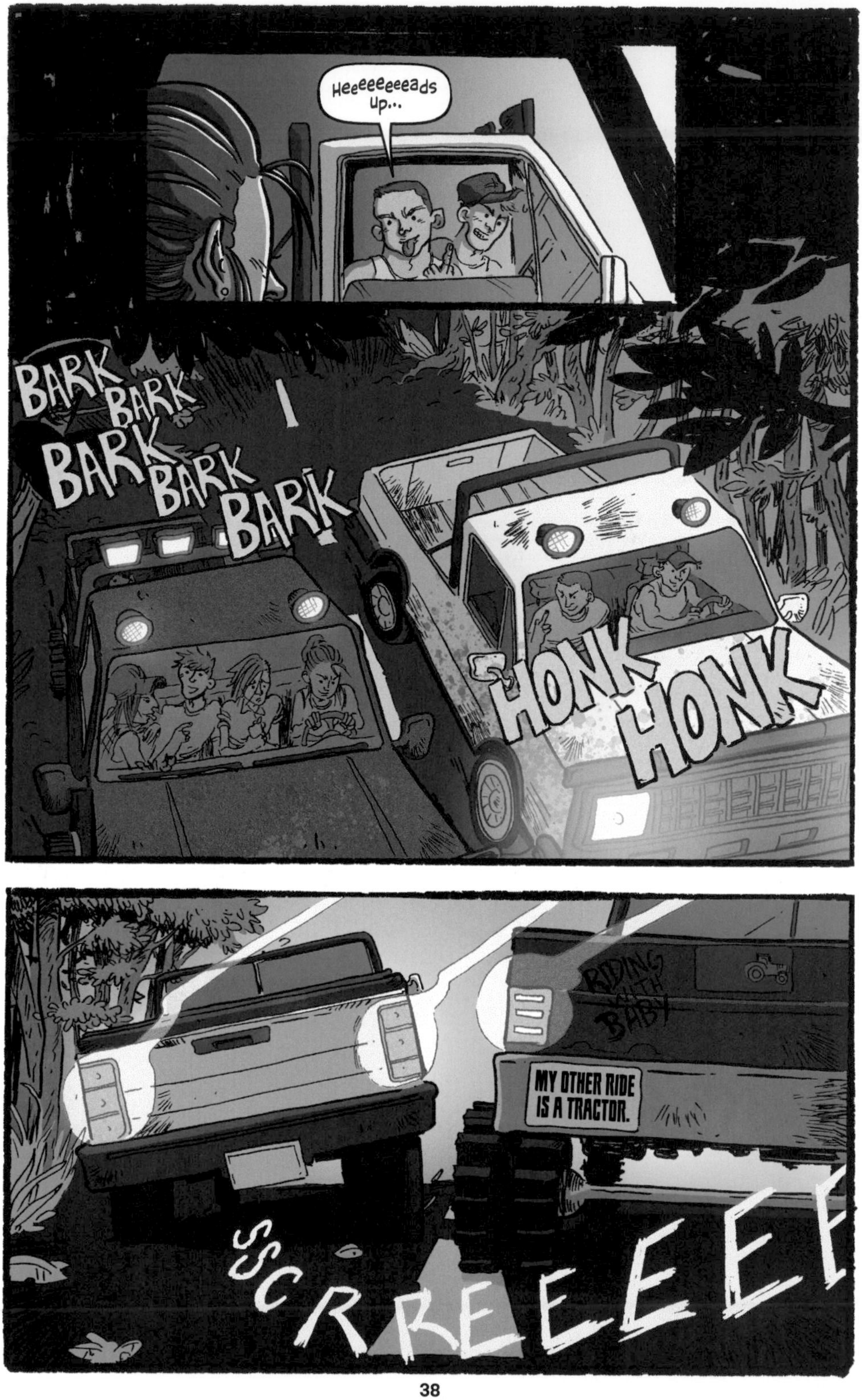
Heeeeeeeeads up...
BARK BARK BARK BARK BARK
HONK HONK
RIDING WITH BABY
MY OTHER RIDE IS A TRACTOR.
SCREEEEEEE

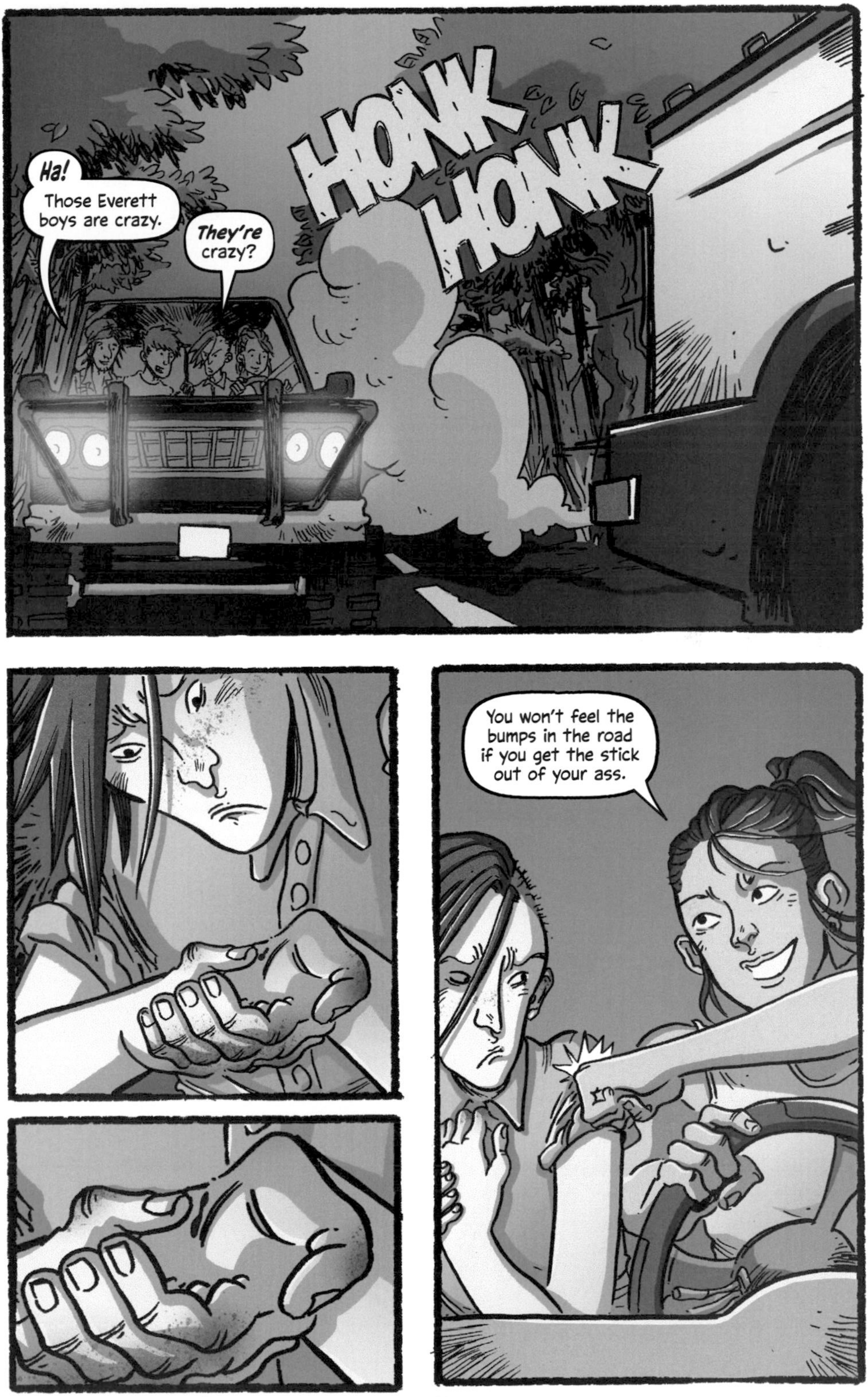
HONK HONK
Ha!
Those Everett boys are crazy.
They're crazy?
You won't feel the bumps in the road if you get the stick out of your ass.

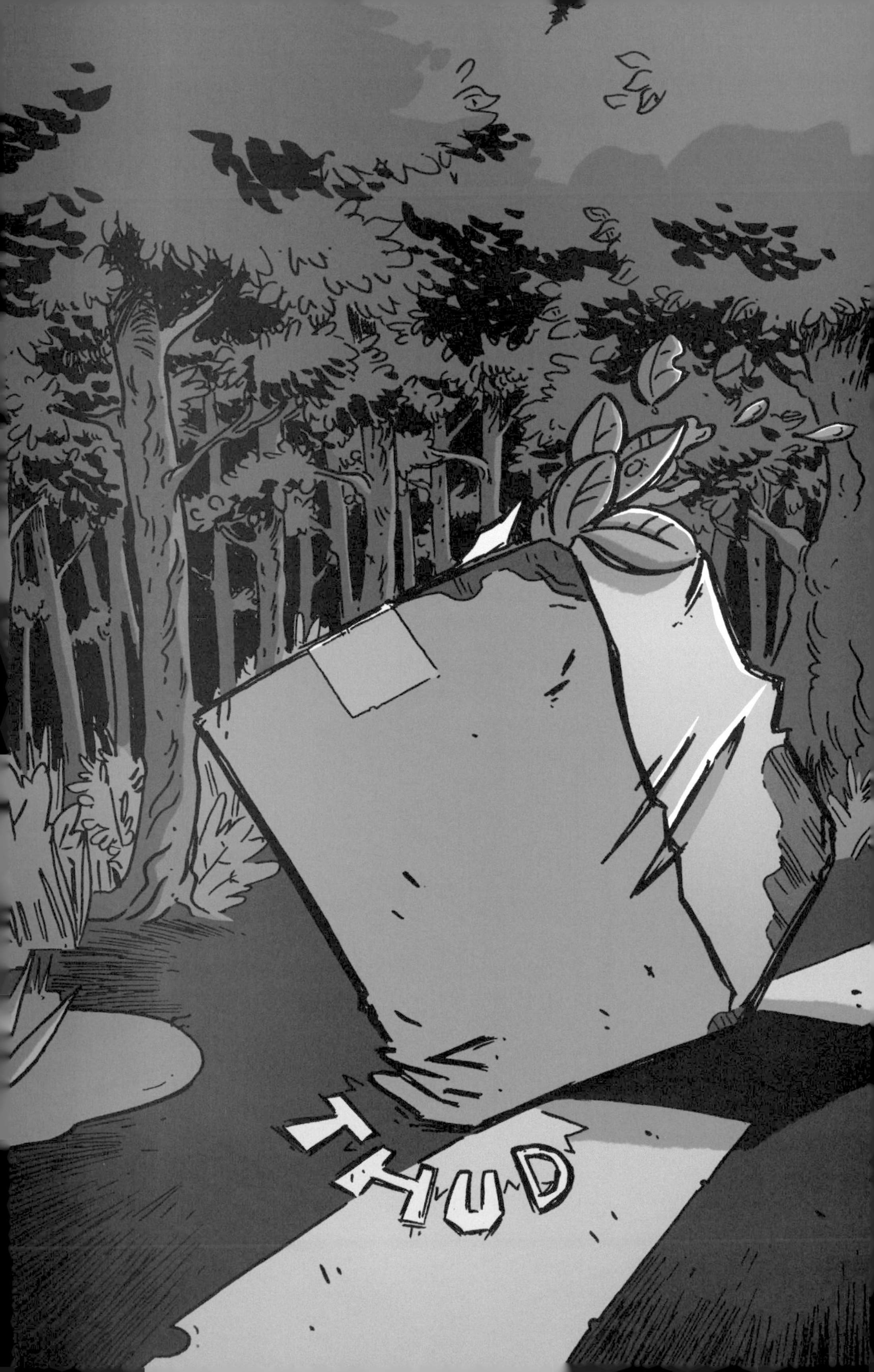
THUD

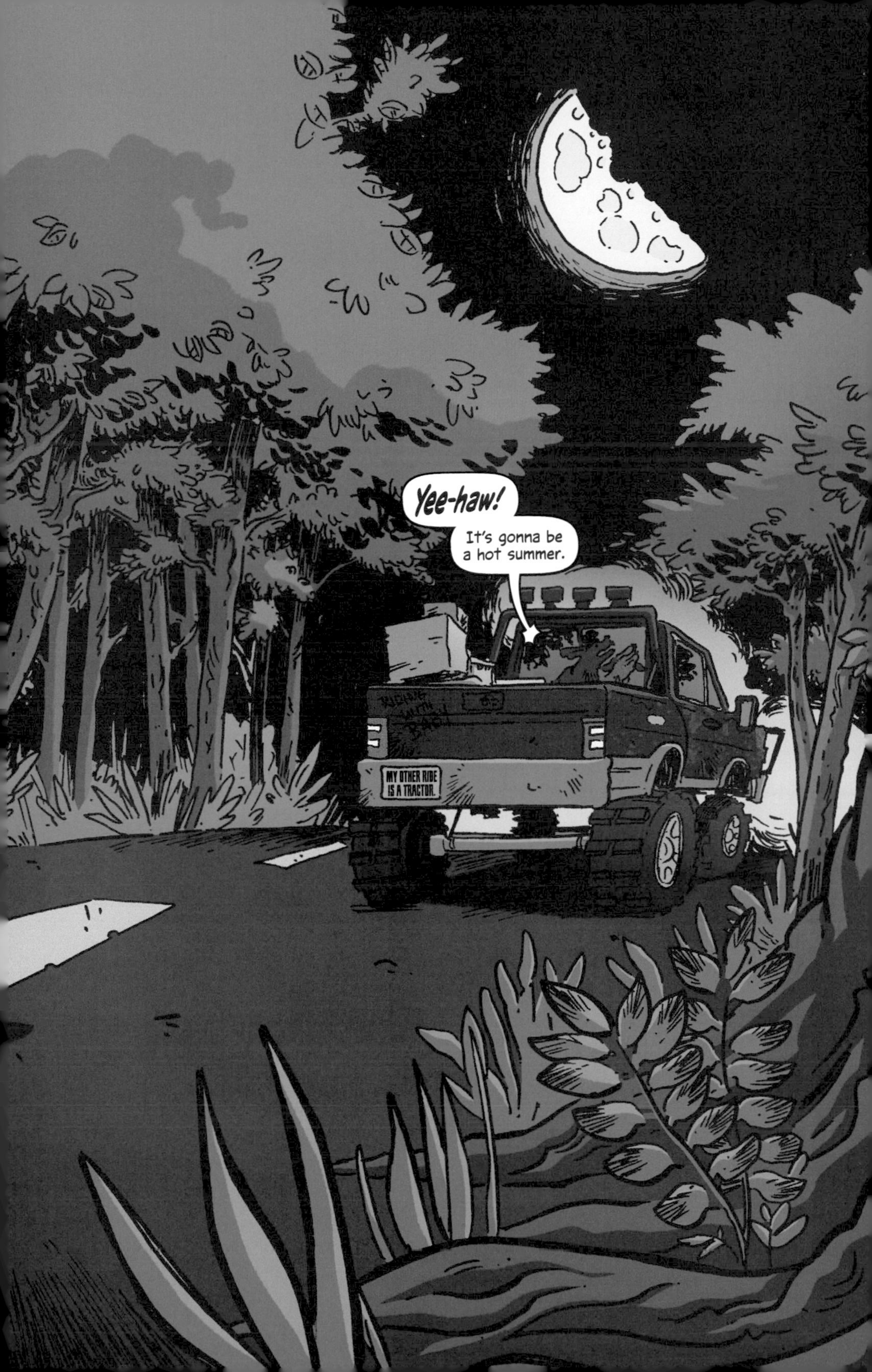
Yee-haw!
It's gonna be a hot summer.
MY OTHER RIDE IS A TRACTOR.

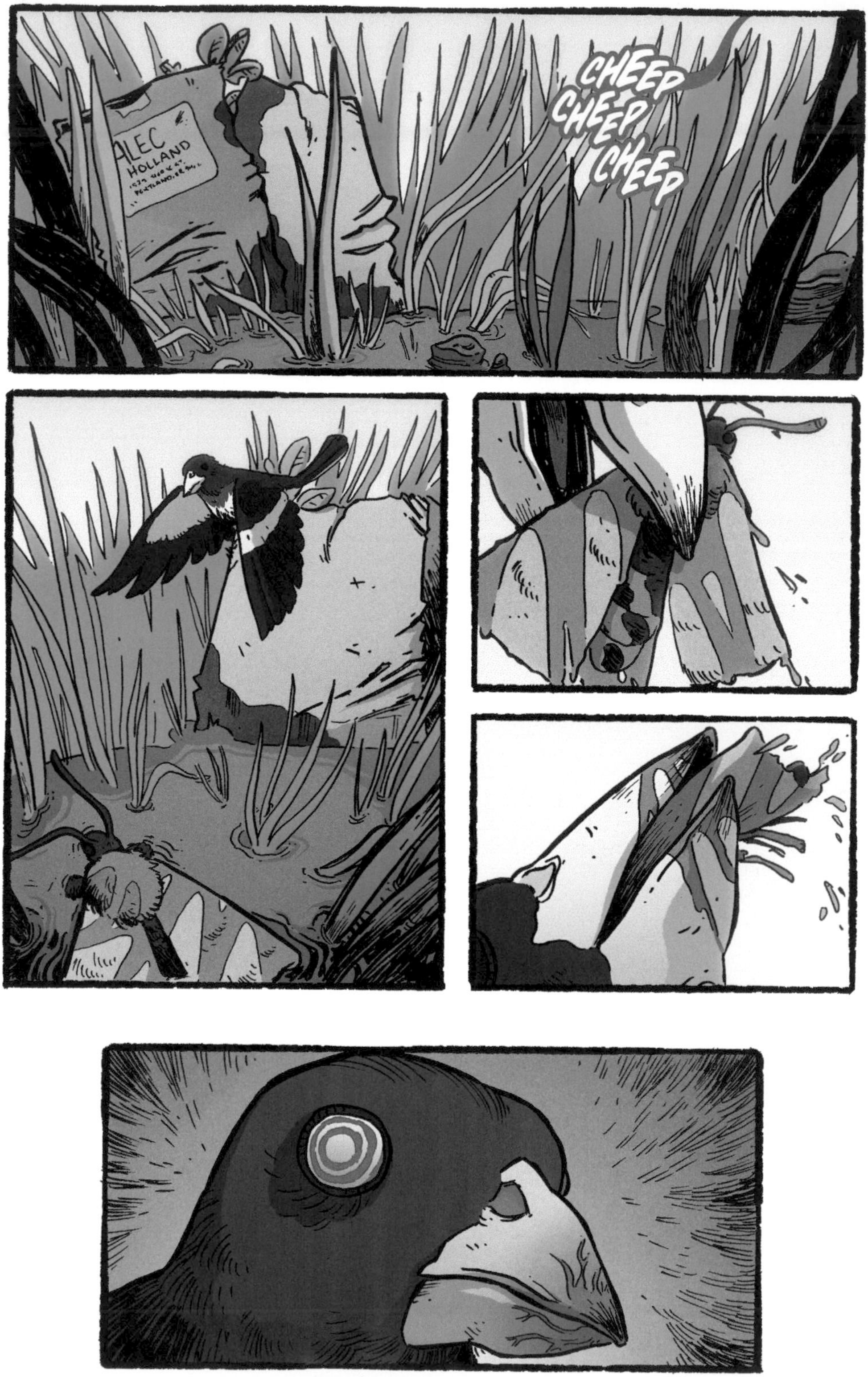
ALEC
HOLLAND
CHEEP
CHEEP
CHEEP

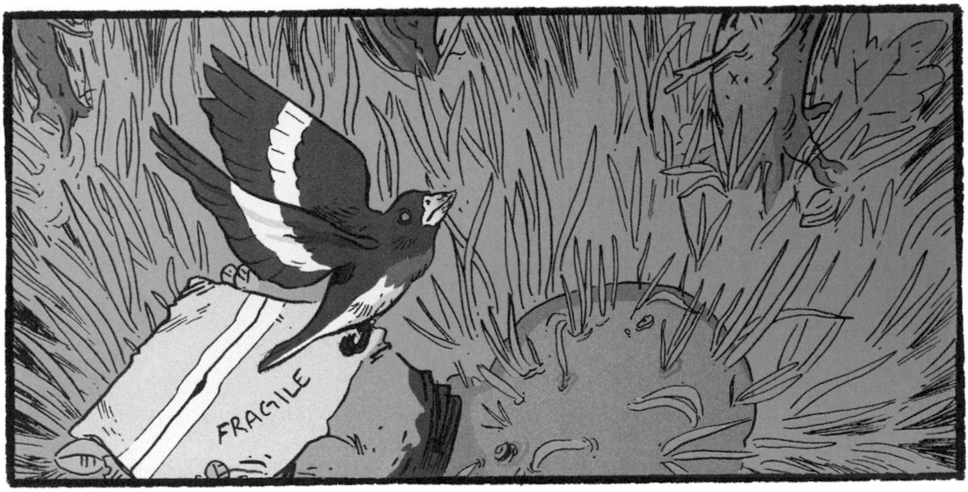
FRAGILE
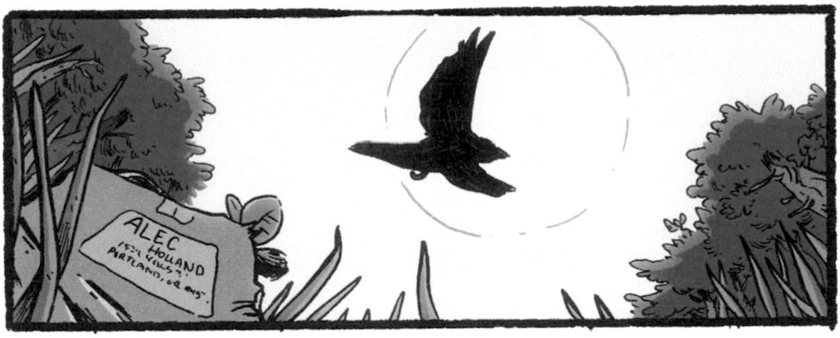
ALEC
HOLLAND
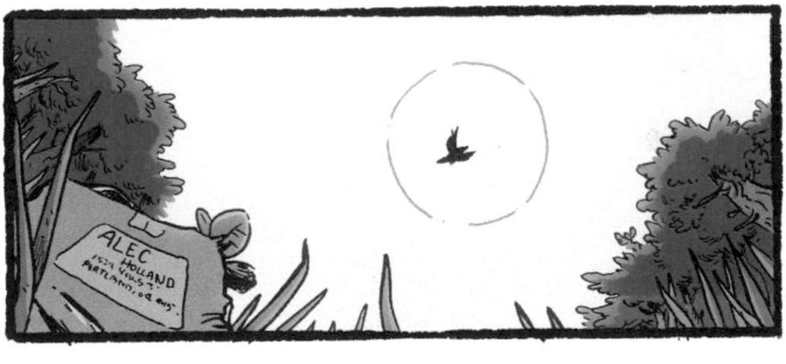
ALEC
HOLLAND
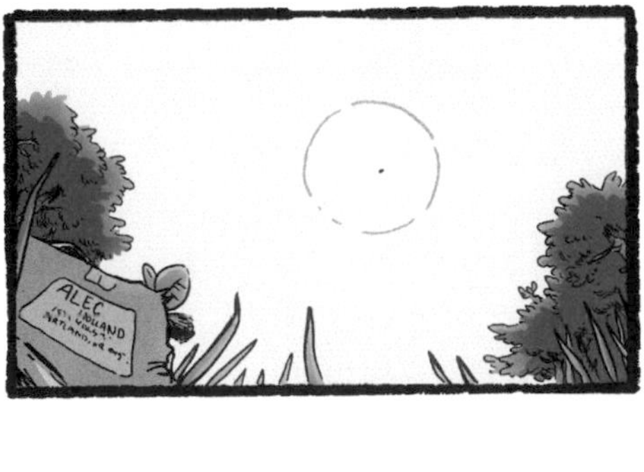
ALEC
HOLLAND

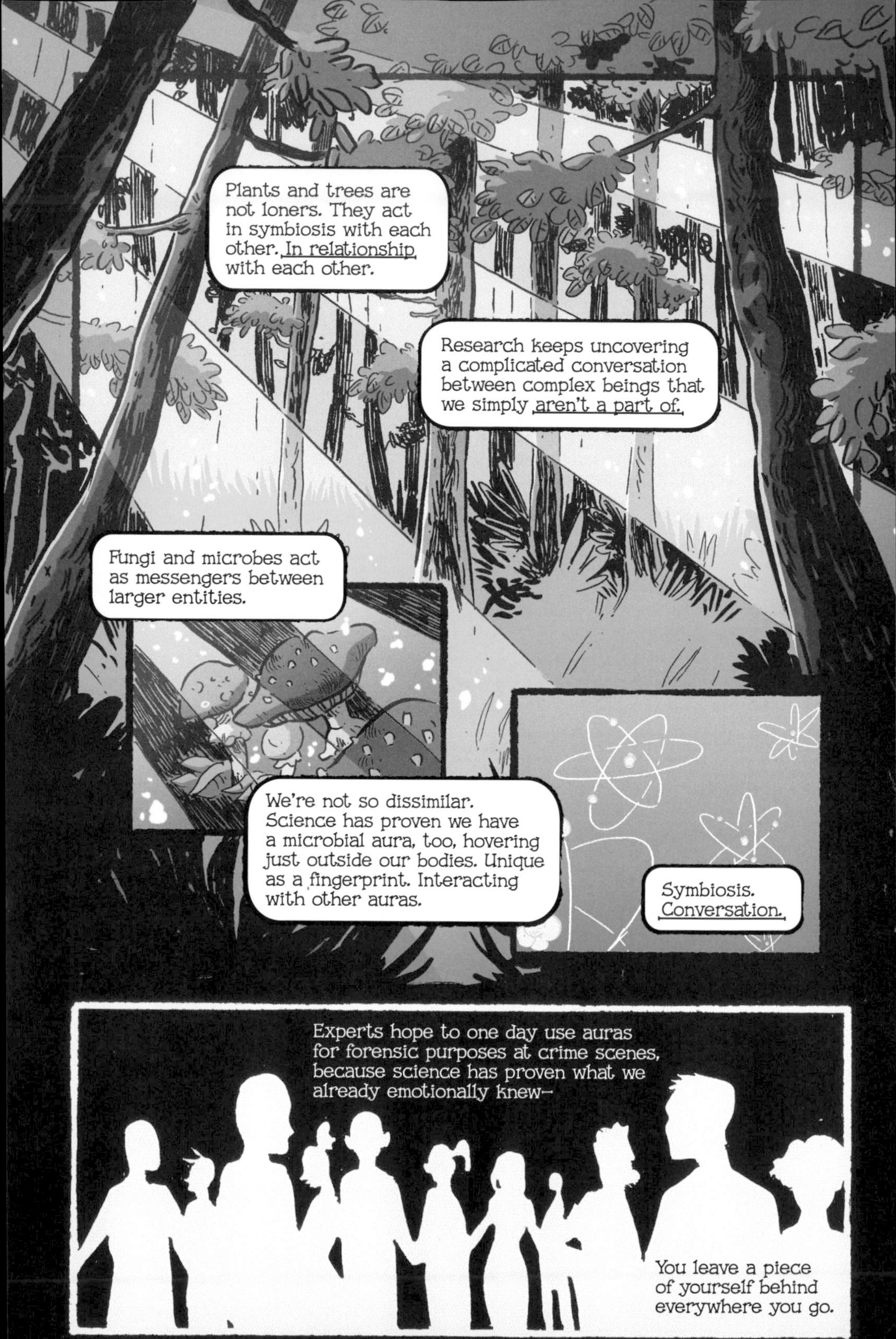
Plants and trees are not loners. They act in symbiosis with each other. In relationship with each other.
Research keeps uncovering a complicated conversation between complex beings that we simply aren't a part of.
Fungi and microbes act as messengers between larger entities.
We're not so dissimilar. Science has proven we have a microbial aura, too, hovering just outside our bodies. Unique as a fingerprint. Interacting with other auras.
Symbiosis. Conversation.
Experts hope to one day use auras for forensic purposes at crime scenes, because science has proven what we already emotionally knew–
You leave a piece of yourself behind everywhere you go.

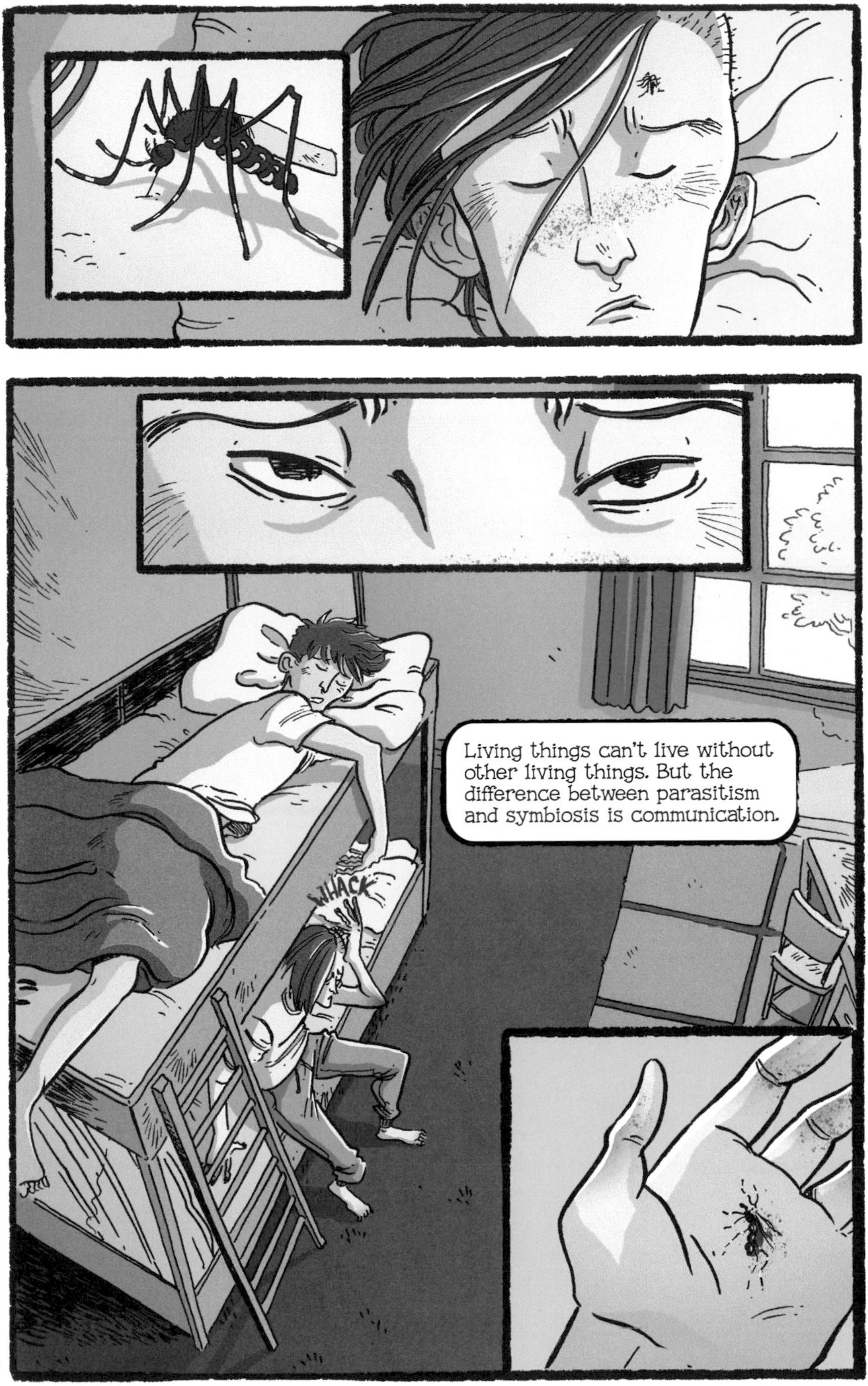
Living things can't live without other living things. But the difference between parasitism and symbiosis is communication.
WHACK

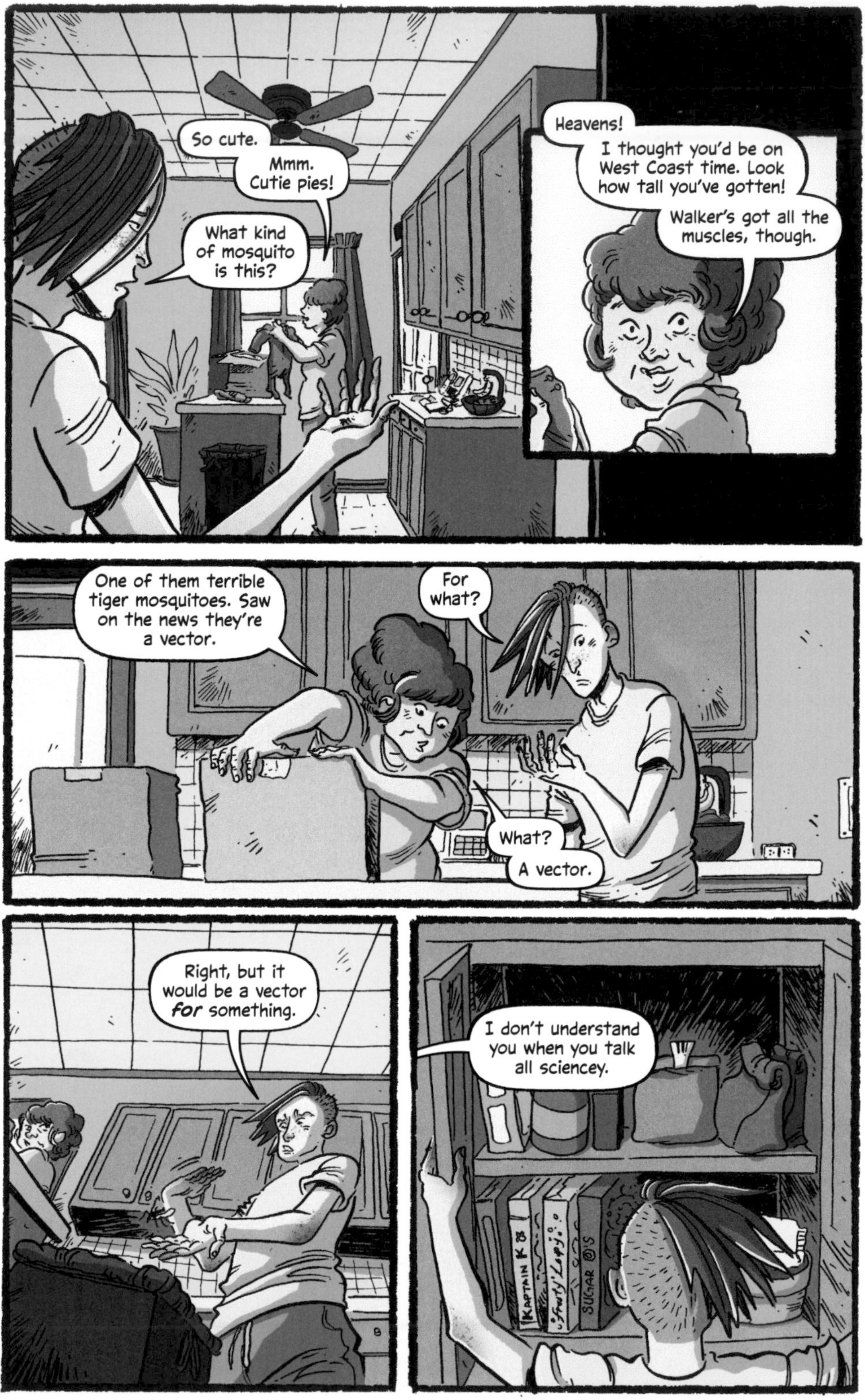
So cute.
Mmm. Cutie pies!
What kind of mosquito is this?
Heavens!
I thought you'd be on West Coast time. Look how tall you've gotten!
Walker's got all the muscles, though.
One of them terrible tiger mosquitoes. Saw on the news they're a vector.
For what?
What?
A vector.
Right, but it would be a vector *for* something.
I don't understand you when you talk all sciencey.

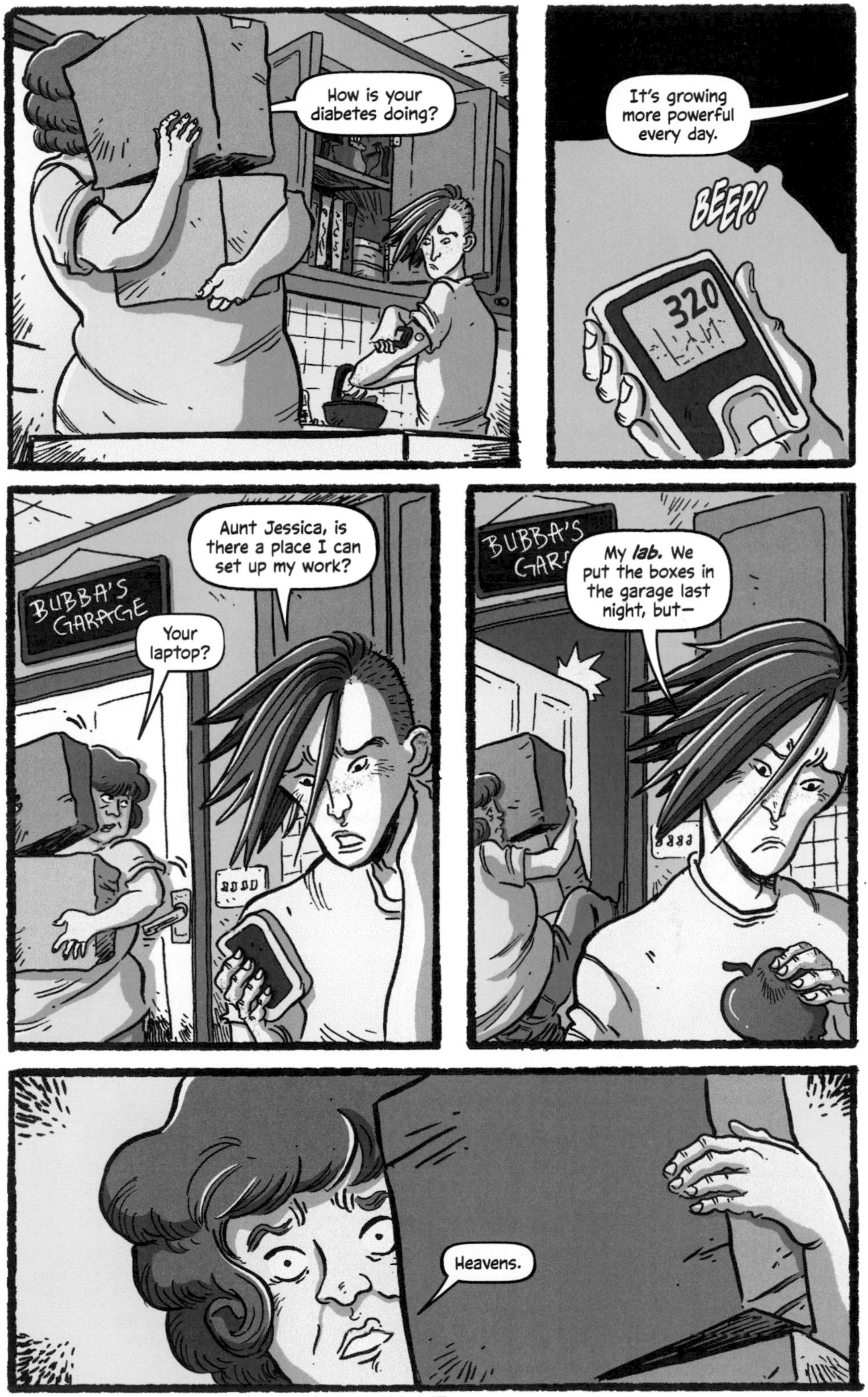
How is your diabetes doing?
It's growing more powerful every day.
BEEP!
320
Aunt Jessica, is there a place I can set up my work?
BUBBA'S GARAGE
Your laptop?
BUBBA'S GARA
My *lab.* We put the boxes in the garage last night, but—
Heavens.

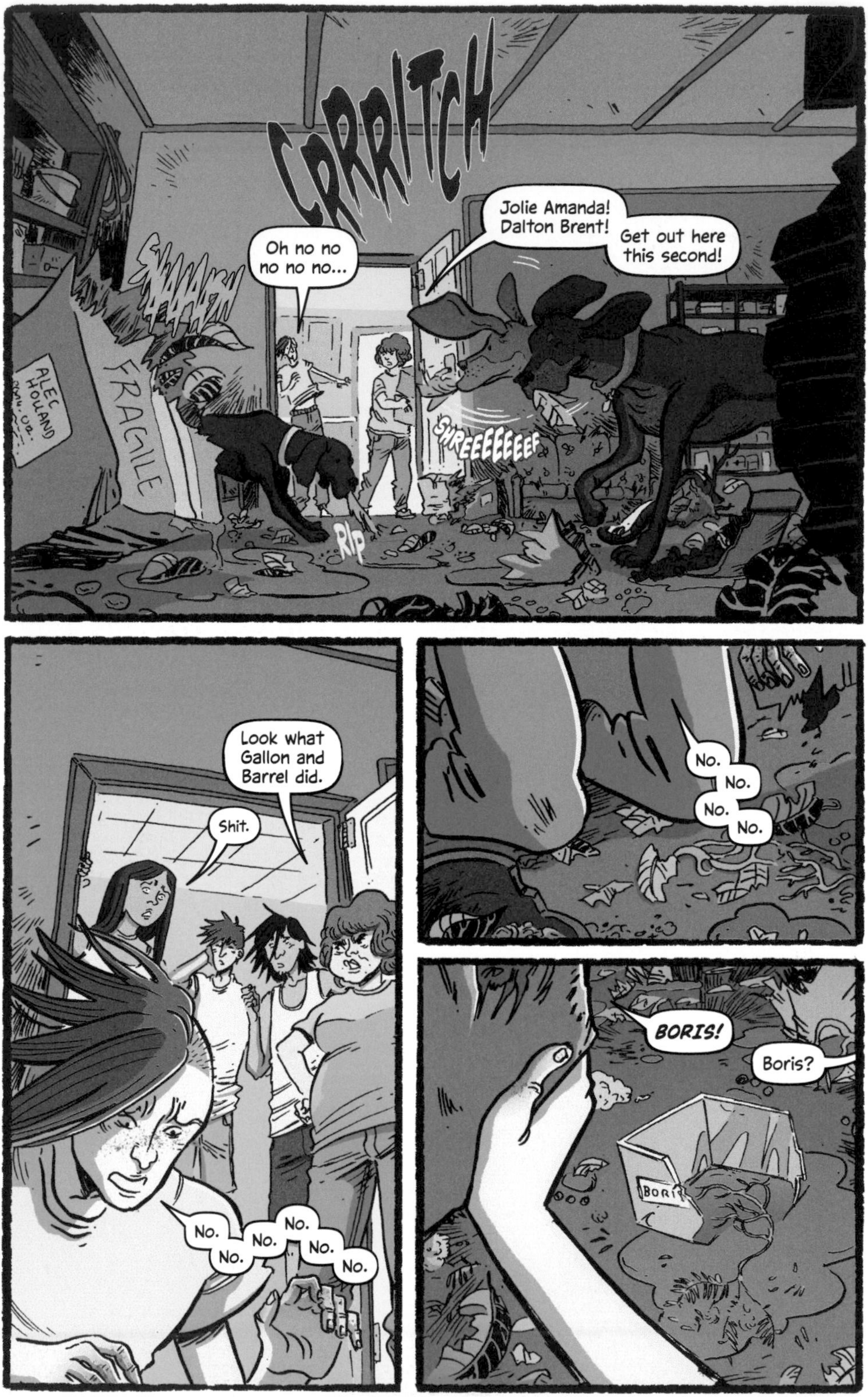
CRRRITCH
SNAAAASH
ALEC HOLLAND
FRAGILE
Oh no no no no no...
Jolie Amanda! Dalton Brent!
Get out here this second!
SHREEEEEEEF
RIP
Look what Gallon and Barrel did.
Shit.
No.
No.
No.
No.
No.
No.
No.
No.
No.
No.
BORIS!
Boris?
BORIS

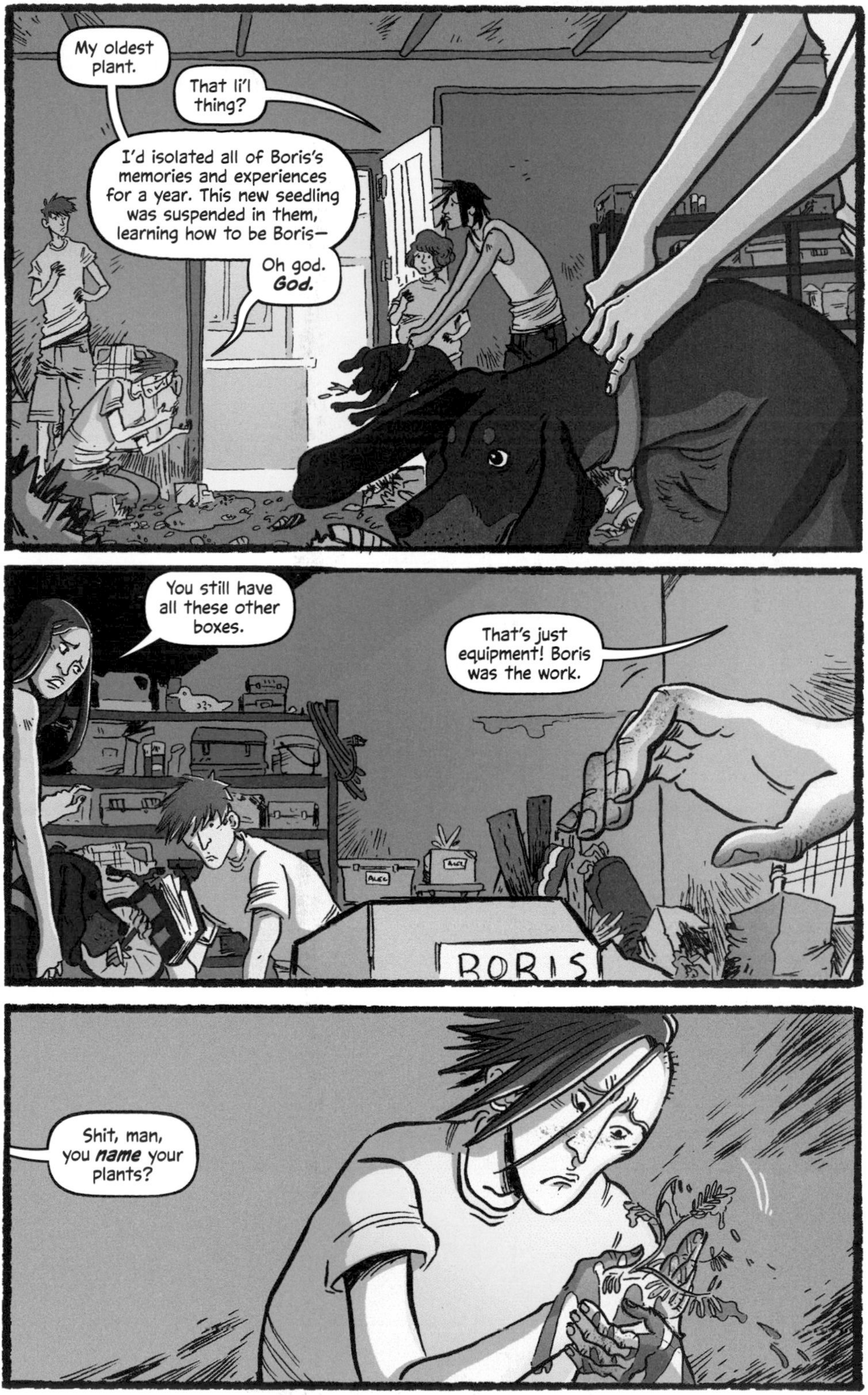
My oldest plant.
That li'l thing?
I'd isolated all of Boris's memories and experiences for a year. This new seedling was suspended in them, learning how to be Boris—
Oh god. ***God.***
You still have all these other boxes.
That's just equipment! Boris was the work.
BORIS
Shit, man, you ***name*** your plants?

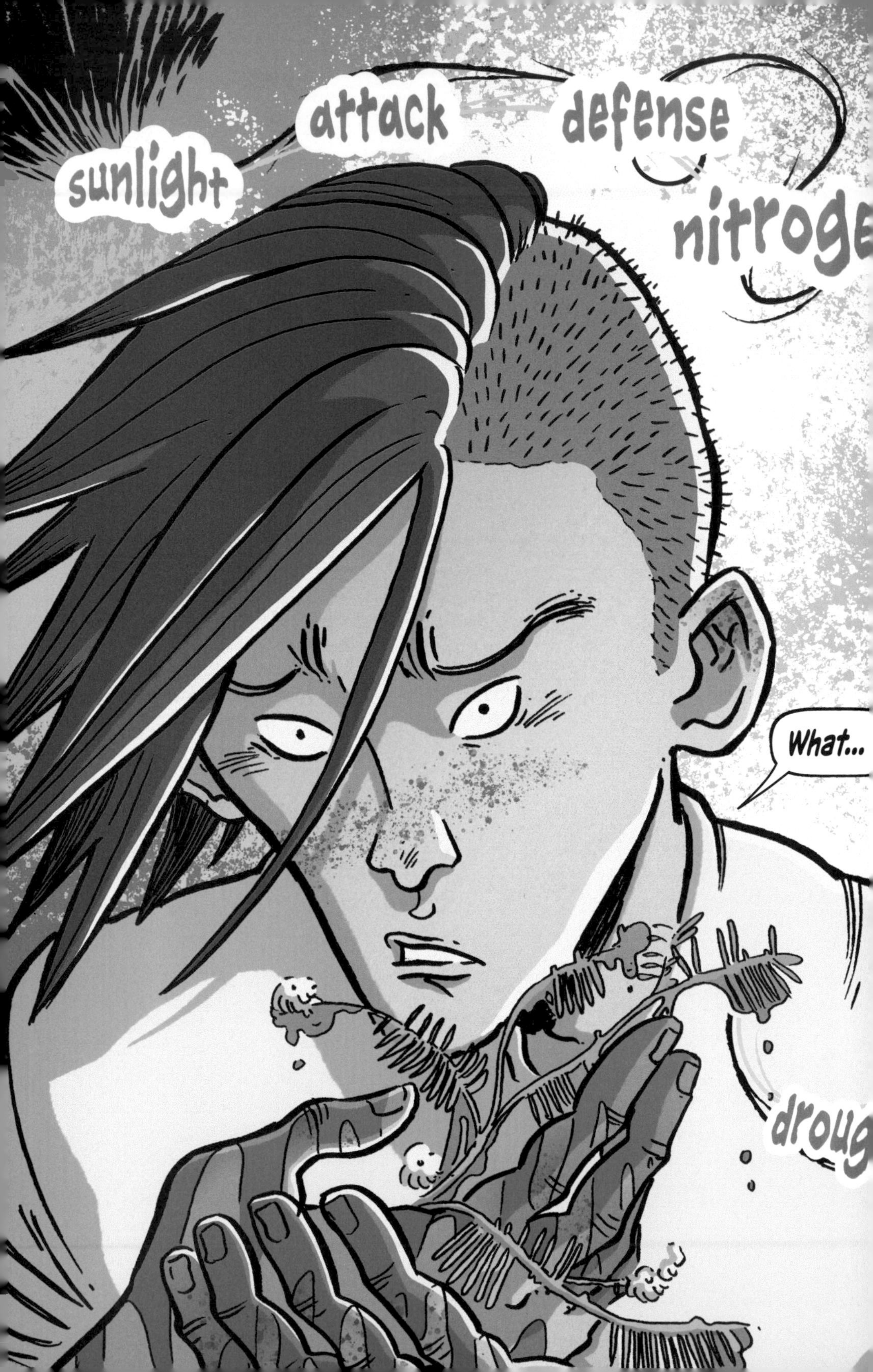
sunlight
attack
defense
nitroge
What...
droug

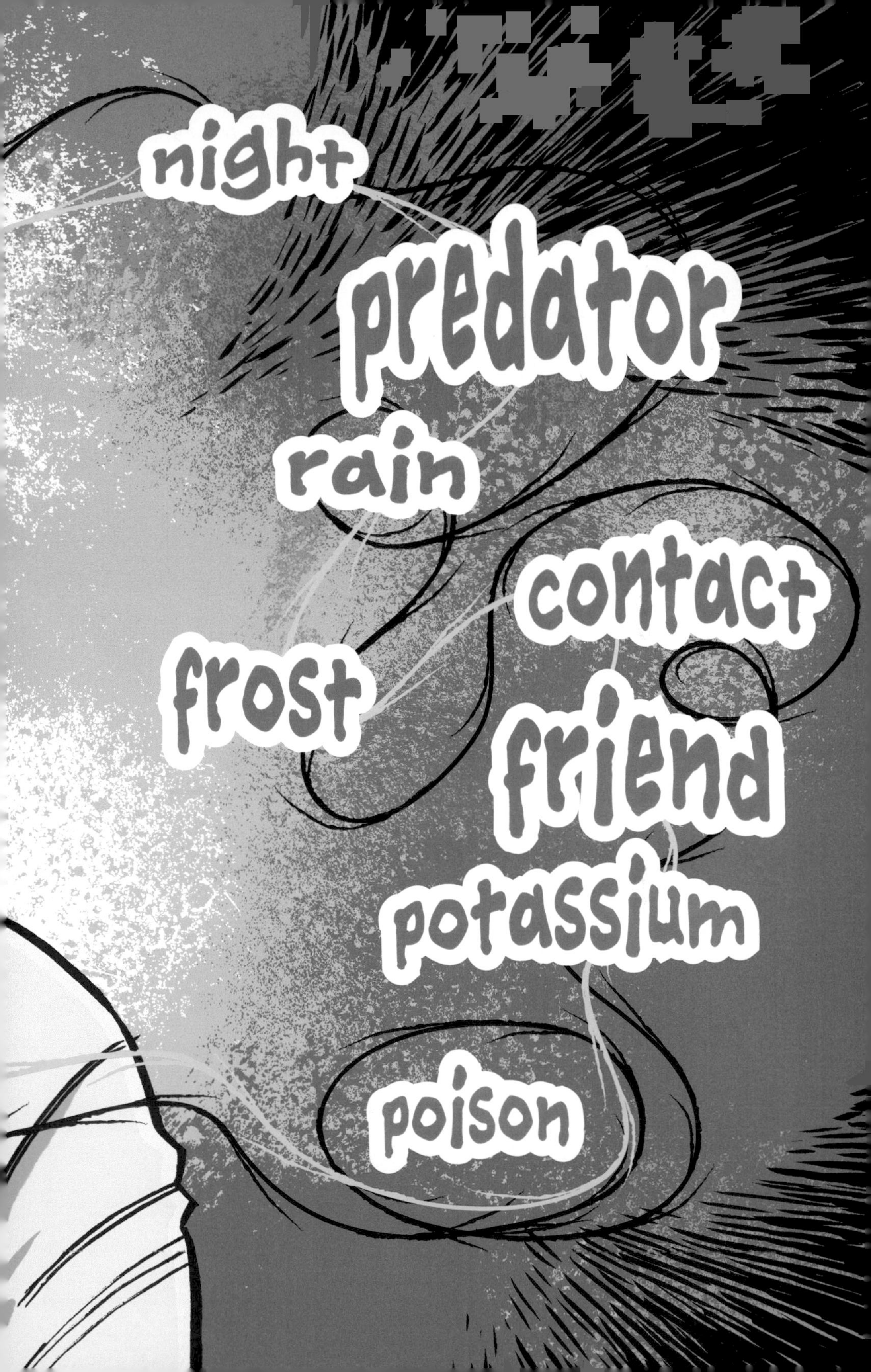
night
predator
rain
contact
frost
friend
potassium
poison

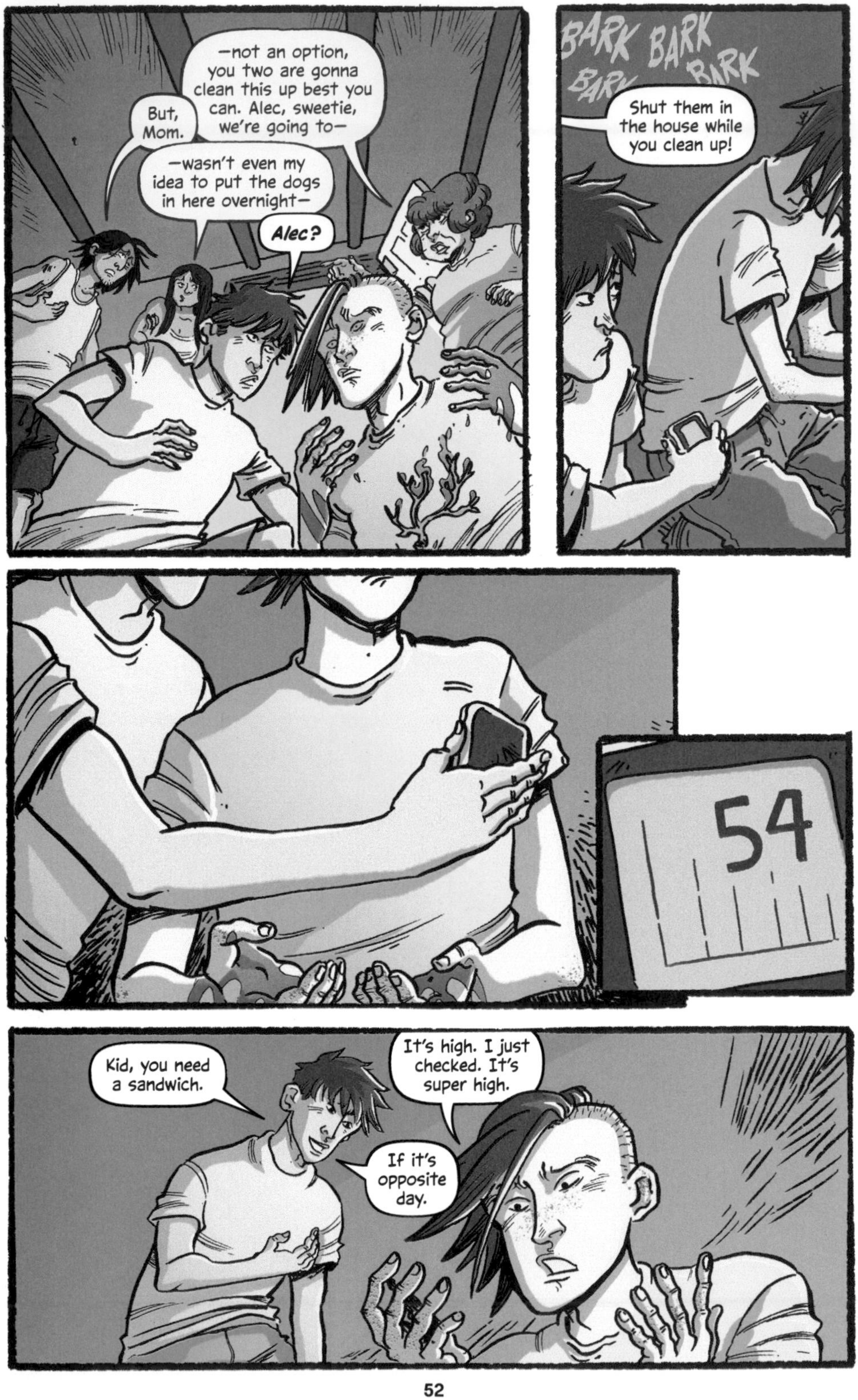
—not an option, you two are gonna clean this up best you can. Alec, sweetie, we're going to—
But, Mom.
—wasn't even my idea to put the dogs in here overnight—
Alec?
BARK BARK
BARK BARK
Shut them in the house while you clean up!
54
Kid, you need a sandwich.
It's high. I just checked. It's super high.
If it's opposite day.

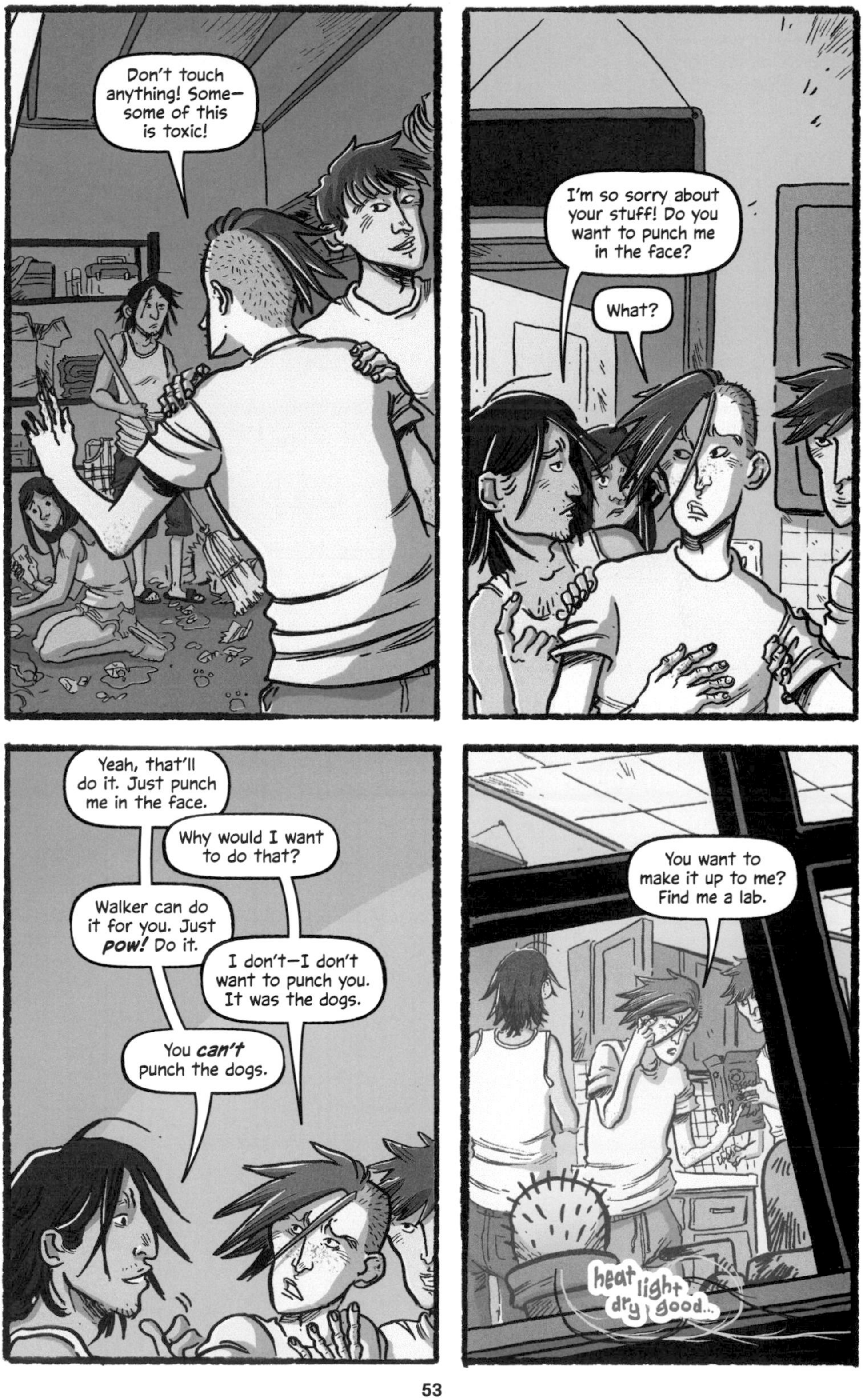
Don't touch anything! Some—some of this is toxic!
I'm so sorry about your stuff! Do you want to punch me in the face?
What?
Yeah, that'll do it. Just punch me in the face.
Why would I want to do that?
Walker can do it for you. Just *pow!* Do it.
I don't—I don't want to punch you. It was the dogs.
You *can't* punch the dogs.
You want to make it up to me? Find me a lab.
heat light dry good...

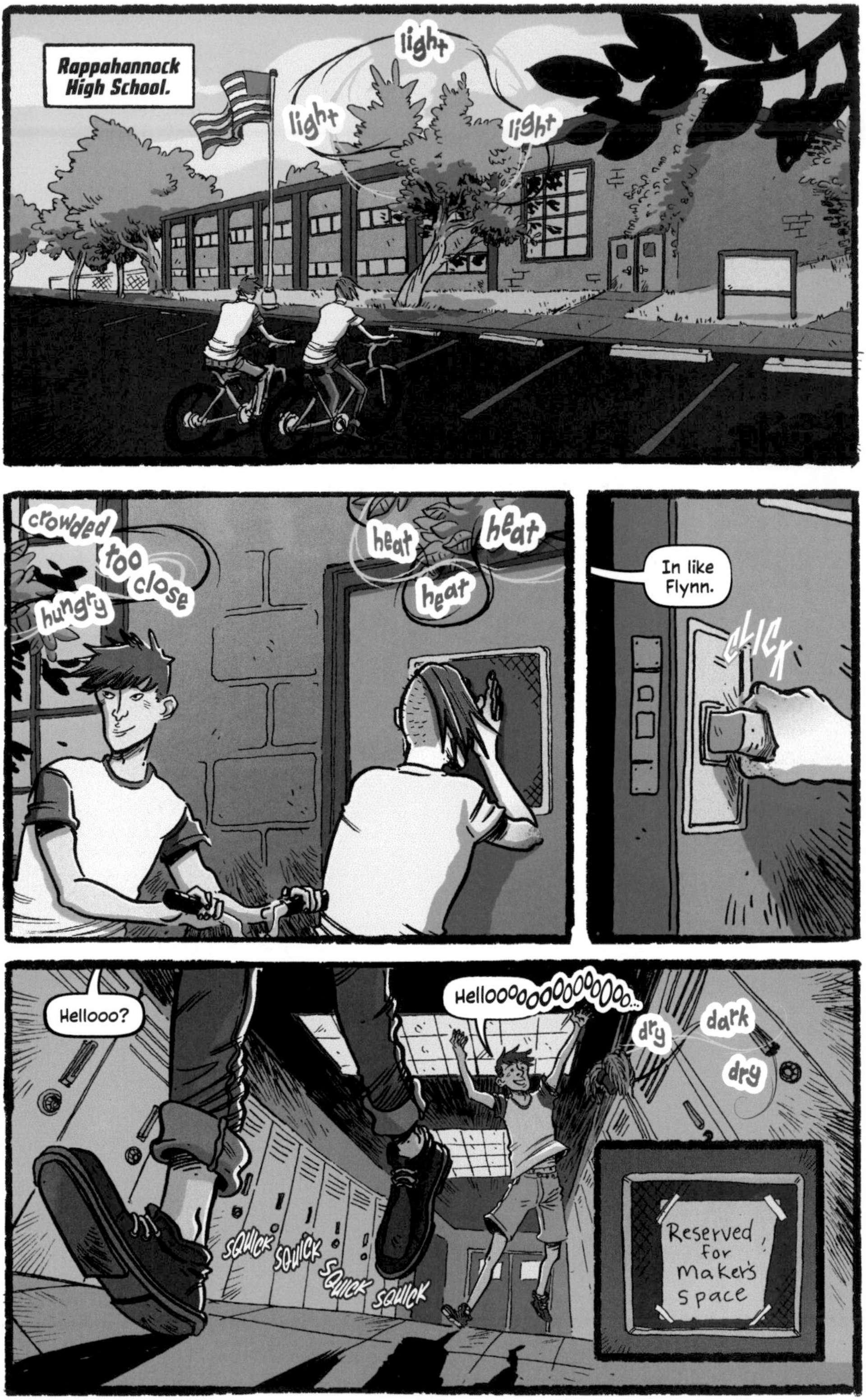
Rappahannock High School.
light
light
light
crowded
too close
hungry
heat
heat
heat
In like Flynn.
CLICK
Hellooo?
Hellooooooooooooooo...
dry
dark
dry
SQUICK SQUICK SQUICK SQUICK
Reserved for Maker's Space

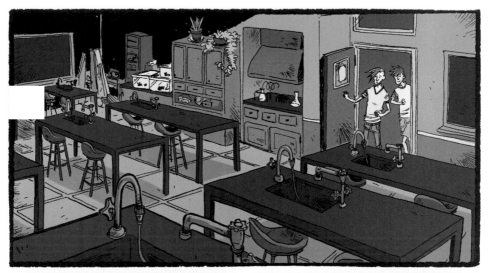

Hm.

Sciencey!

Hm.

Beakery!

CLINK

Hm.

Rodenty!

WHOA, *SCARY!*

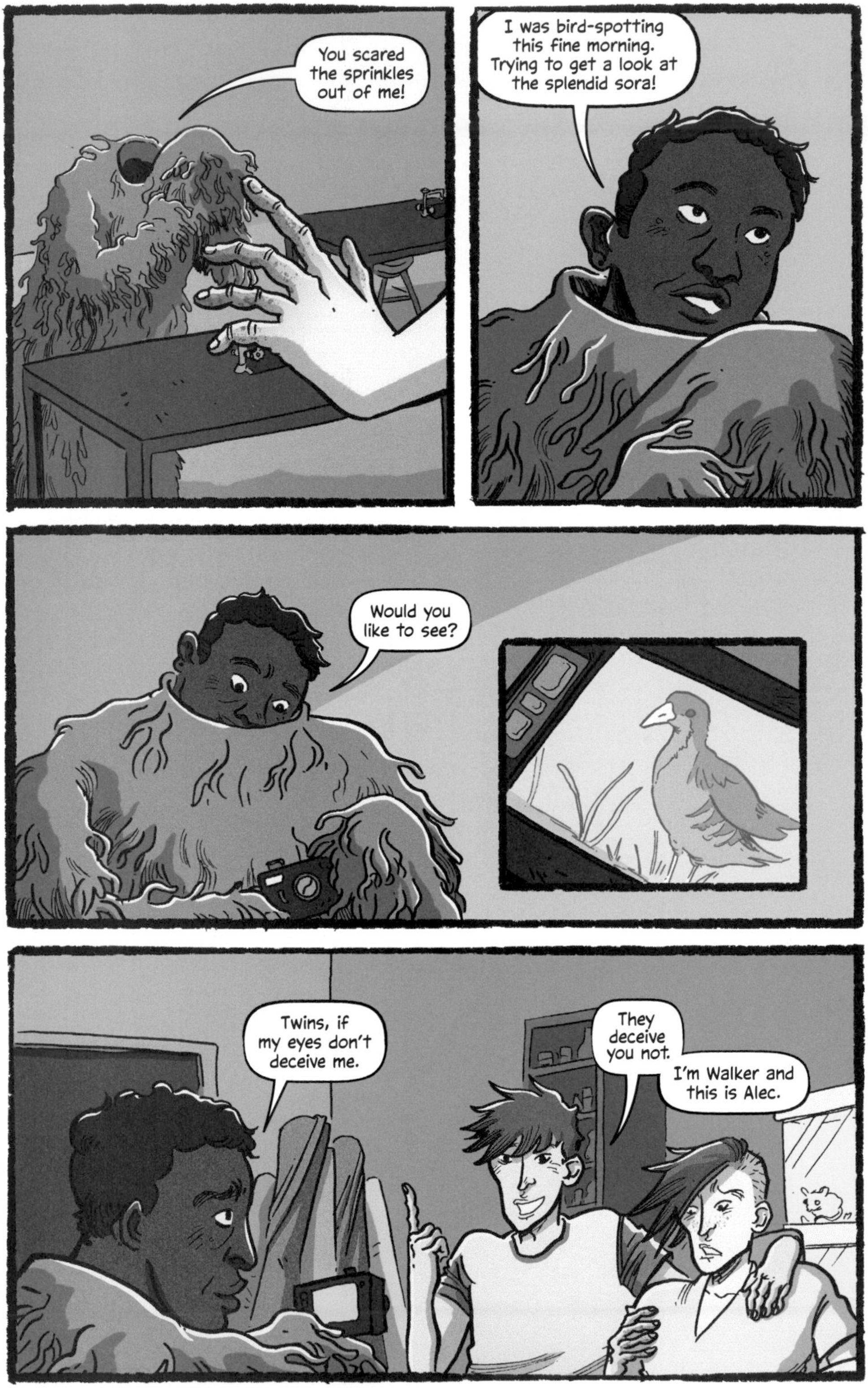
You scared the sprinkles out of me!
I was bird-spotting this fine morning. Trying to get a look at the splendid sora!
Would you like to see?
Twins, if my eyes don't deceive me.
They deceive you not.
I'm Walker and this is Alec.

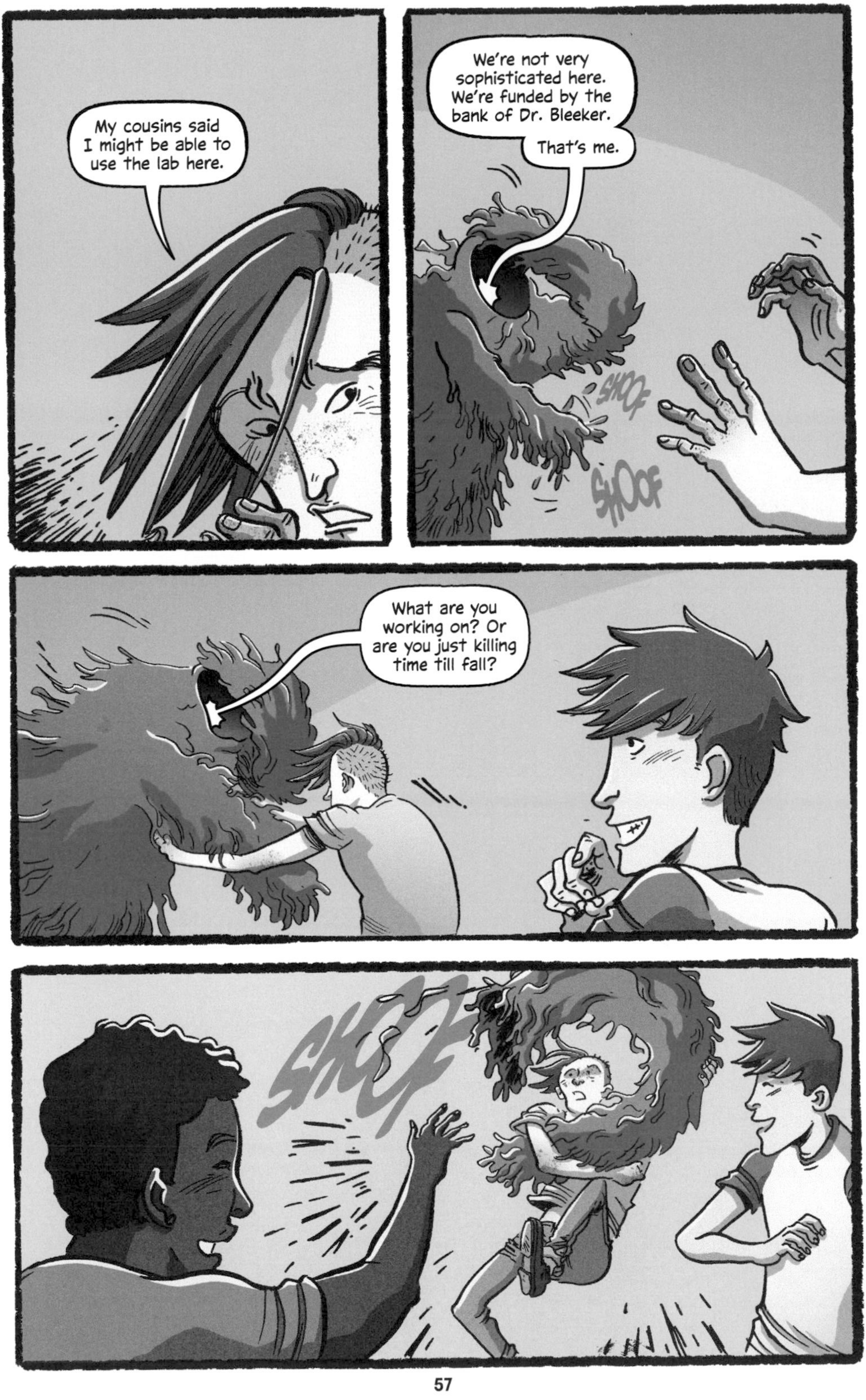
My cousins said I might be able to use the lab here.
We're not very sophisticated here. We're funded by the bank of Dr. Bleeker.
That's me.
SHOOF
SHOOF
What are you working on? Or are you just killing time till fall?
SHOOF

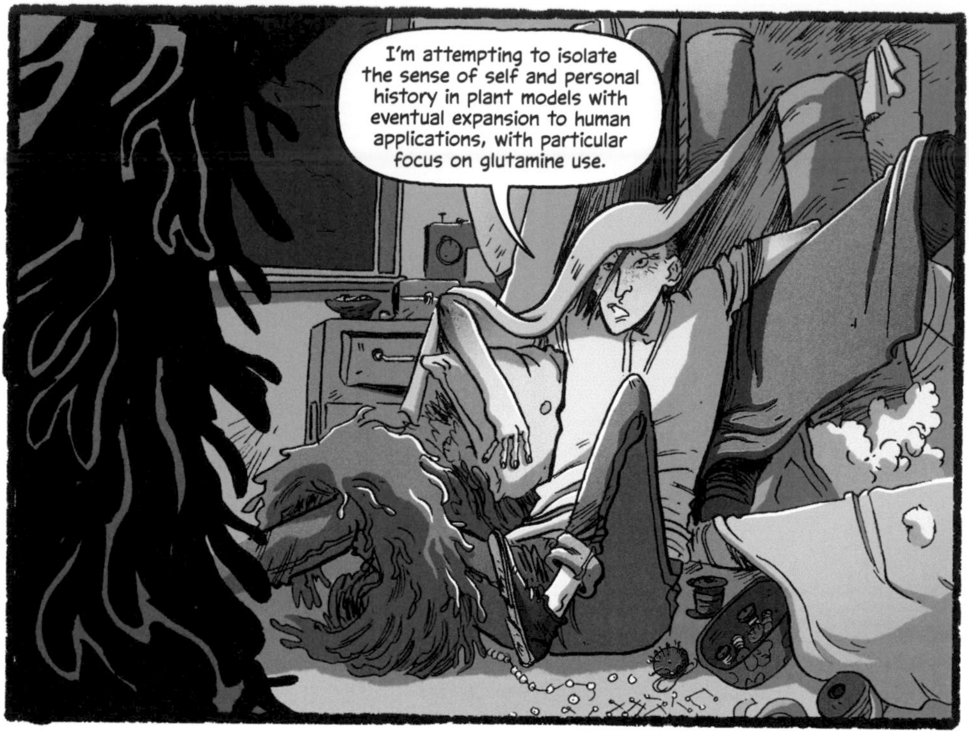
I'm attempting to isolate the sense of self and personal history in plant models with eventual expansion to human applications, with particular focus on glutamine use.

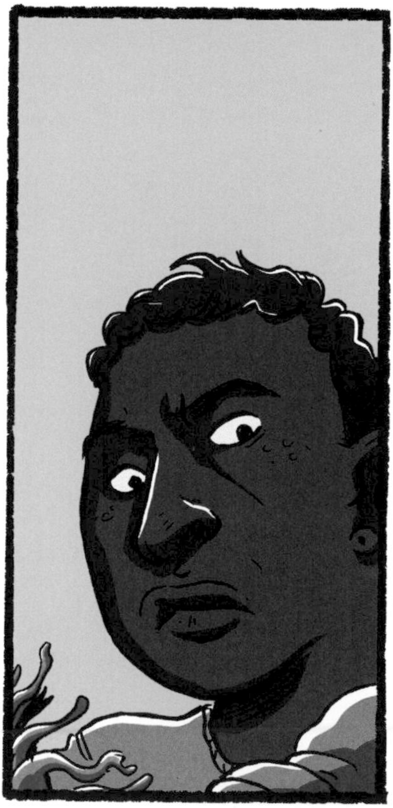

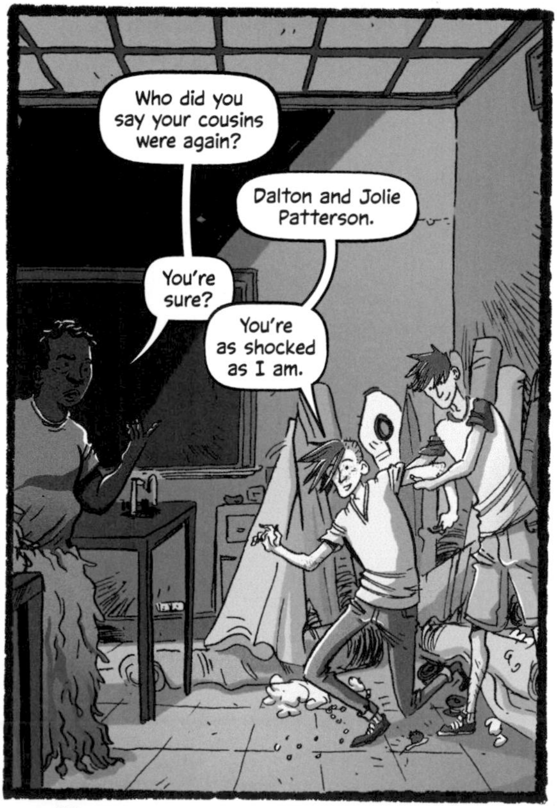
Who did you say your cousins were again?
Dalton and Jolie Patterson.
You're sure?
You're as shocked as I am.

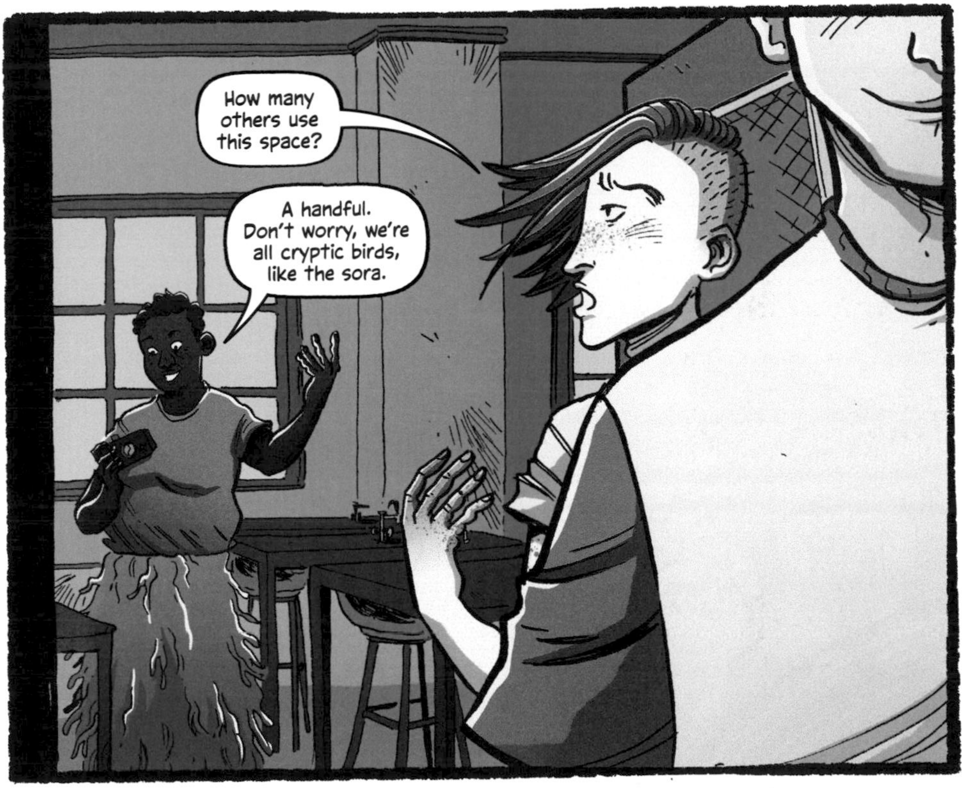
How many others use this space?
A handful. Don't worry, we're all cryptic birds, like the sora.

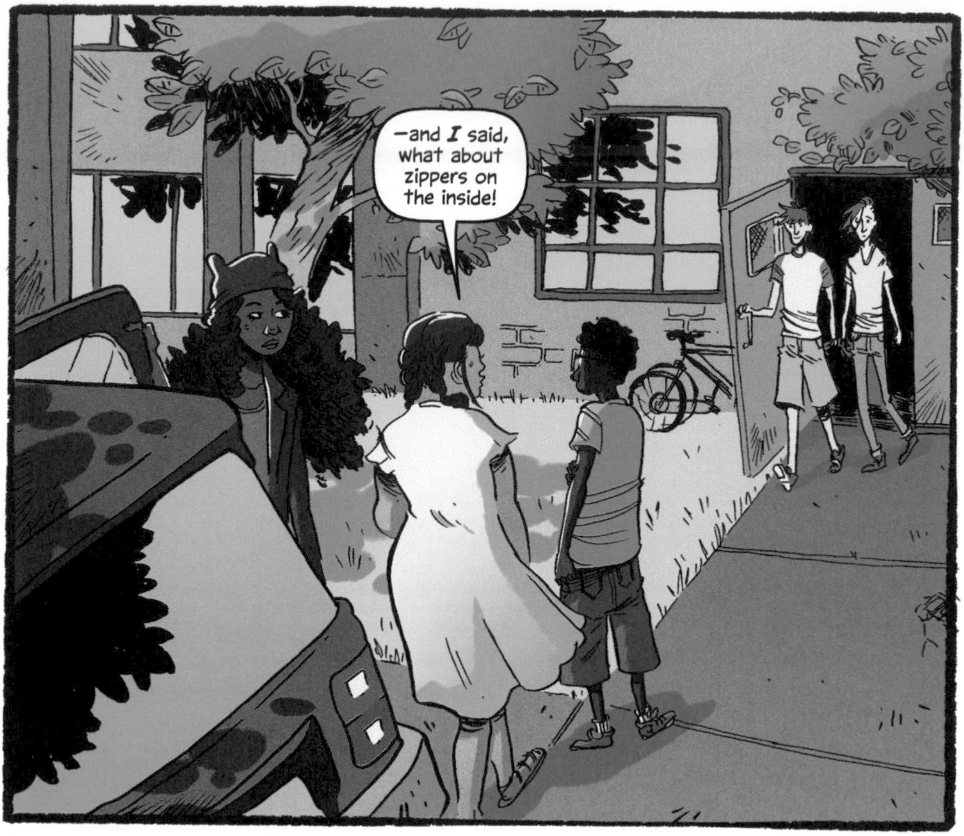
—and I said, what about zippers on the inside!

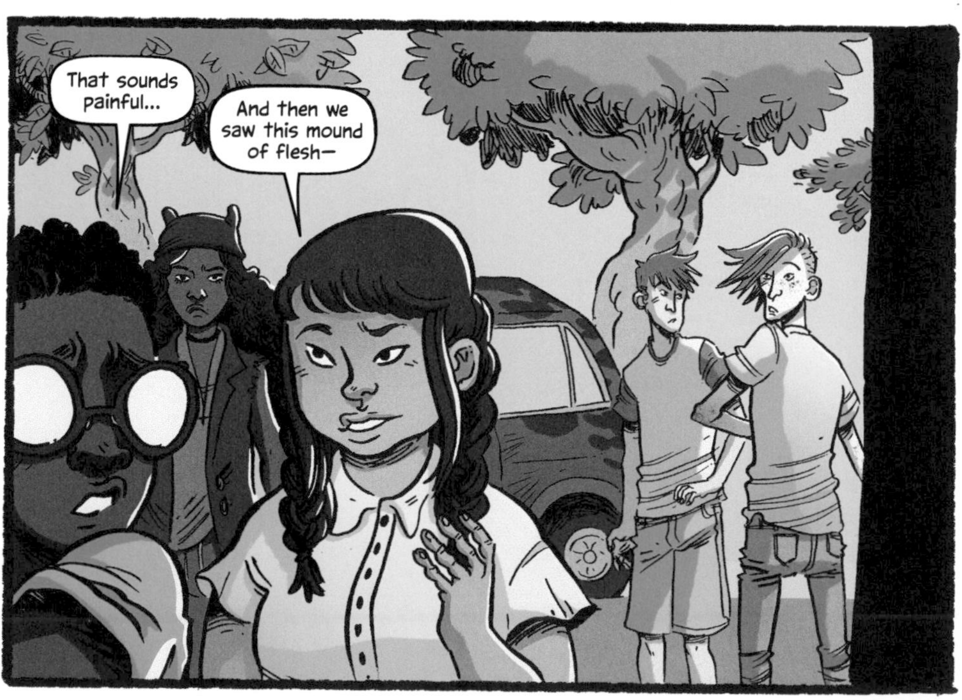
That sounds painful...
And then we saw this mound of flesh—

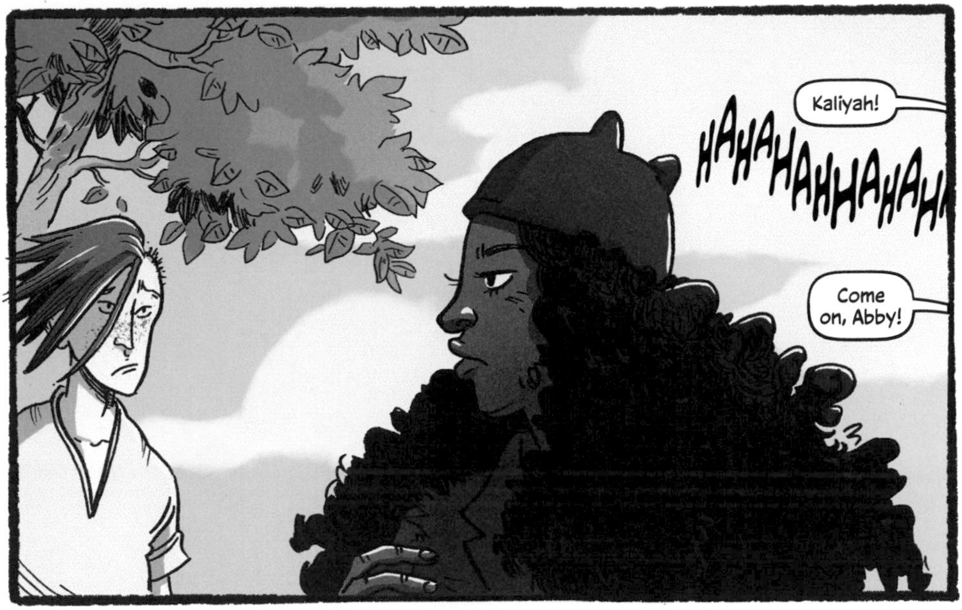
Kaliyah!
HAHAHAHHAHAHAH
Come on, Abby!

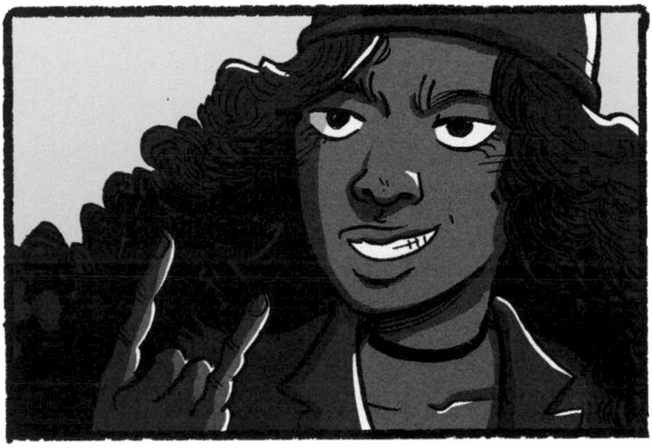

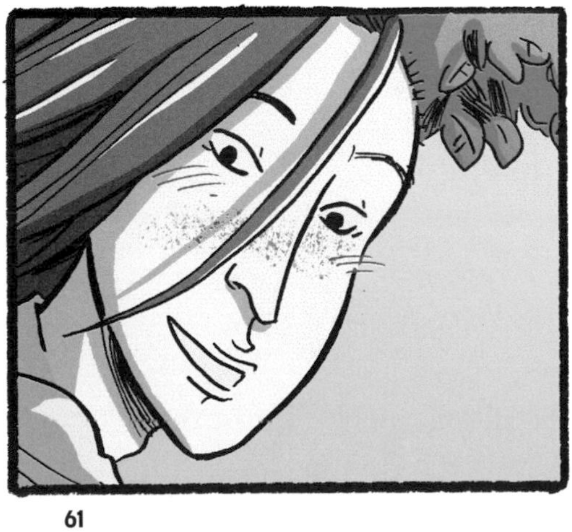

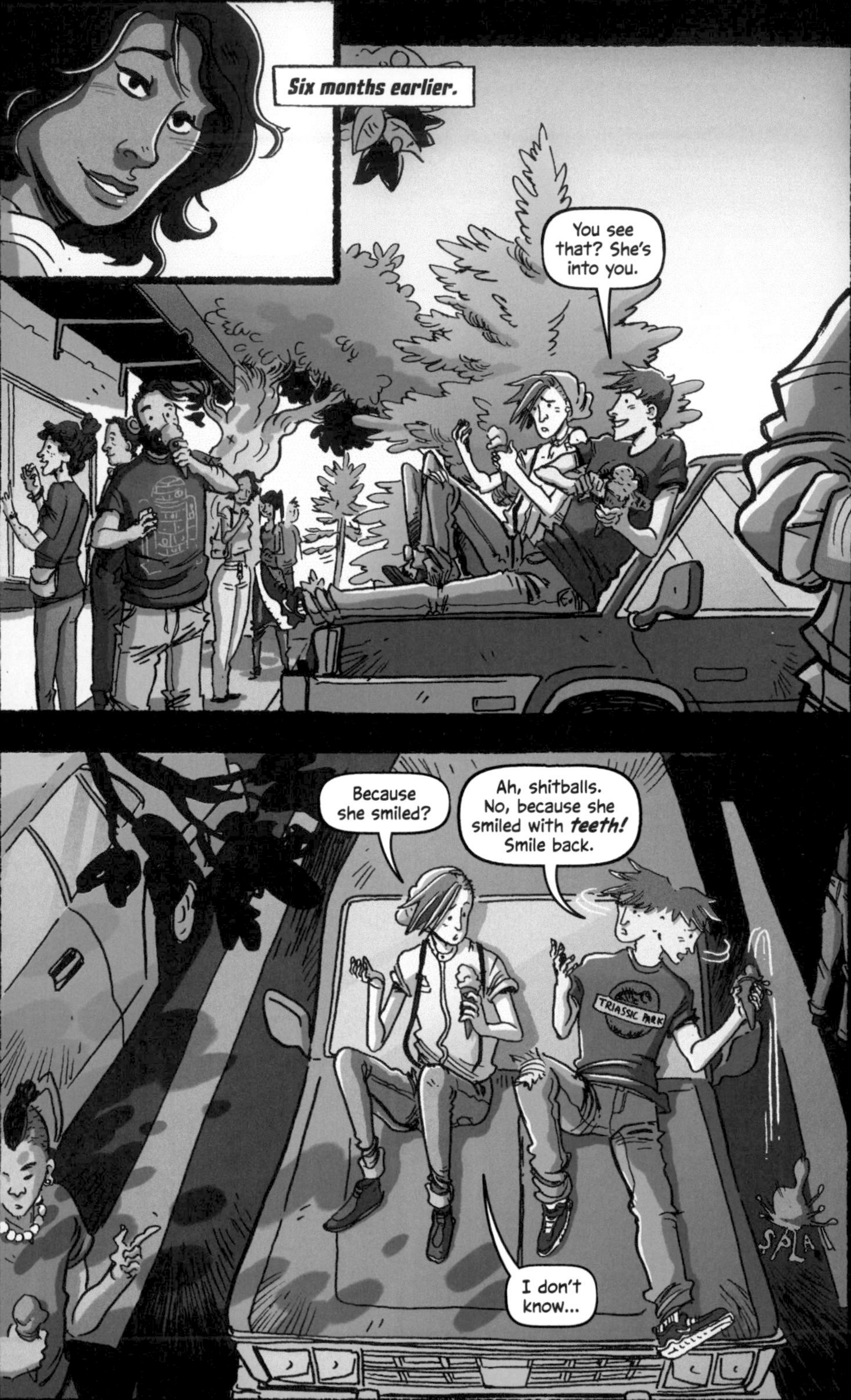
Six months earlier.
You see that? She's into you.
Because she smiled?
Ah, shitballs. No, because she smiled with *teeth!* Smile back.
I don't know...
SPLAT

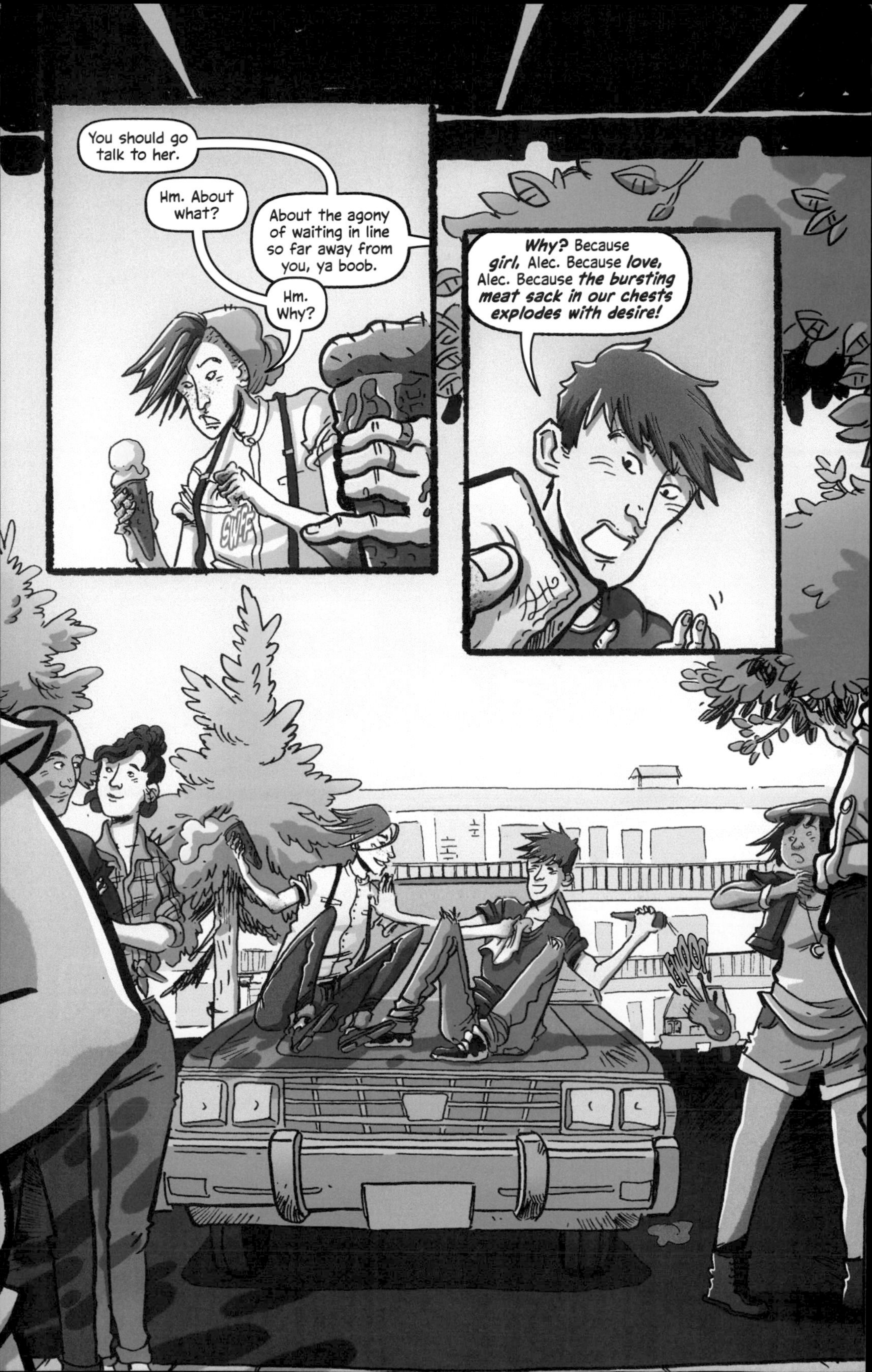
You should go talk to her.
Hm. About what?
About the agony of waiting in line so far away from you, ya boob.
Hm. Why?
Why? Because *girl,* Alec. Because *love,* Alec. Because *the bursting meat sack in our chests explodes with desire!*
FWOOP!

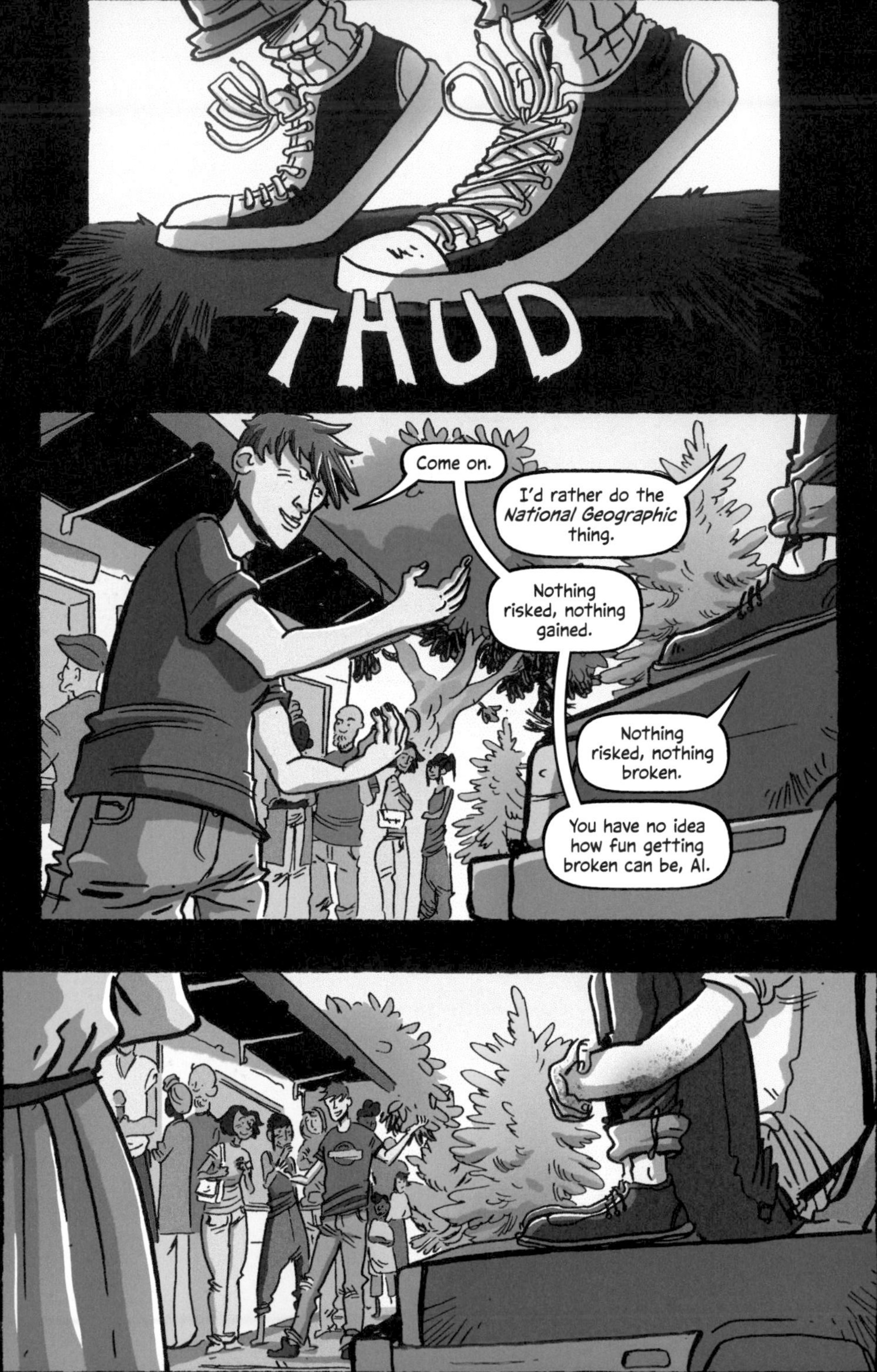
THUD
Come on.
I'd rather do the *National Geographic* thing.
Nothing risked, nothing gained.
Nothing risked, nothing broken.
You have no idea how fun getting broken can be, Al.

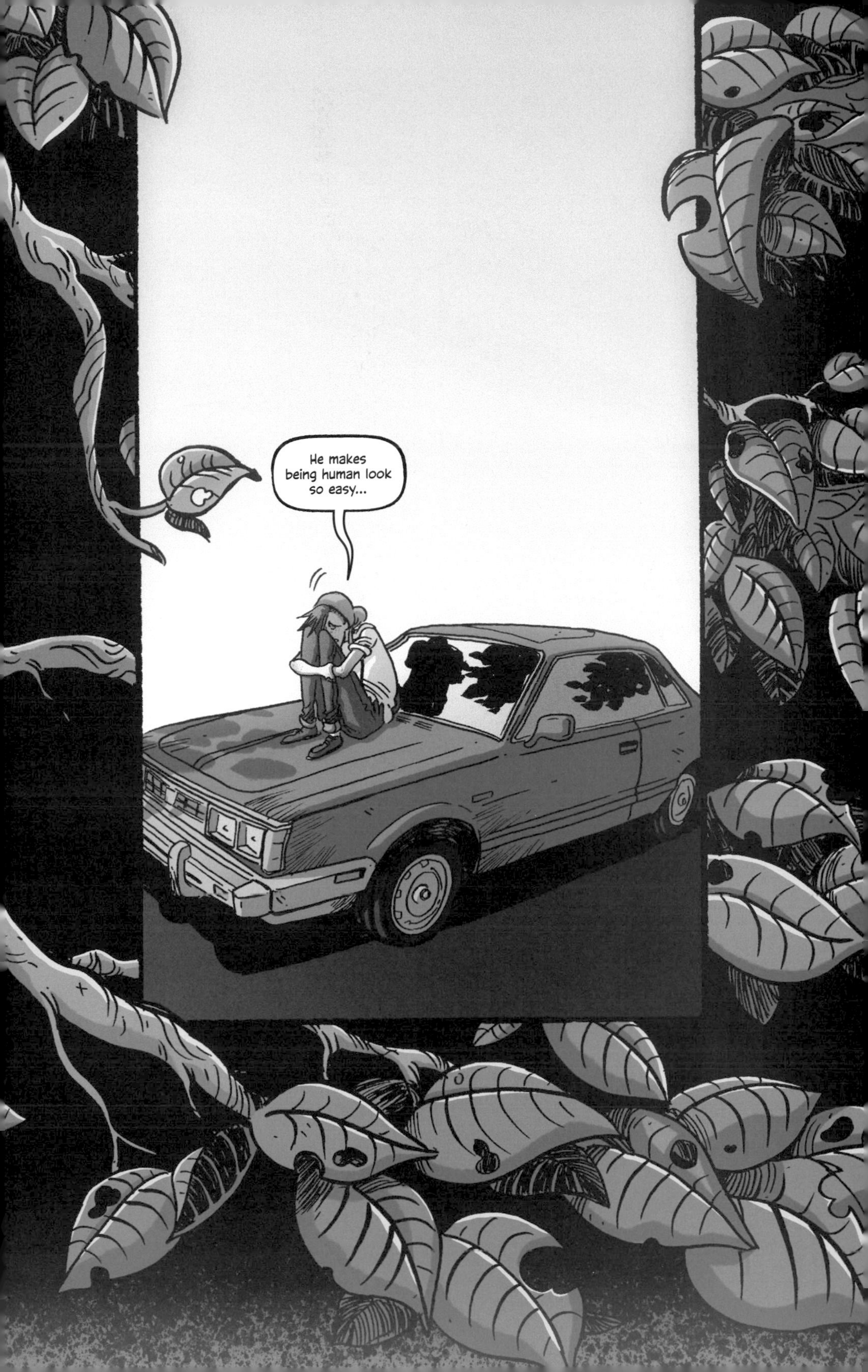
He makes being human look so easy...

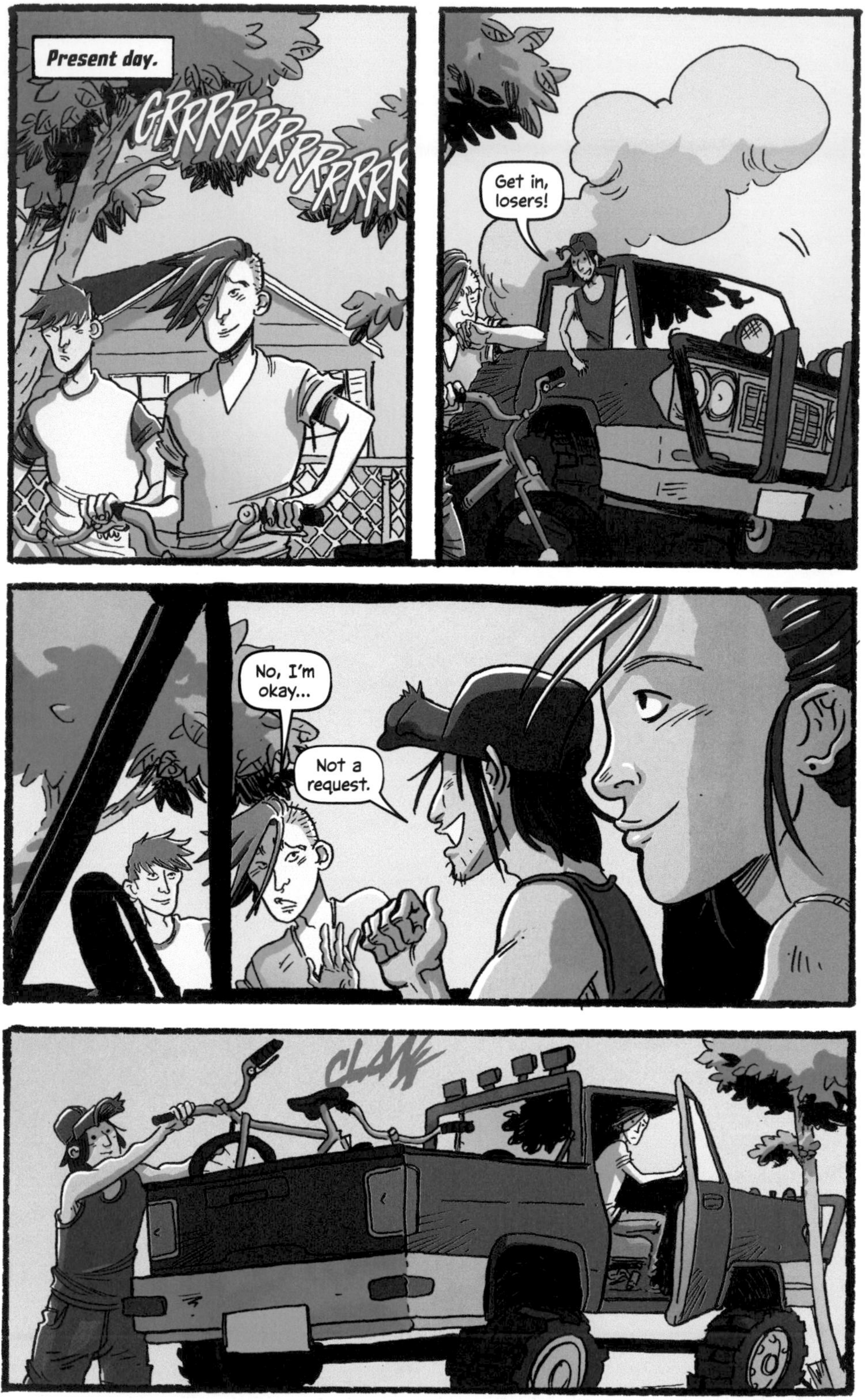
Present day.
GRRRRRRRRRRRRRR
Get in, losers!
No, I'm okay...
Not a request.
CLANK

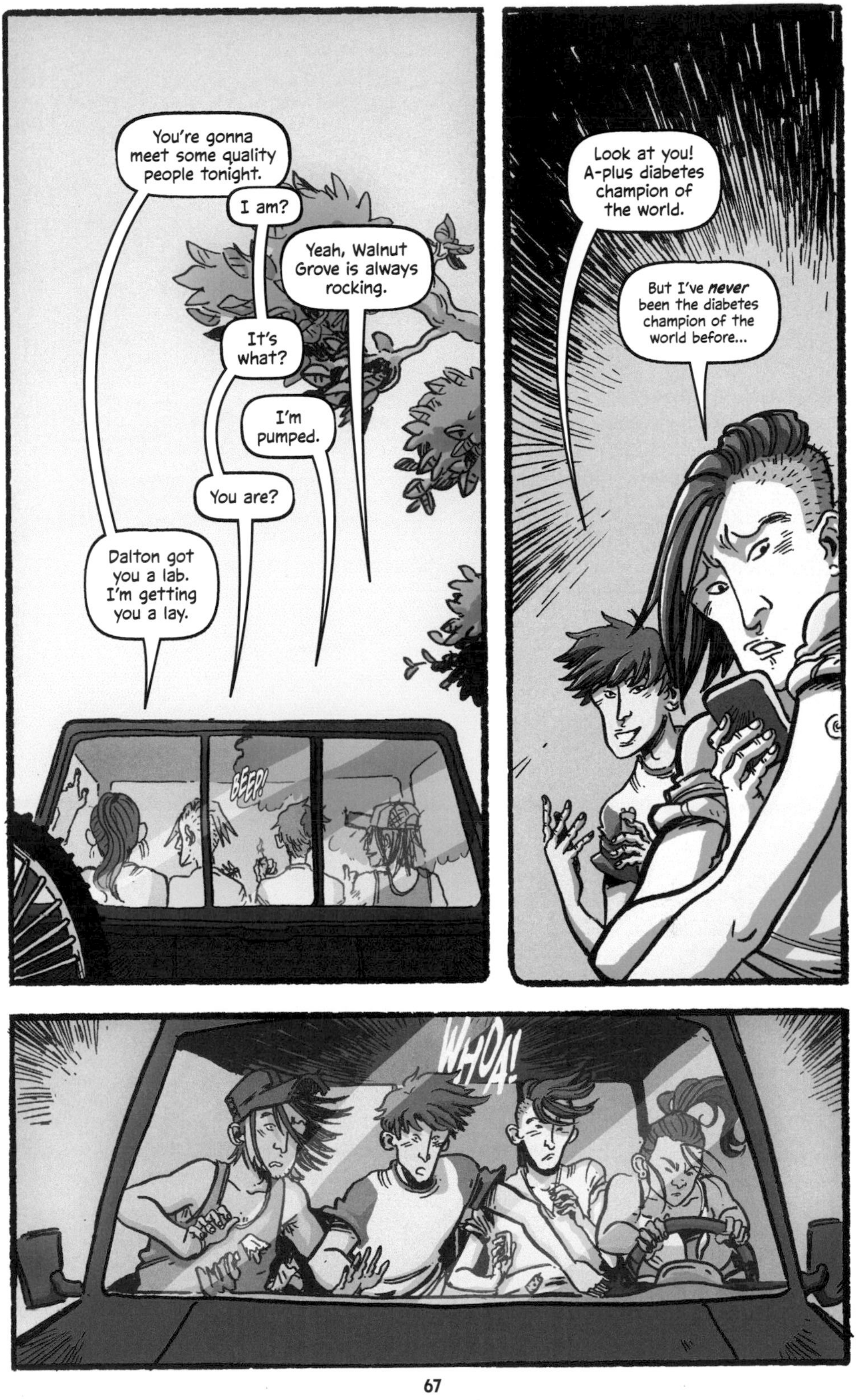

You're gonna meet some quality people tonight.
I am?
Yeah, Walnut Grove is always rocking.
It's what?
I'm pumped.
You are?
Dalton got you a lab. I'm getting you a lay.
BEEP!
Look at you! A-plus diabetes champion of the world.
But I've ***never*** been the diabetes champion of the world before...
WHOA!

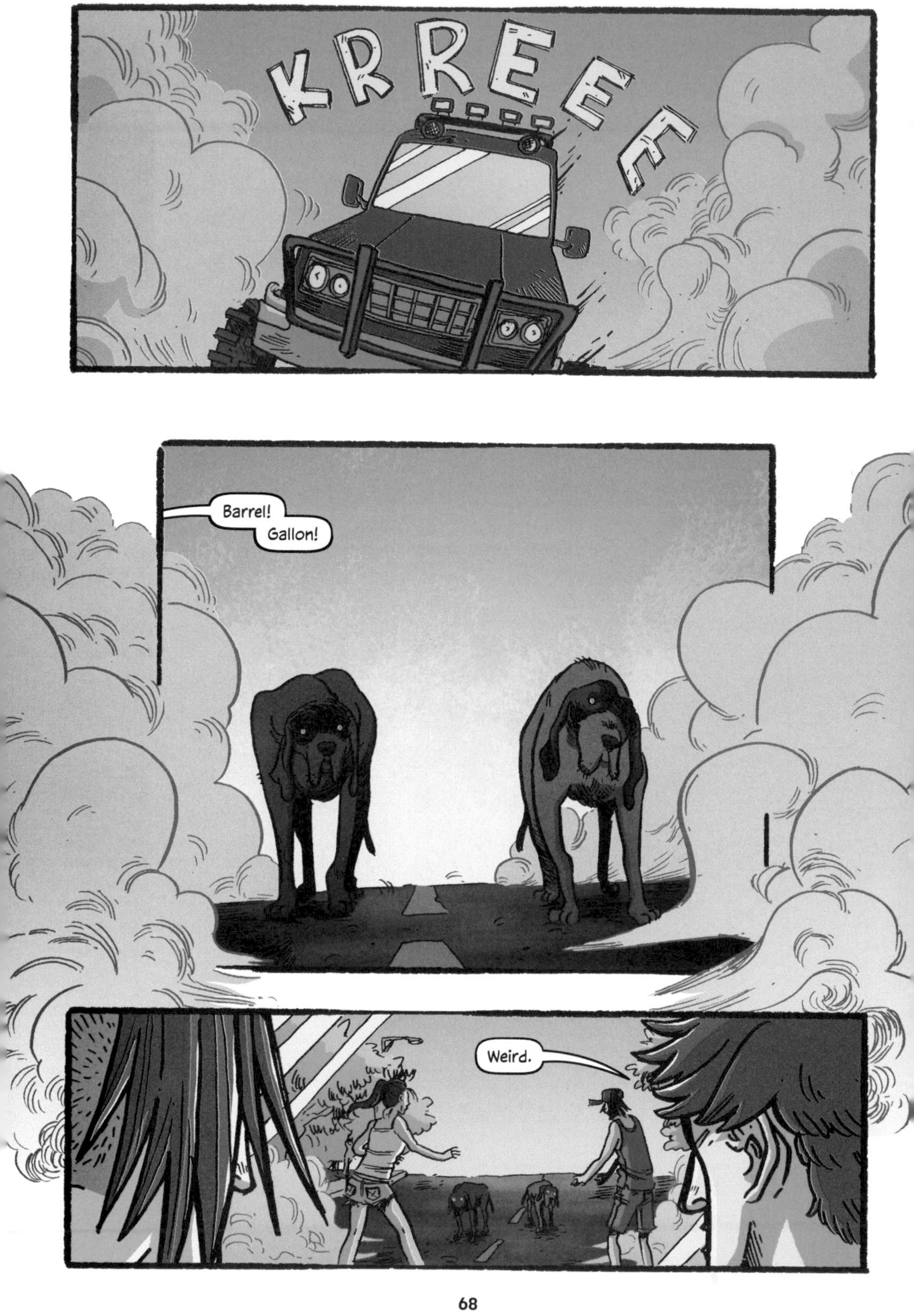
KRREEE
Barrel!
Gallon!
Weird.

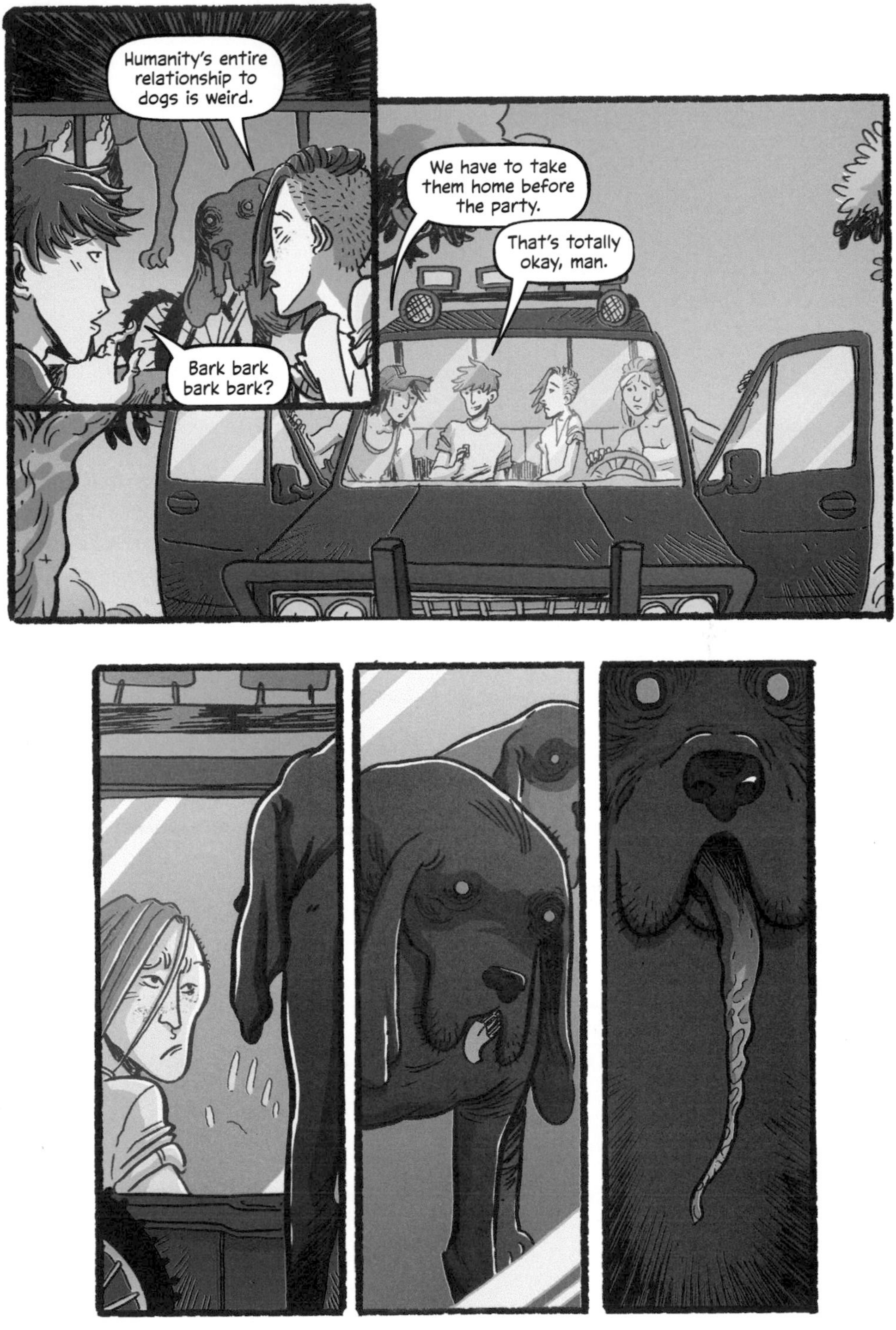
Humanity's entire relationship to dogs is weird.
Bark bark bark bark?
We have to take them home before the party.
That's totally okay, man.

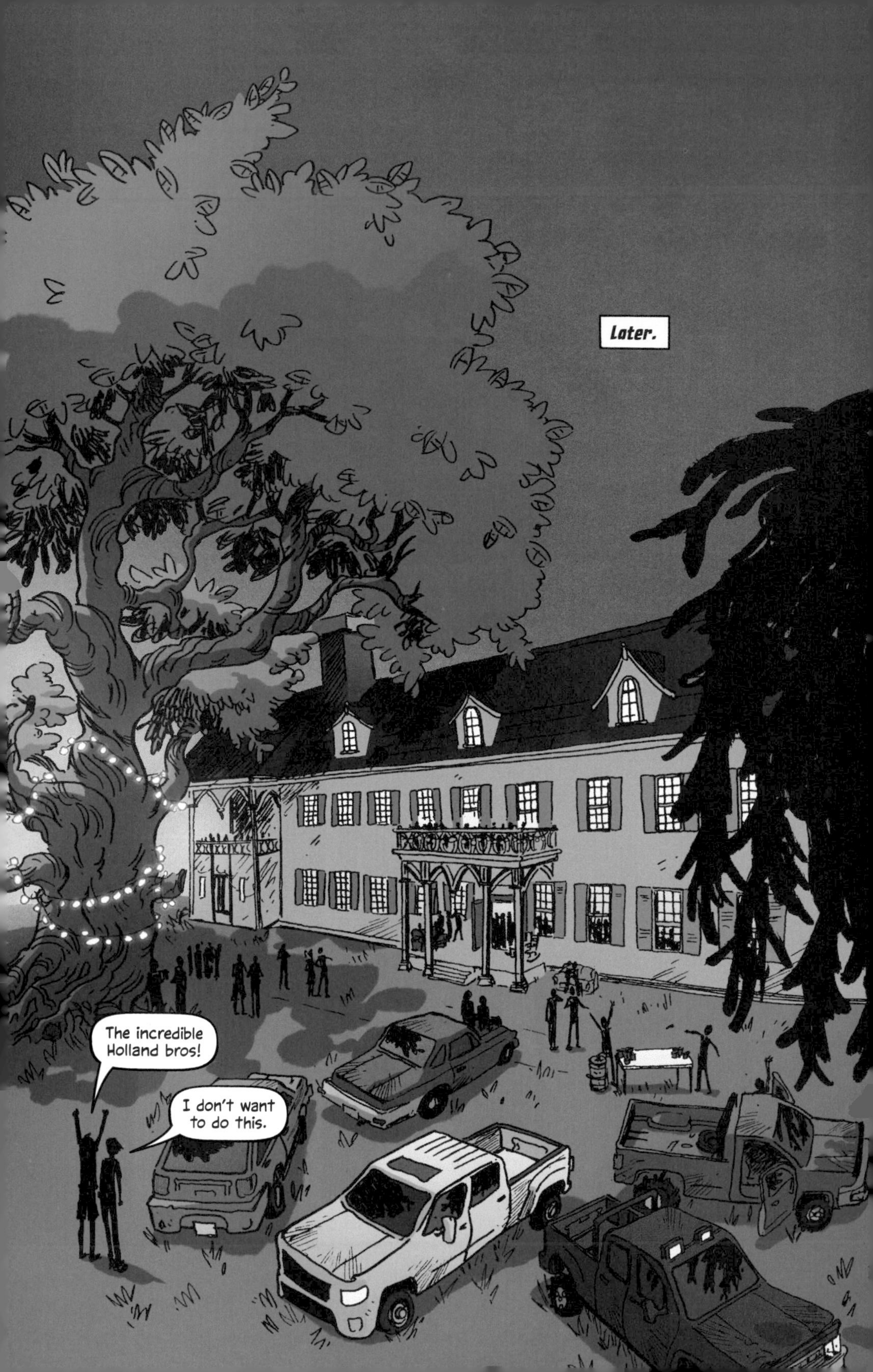
Later.
The incredible Holland bros!
I don't want to do this.

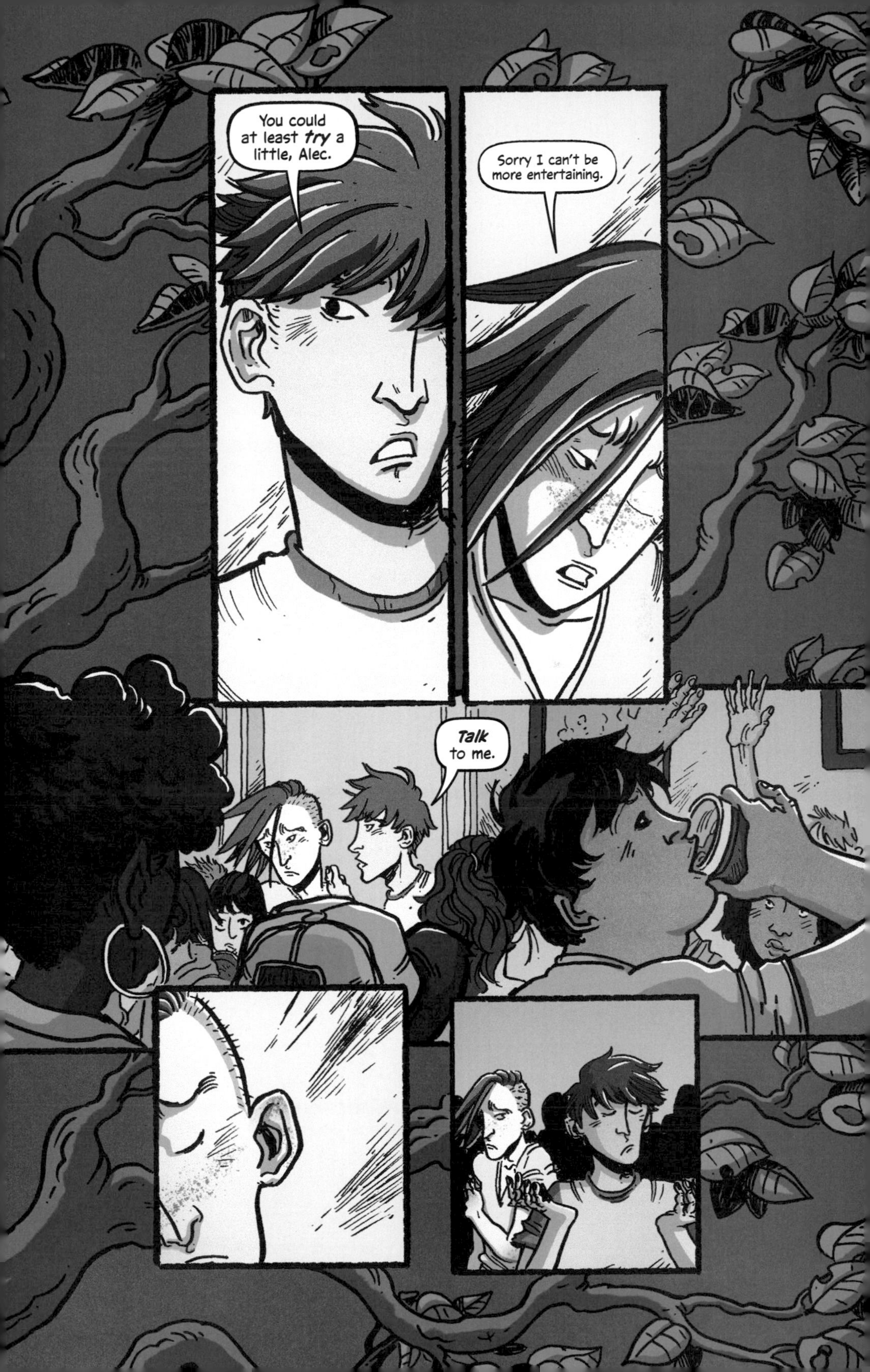
You could at least *try* a little, Alec.
Sorry I can't be more entertaining.
Talk to me.

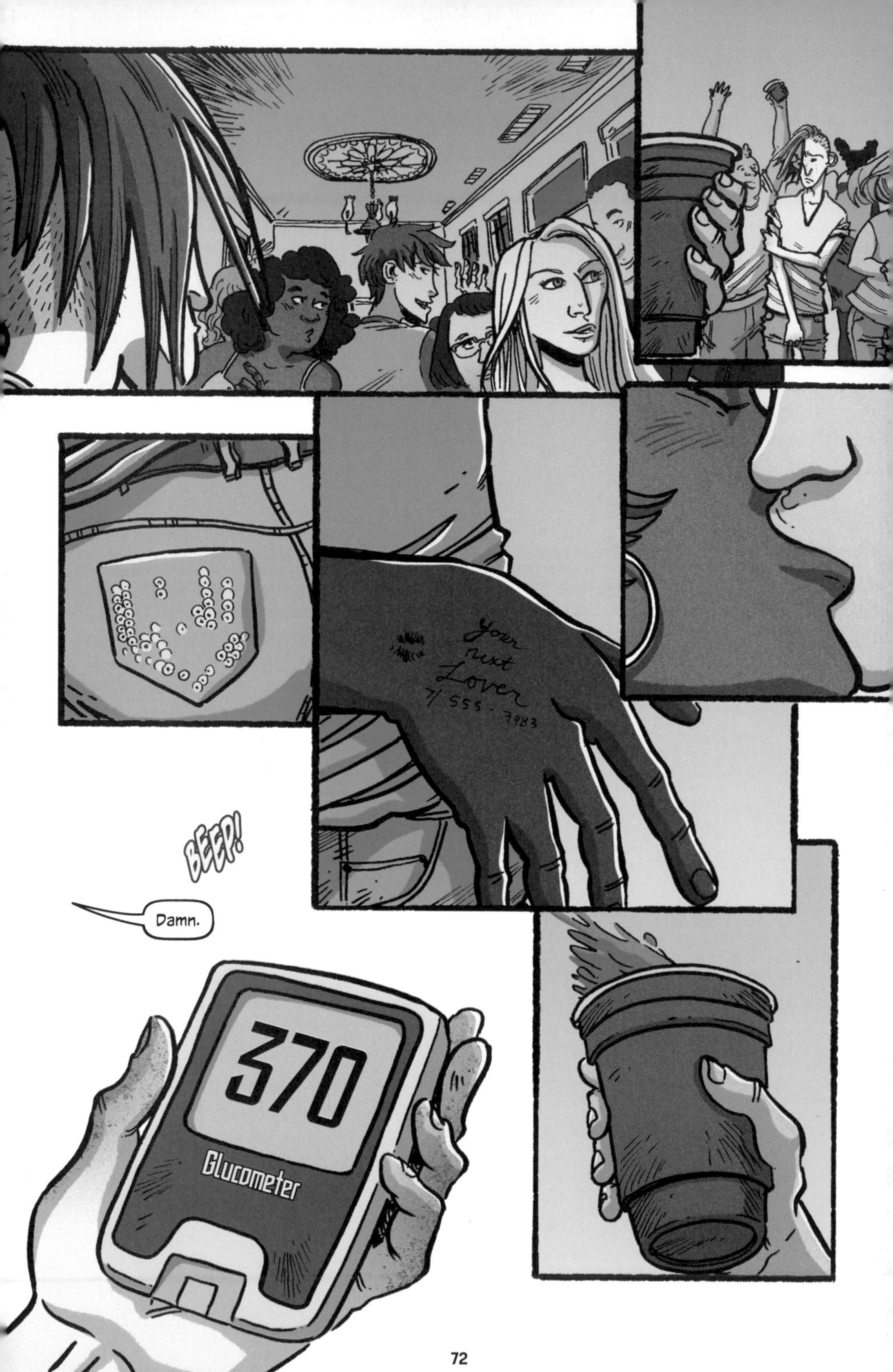
Your next Lover
7/ 555-7983
BEEP!
Damn.
370
Glucometer

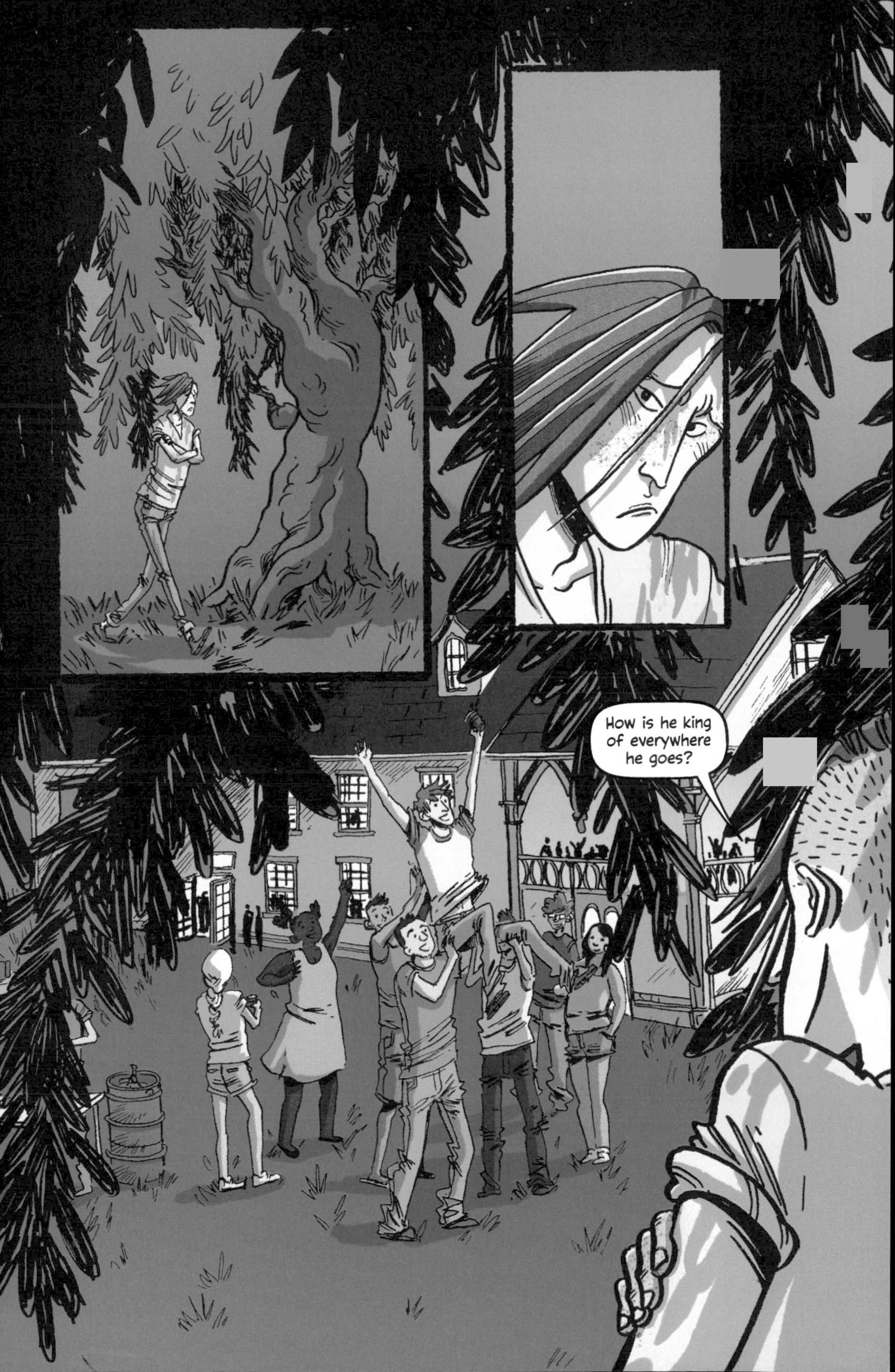
How is he king of everywhere he goes?

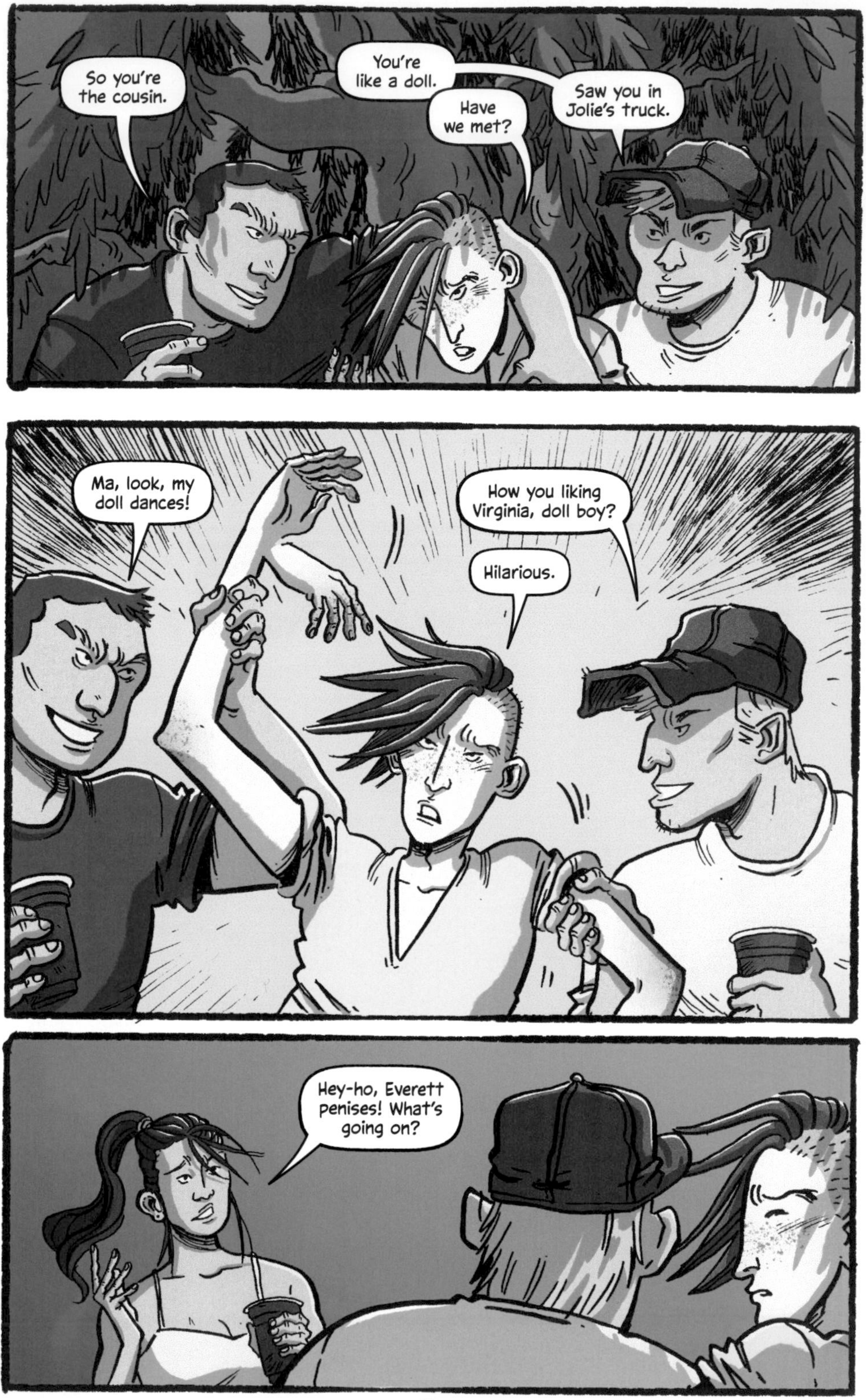
So you're the cousin.
You're like a doll.
Saw you in Jolie's truck.
Have we met?
Ma, look, my doll dances!
How you liking Virginia, doll boy?
Hilarious.
Hey-ho, Everett penises! What's going on?

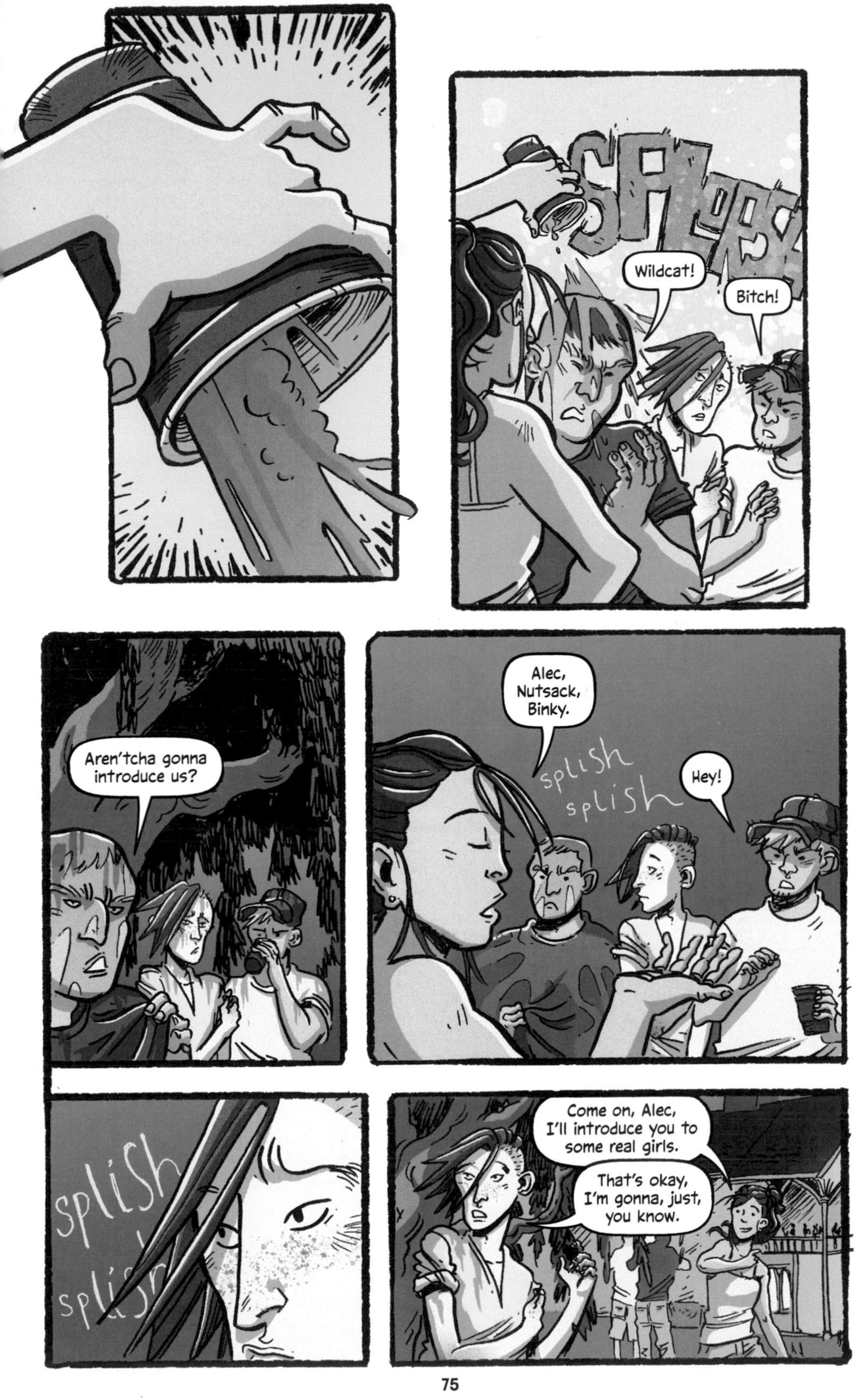
Wildcat!
Bitch!
Aren'tcha gonna introduce us?
Alec, Nutsack, Binky.
splish splish
Hey!
splish splish
Come on, Alec, I'll introduce you to some real girls.
That's okay, I'm gonna, just, you know.

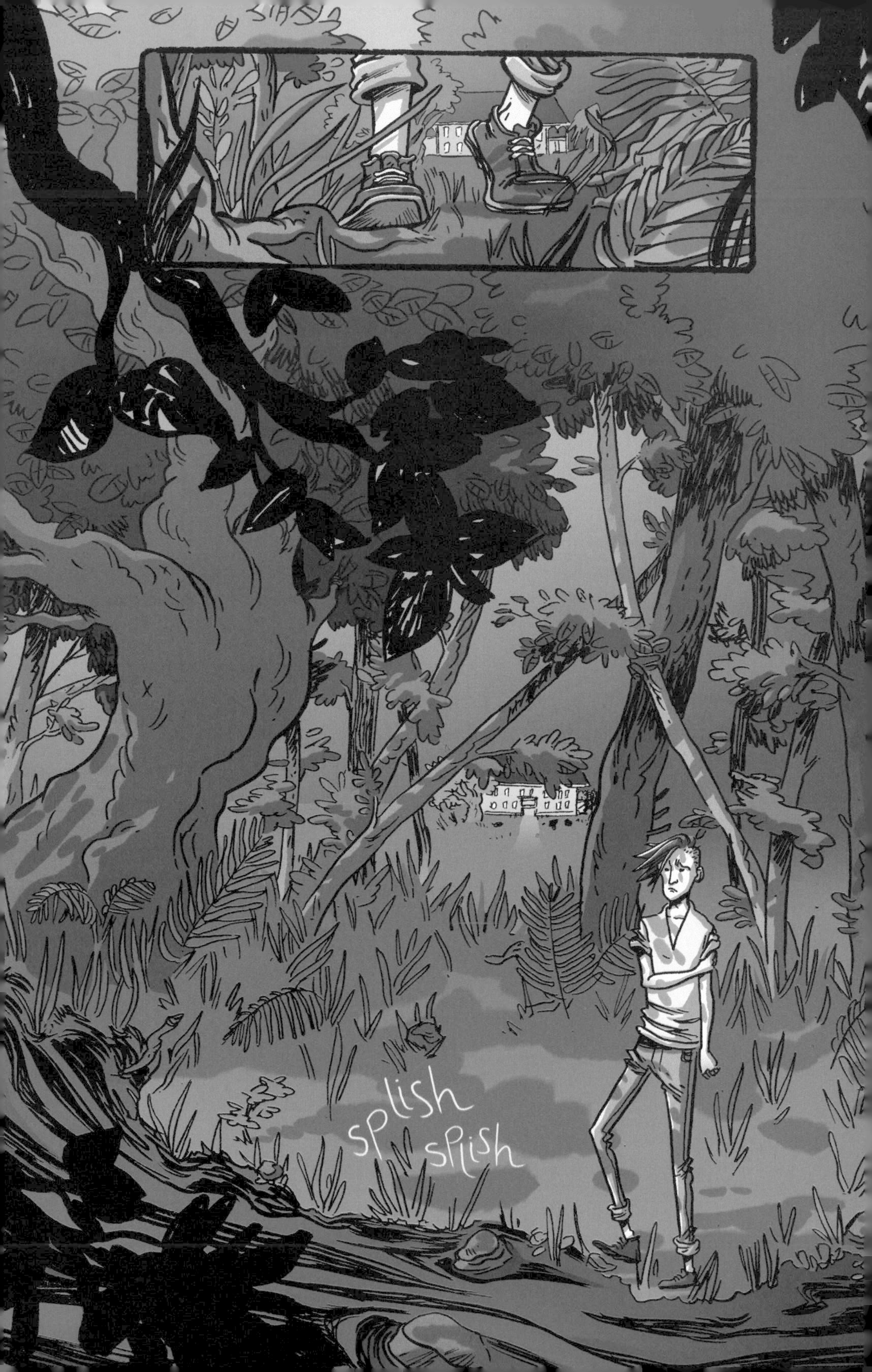
splish
splish
splish

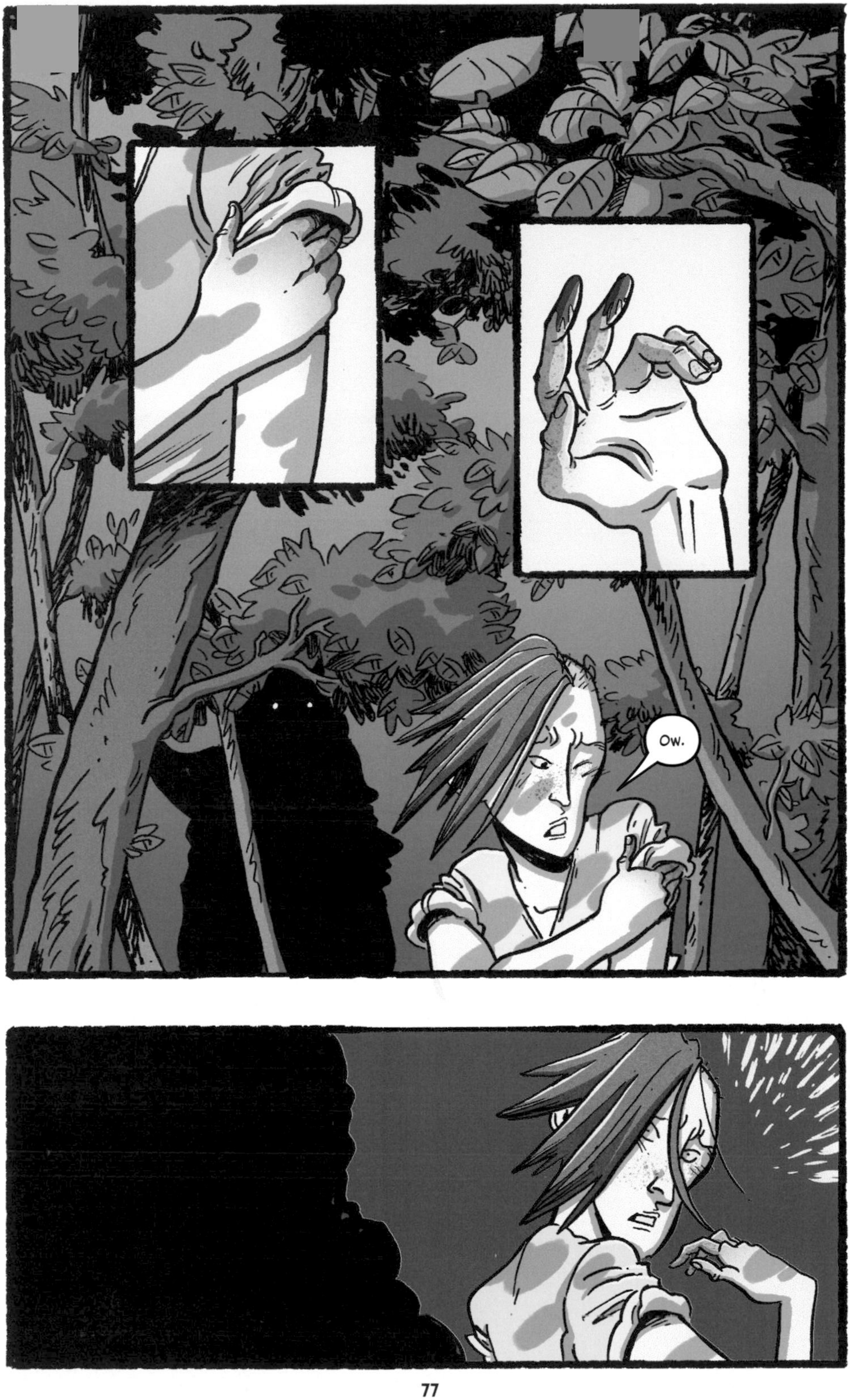
OW.

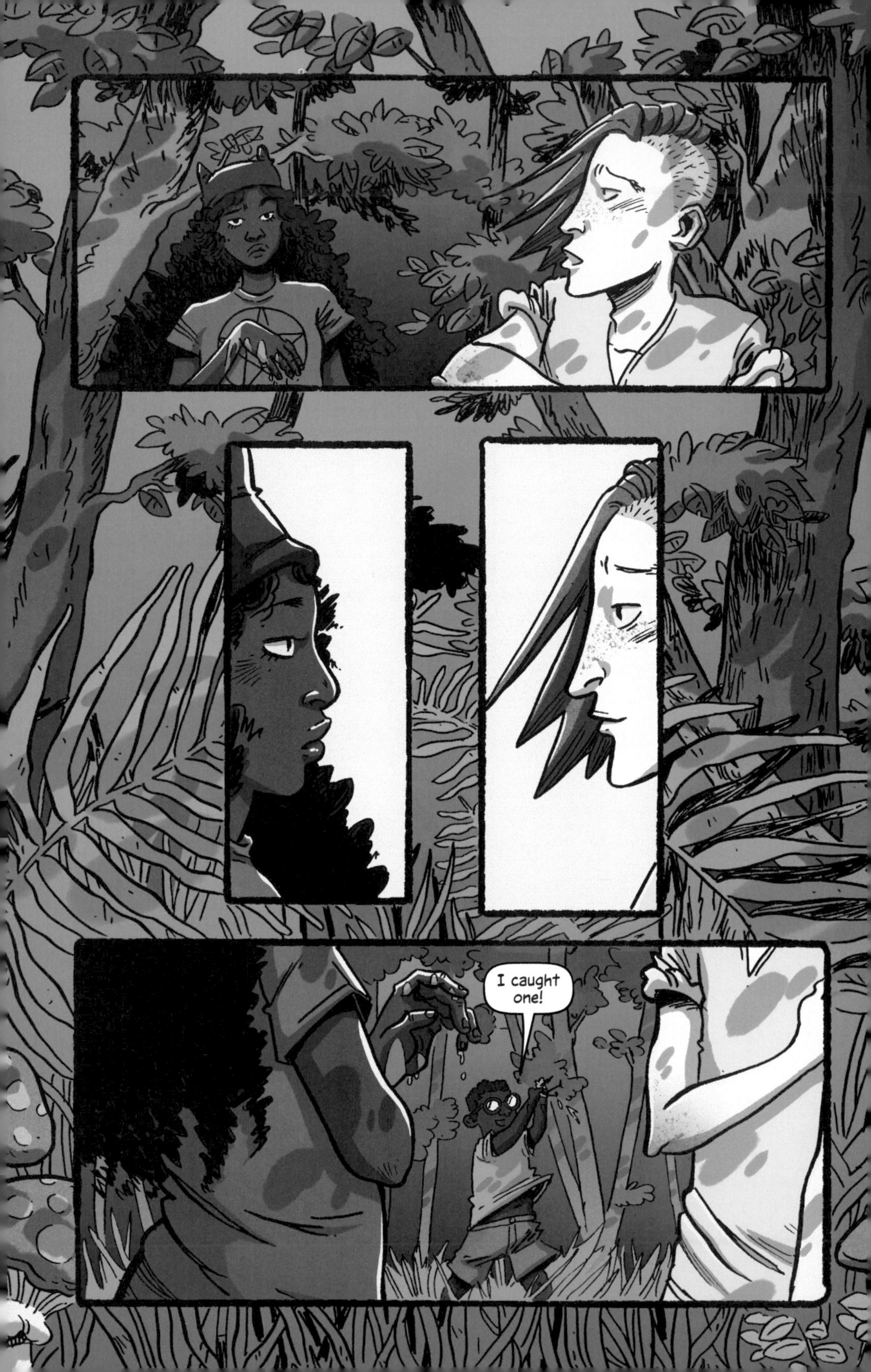
I caught one!

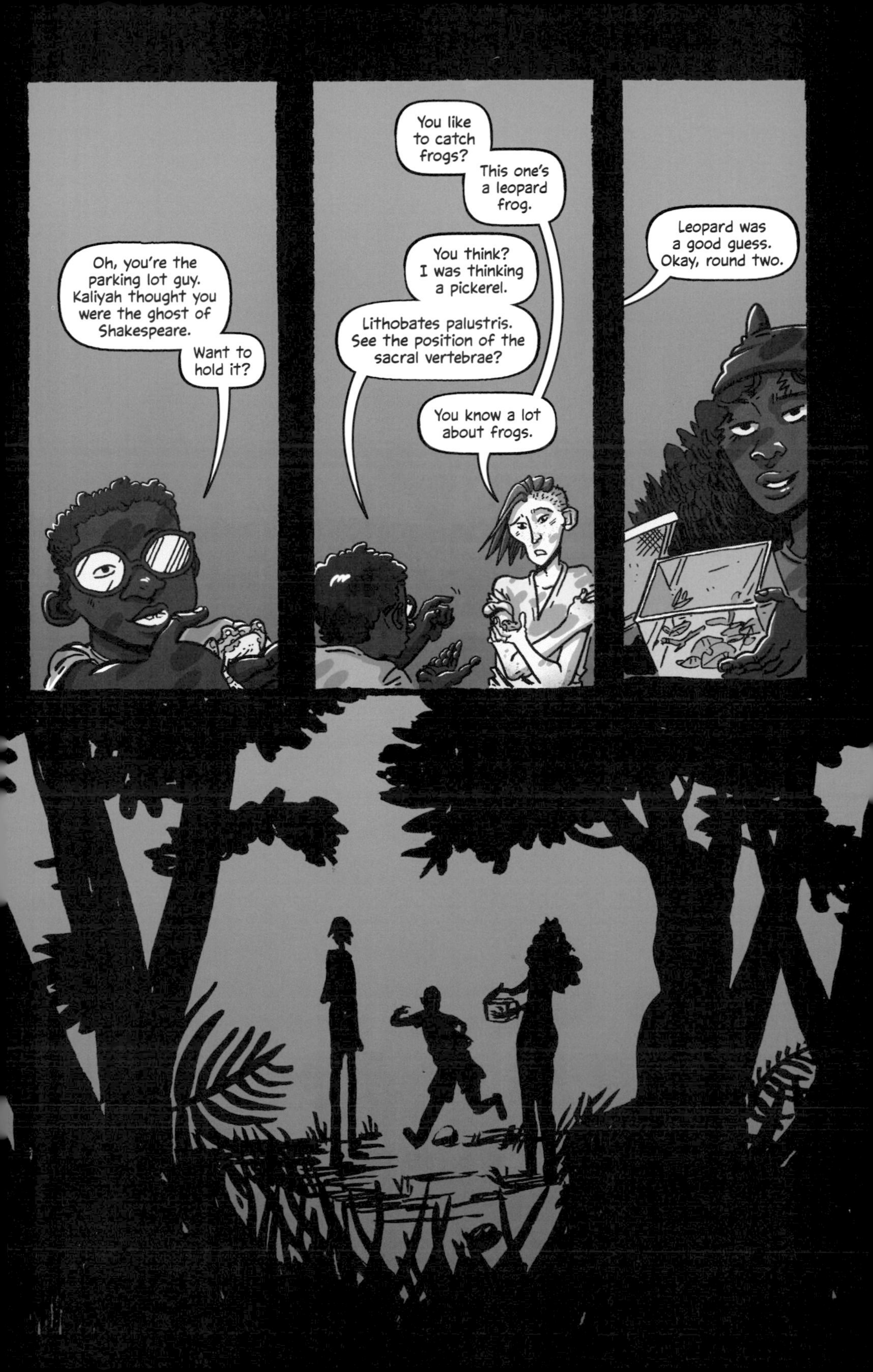
Oh, you're the parking lot guy. Kaliyah thought you were the ghost of Shakespeare.
Want to hold it?
You like to catch frogs?
This one's a leopard frog.
You think? I was thinking a pickerel.
Lithobates palustris. See the position of the sacral vertebrae?
You know a lot about frogs.
Leopard was a good guess. Okay, round two.

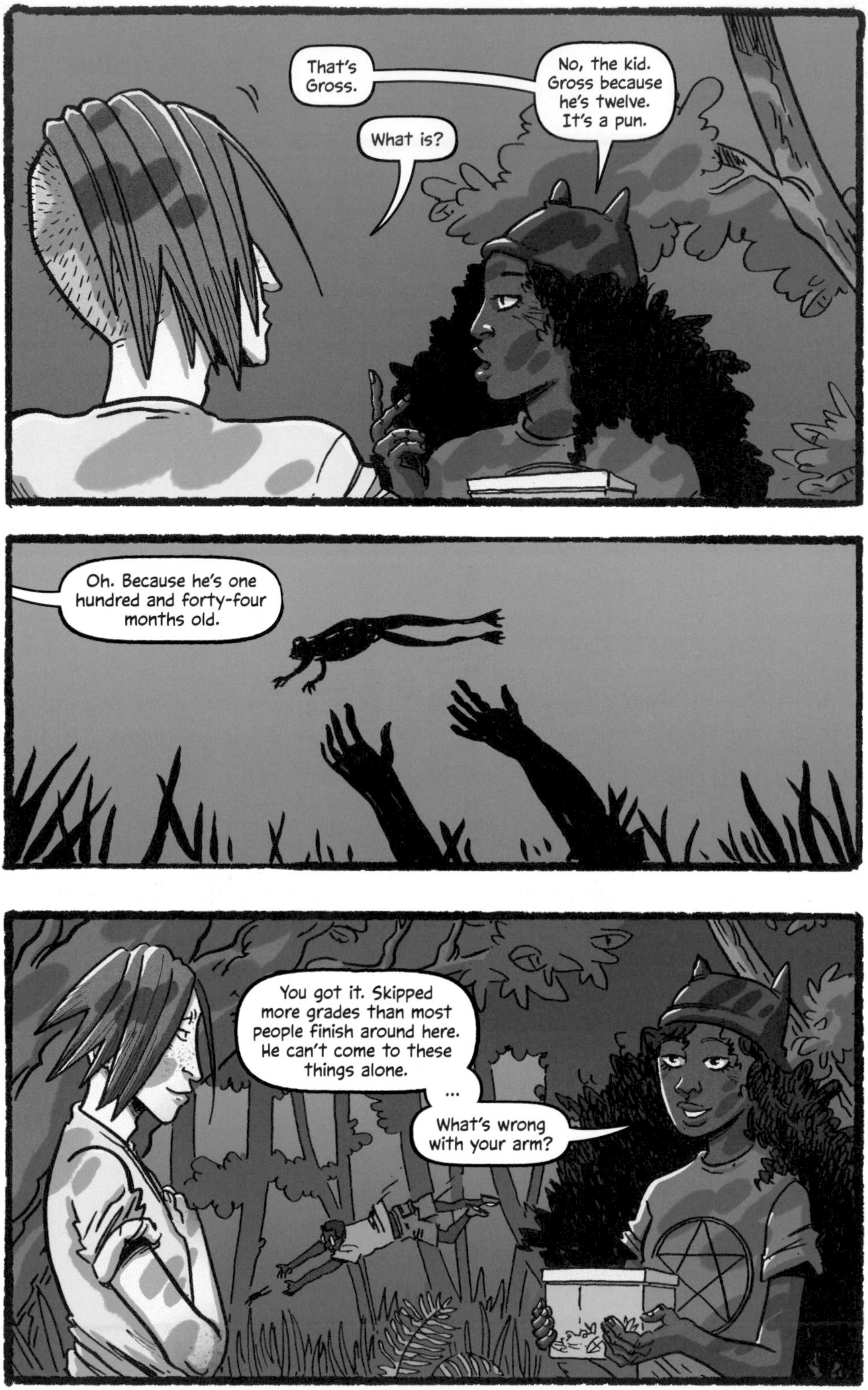
That's Gross.
What is?
No, the kid. Gross because he's twelve. It's a pun.
Oh. Because he's one hundred and forty-four months old.
You got it. Skipped more grades than most people finish around here. He can't come to these things alone.
...
What's wrong with your arm?

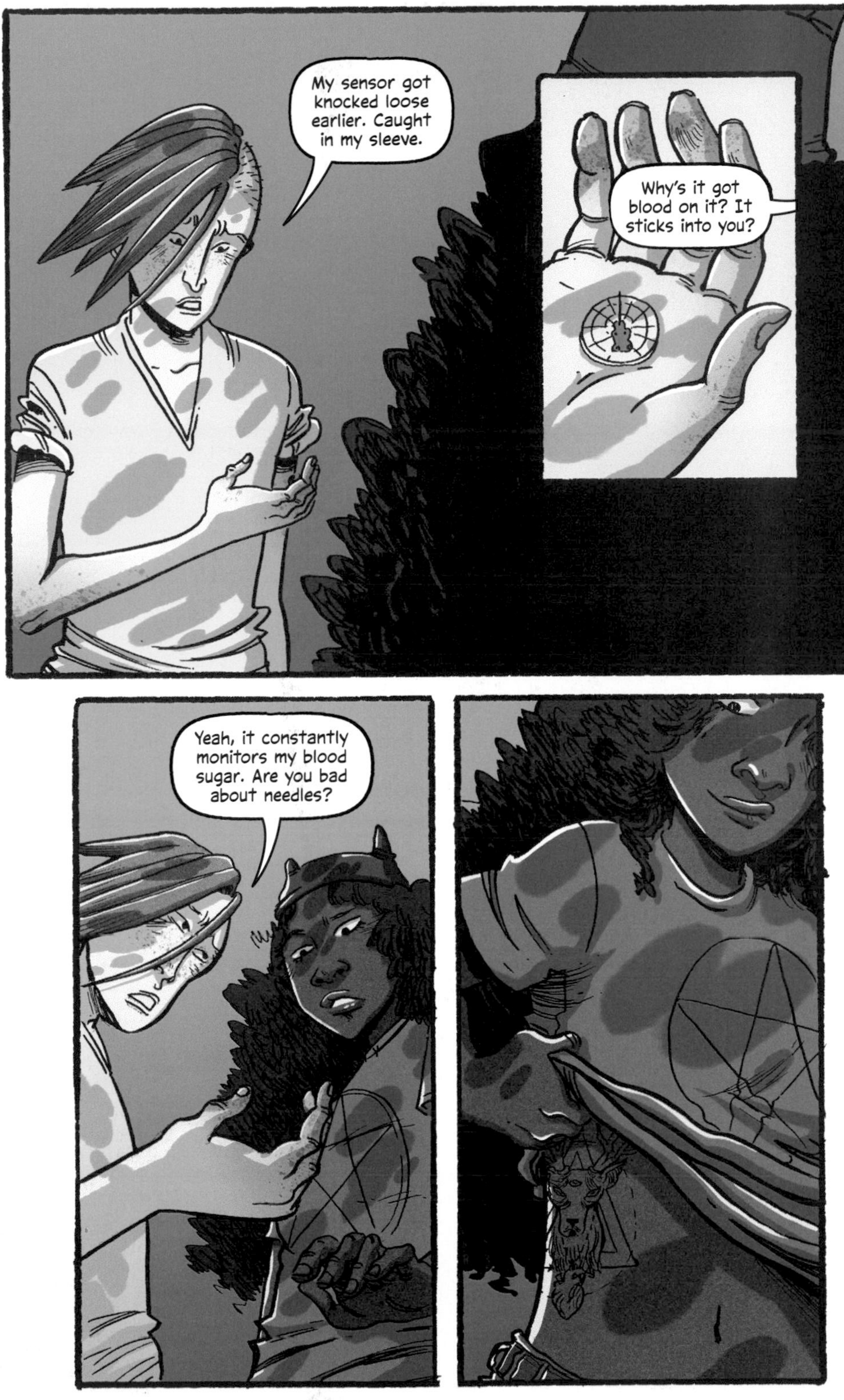
My sensor got knocked loose earlier. Caught in my sleeve.
Why's it got blood on it? It sticks into you?
Yeah, it constantly monitors my blood sugar. Are you bad about needles?

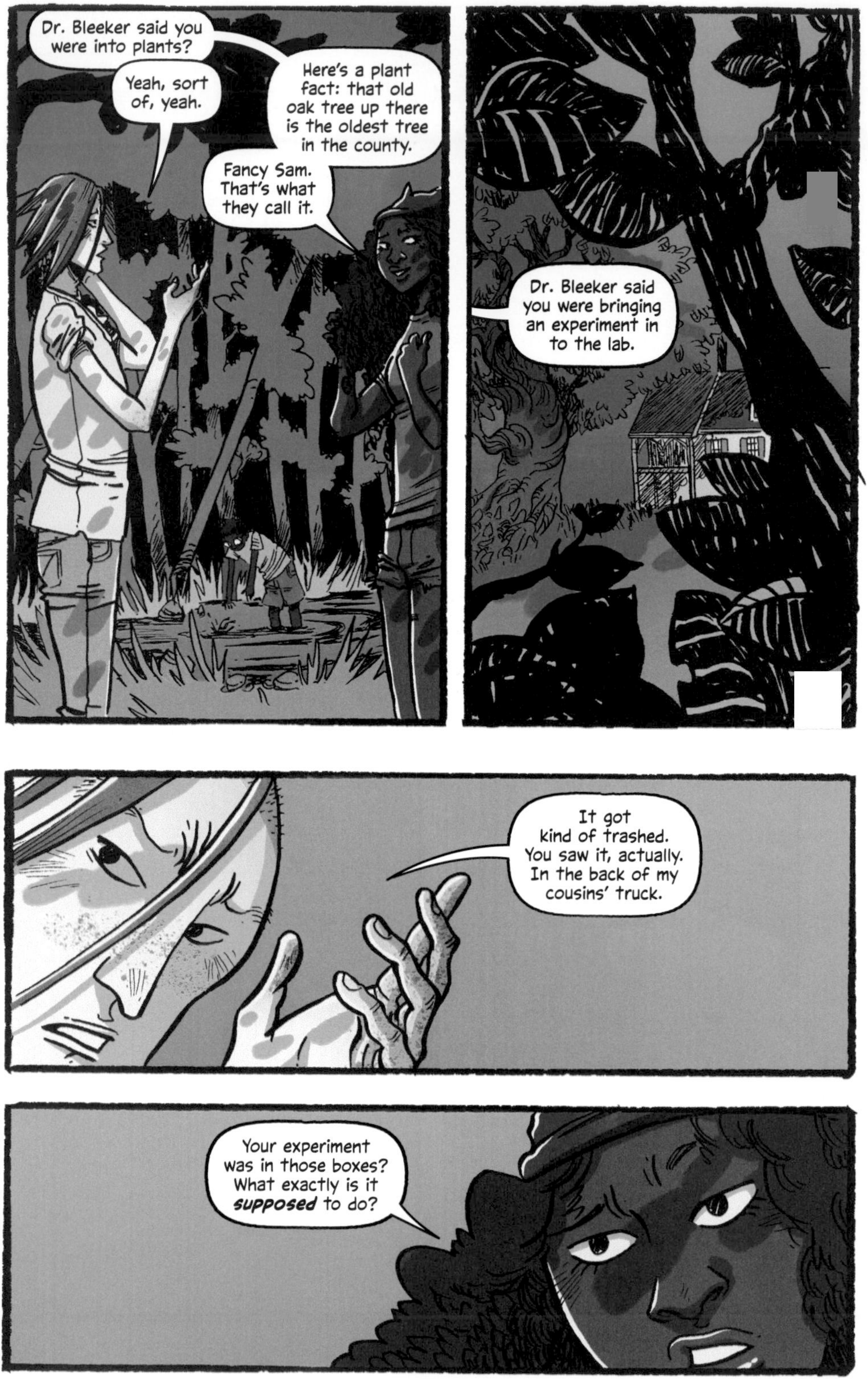
Dr. Bleeker said you were into plants?
Yeah, sort of, yeah.
Here's a plant fact: that old oak tree up there is the oldest tree in the county.
Fancy Sam. That's what they call it.
Dr. Bleeker said you were bringing an experiment in to the lab.
It got kind of trashed. You saw it, actually. In the back of my cousins' truck.
Your experiment was in those boxes? What exactly is it *supposed* to do?

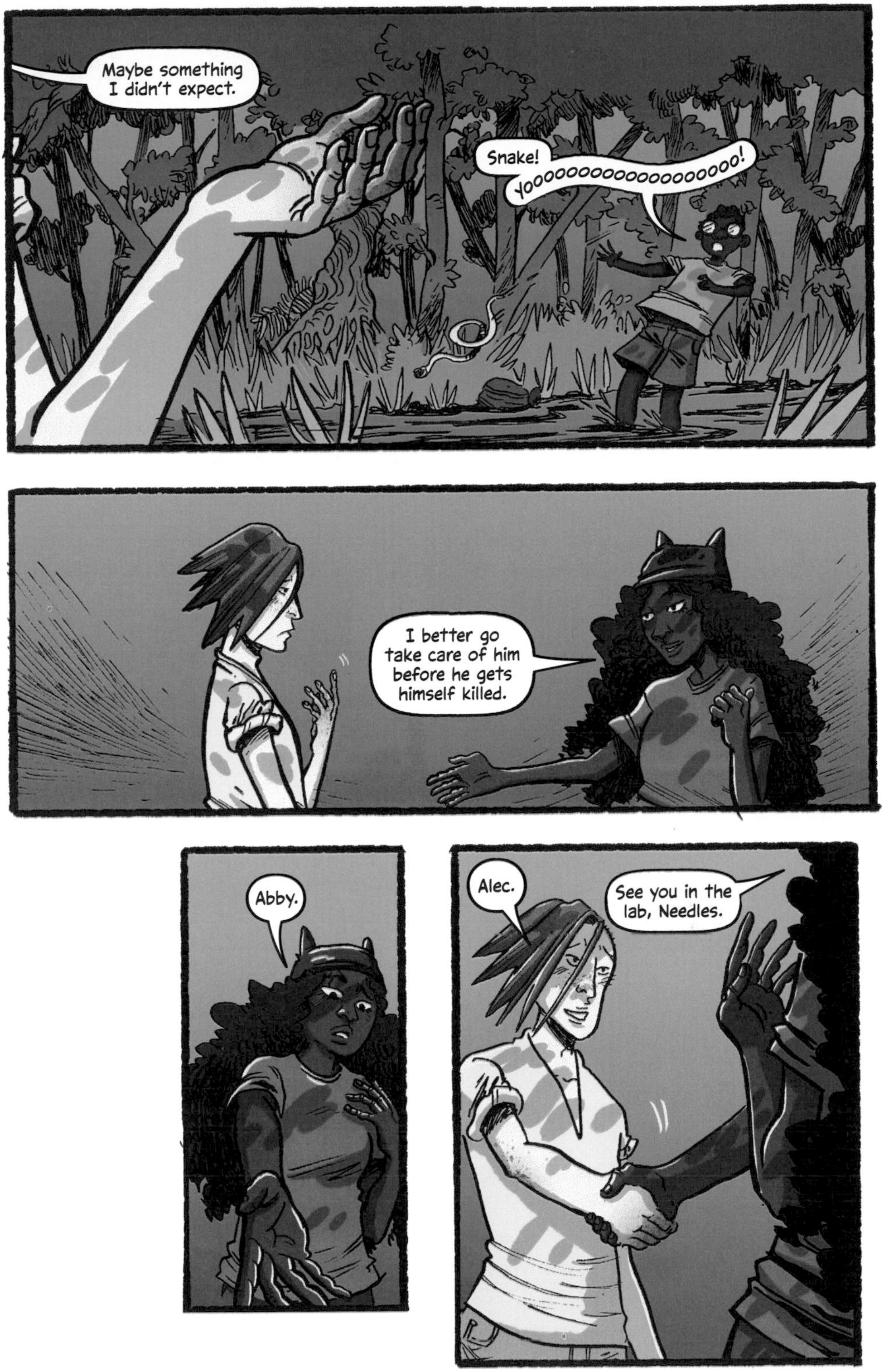
Maybe something I didn't expect.
Snake!
Yoooooooooooooooooooo!
I better go take care of him before he gets himself killed.
Abby.
Alec.
See you in the lab, Needles.

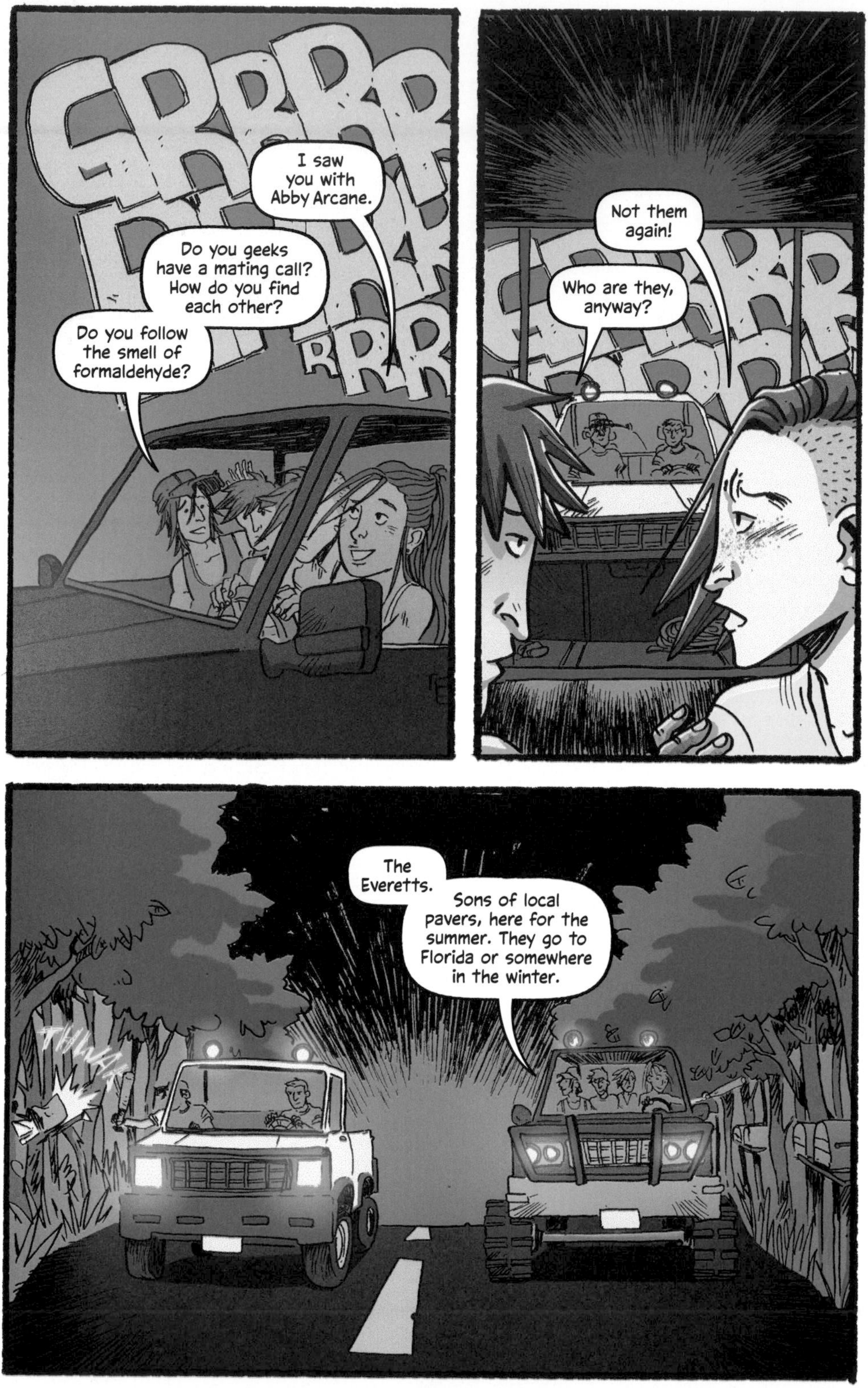
GRRRR
I saw you with Abby Arcane.
Do you geeks have a mating call? How do you find each other?
Do you follow the smell of formaldehyde?
Not them again!
Who are they, anyway?
The Everetts.
Sons of local pavers, here for the summer. They go to Florida or somewhere in the winter.
THWAK

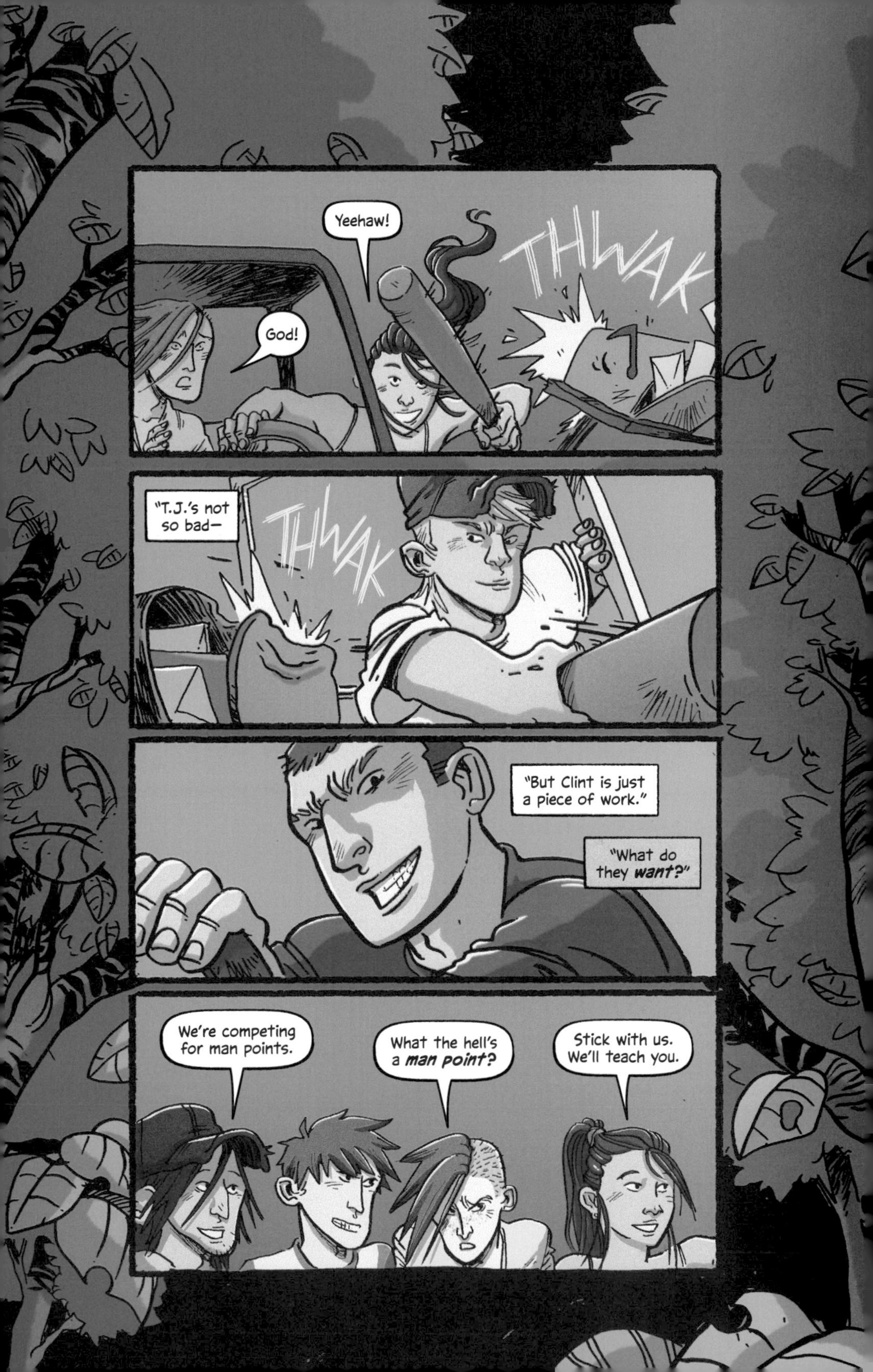
Yeehaw!
God!
THWAK
"T.J.'s not so bad—
THWAK
"But Clint is just a piece of work."
"What do they *want?*"
We're competing for man points.
What the hell's a ***man point?***
Stick with us. We'll teach you.

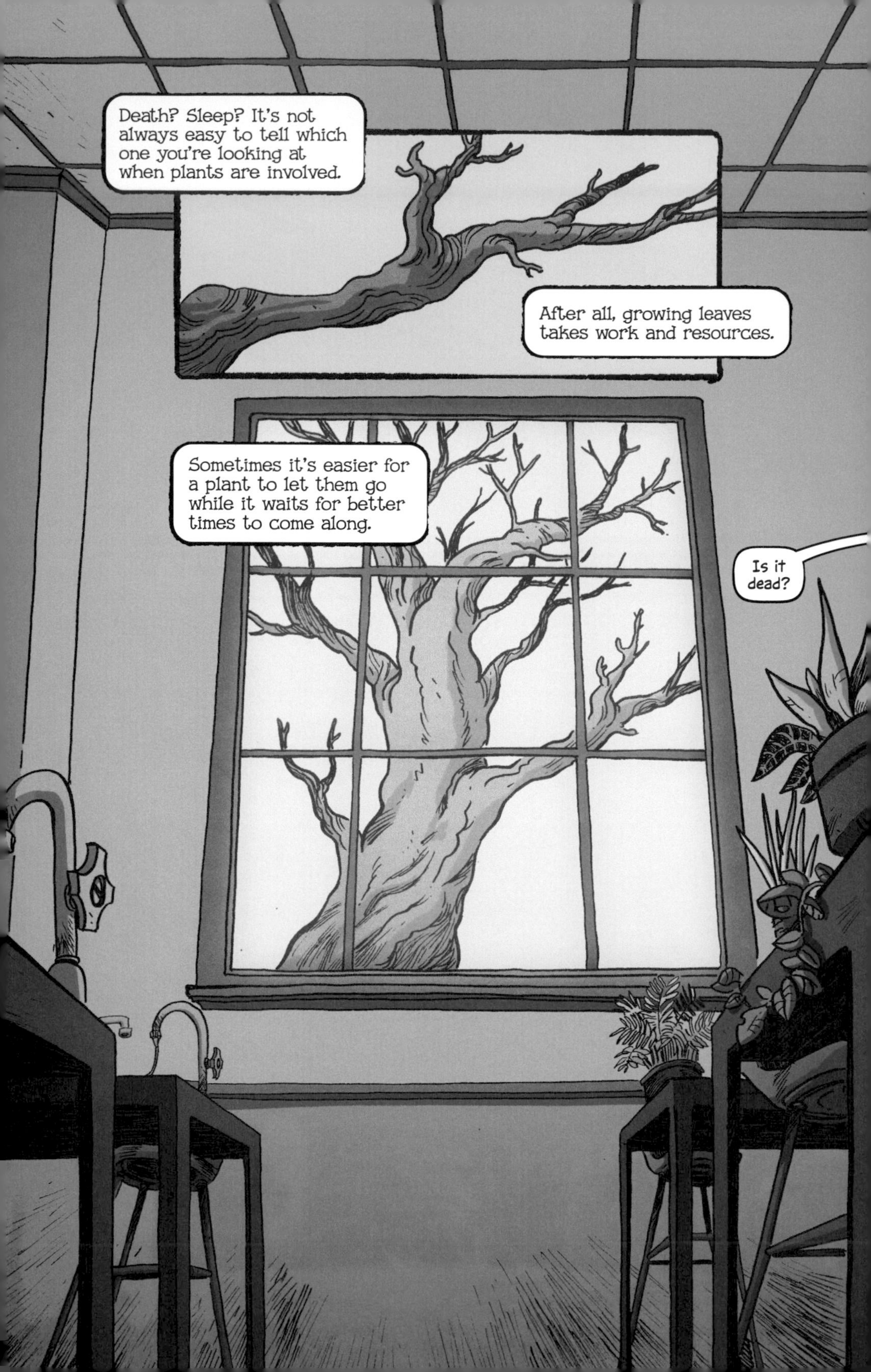
Death? Sleep? It's not always easy to tell which one you're looking at when plants are involved.
After all, growing leaves takes work and resources.
Sometimes it's easier for a plant to let them go while it waits for better times to come along.
Is it dead?

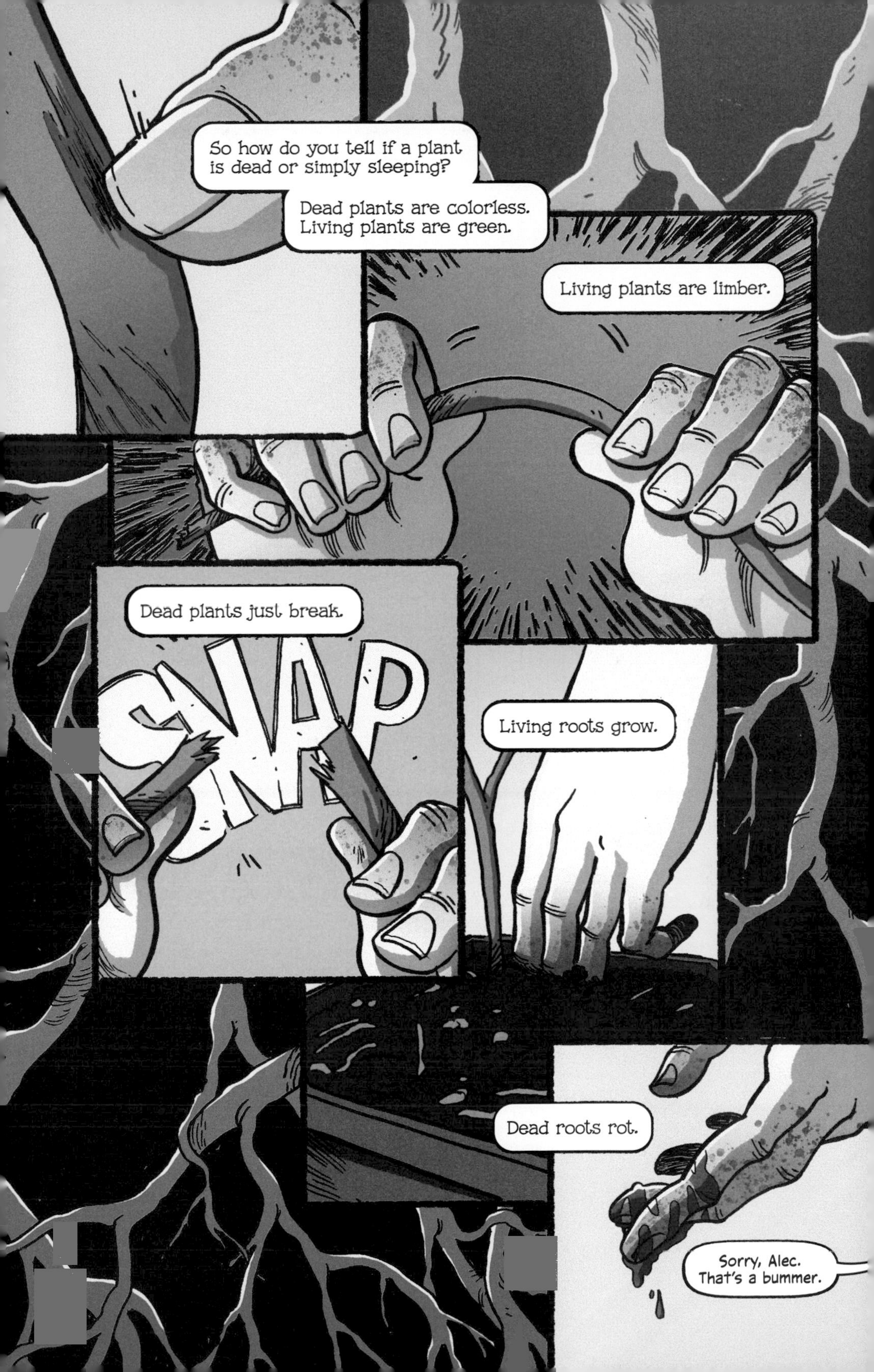
So how do you tell if a plant is dead or simply sleeping?
Dead plants are colorless. Living plants are green.
Living plants are limber.
Dead plants just break.
SNAP
Living roots grow.
Dead roots rot.
Sorry, Alec. That's a bummer.

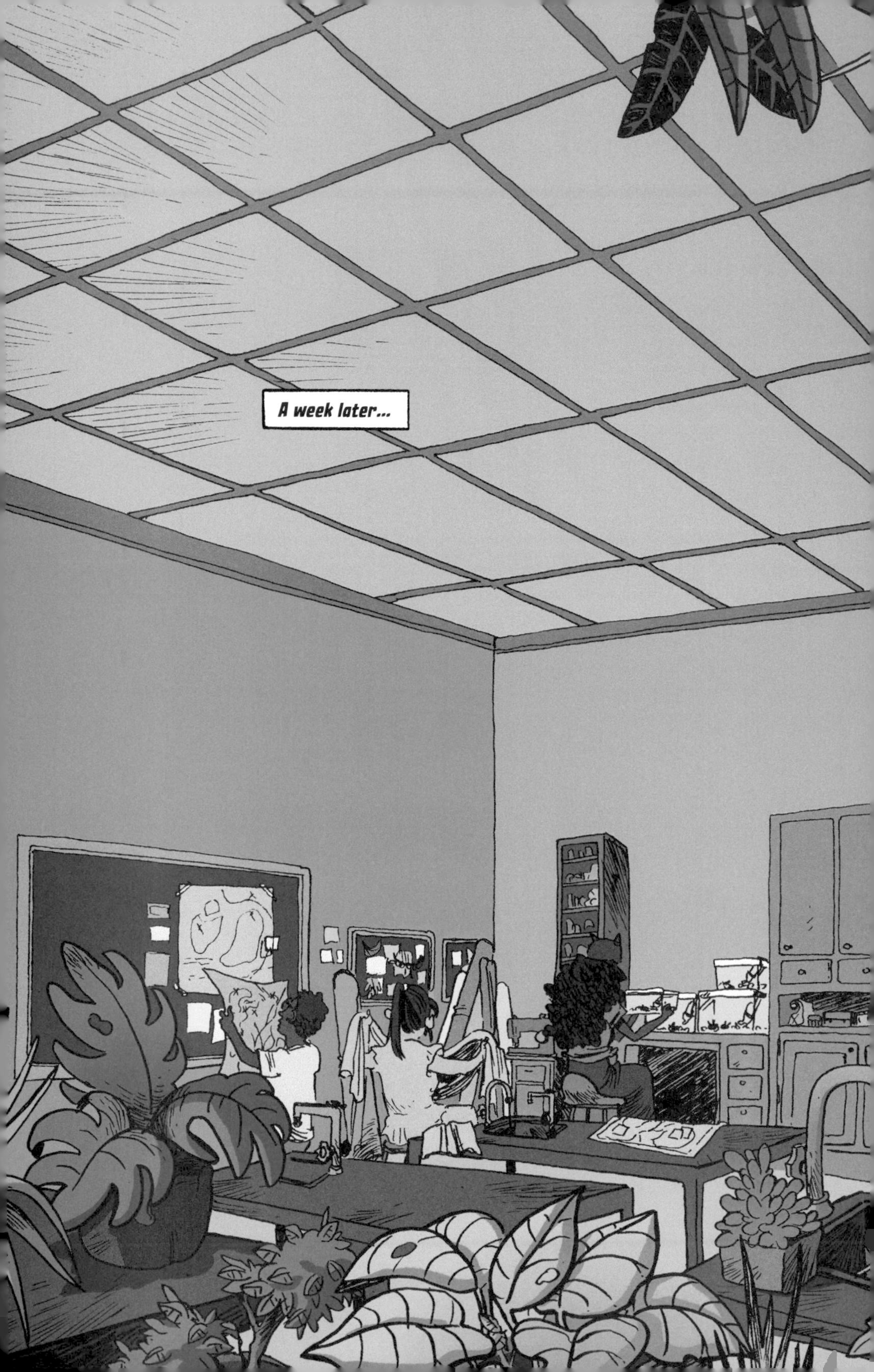
A week later...

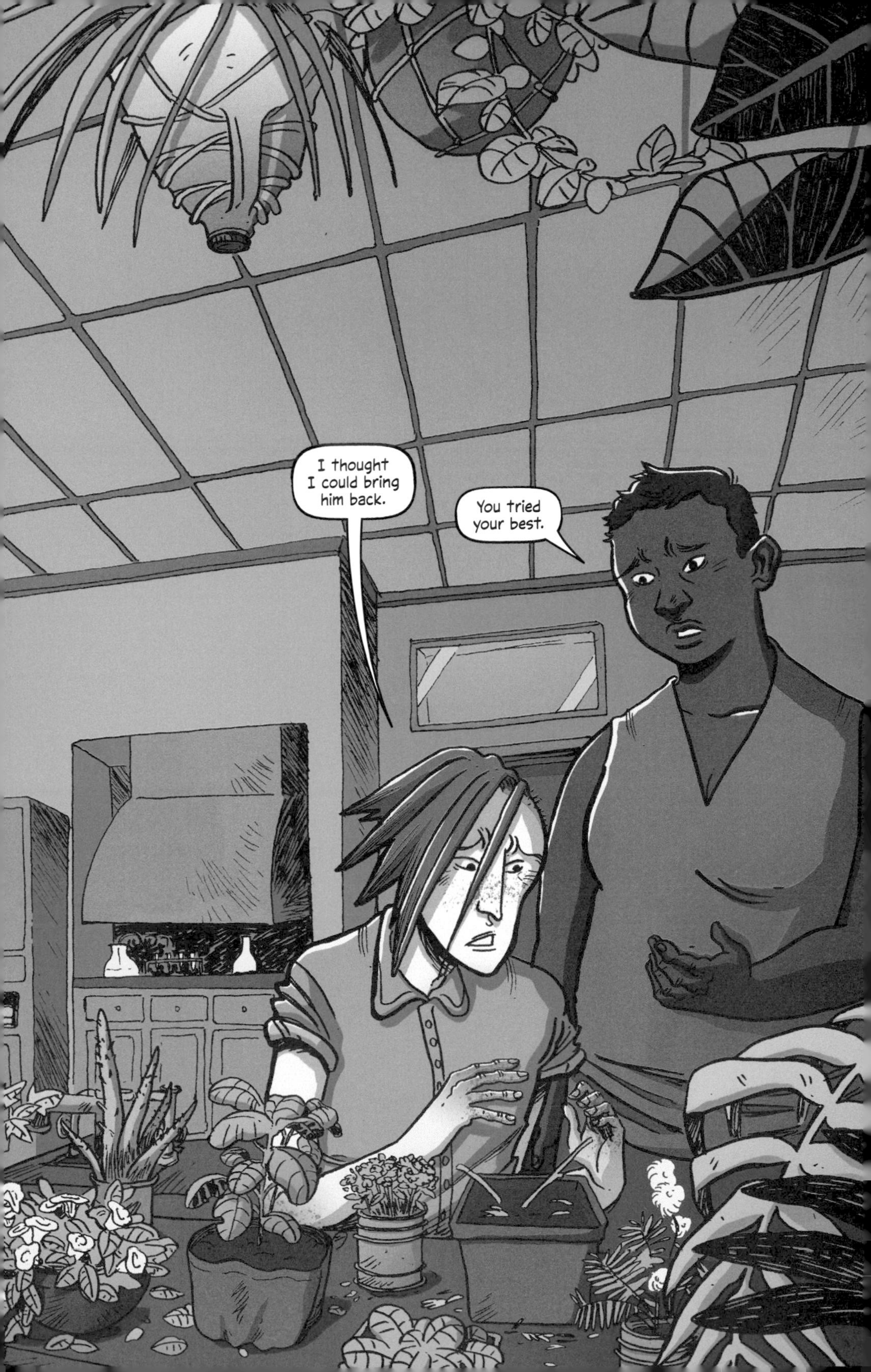
I thought I could bring him back.
You tried your best.

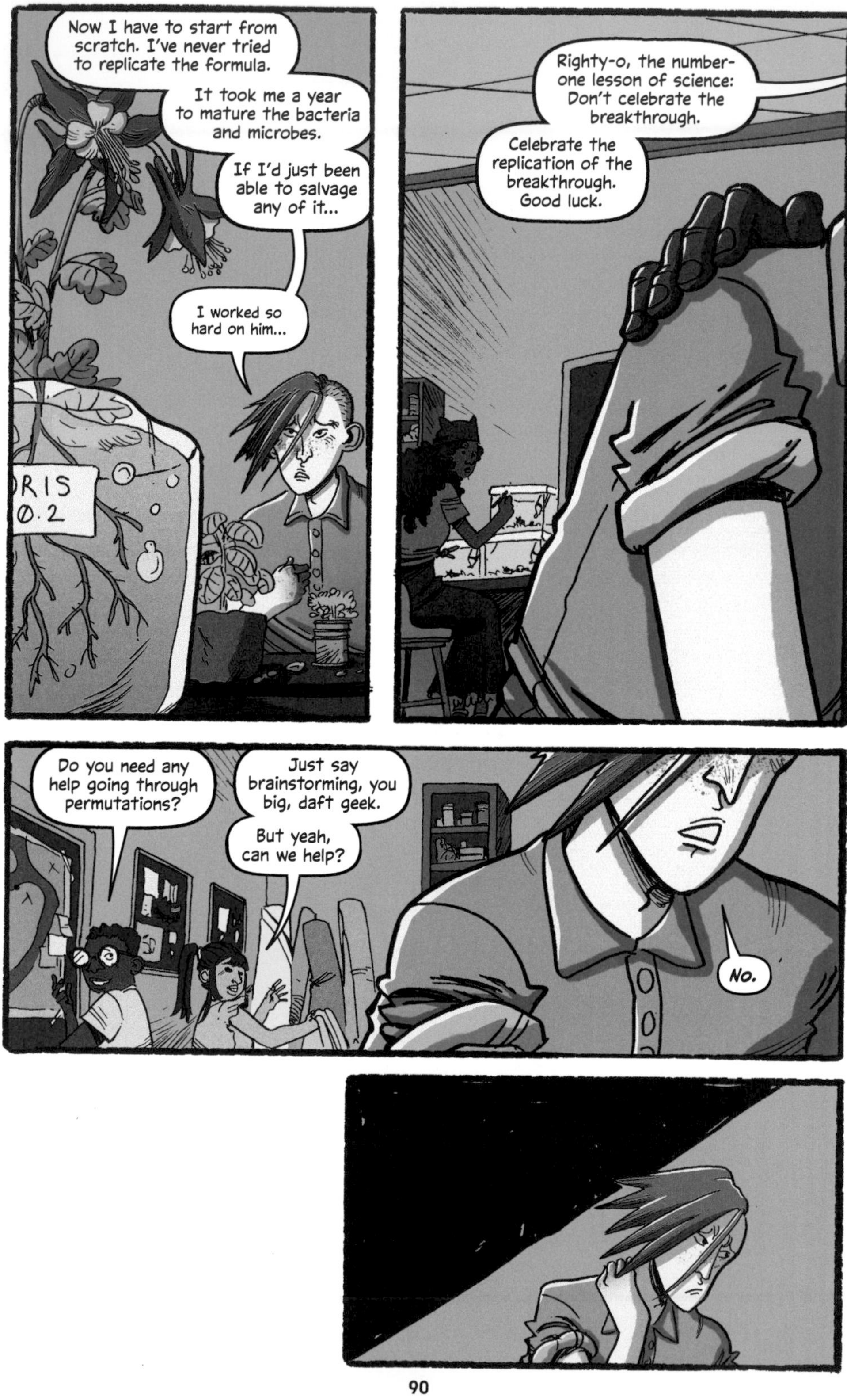
Now I have to start from scratch. I've never tried to replicate the formula.
It took me a year to mature the bacteria and microbes.
If I'd just been able to salvage any of it...
I worked so hard on him...
RIS
0.2
Righty-o, the number-one lesson of science: Don't celebrate the breakthrough.
Celebrate the replication of the breakthrough. Good luck.
Do you need any help going through permutations?
Just say brainstorming, you big, daft geek.
But yeah, can we help?
No.

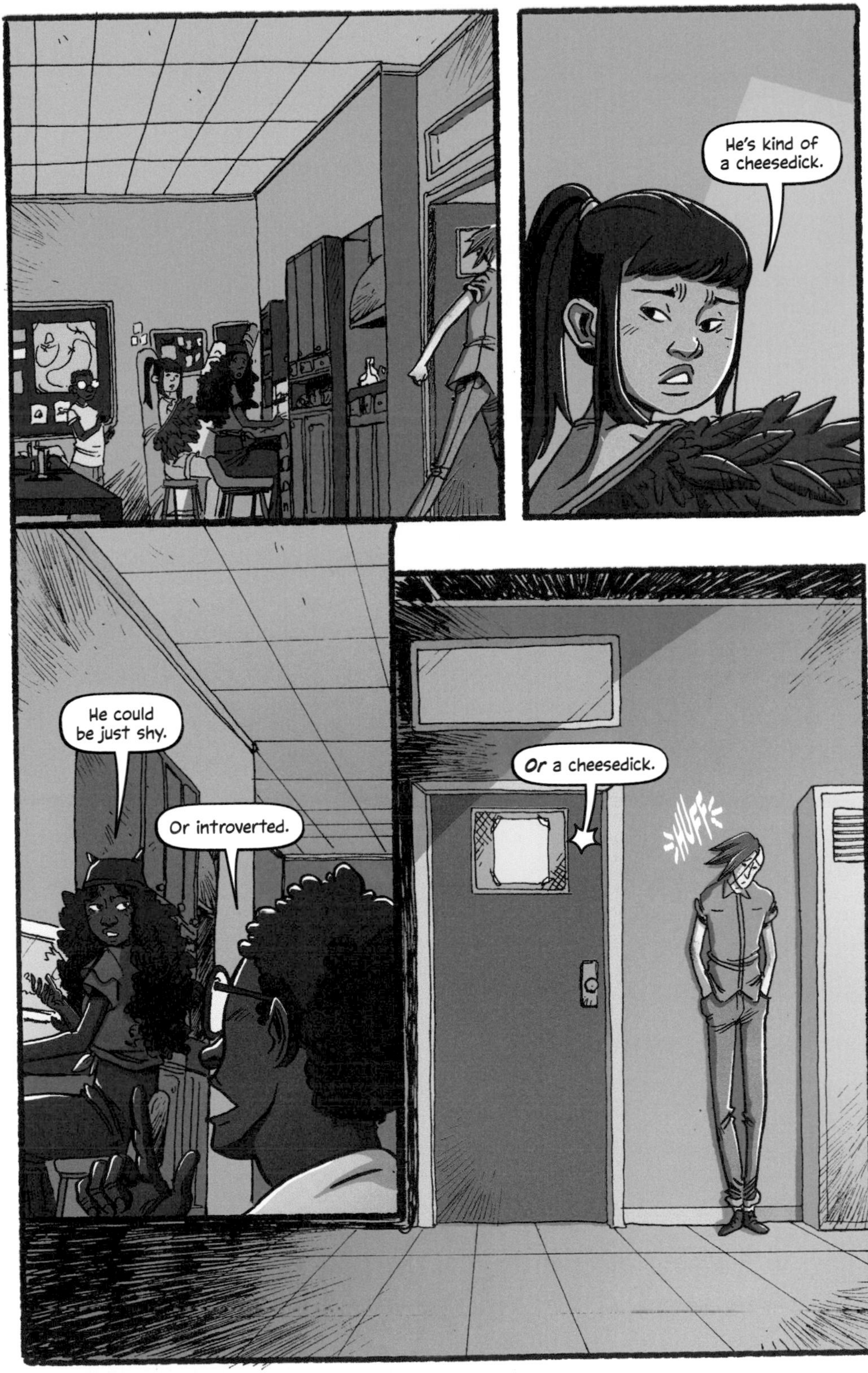
He's kind of a cheesedick.
He could be just shy.
Or introverted.
Or a cheesedick.
HUFF

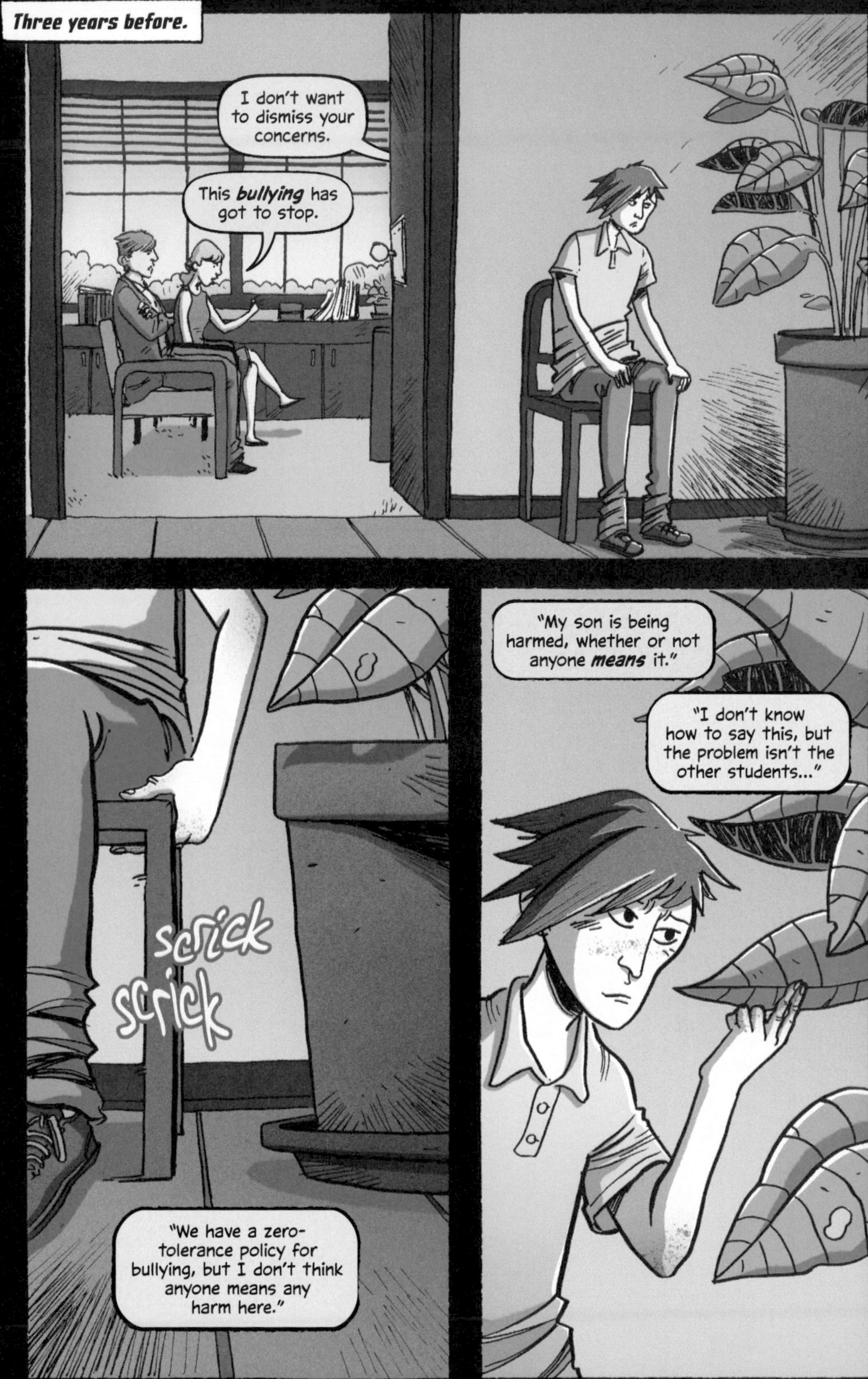
Three years before.
I don't want to dismiss your concerns.
This bullying has got to stop.
scrick
scrick
"We have a zero-tolerance policy for bullying, but I don't think anyone means any harm here."
"My son is being harmed, whether or not anyone means it."
"I don't know how to say this, but the problem isn't the other students..."

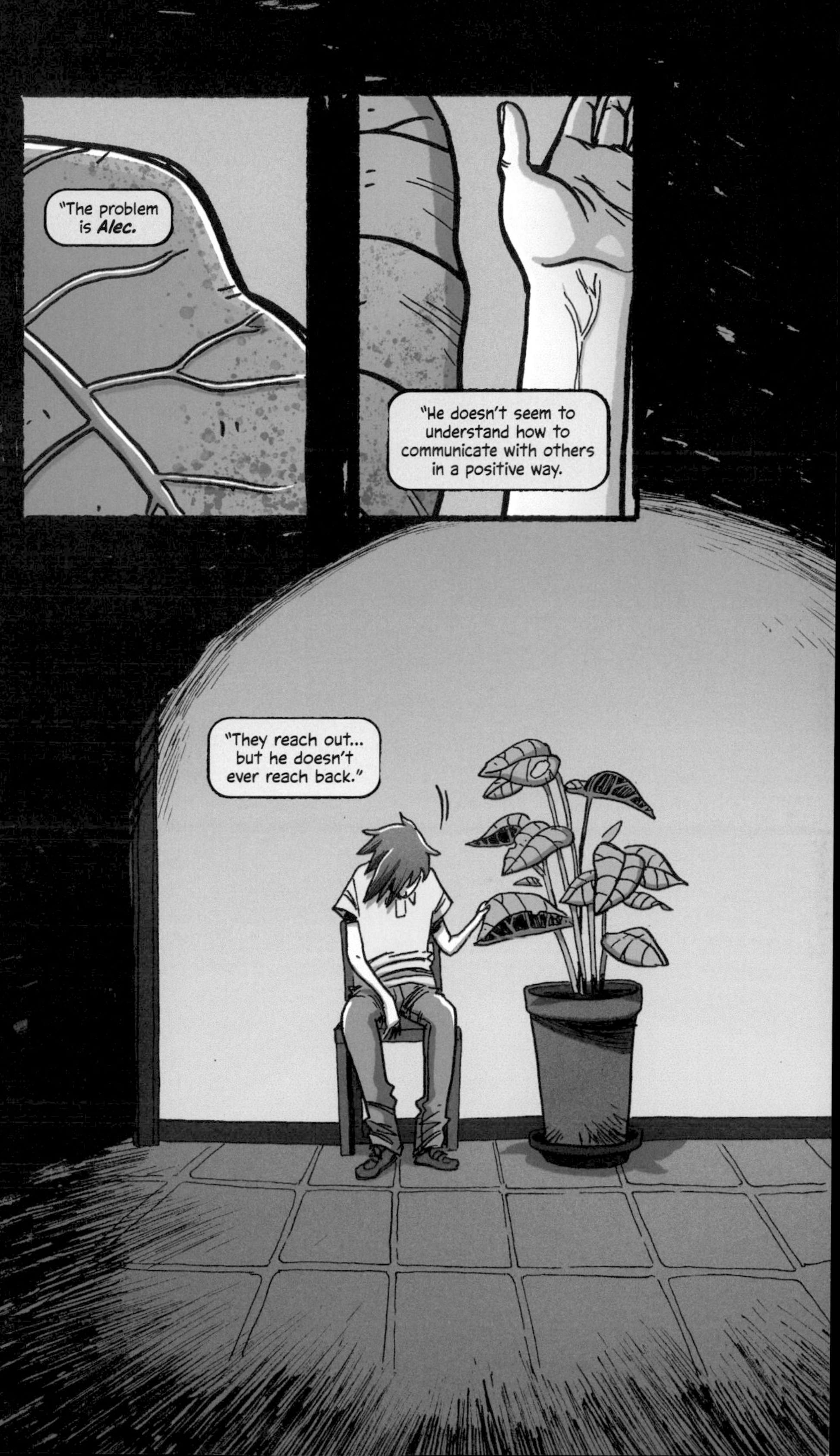
"The problem is *Alec.*
"He doesn't seem to understand how to communicate with others in a positive way.
"They reach out... but he doesn't ever reach back."

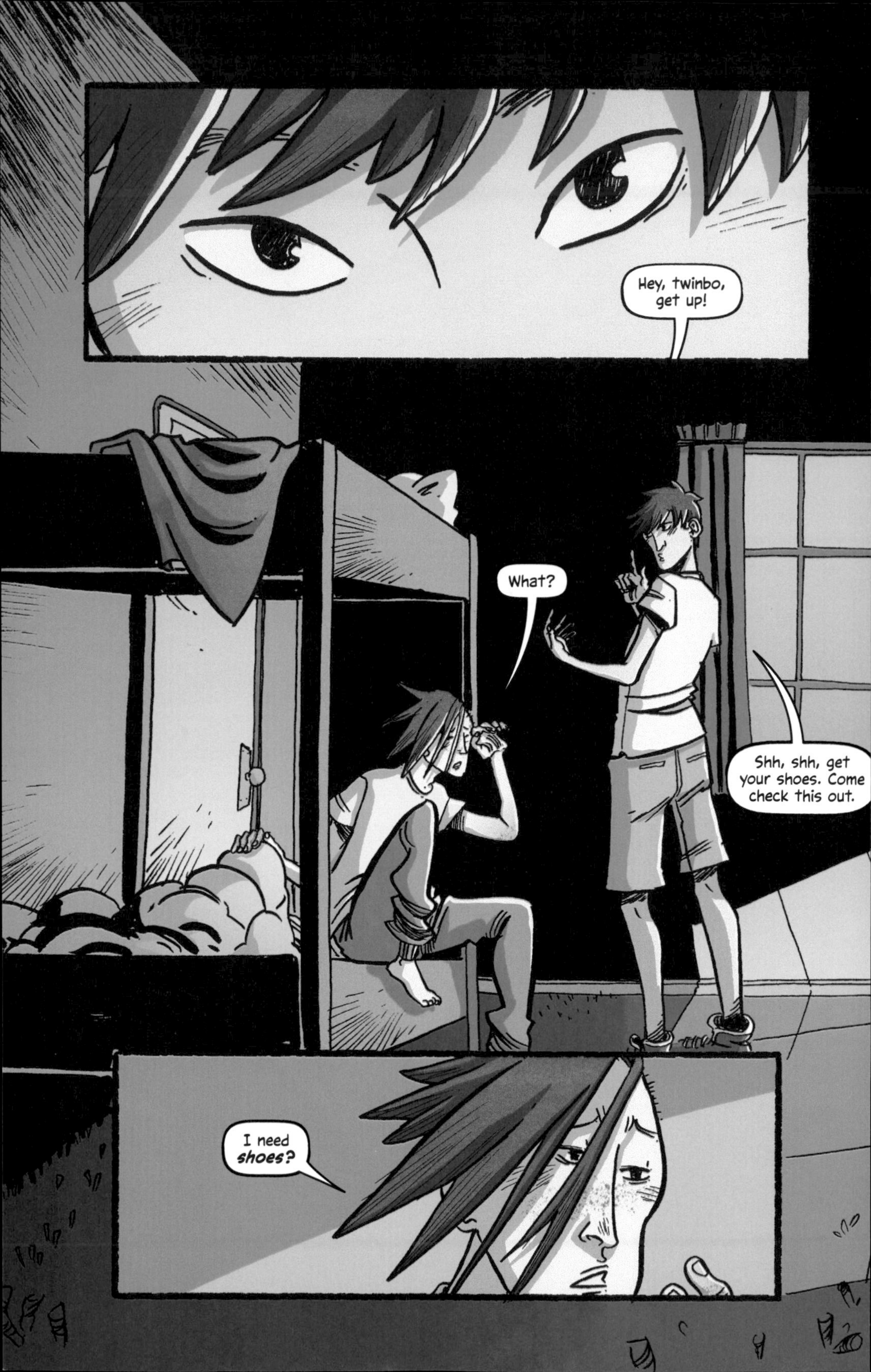
Hey, twinbo, get up!
What?
Shh, shh, get your shoes. Come check this out.
I need *shoes?*

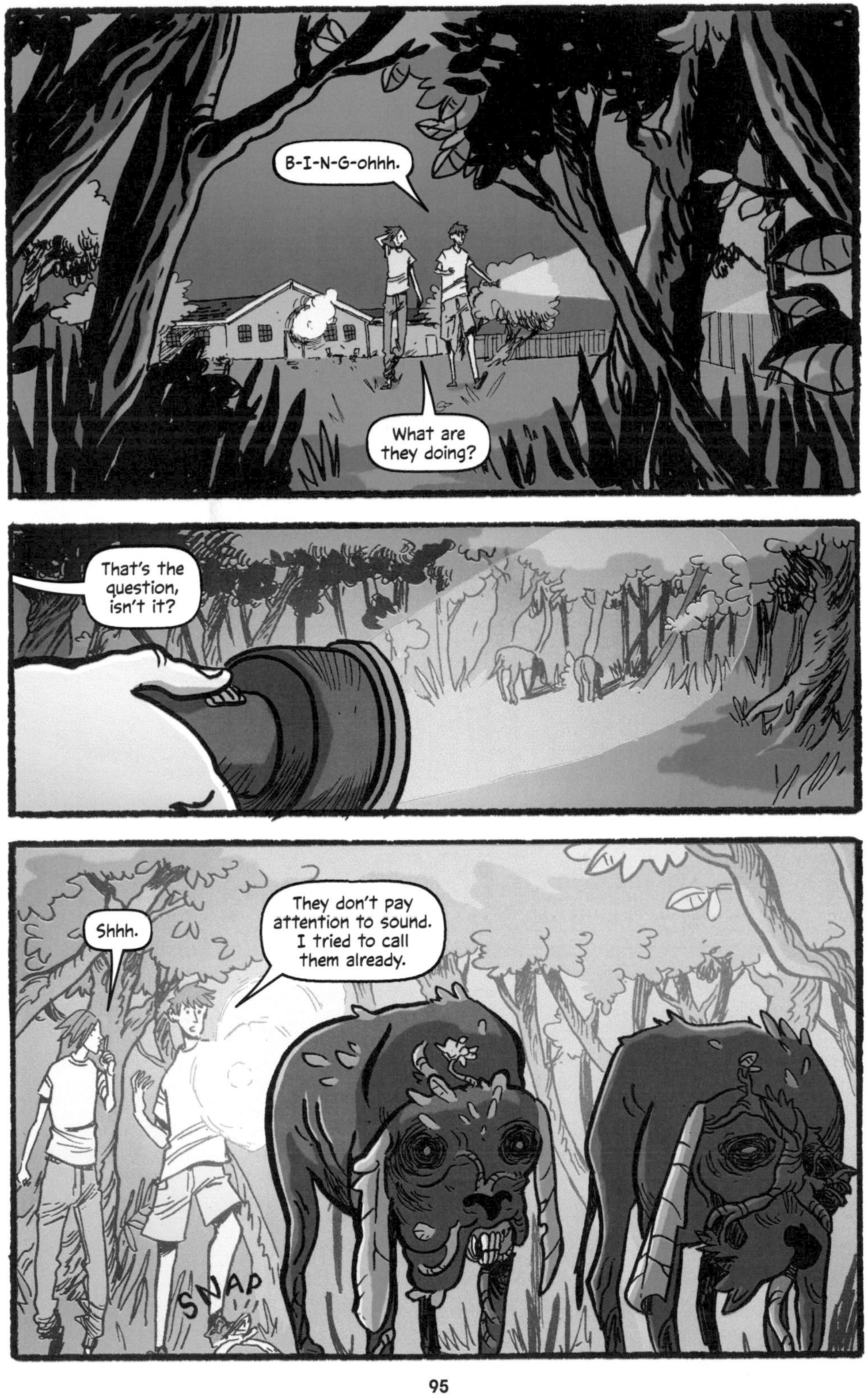
B-I-N-G-ohhh.
What are they doing?
That's the question, isn't it?
Shhh.
They don't pay attention to sound. I tried to call them already.
SNAP

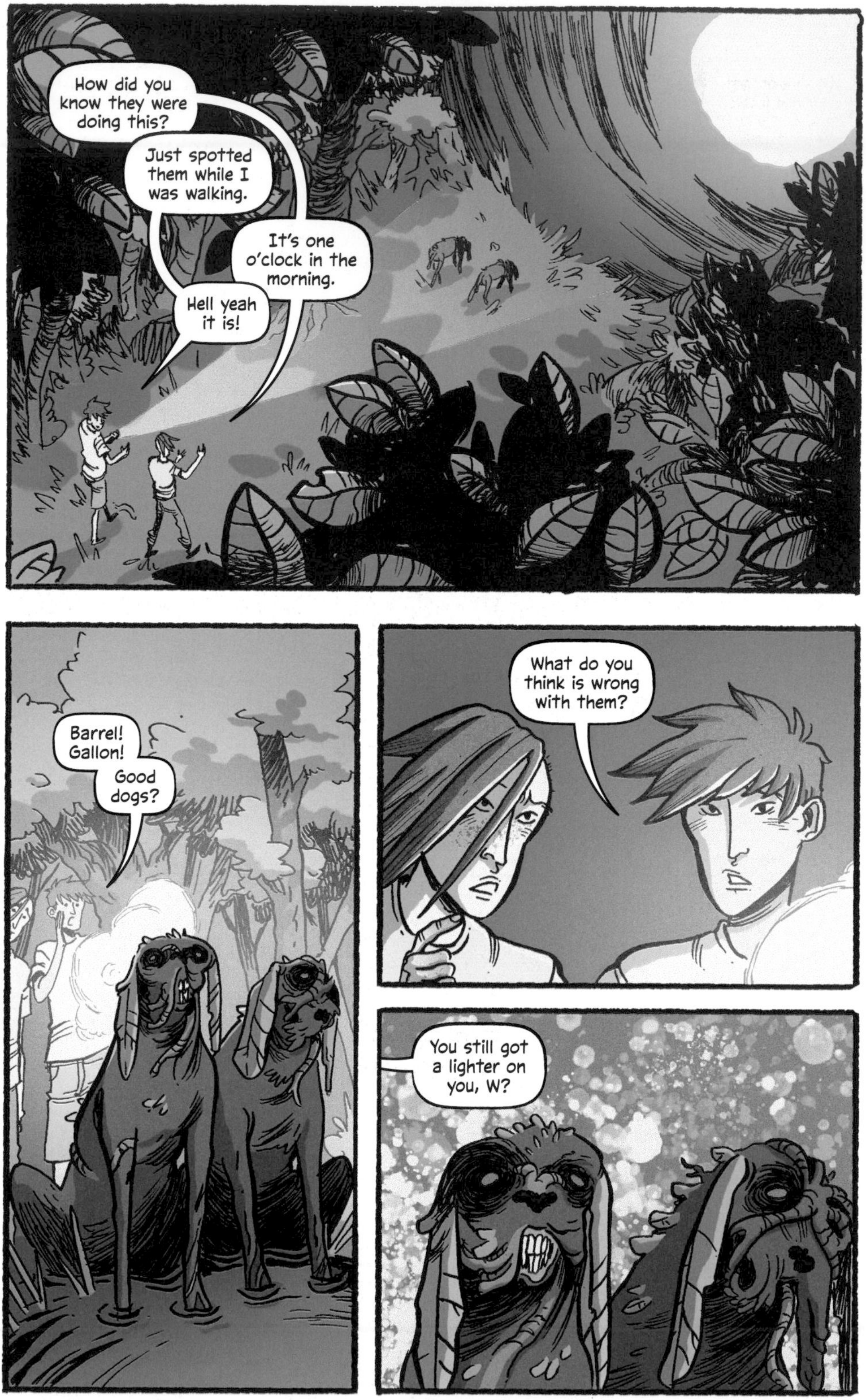
How did you know they were doing this?
Just spotted them while I was walking.
It's one o'clock in the morning.
Hell yeah it is!
Barrel! Gallon!
Good dogs?
What do you think is wrong with them?
You still got a lighter on you, W?

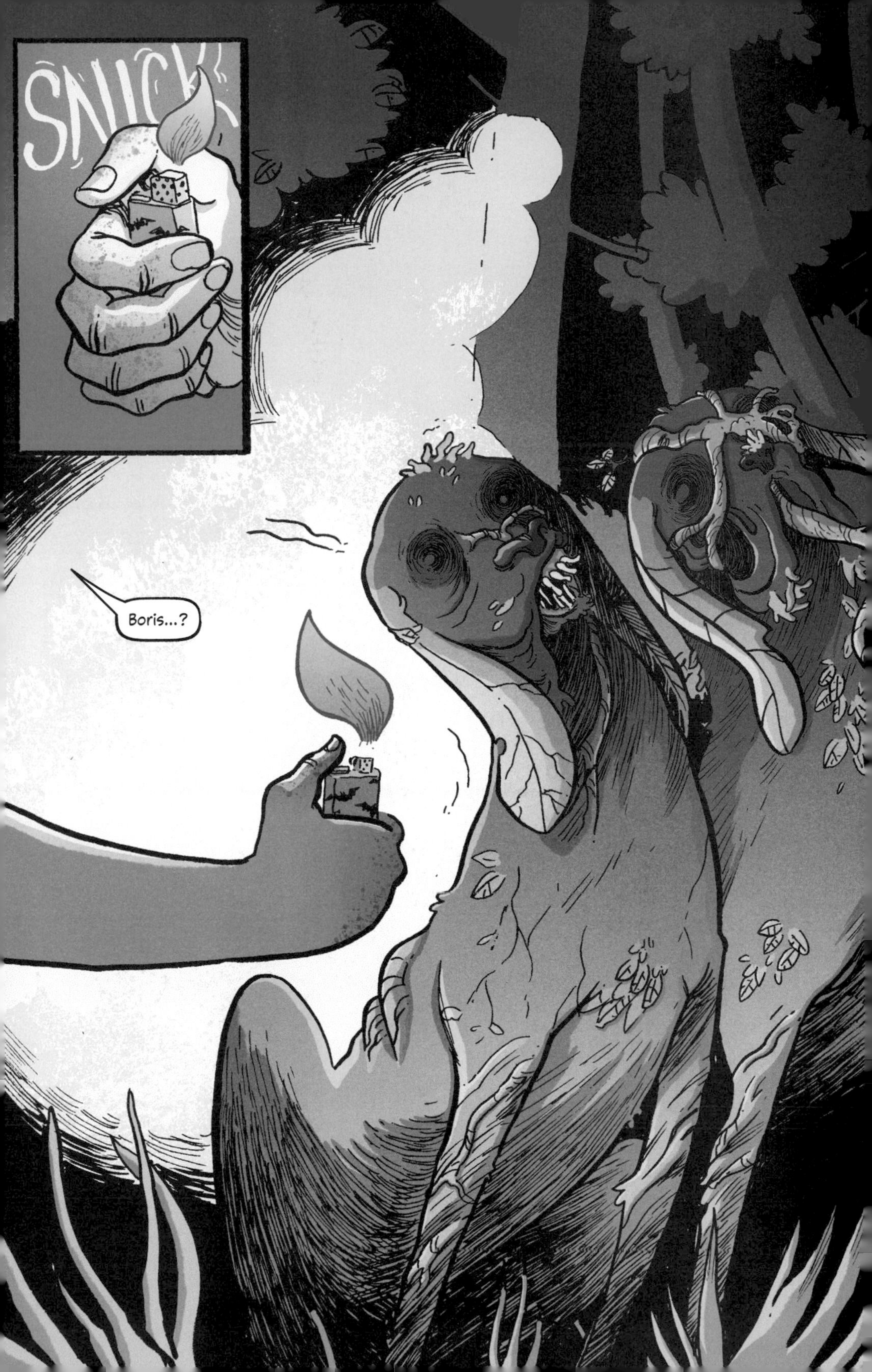
SNICK
Boris...?

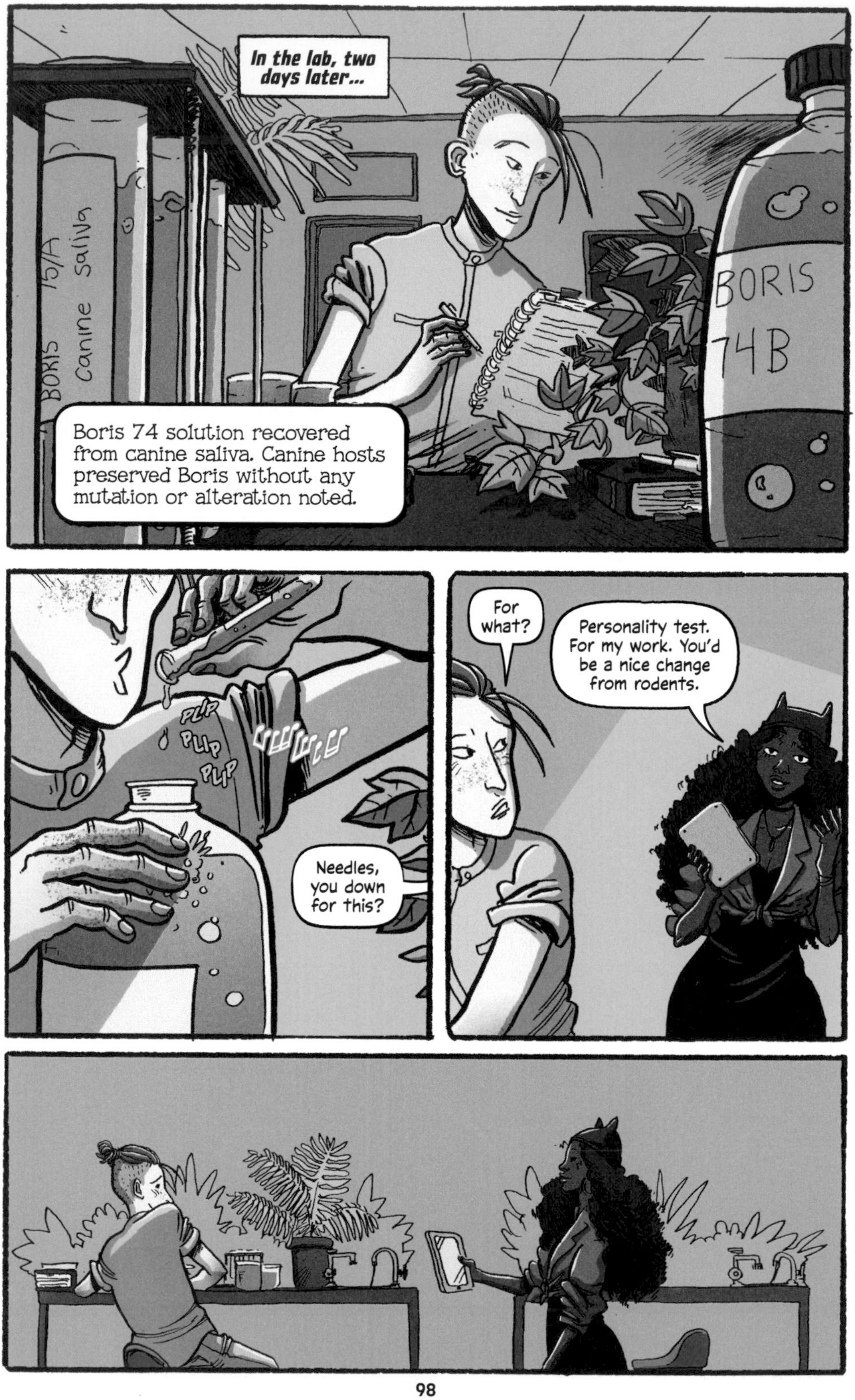
In the lab, two days later...
BORIS 15/A Canine Saliva
BORIS 74B
Boris 74 solution recovered from canine saliva. Canine hosts preserved Boris without any mutation or alteration noted.
PLIP PLIP PLIP
SCRITCH
Needles, you down for this?
For what?
Personality test. For my work. You'd be a nice change from rodents.

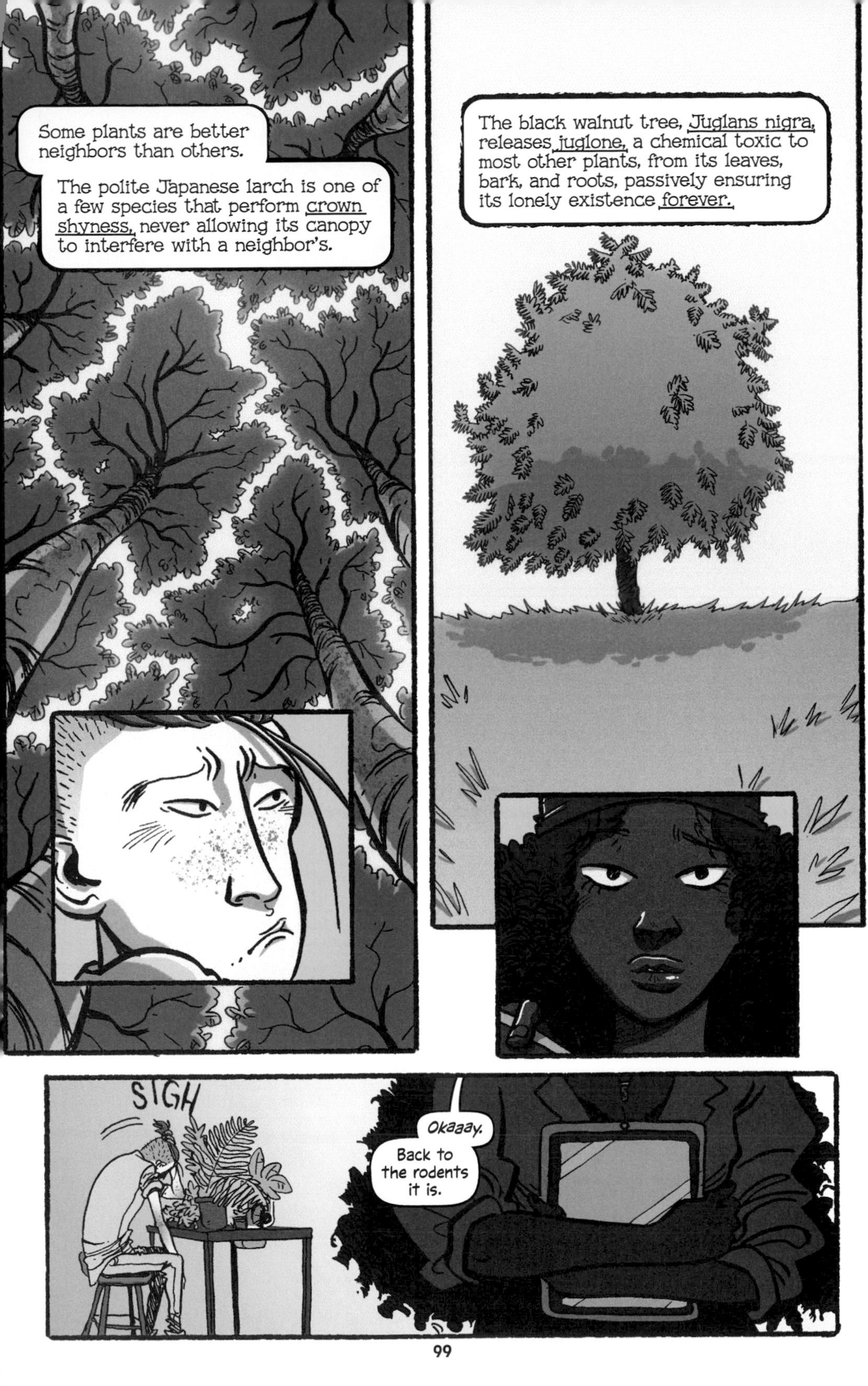
Some plants are better neighbors than others.
The polite Japanese larch is one of a few species that perform crown shyness, never allowing its canopy to interfere with a neighbor's.
The black walnut tree, Juglans nigra, releases juglone, a chemical toxic to most other plants, from its leaves, bark, and roots, passively ensuring its lonely existence forever.
SIGH
Okaaay.
Back to the rodents it is.

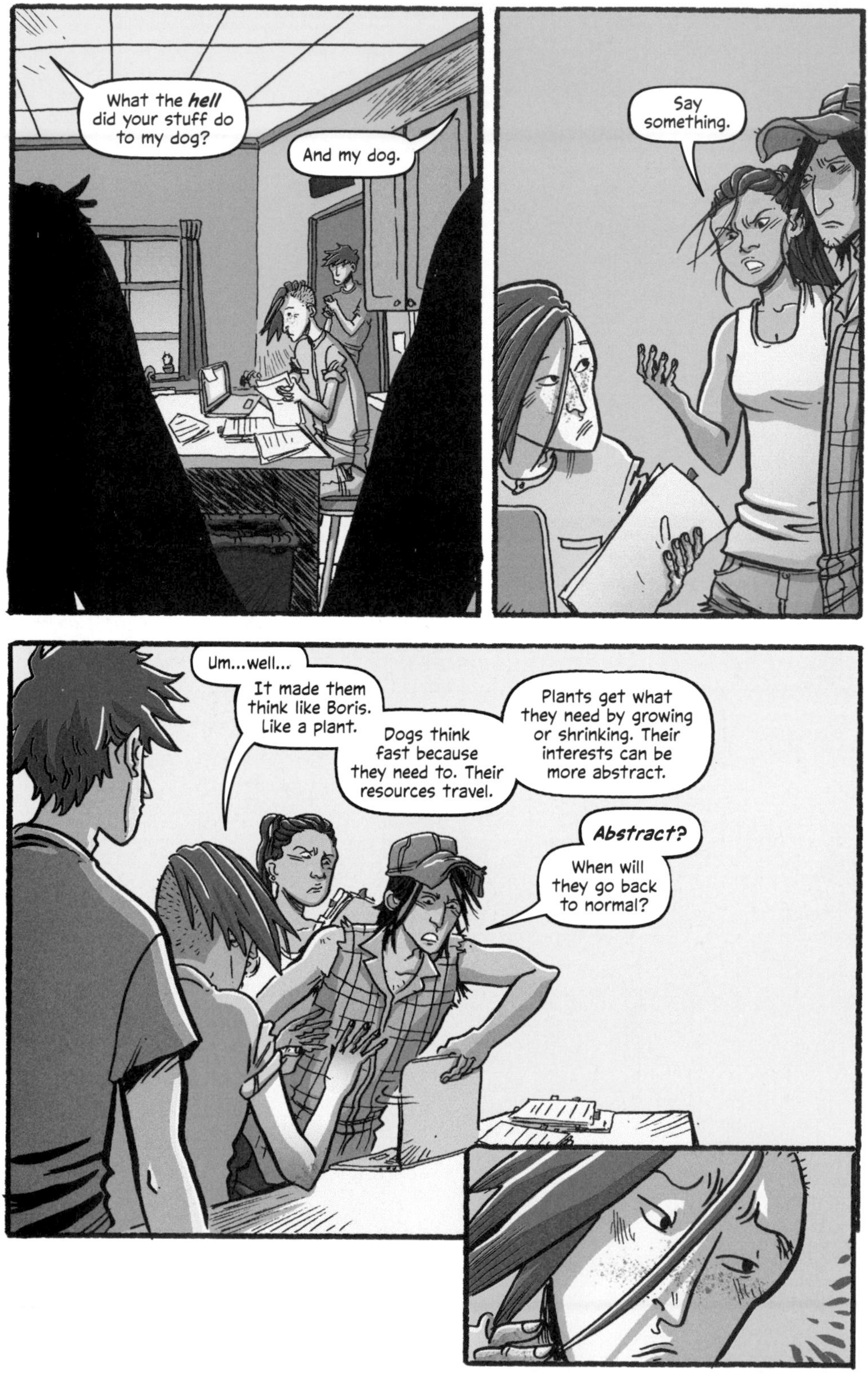
What the *hell* did your stuff do to my dog?
And my dog.
Say something.
Um...well...
It made them think like Boris. Like a plant.
Dogs think fast because they need to. Their resources travel.
Plants get what they need by growing or shrinking. Their interests can be more abstract.
Abstract?
When will they go back to normal?

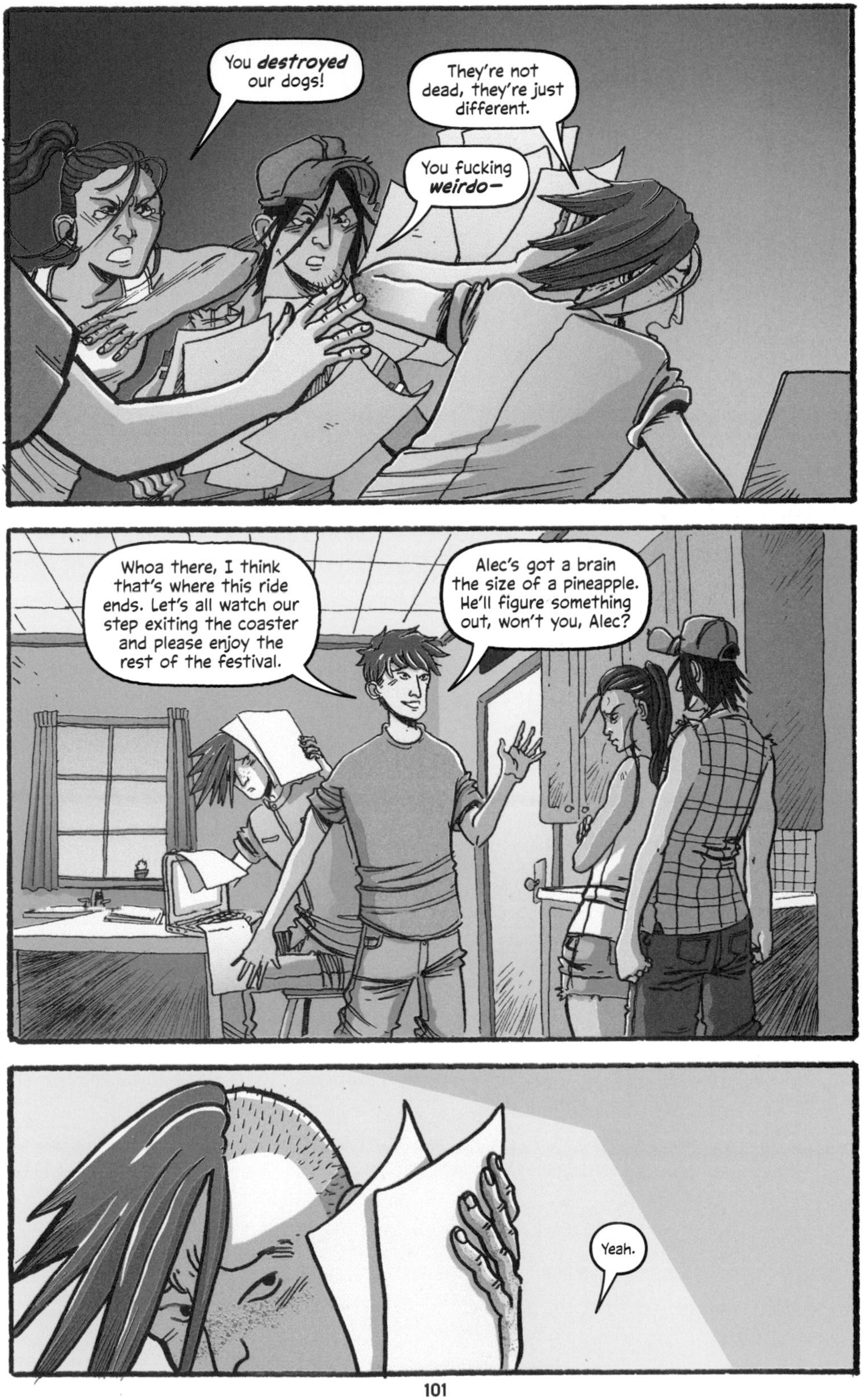
You *destroyed* our dogs!
They're not dead, they're just different.
You fucking *weirdo*—
Whoa there, I think that's where this ride ends. Let's all watch our step exiting the coaster and please enjoy the rest of the festival.
Alec's got a brain the size of a pineapple. He'll figure something out, won't you, Alec?
Yeah.

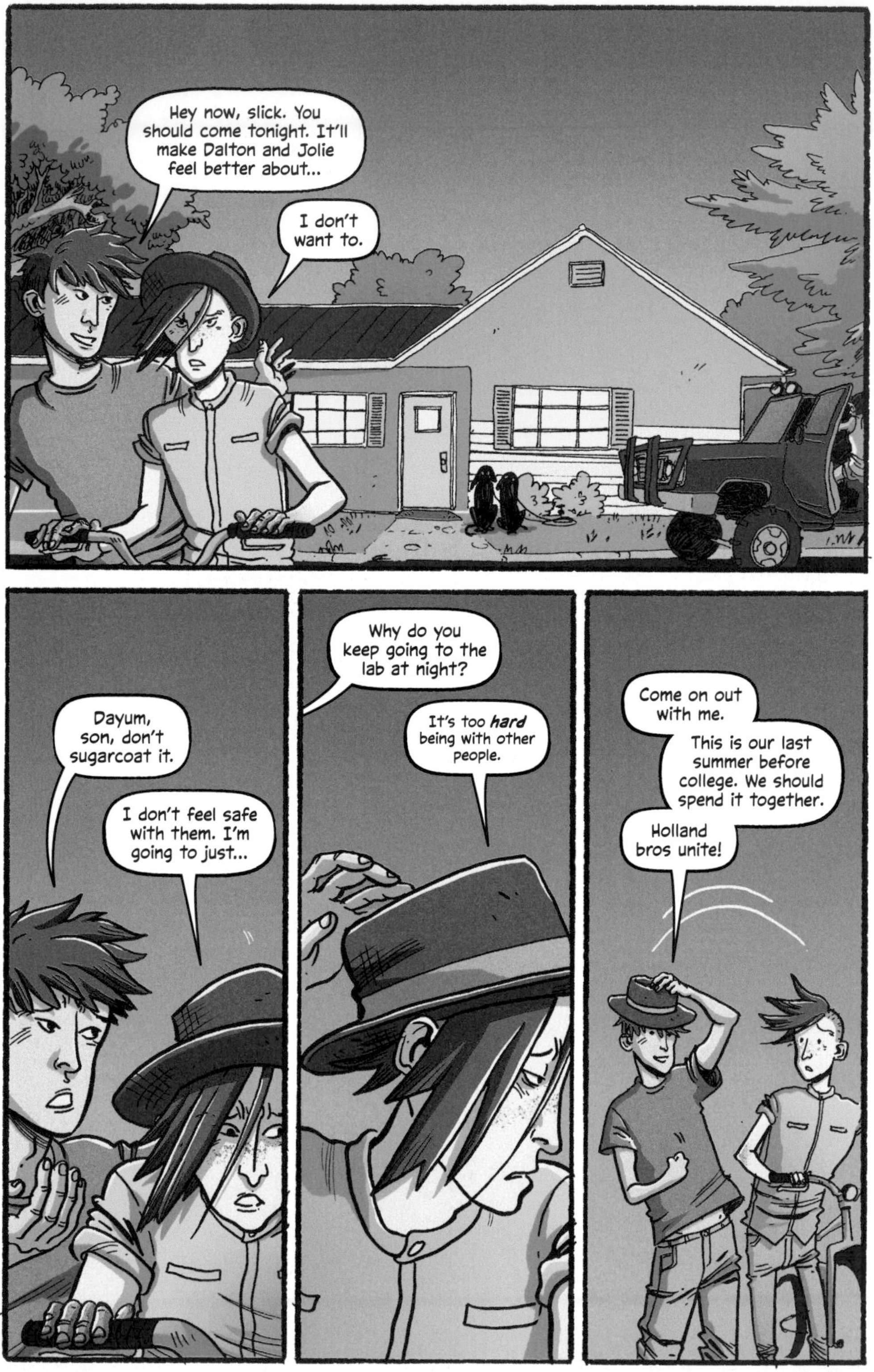
Hey now, slick. You should come tonight. It'll make Dalton and Jolie feel better about...
I don't want to.
Dayum, son, don't sugarcoat it.
I don't feel safe with them. I'm going to just...
Why do you keep going to the lab at night?
It's too **hard** being with other people.
Come on out with me.
This is our last summer before college. We should spend it together.
Holland bros unite!

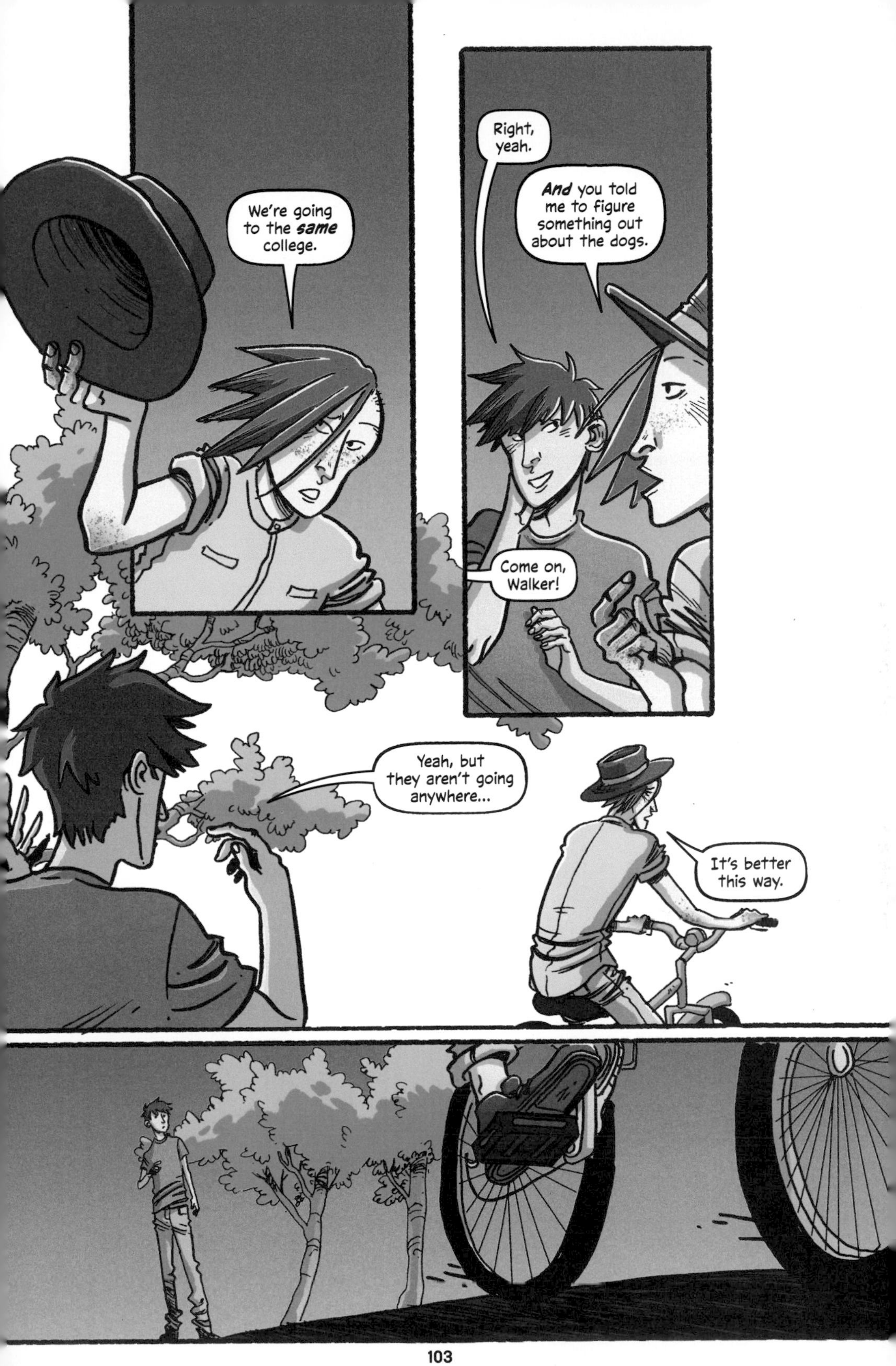
We're going to the *same* college.
Right, yeah.
And you told me to figure something out about the dogs.
Come on, Walker!
Yeah, but they aren't going anywhere...
It's better this way.

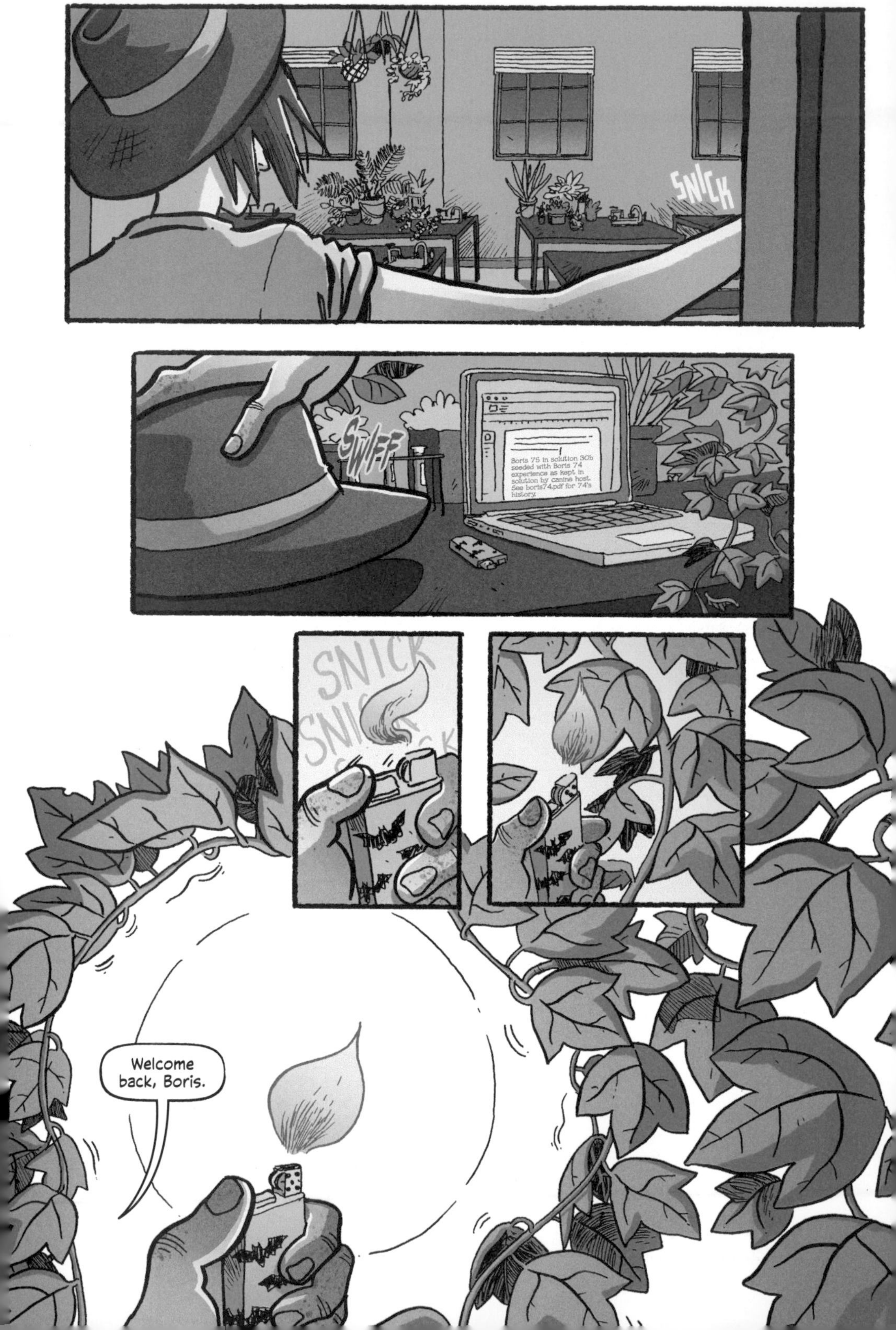
SNICK
SWIFF
Boris 75 in solution 30b seeded with Boris 74 experience as kept in solution by canine host. See boris74.pdf for 74's history.
SNICK
Welcome back, Boris.

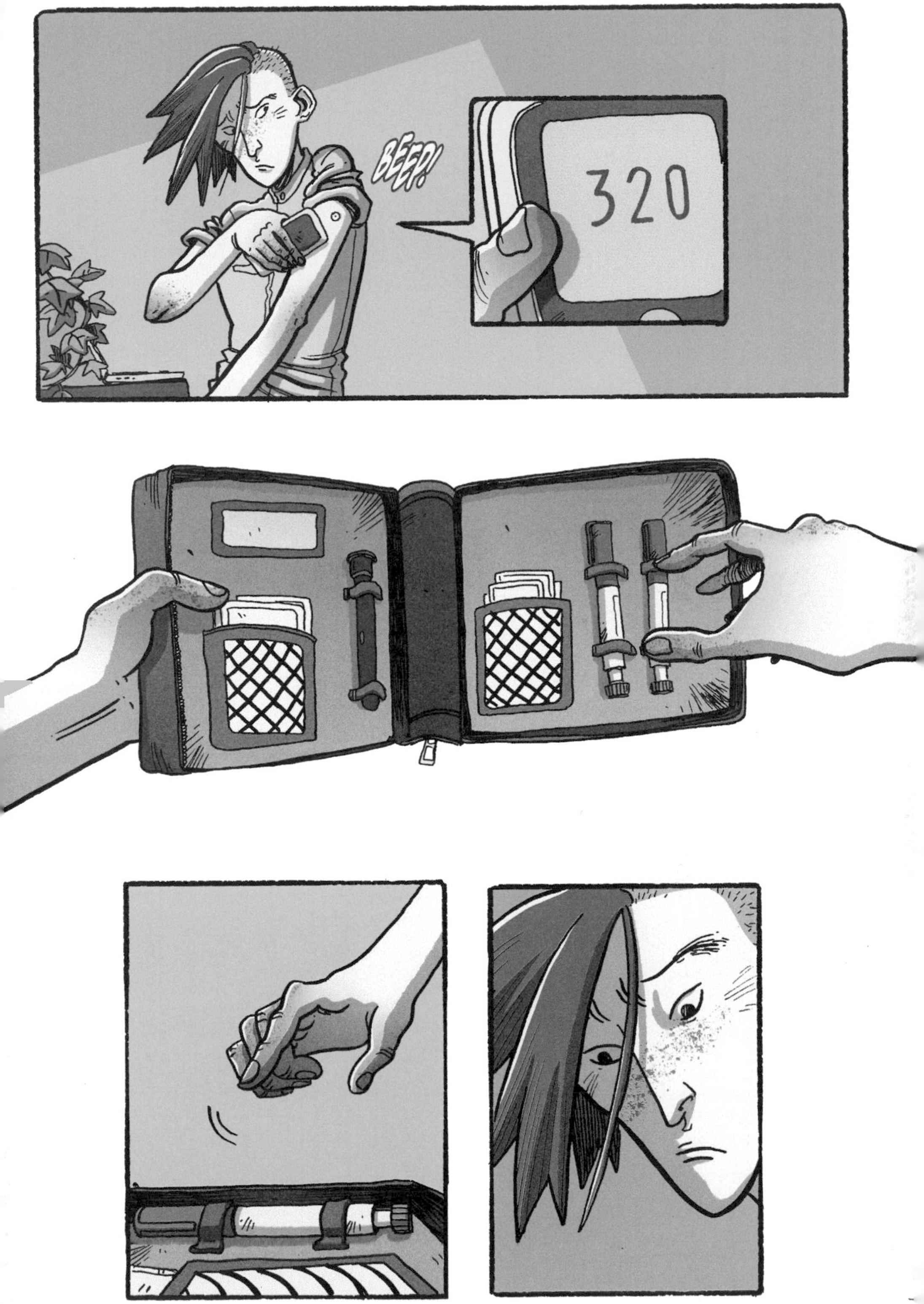
BEEP!
320

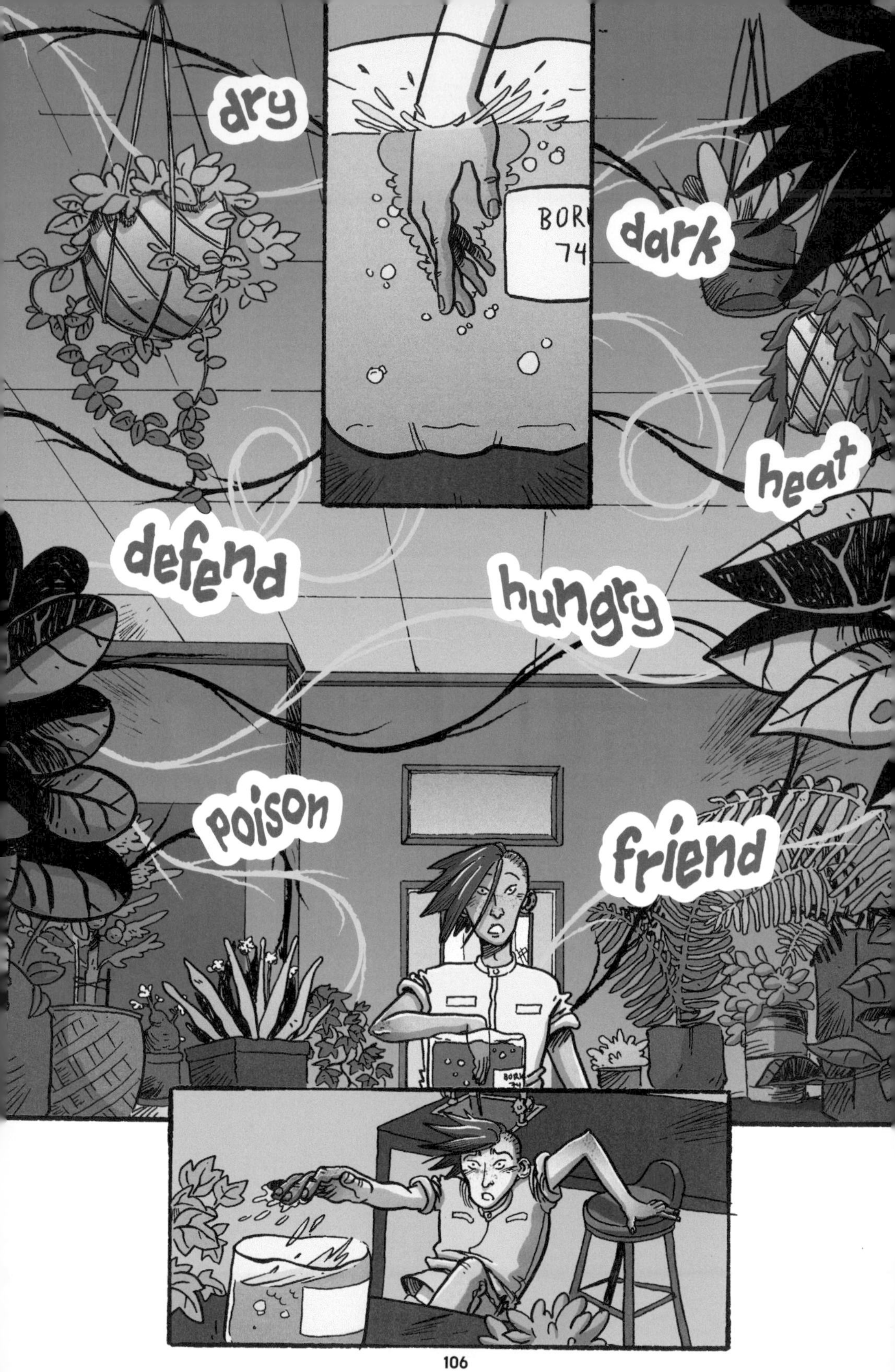
dry
dark
BORK
74
heat
defend
hungry
poison
friend

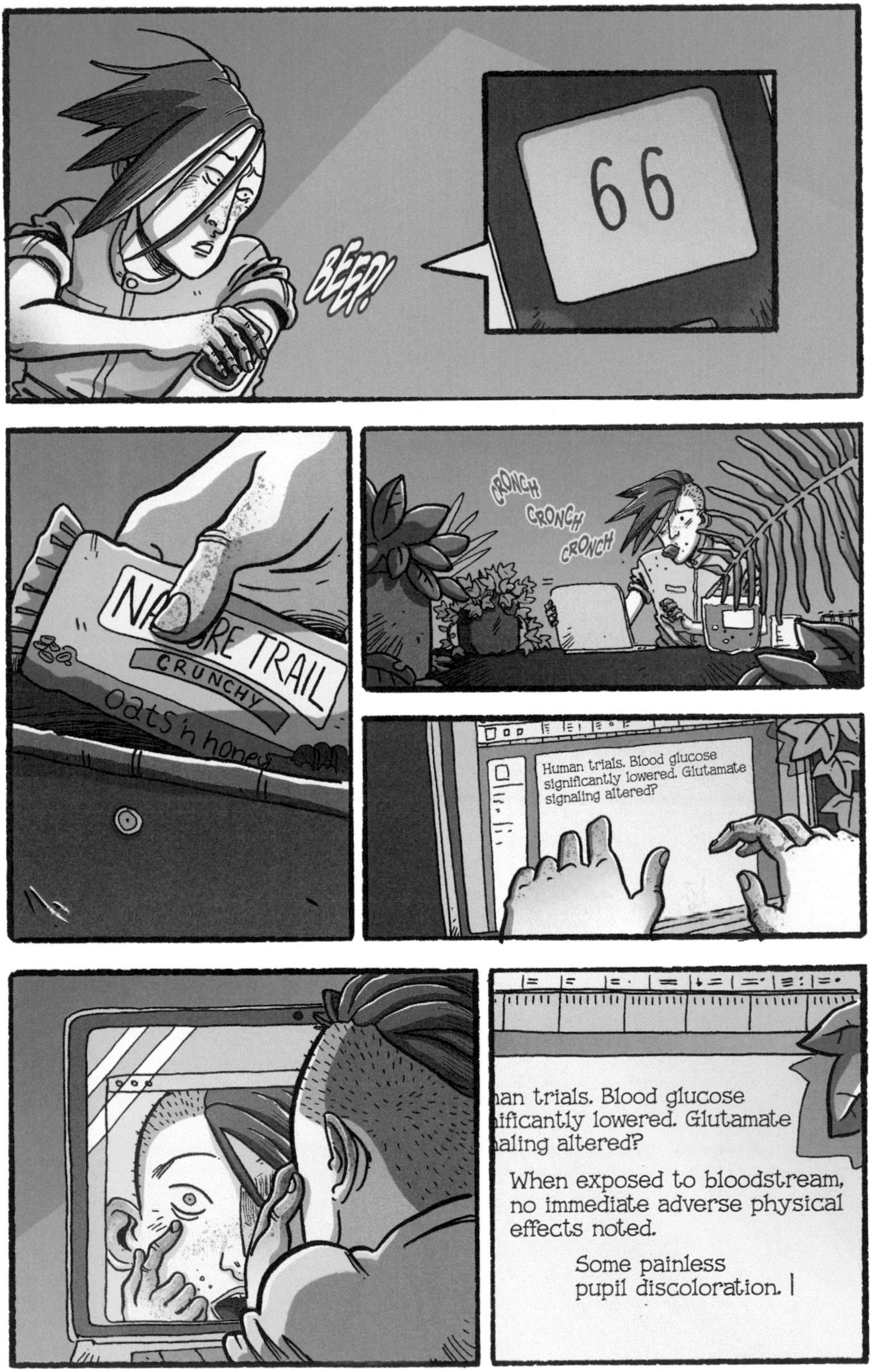
66
BEEP!
NATURE TRAIL
CRUNCHY
oats'n honey
CRONCH
CRONCH
CRONCH
Human trials. Blood glucose significantly lowered. Glutamate signaling altered?
man trials. Blood glucose
nificantly lowered. Glutamate
naling altered?
When exposed to bloodstream, no immediate adverse physical effects noted.
Some painless pupil discoloration.

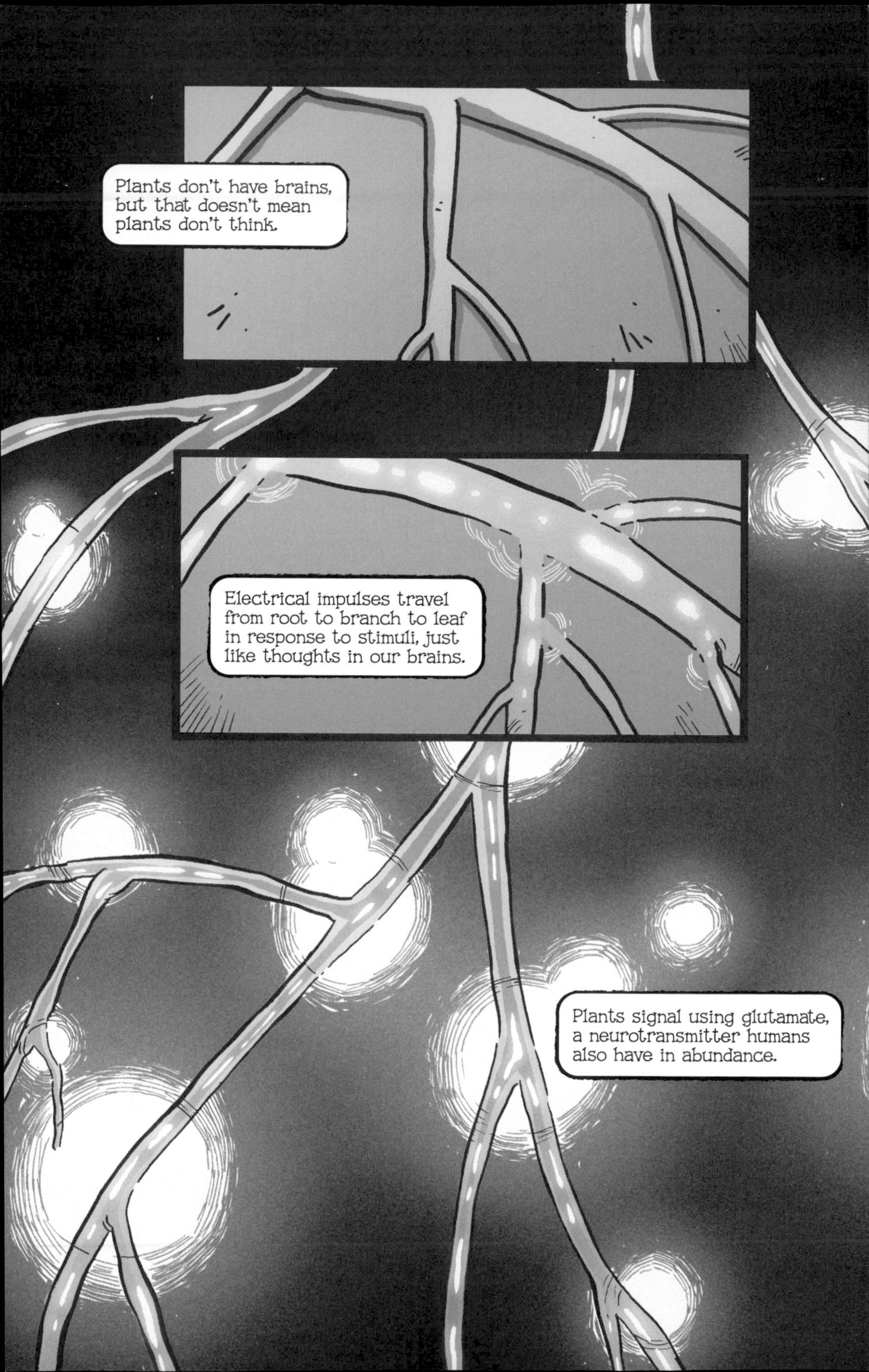
Plants don't have brains, but that doesn't mean plants don't think.
Electrical impulses travel from root to branch to leaf in response to stimuli, just like thoughts in our brains.
Plants signal using glutamate, a neurotransmitter humans also have in abundance.

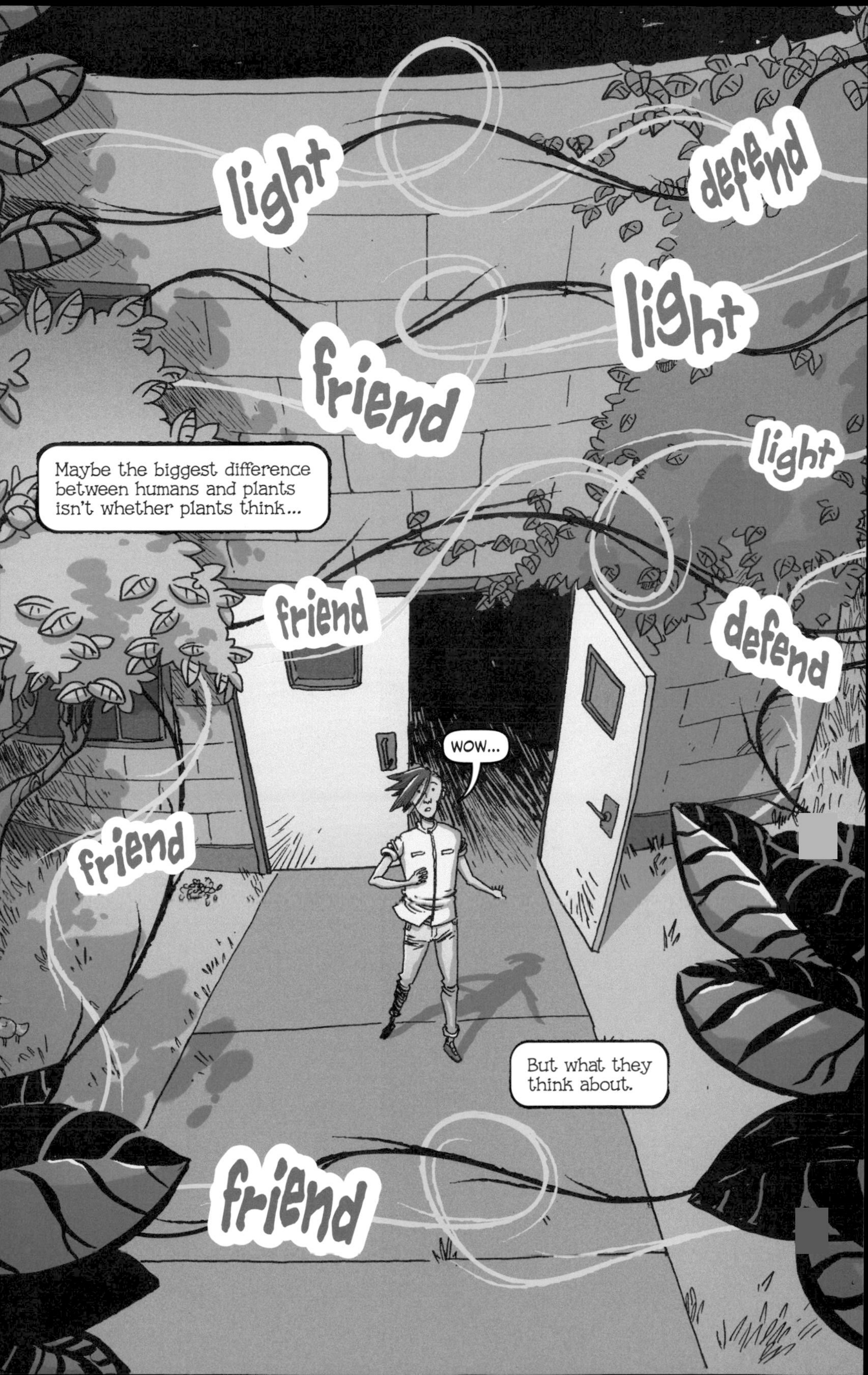
light
defend
light
friend
light
Maybe the biggest difference between humans and plants isn't whether plants think...
friend
defend
WOW...
friend
But what they think about.
friend

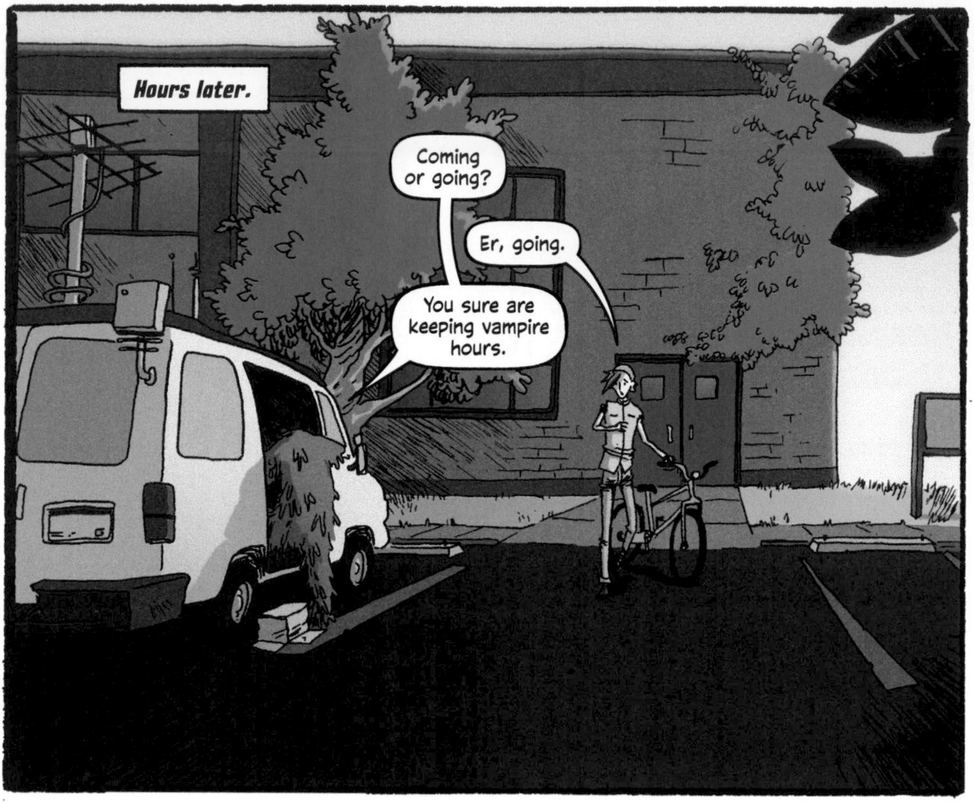
Hours later.
Coming or going?
Er, going.
You sure are keeping vampire hours.

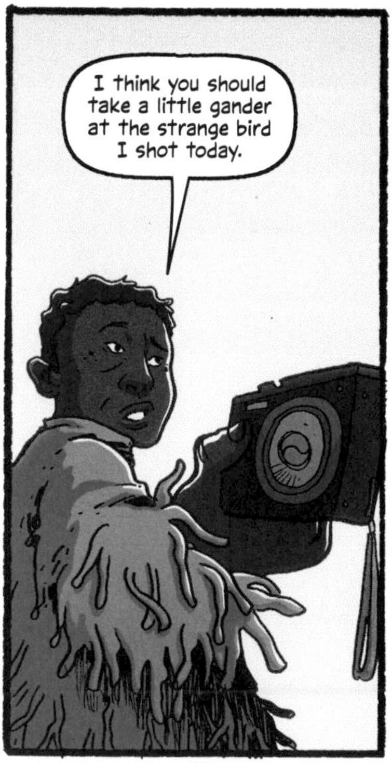
I think you should take a little gander at the strange bird I shot today.

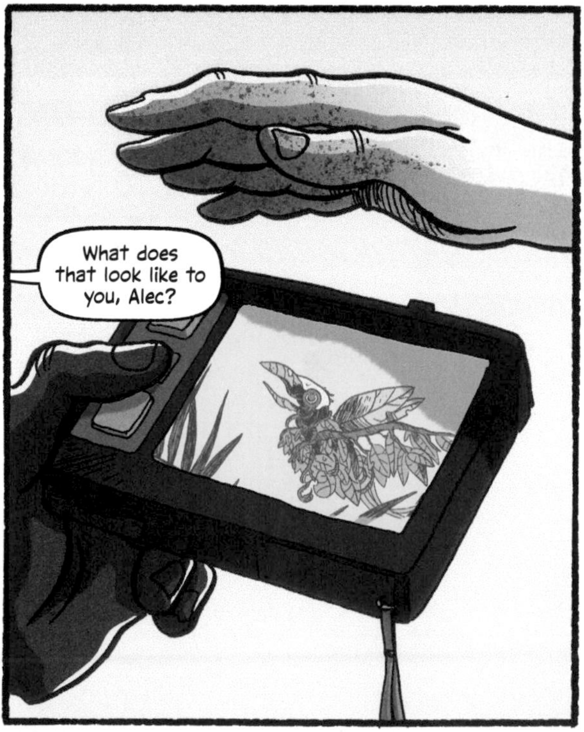
What does that look like to you, Alec?

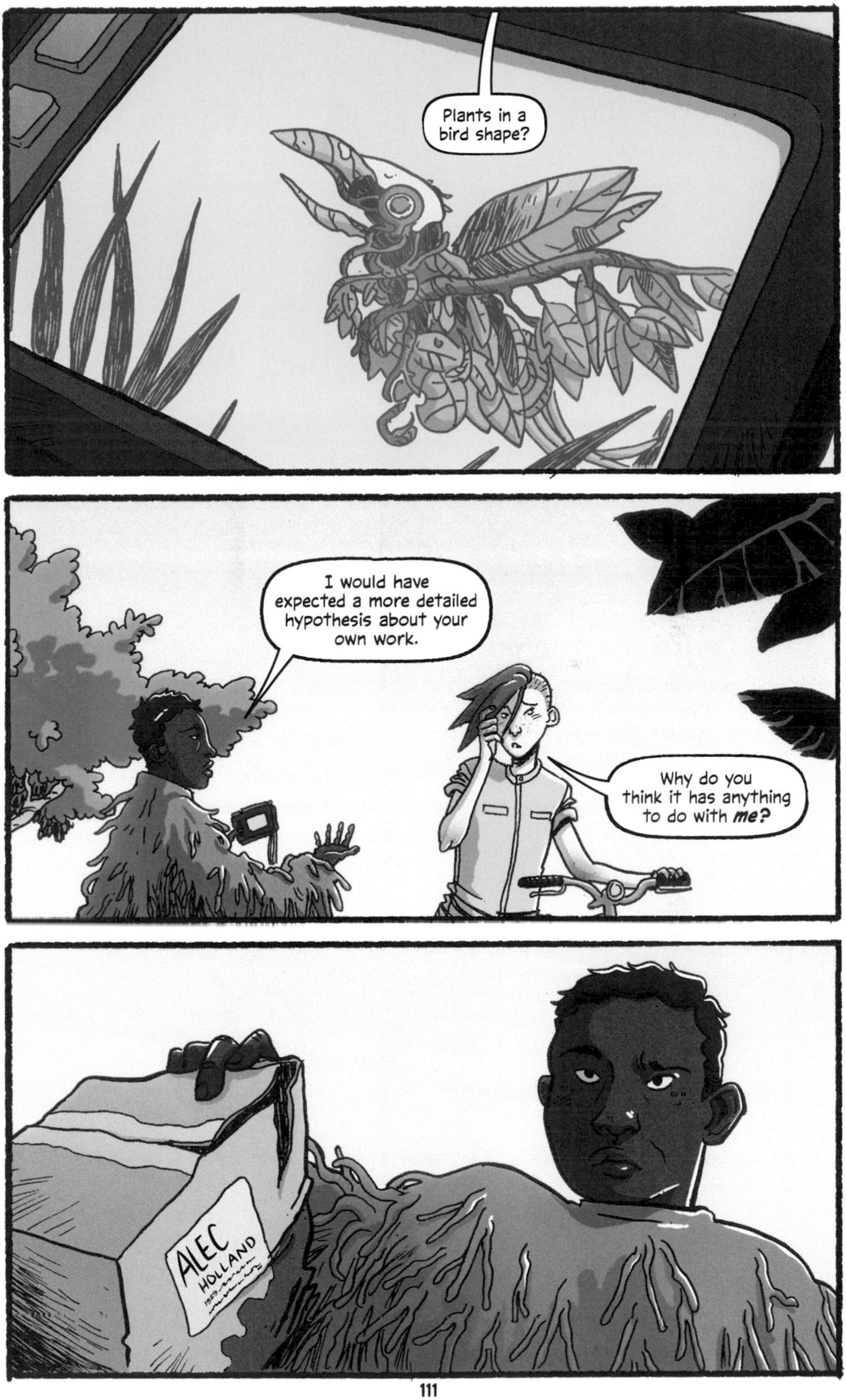
Plants in a bird shape?
I would have expected a more detailed hypothesis about your own work.
Why do you think it has anything to do with *me?*
ALEC HOLLAND

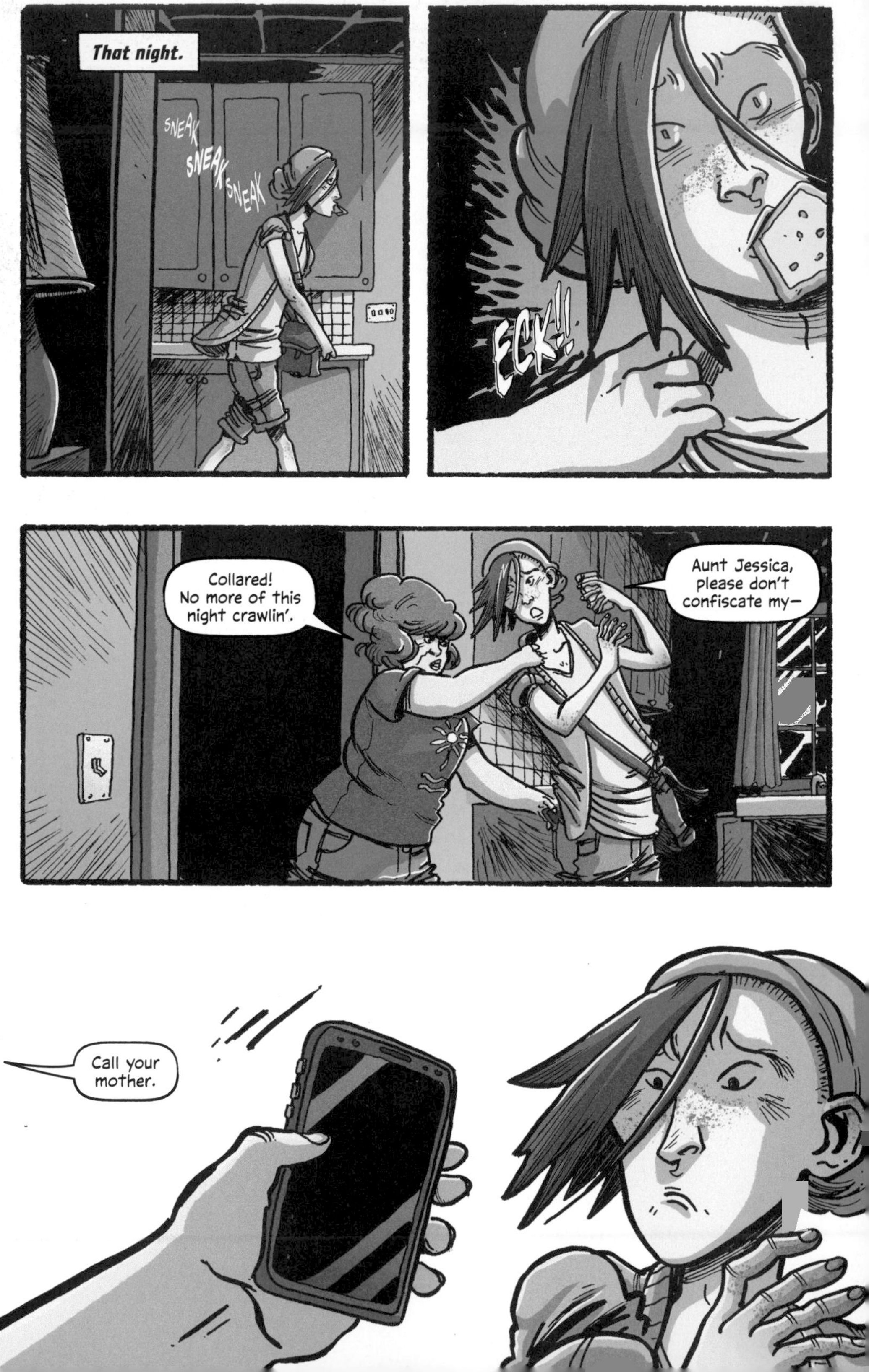
That night.
SNEAK
SNEAK
SNEAK
ECK!!
Collared! No more of this night crawlin'.
Aunt Jessica, please don't confiscate my—
Call your mother.

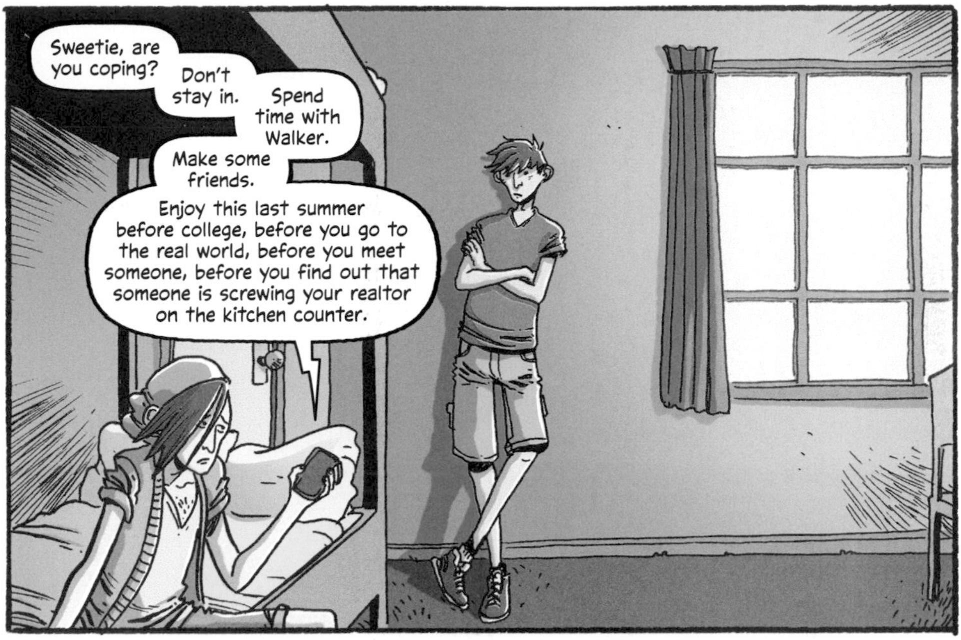
Sweetie, are you coping?
Don't stay in.
Spend time with Walker.
Make some friends.
Enjoy this last summer before college, before you go to the real world, before you meet someone, before you find out that someone is screwing your realtor on the kitchen counter.

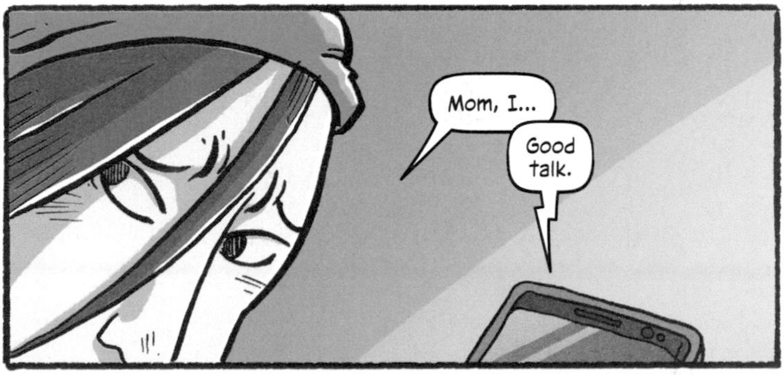
Mom, I...
Good talk.

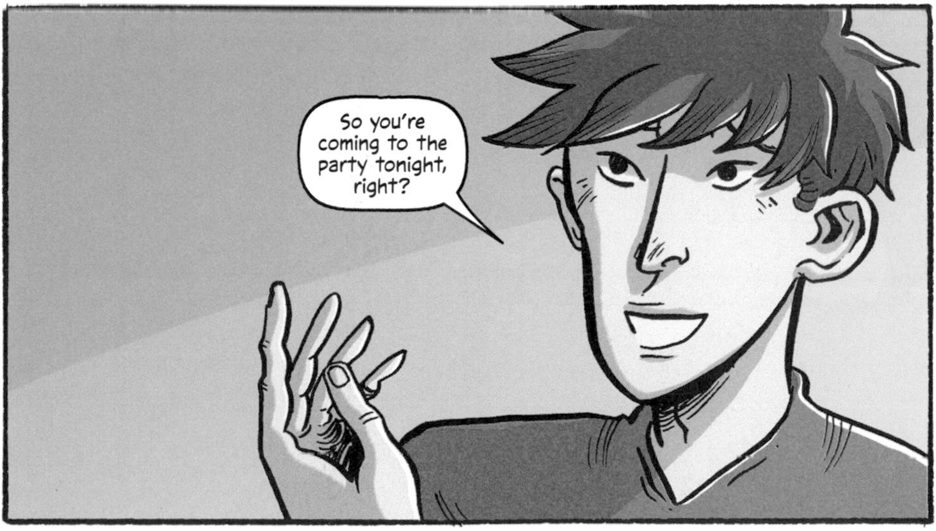
So you're coming to the party tonight, right?

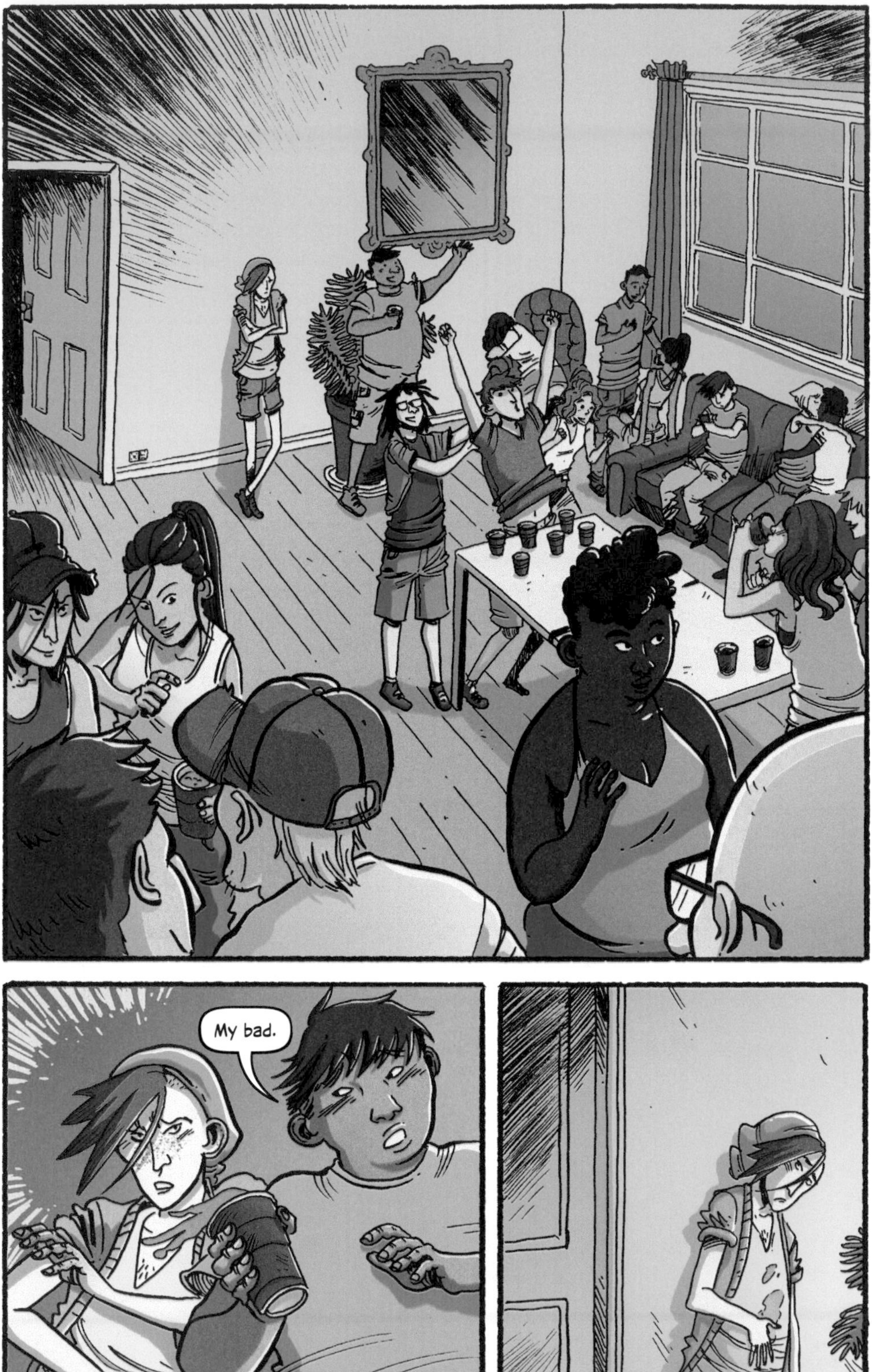
My bad.

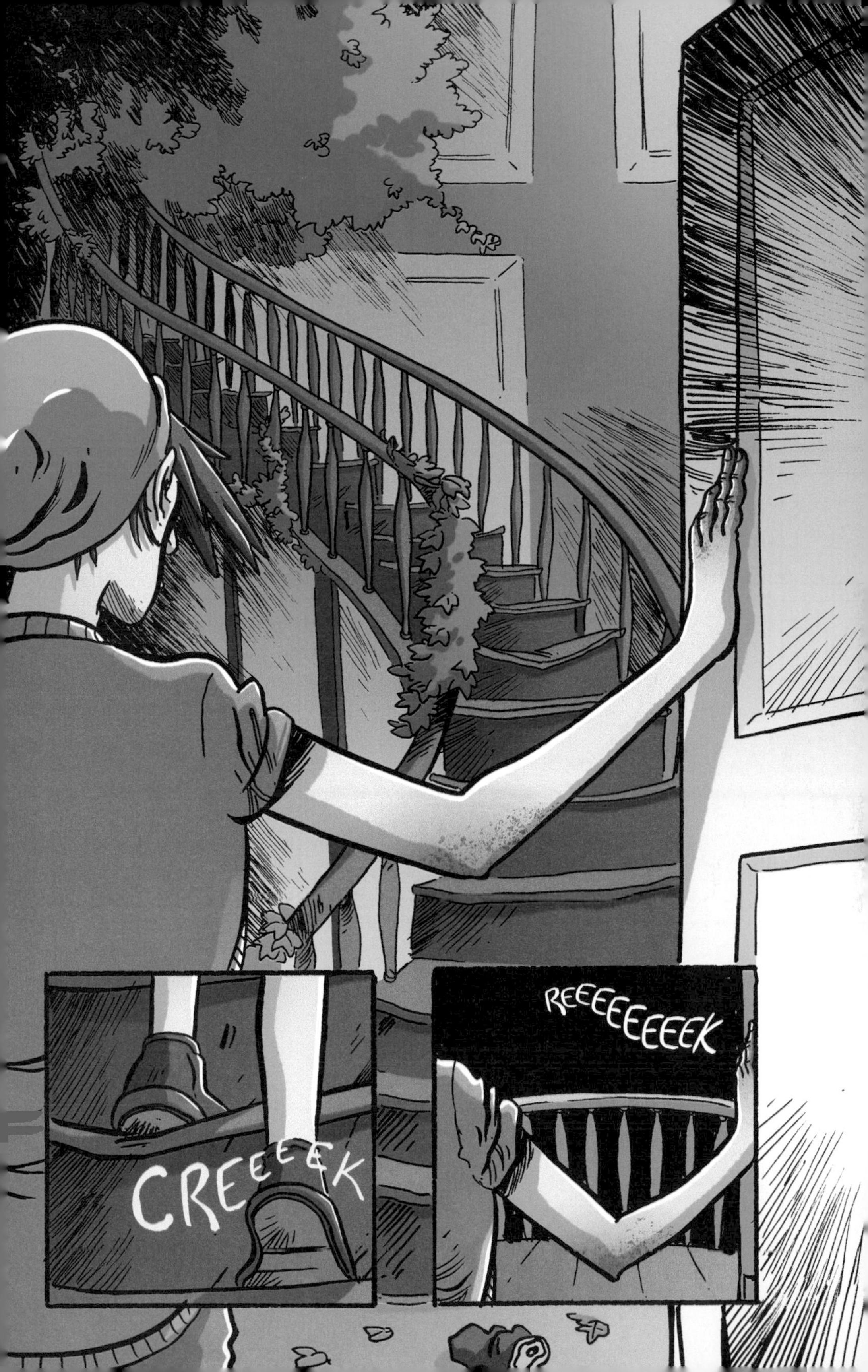
CREEEEK
REEEEEEEEEK

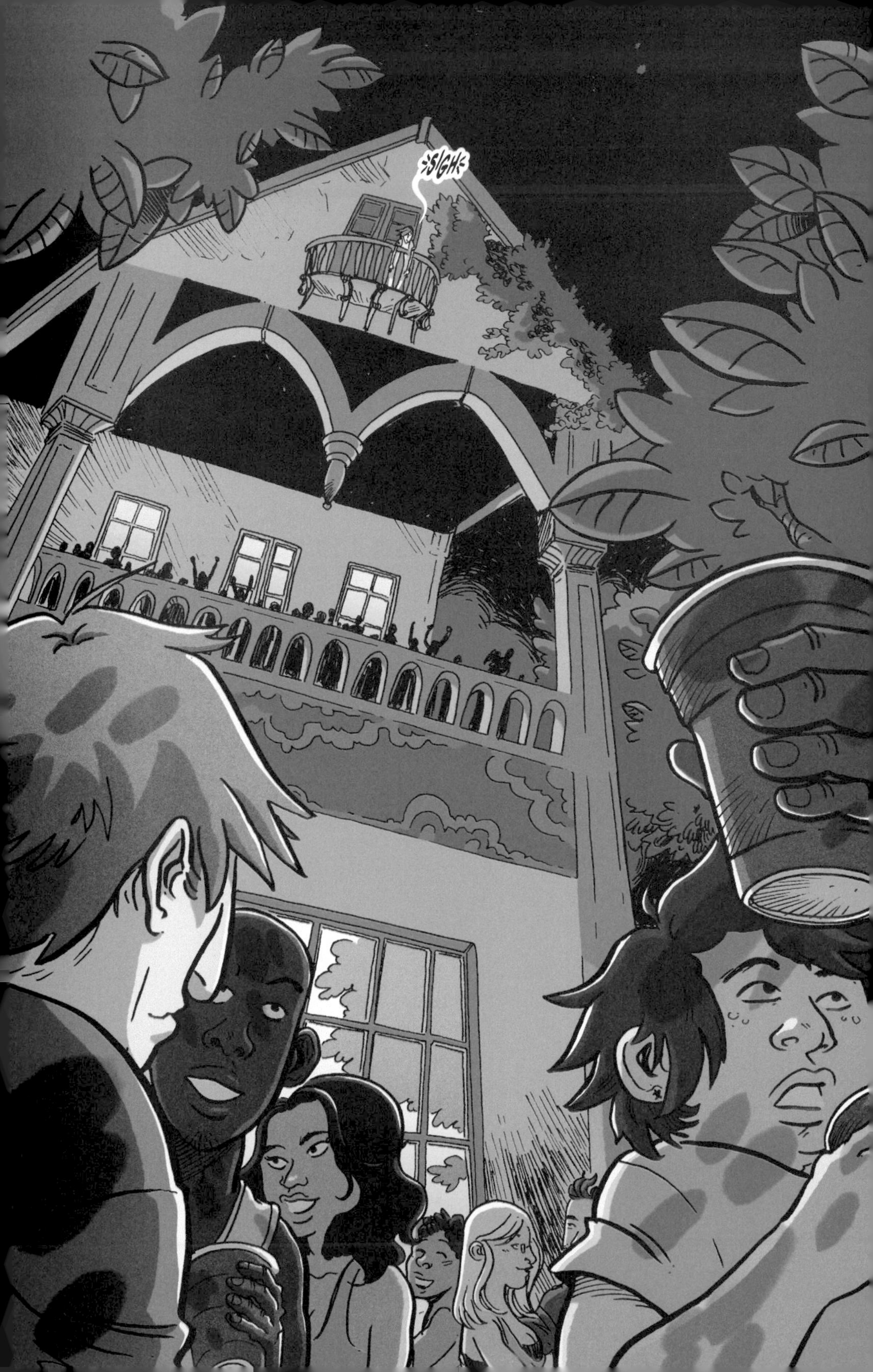
SIGH

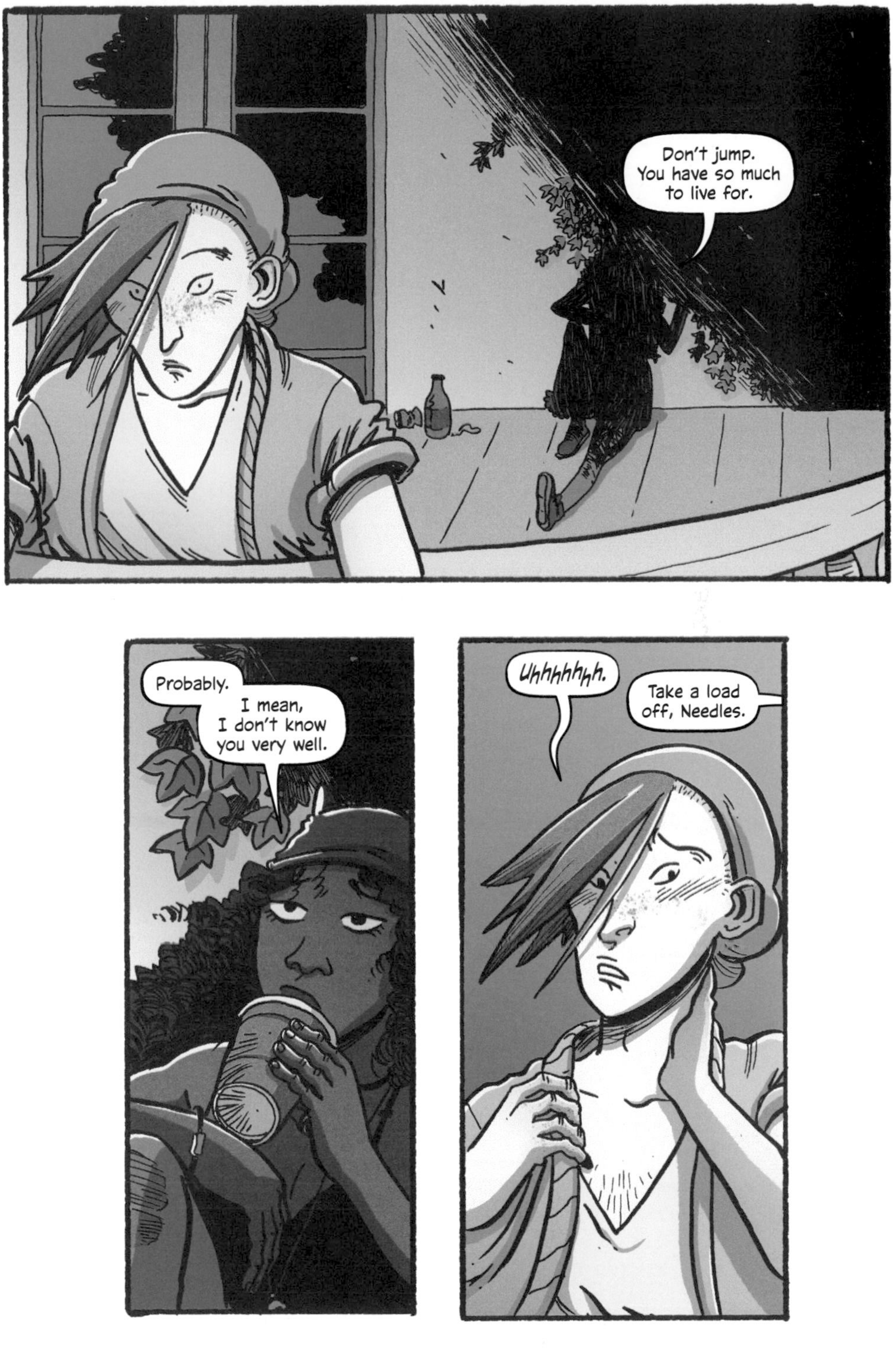
Don't jump. You have so much to live for.
Probably.
I mean, I don't know you very well.
Uhhhhhh.
Take a load off, Needles.

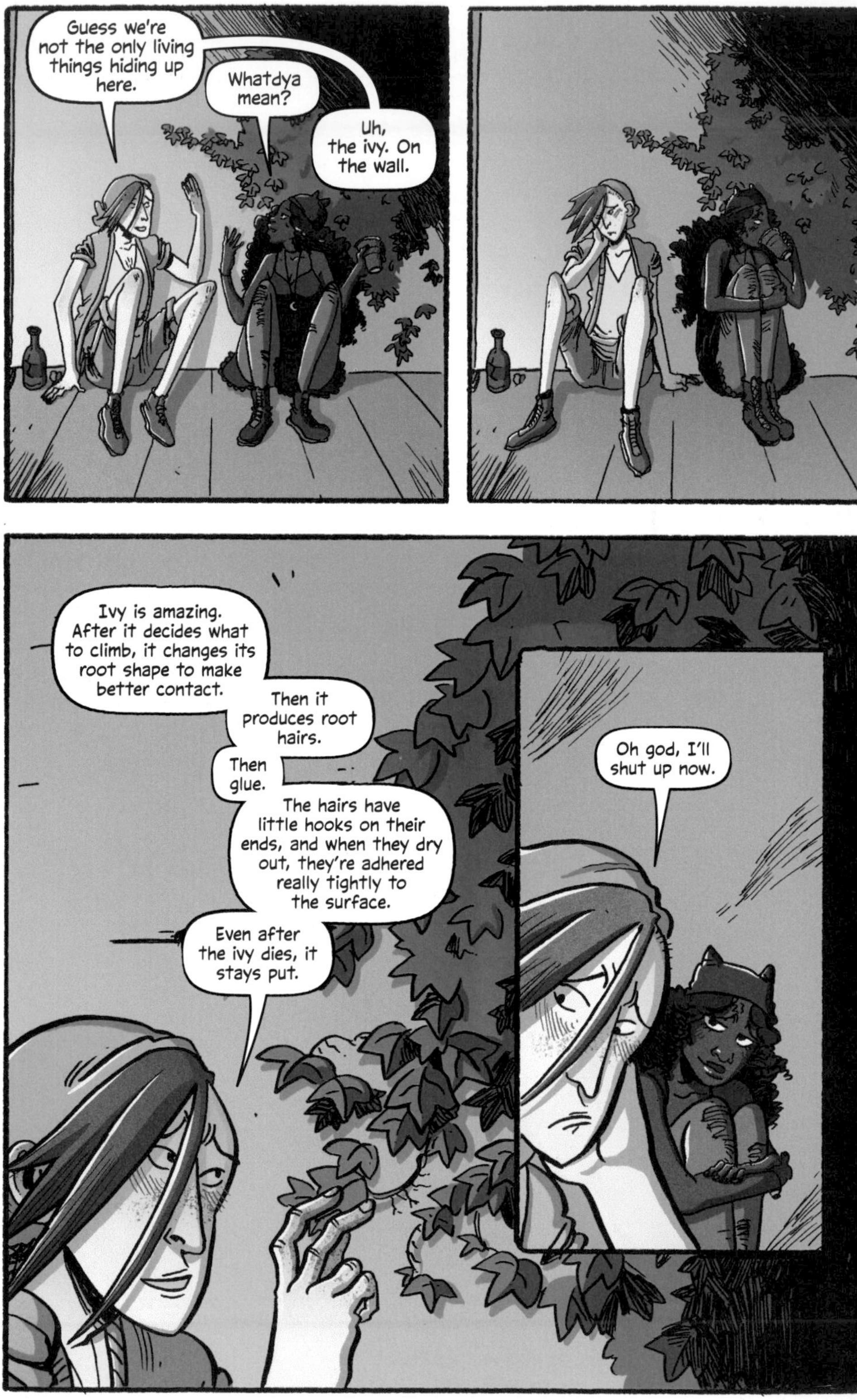

Guess we're not the only living things hiding up here.
Whatdya mean?
Uh, the ivy. On the wall.
Ivy is amazing. After it decides what to climb, it changes its root shape to make better contact.
Then it produces root hairs.
Then glue.
The hairs have little hooks on their ends, and when they dry out, they're adhered really tightly to the surface.
Even after the ivy dies, it stays put.
Oh god, I'll shut up now.

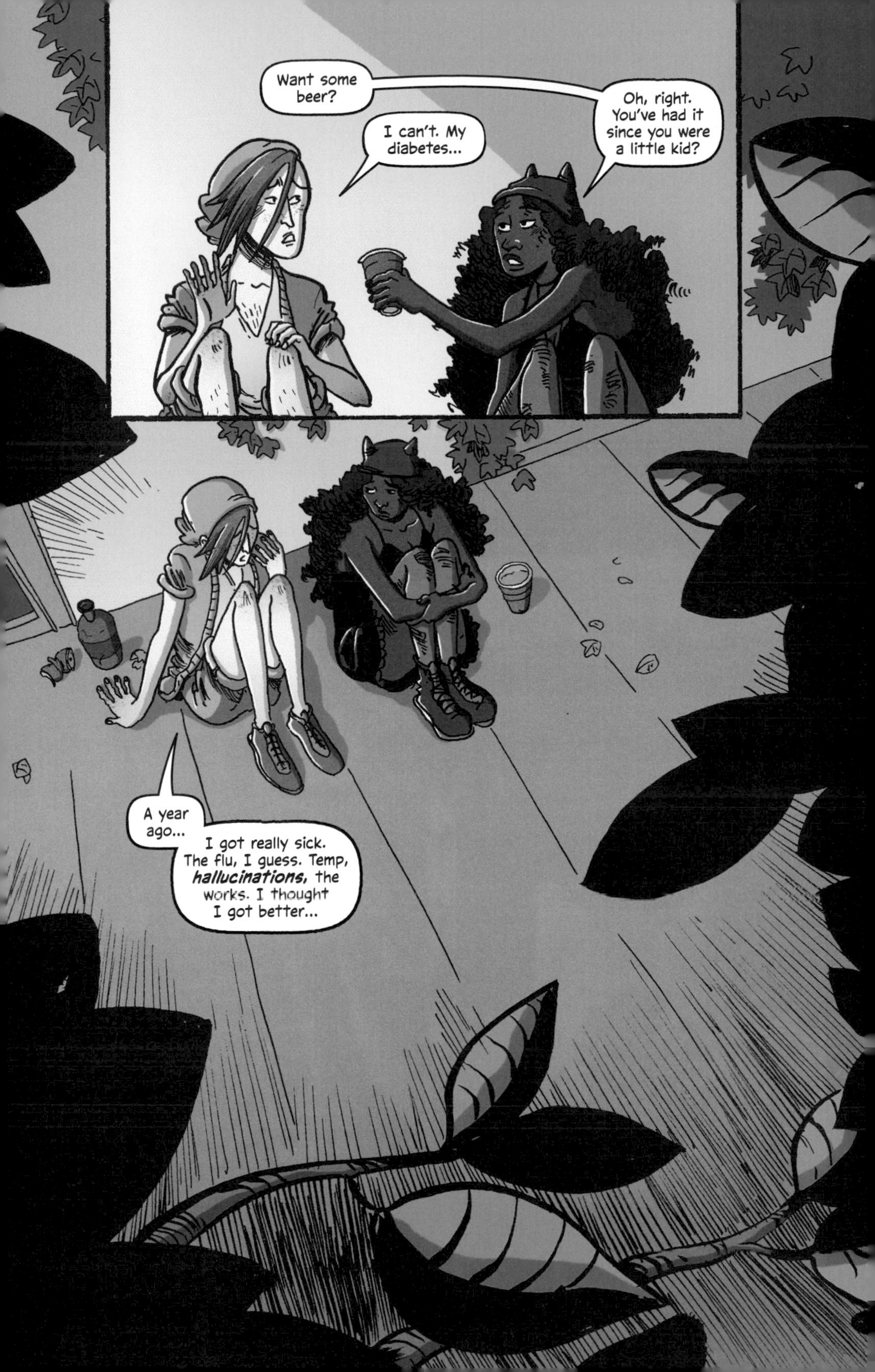
Want some beer?
I can't. My diabetes...
Oh, right. You've had it since you were a little kid?
A year ago...
I got really sick. The flu, I guess. Temp, ***hallucinations,*** the works. I thought I got better...

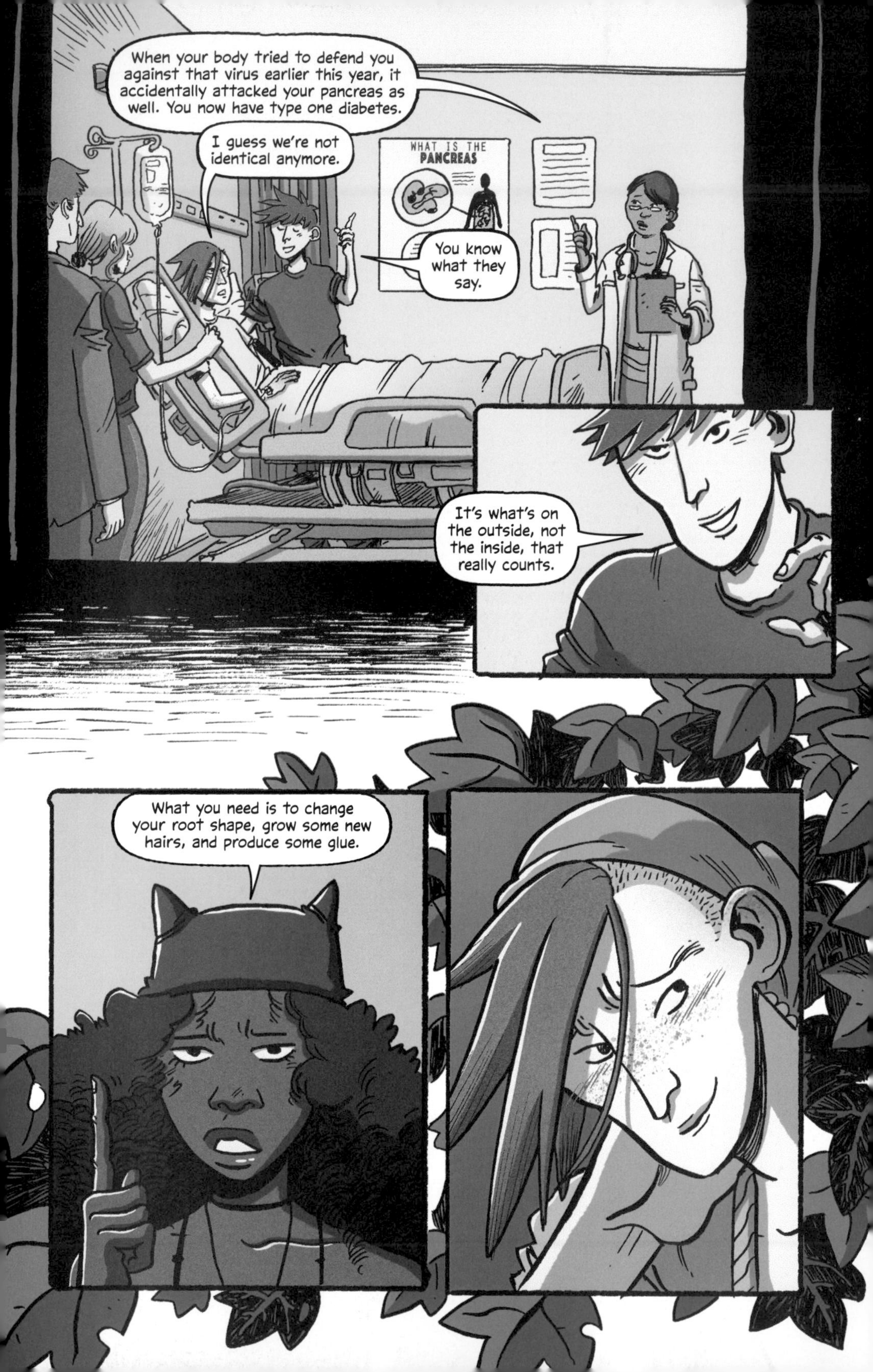
When your body tried to defend you against that virus earlier this year, it accidentally attacked your pancreas as well. You now have type one diabetes.
I guess we're not identical anymore.
WHAT IS THE PANCREAS
You know what they say.
It's what's on the outside, not the inside, that really counts.
What you need is to change your root shape, grow some new hairs, and produce some glue.

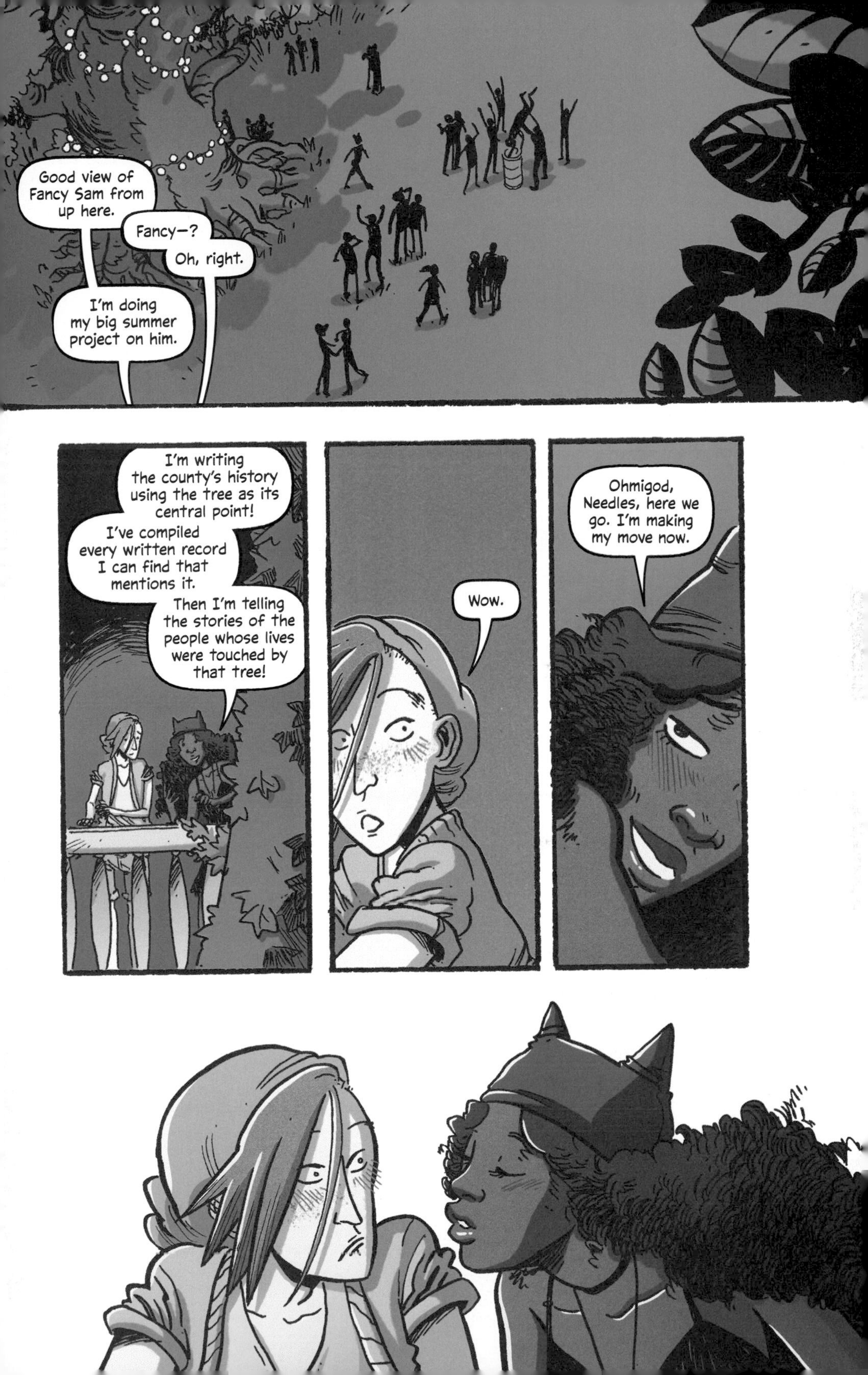

Good view of Fancy Sam from up here.
Fancy—?
Oh, right.
I'm doing my big summer project on him.
I'm writing the county's history using the tree as its central point!
I've compiled every written record I can find that mentions it.
Then I'm telling the stories of the people whose lives were touched by that tree!
Wow.
Ohmigod, Needles, here we go. I'm making my move now.

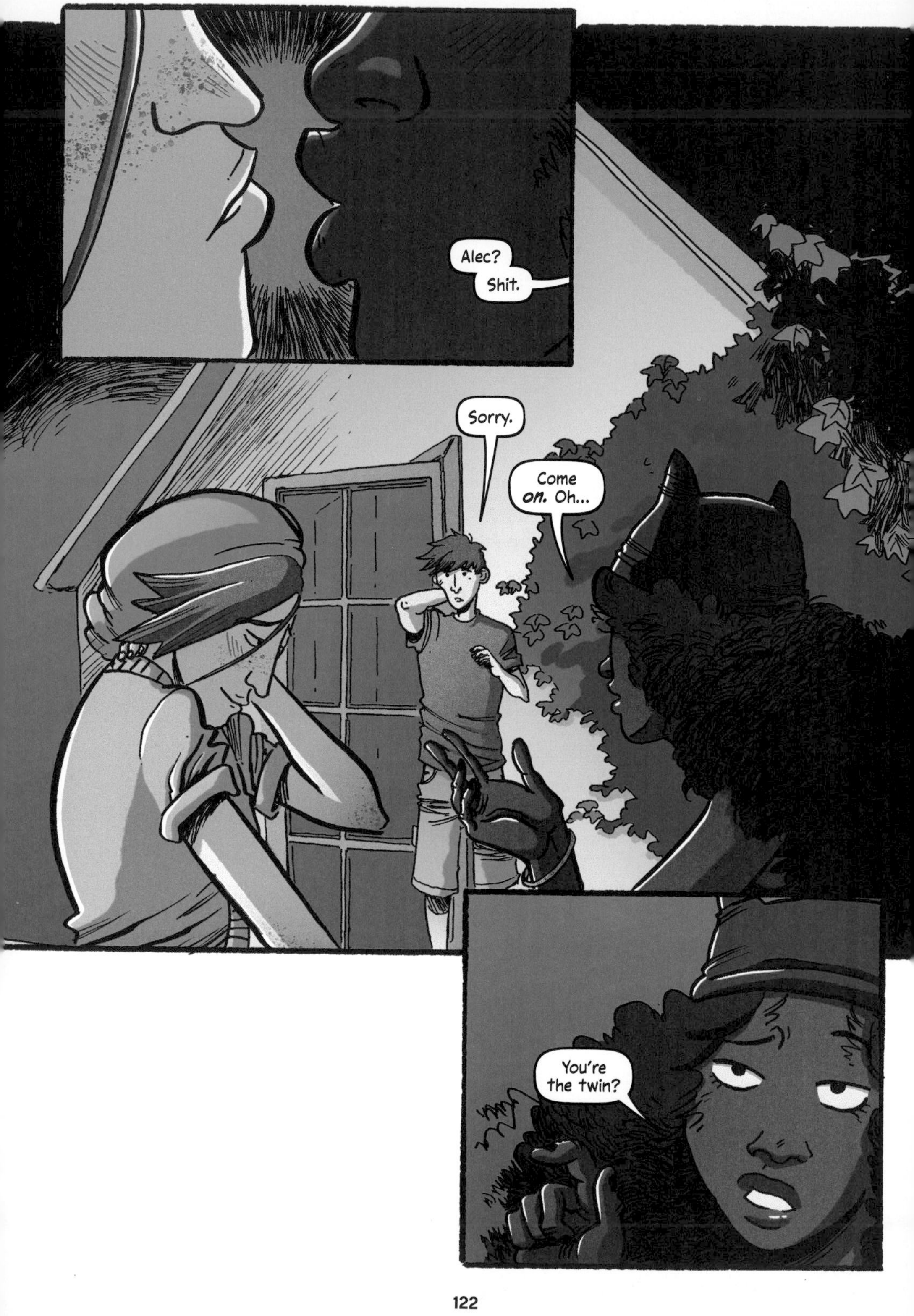
Alec?
Shit.
Sorry.
Come on. Oh...
You're the twin?

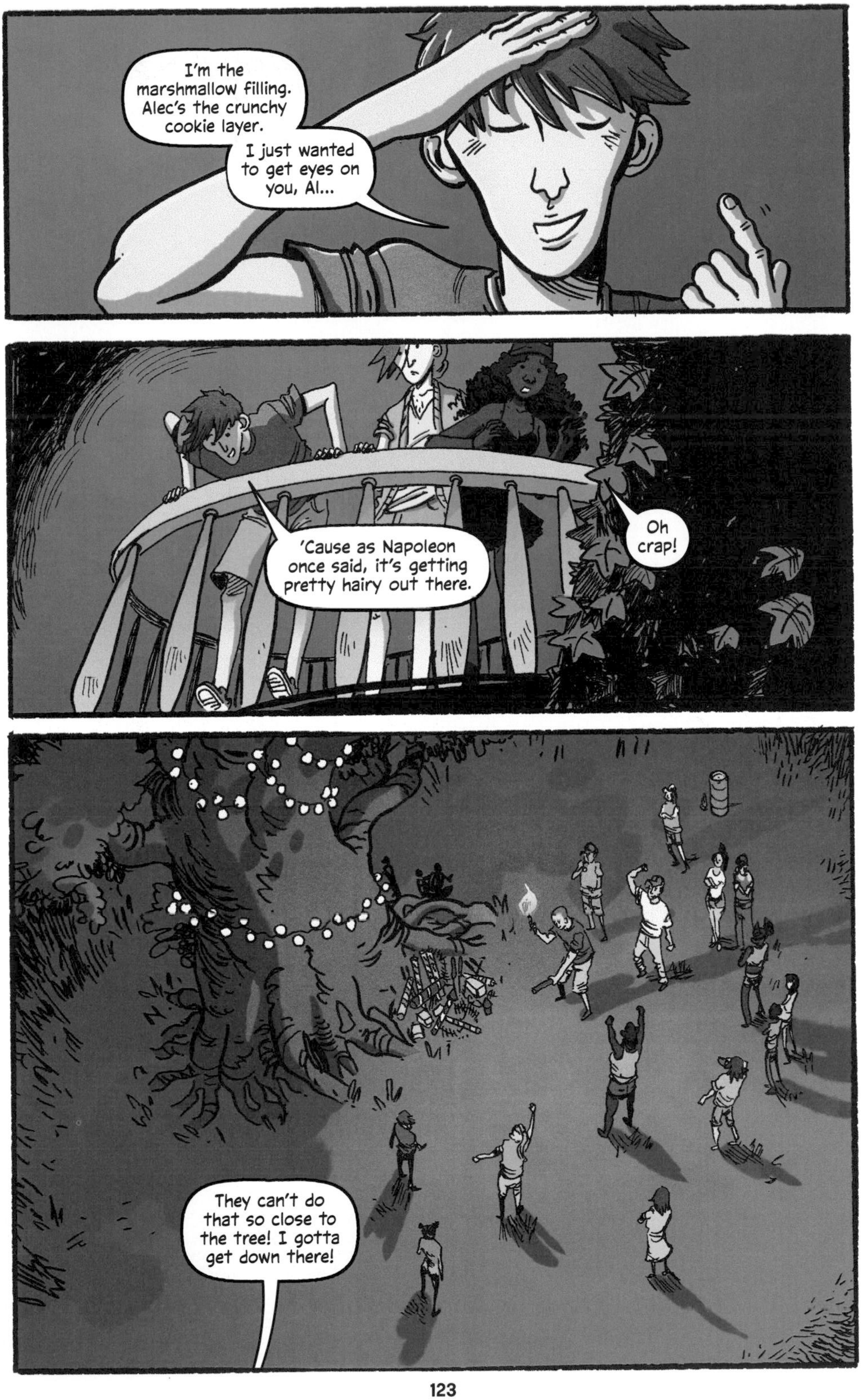
I'm the marshmallow filling. Alec's the crunchy cookie layer.
I just wanted to get eyes on you, Al...
'Cause as Napoleon once said, it's getting pretty hairy out there.
Oh crap!
They can't do that so close to the tree! I gotta get down there!

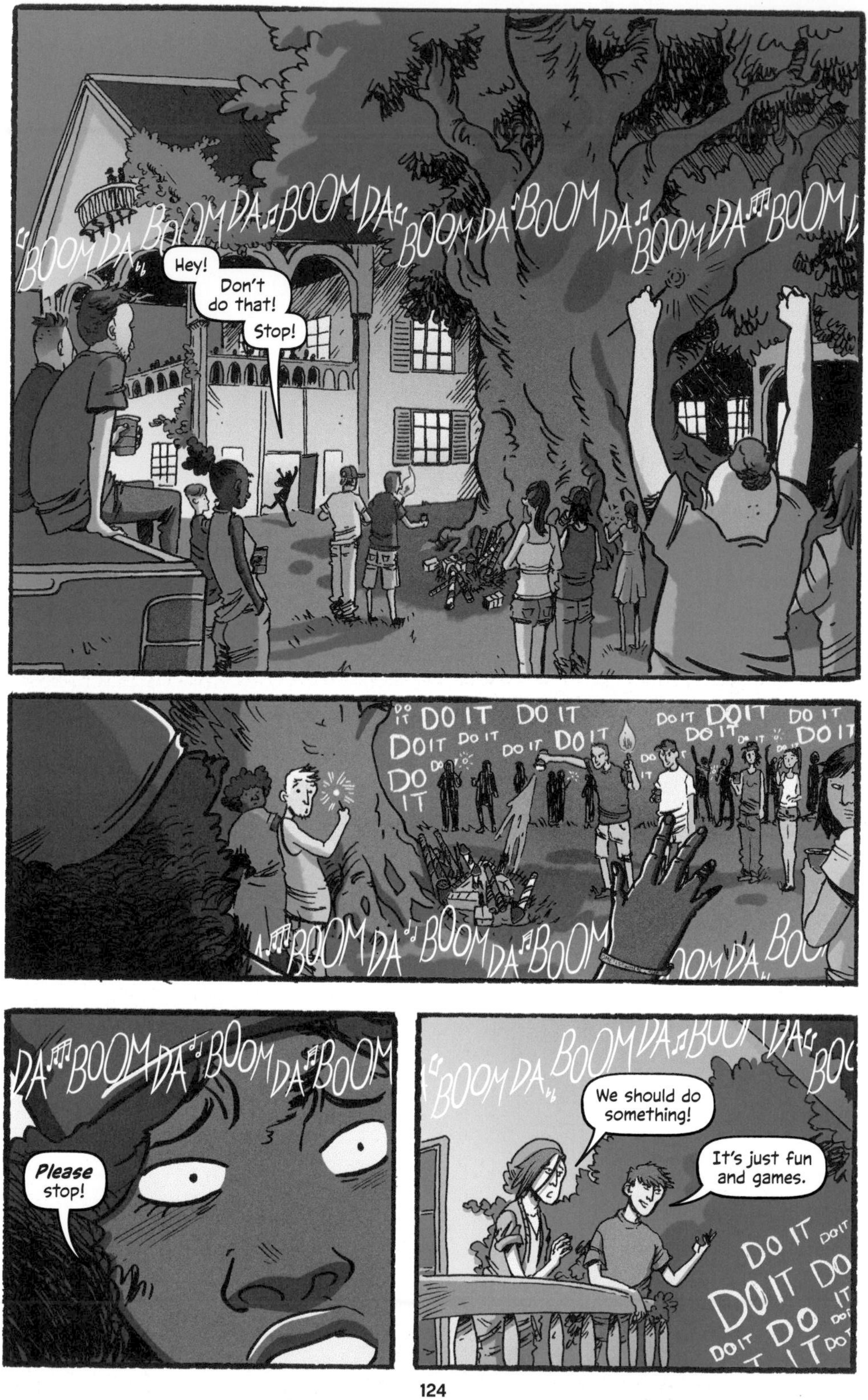
BOOM DA BOOM DA BOOM DA BOOM DA BOOM DA BOOM DA BOOM DA BOOM
Hey!
Don't do that!
Stop!
DO IT DO IT DO IT DO IT DO IT DO IT DO IT DO IT DO IT
BOOM DA BOOM DA BOOM
Please stop!
BOOM DA BOOM DA BOOM DA BOOM DA
We should do something!
It's just fun and games.
DO IT DO IT DO IT DO IT

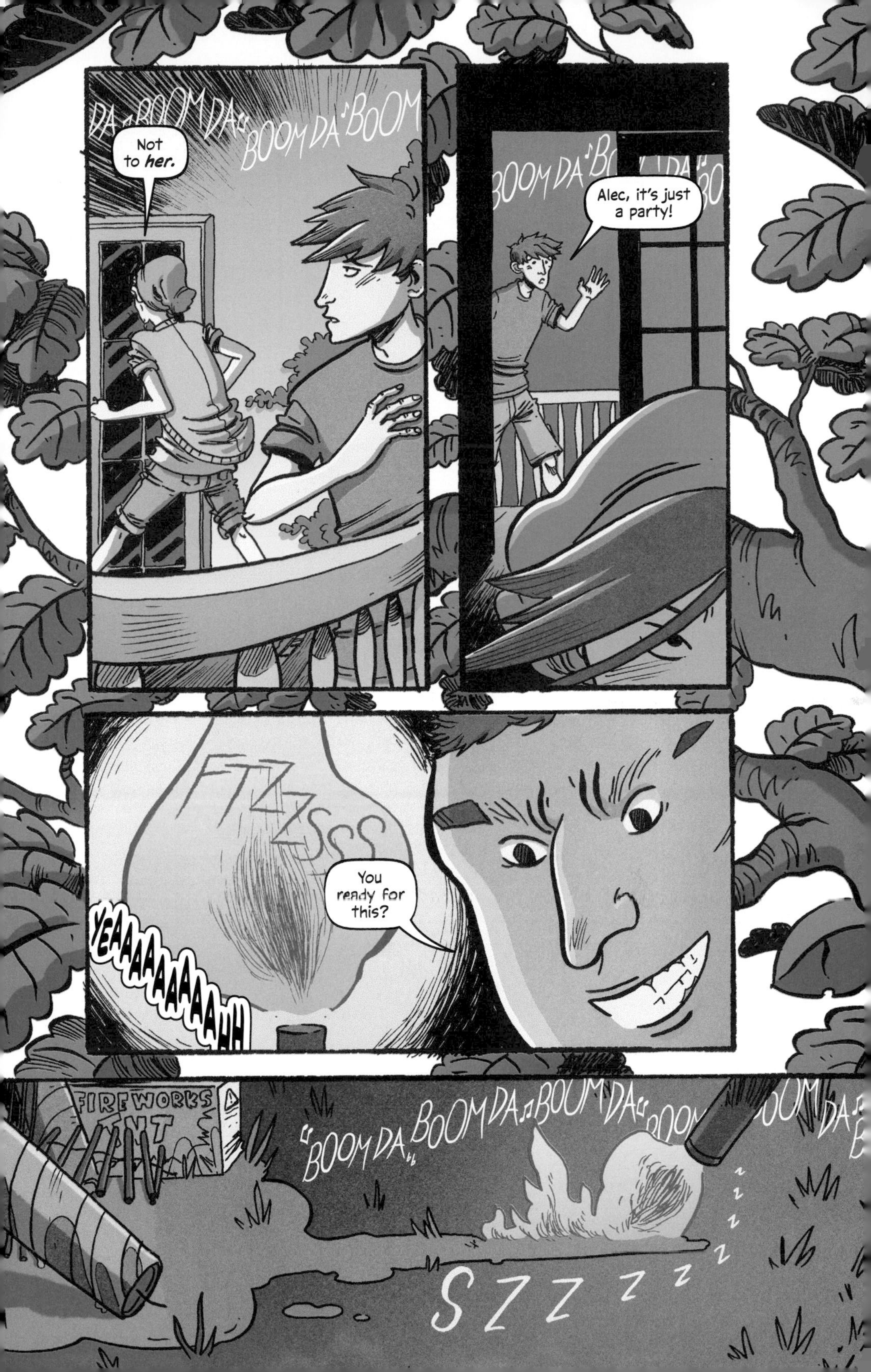
DA BOOM DA BOOM DA BOOM
Not to *her.*
BOOM DA BO DA BO
Alec, it's just a party!
FTZZSSS
You ready for this?
YEAAAAAAAAAAHH
FIREWORKS TNT
BOOM DA BOOM DA BOOM DA BOOM DA
SZZ Z Z Z Z

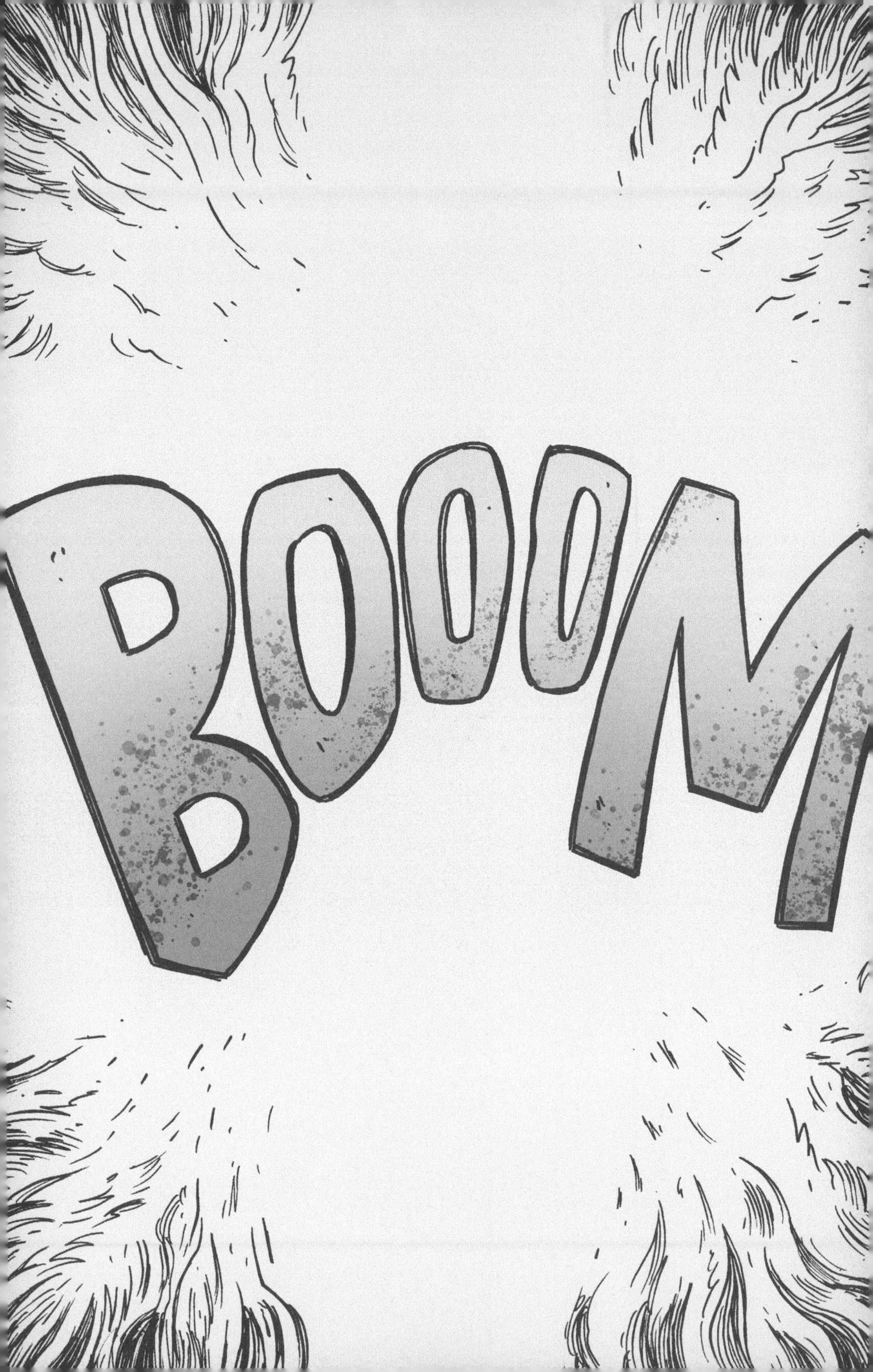
BOOOM

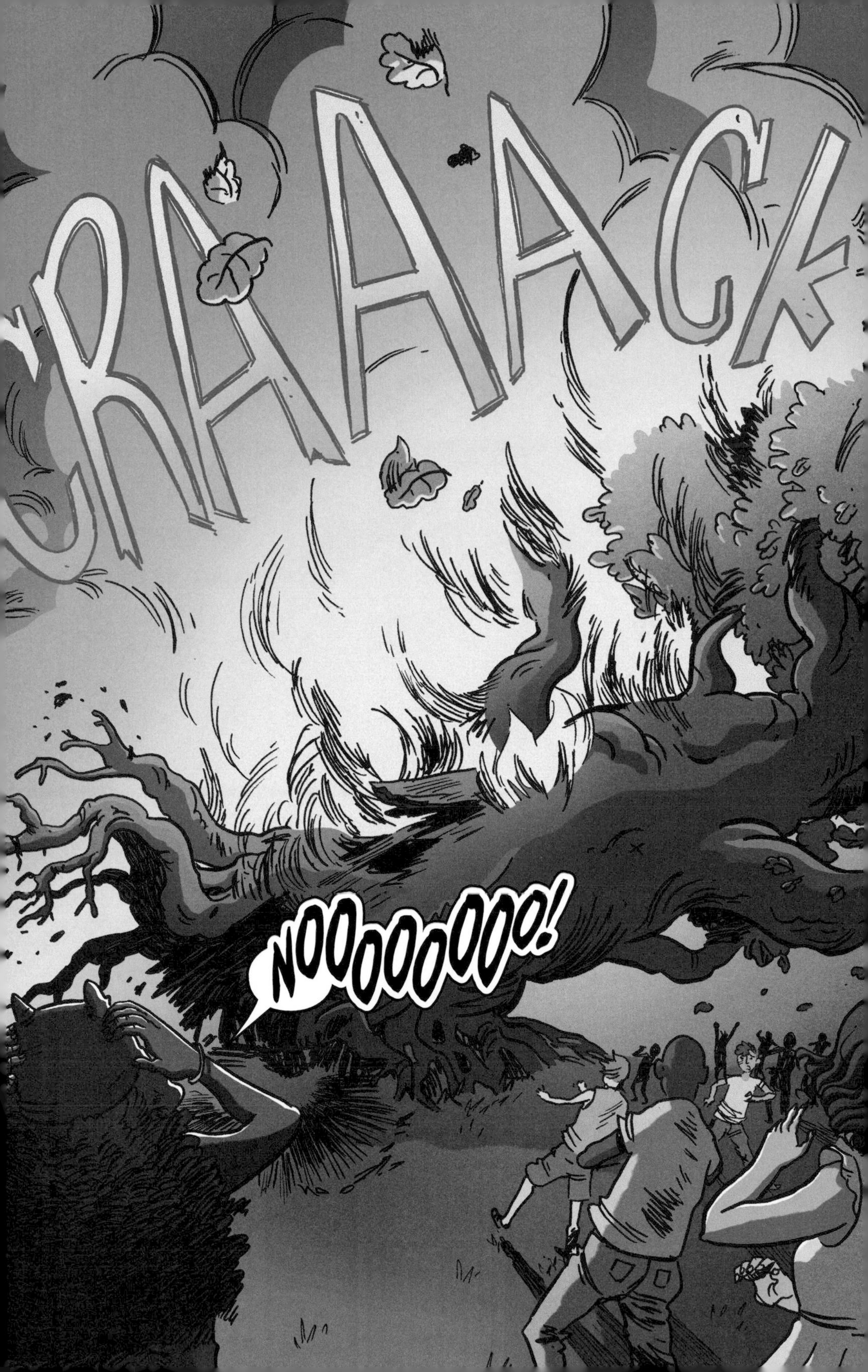
CRAAACK
NOOOOOOOO!

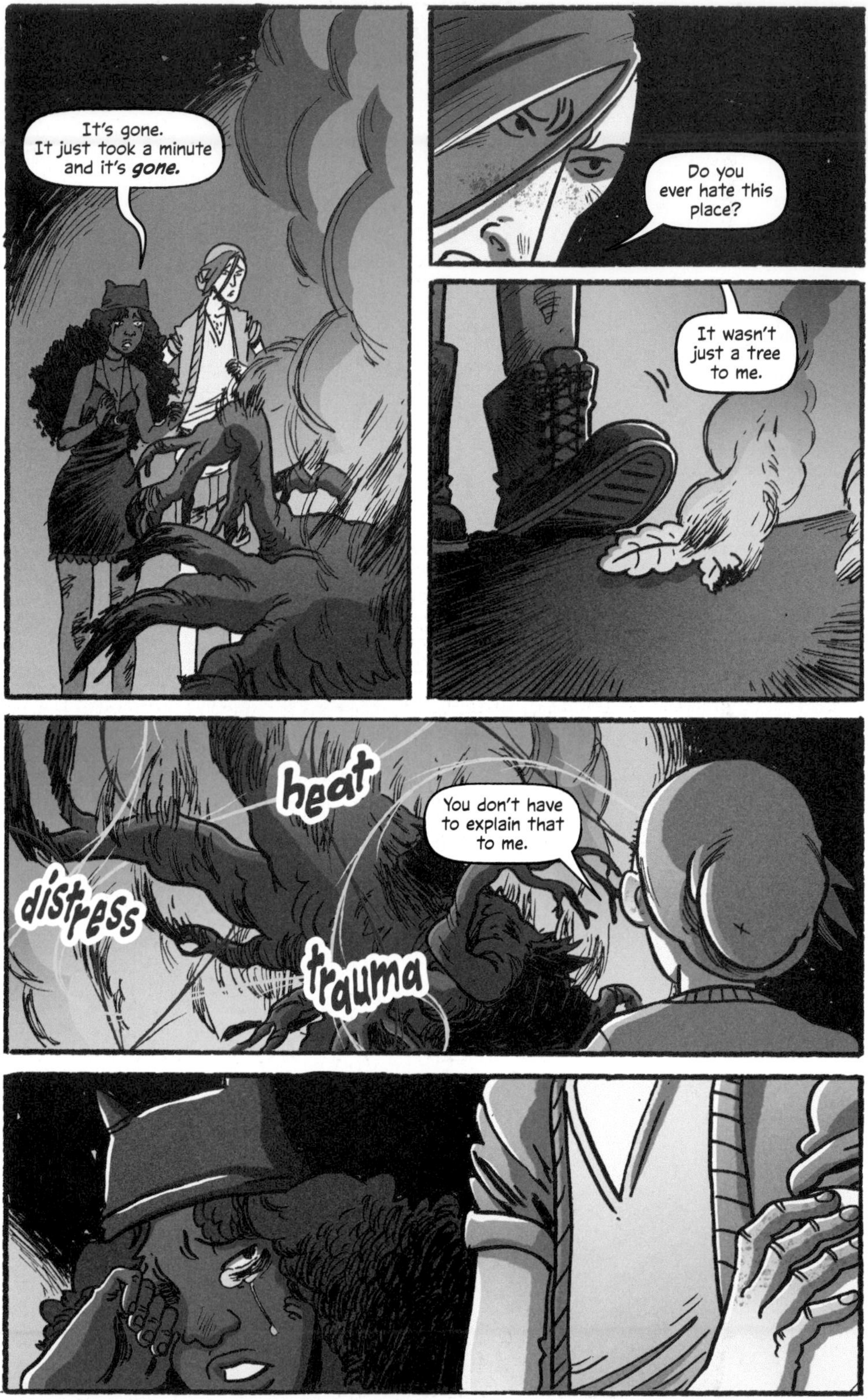
It's gone.
It just took a minute
and it's ***gone.***
Do you
ever hate this
place?
It wasn't
just a tree
to me.
heat
You don't have
to explain that
to me.
distress
trauma

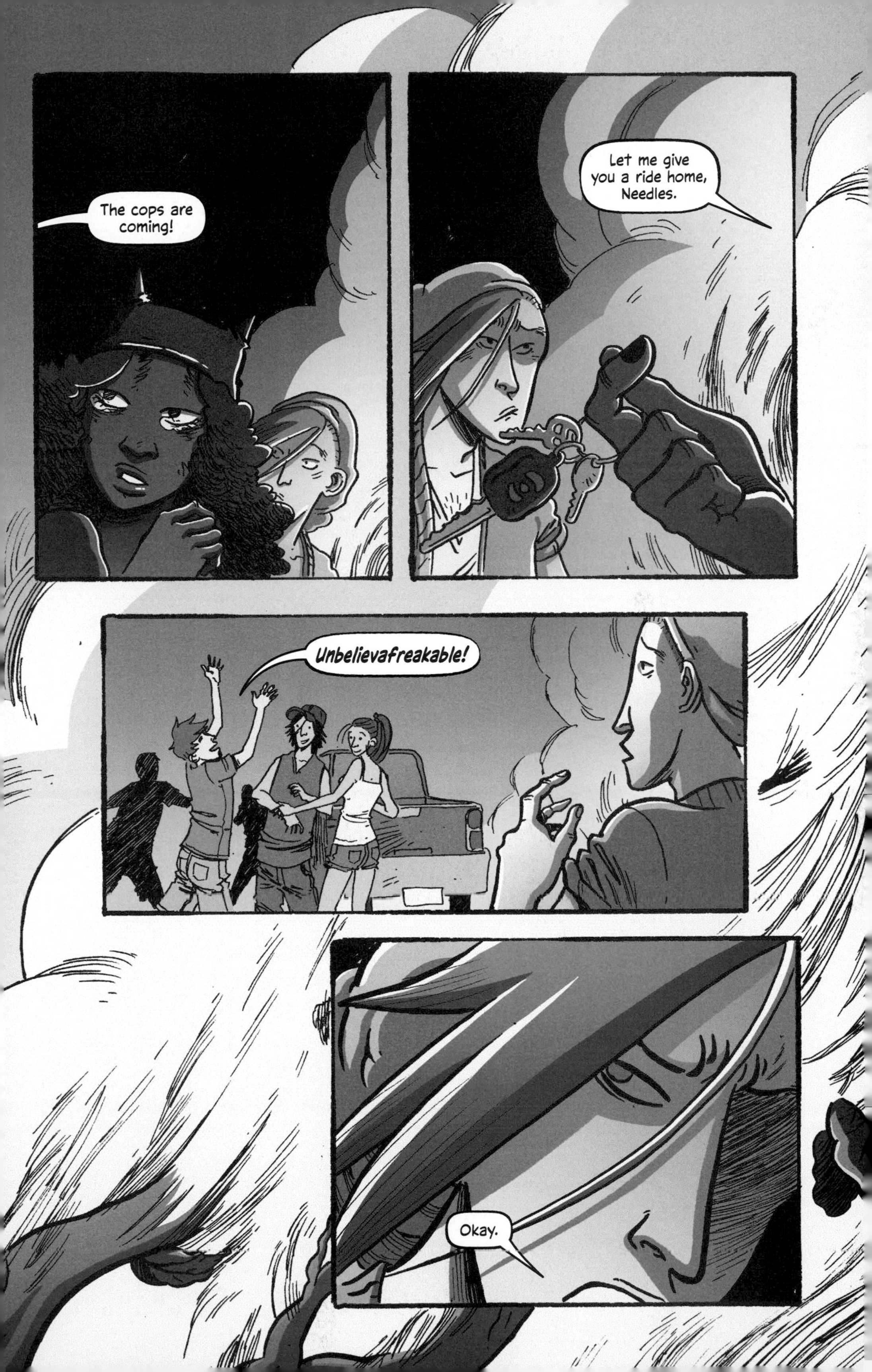
The cops are coming!
Let me give you a ride home, Needles.
Unbelievafreakable!
Okay.

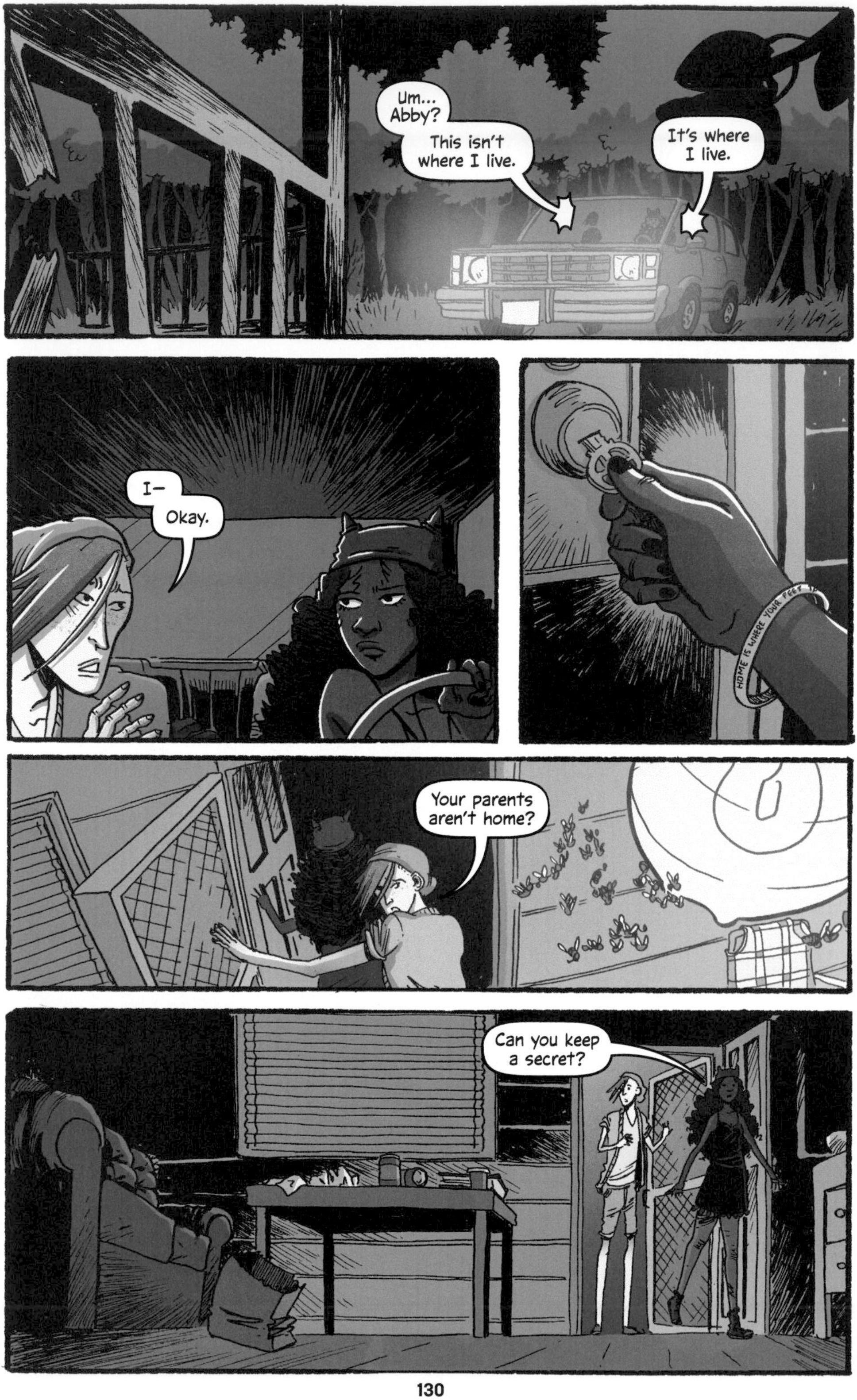
Um... Abby?
This isn't where I live.
It's where I live.
I—
Okay.
Your parents aren't home?
Can you keep a secret?

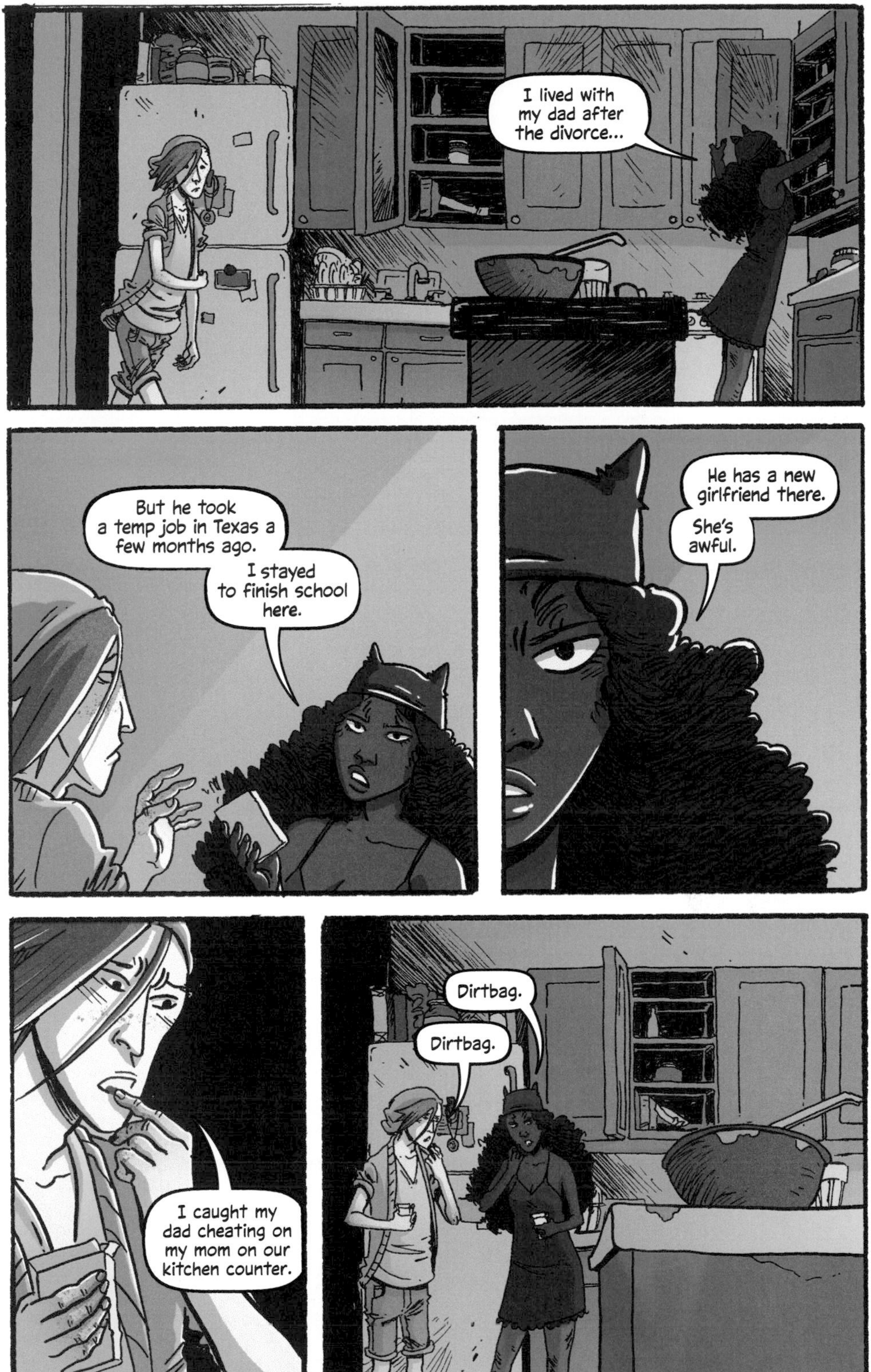
I lived with my dad after the divorce...
But he took a temp job in Texas a few months ago.
I stayed to finish school here.
He has a new girlfriend there.
She's awful.
I caught my dad cheating on my mom on our kitchen counter.
Dirtbag.
Dirtbag.

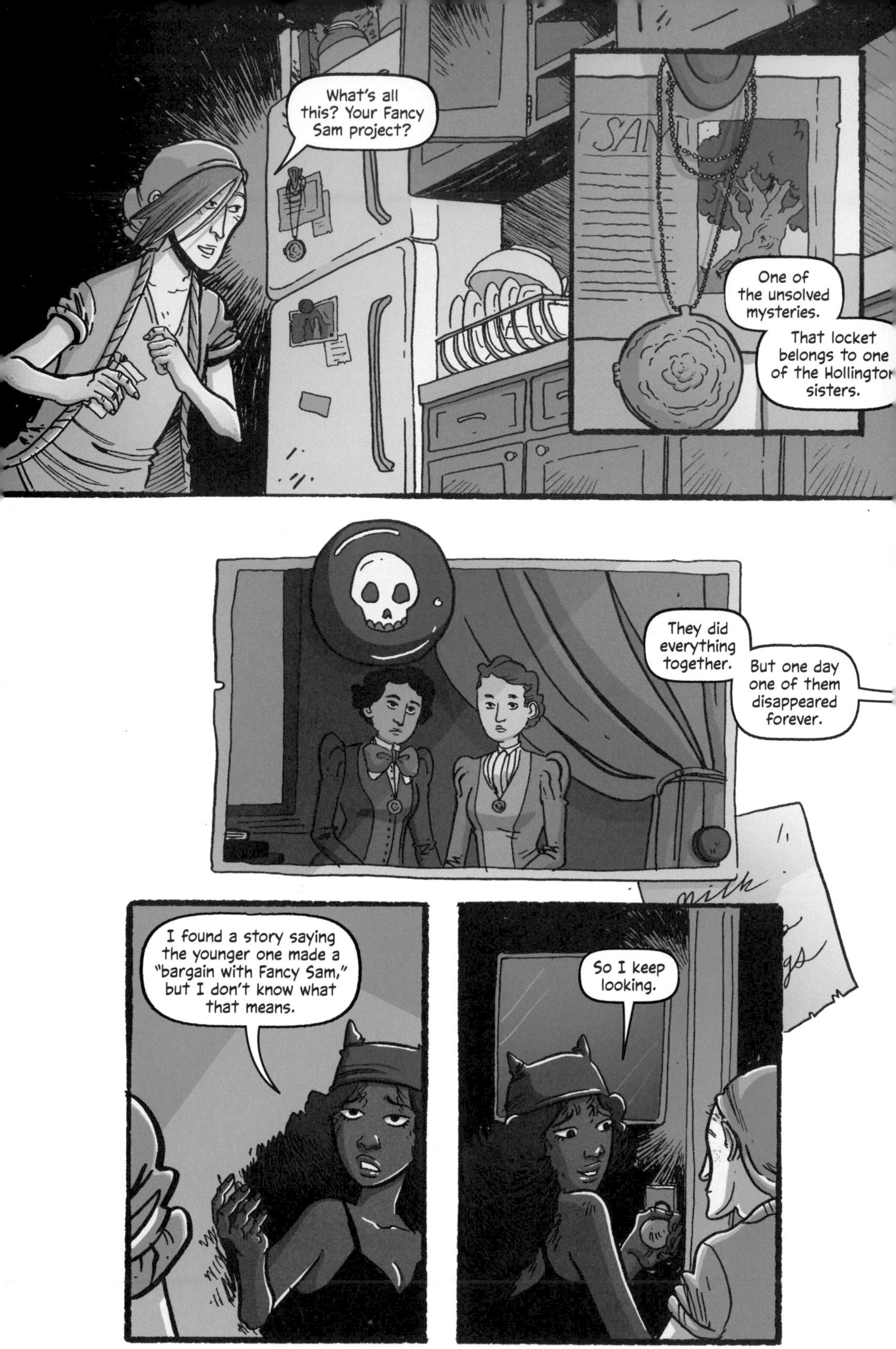
What's all this? Your Fancy Sam project?
One of the unsolved mysteries.
That locket belongs to one of the Hollingtor sisters.
They did everything together.
But one day one of them disappeared forever.
I found a story saying the younger one made a "bargain with Fancy Sam," but I don't know what that means.
So I keep looking.

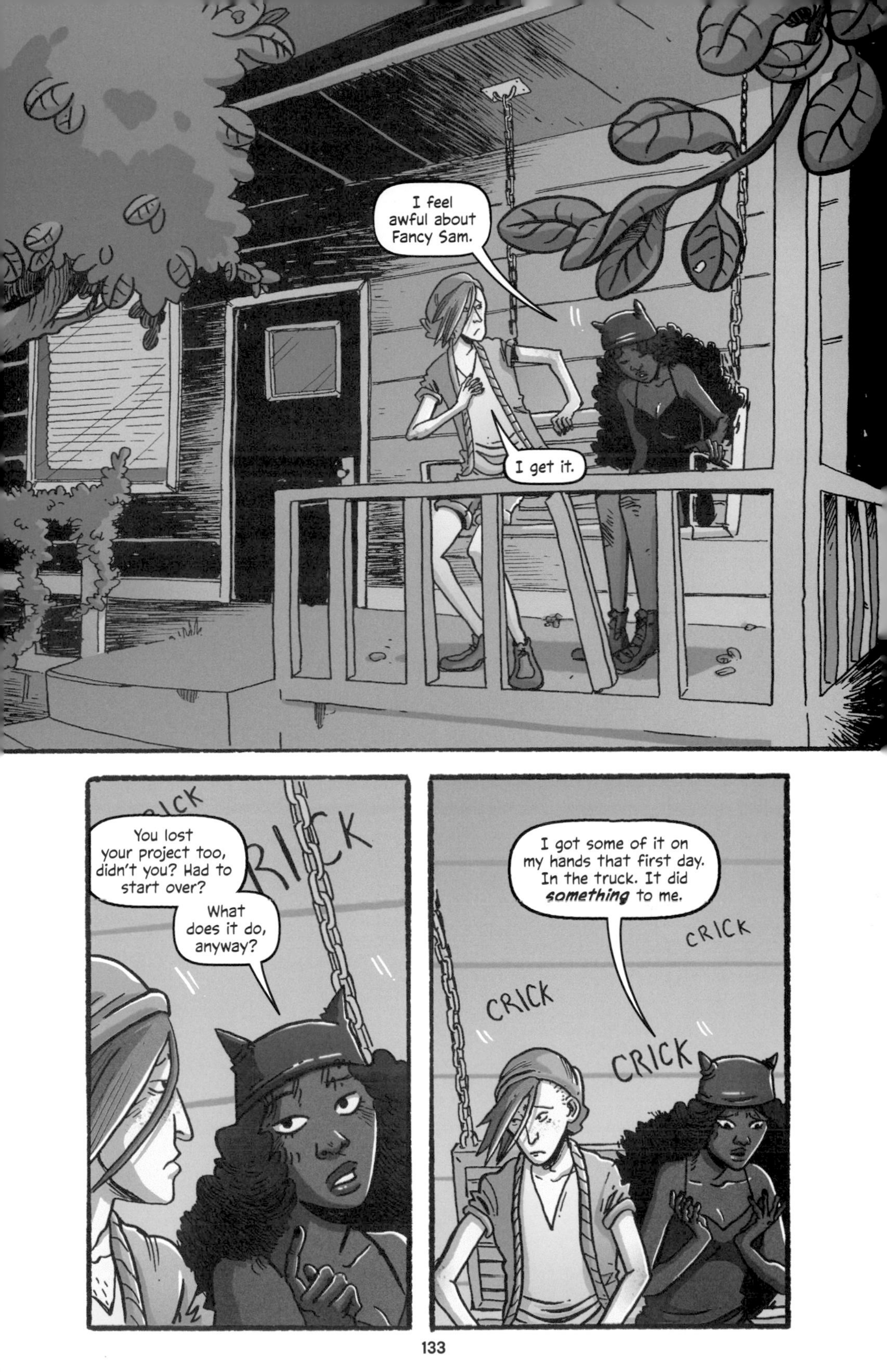
I feel awful about Fancy Sam.
I get it.
RICK
You lost your project too, didn't you? Had to start over?
What does it do, anyway?
I got some of it on my hands that first day. In the truck. It did *something* to me.
CRICK
CRICK
CRICK

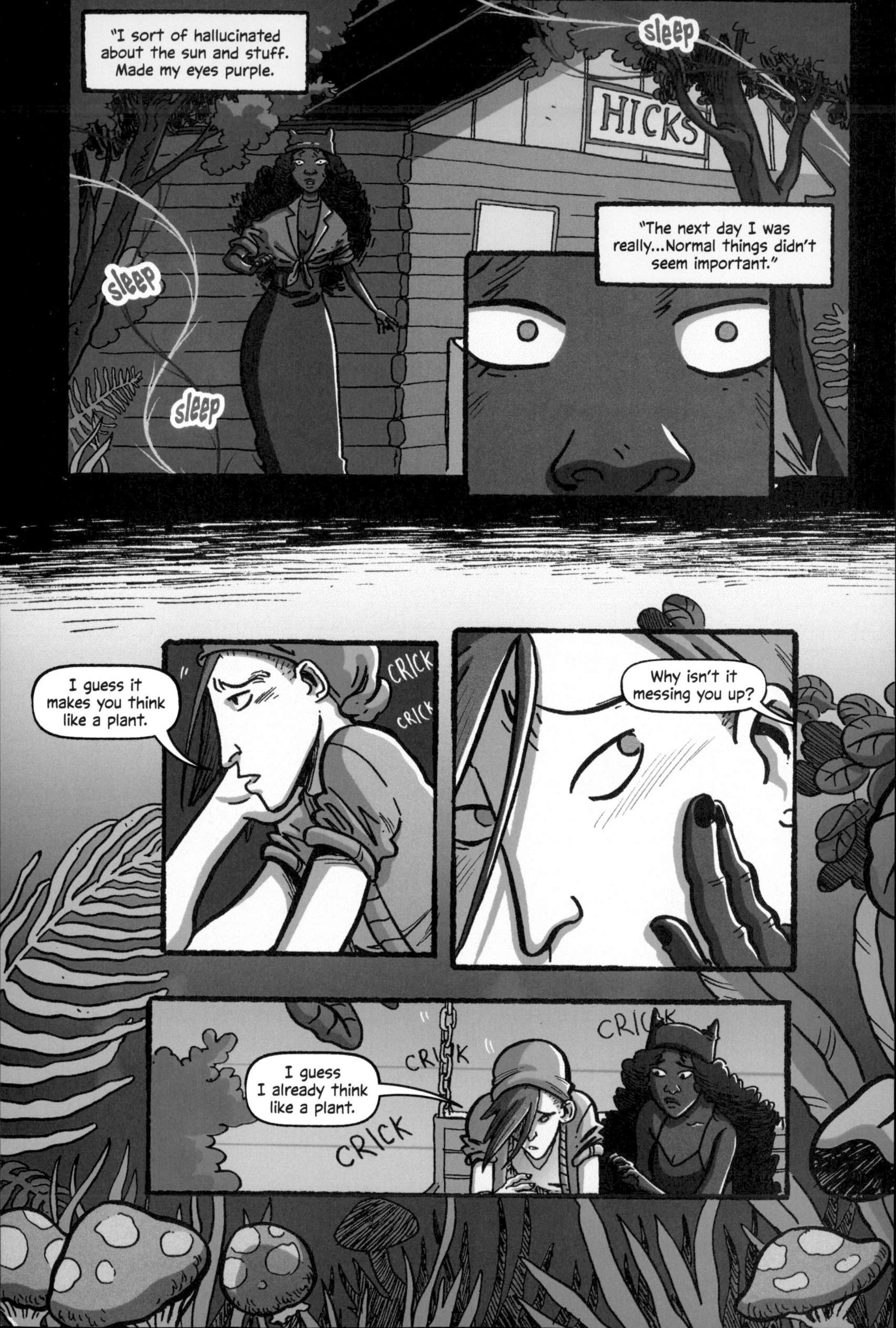
"I sort of hallucinated about the sun and stuff. Made my eyes purple.
sleep
HICKS
sleep
sleep
"The next day I was really...Normal things didn't seem important."
I guess it makes you think like a plant.
CRICK
CRICK
Why isn't it messing you up?
CRICK
CRICK
I guess I already think like a plant.
CRICK

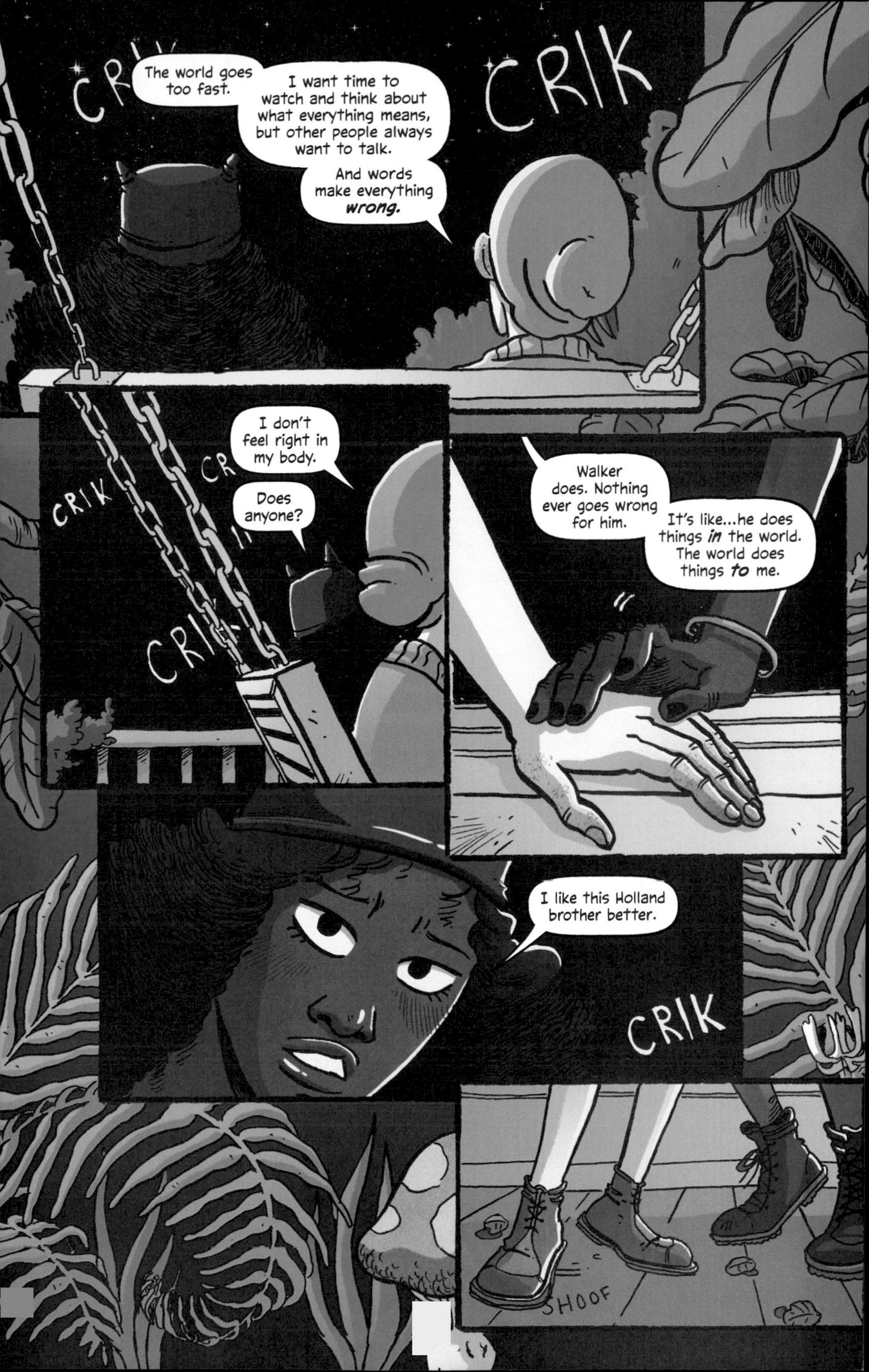
CRIK
The world goes too fast.
I want time to watch and think about what everything means, but other people always want to talk.
And words make everything *wrong.*
CRIK
I don't feel right in my body.
Does anyone?
CRIK
CR
CRIK
Walker does. Nothing ever goes wrong for him.
It's like...he does things *in* the world. The world does things *to* me.
I like this Holland brother better.
CRIK
SHOOF

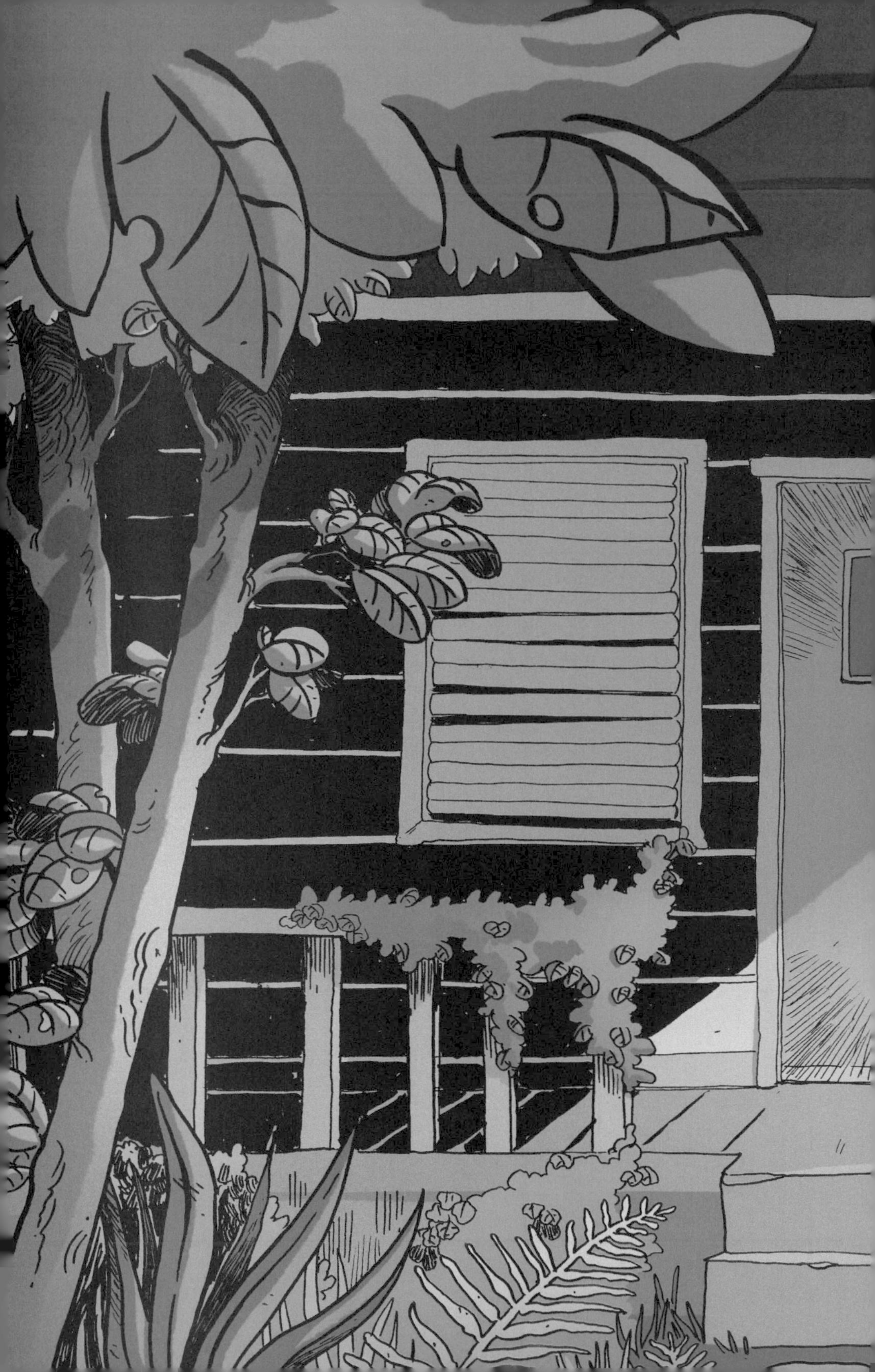

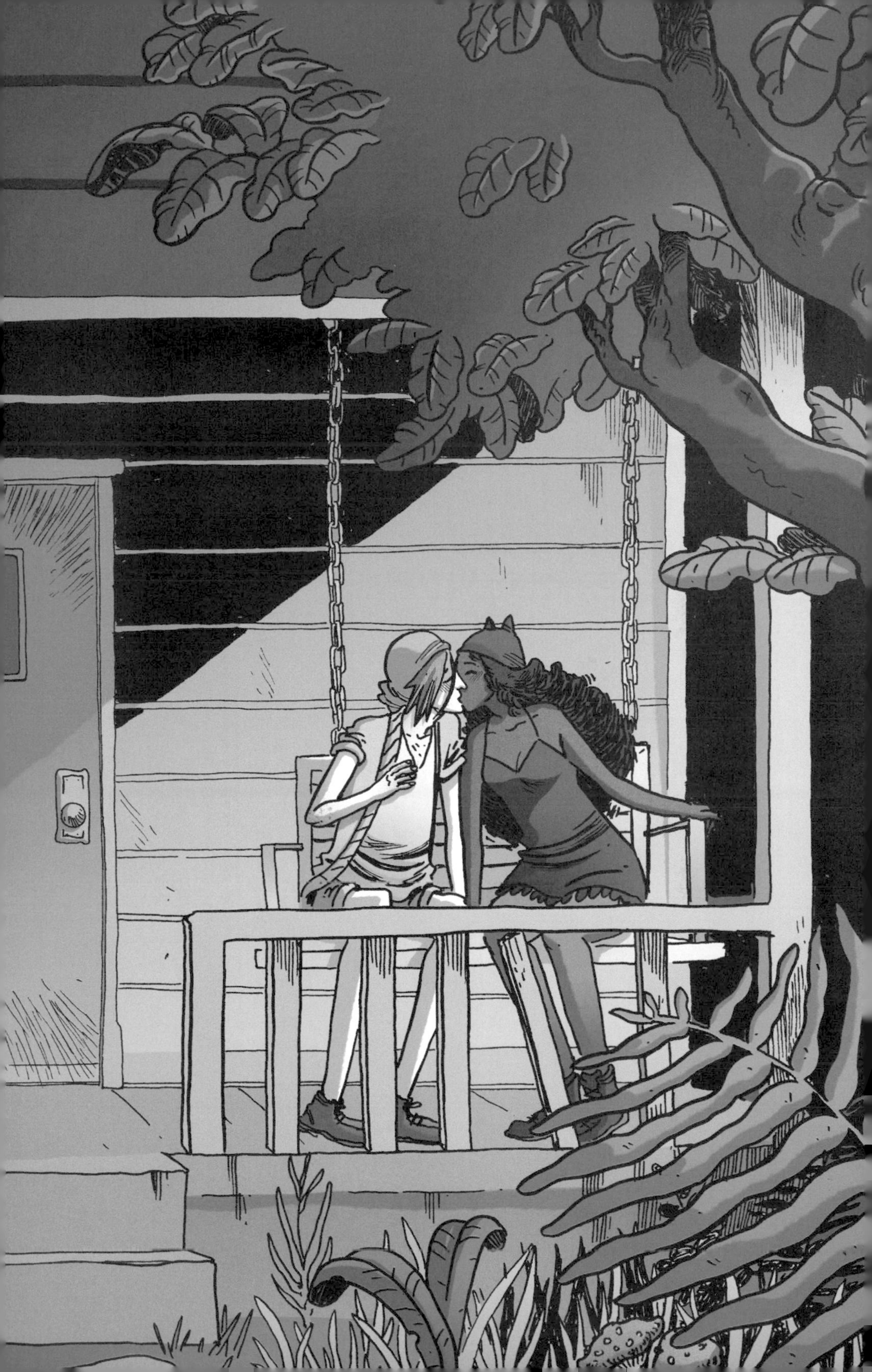

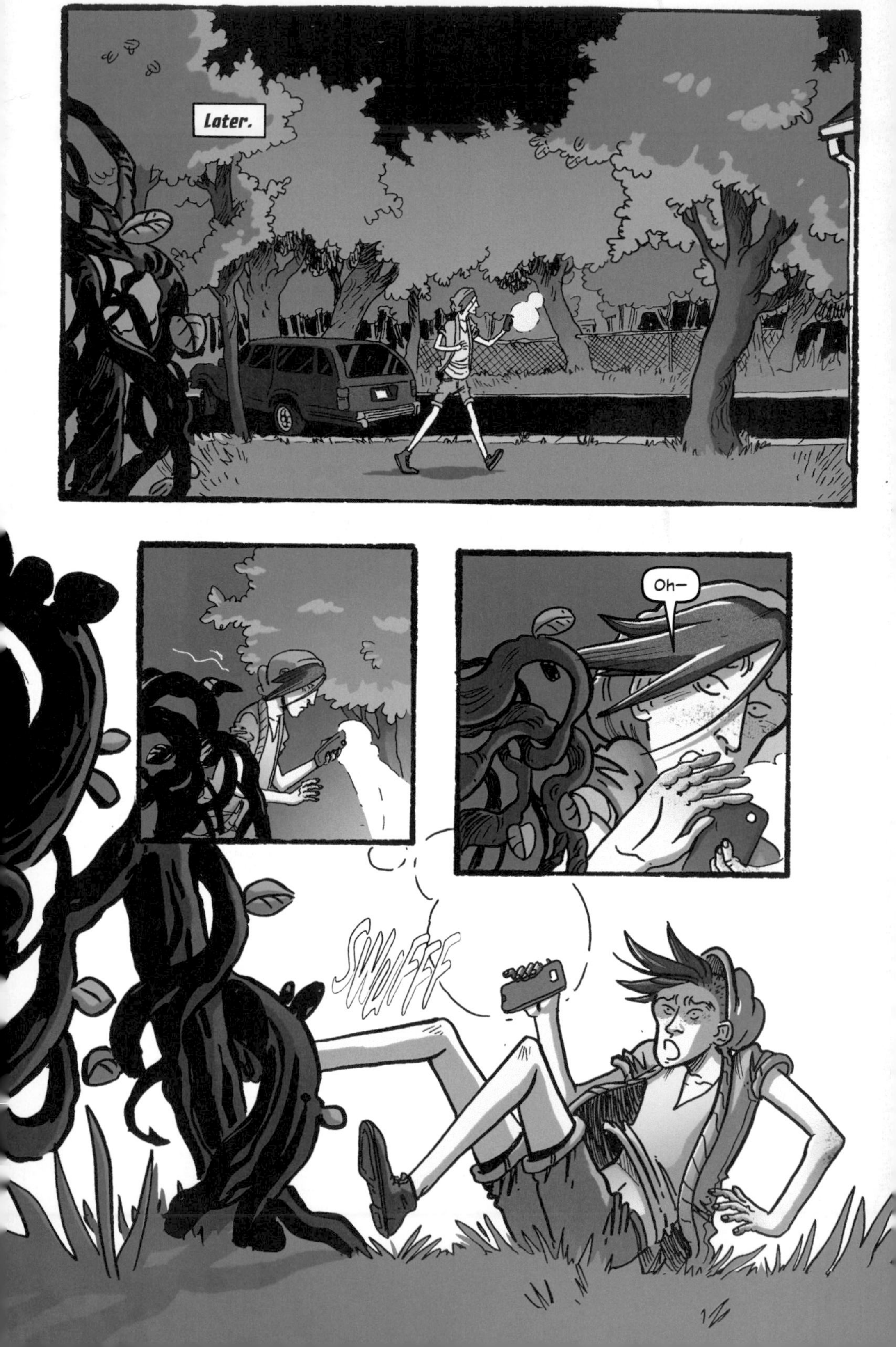
Later.
Oh–

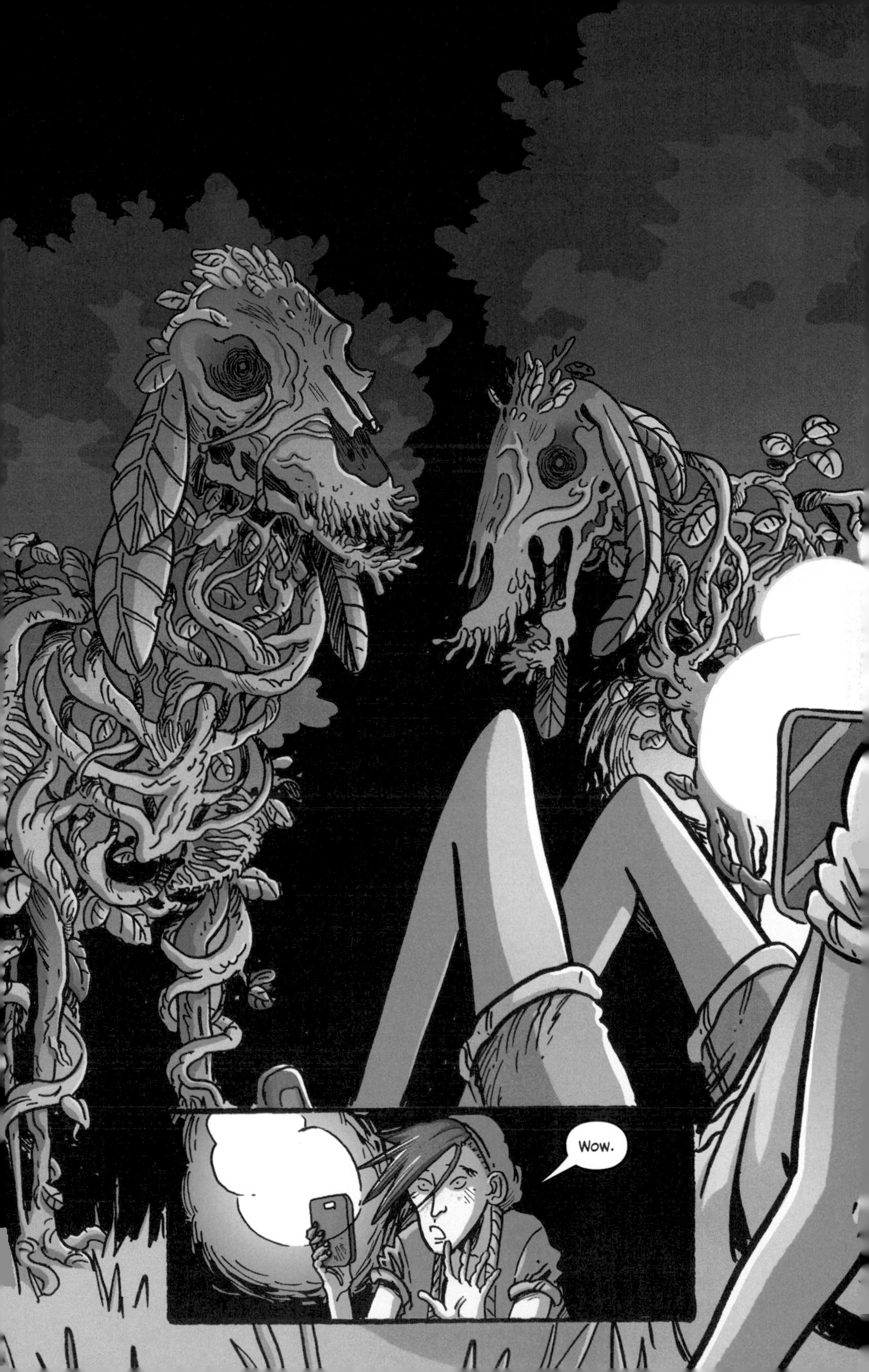
WOW.

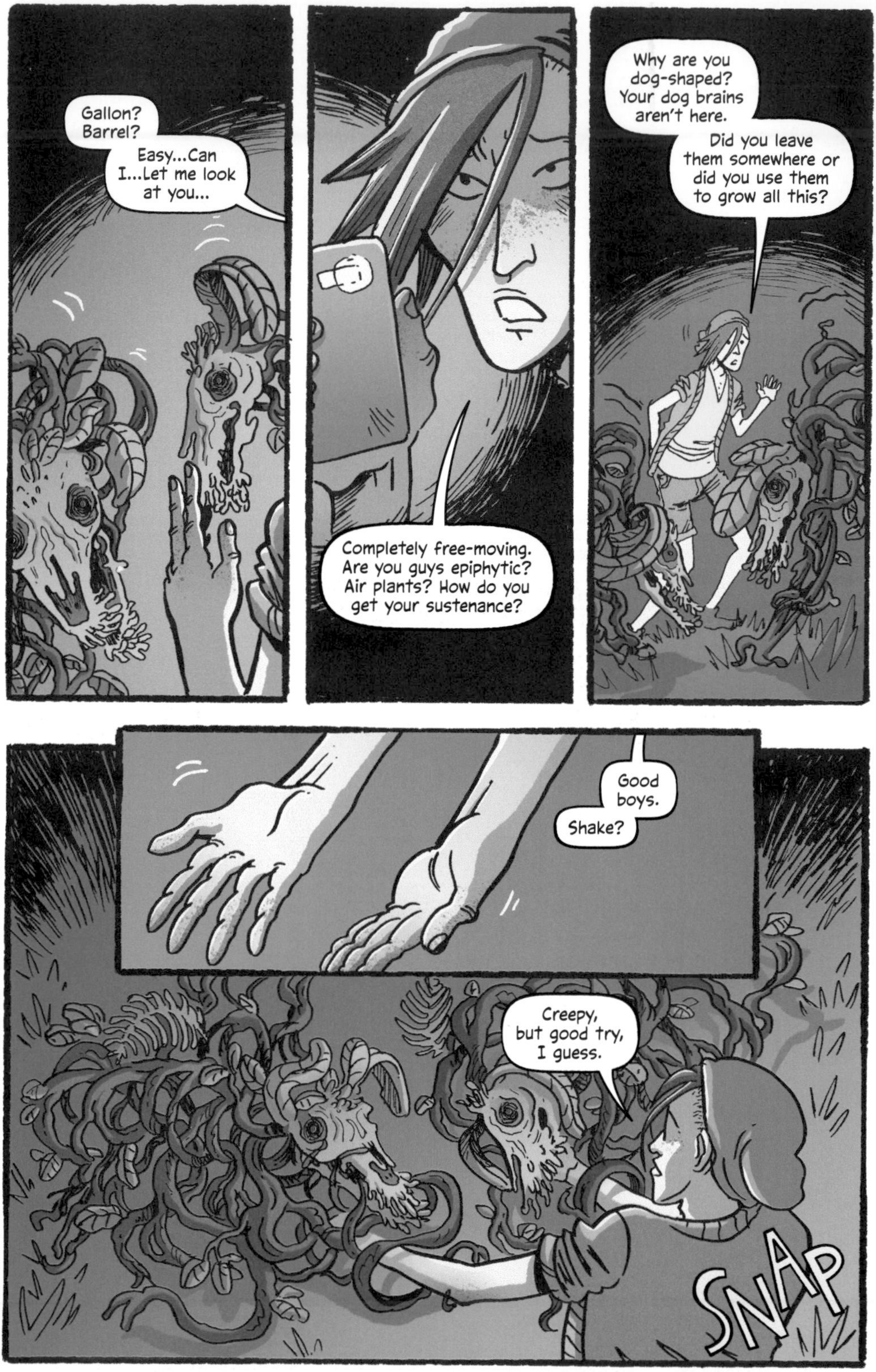
Gallon? Barrel?
Easy...Can I...Let me look at you...
Completely free-moving. Are you guys epiphytic? Air plants? How do you get your sustenance?
Why are you dog-shaped? Your dog brains aren't here.
Did you leave them somewhere or did you use them to grow all this?
Good boys.
Shake?
Creepy, but good try, I guess.
SNAP

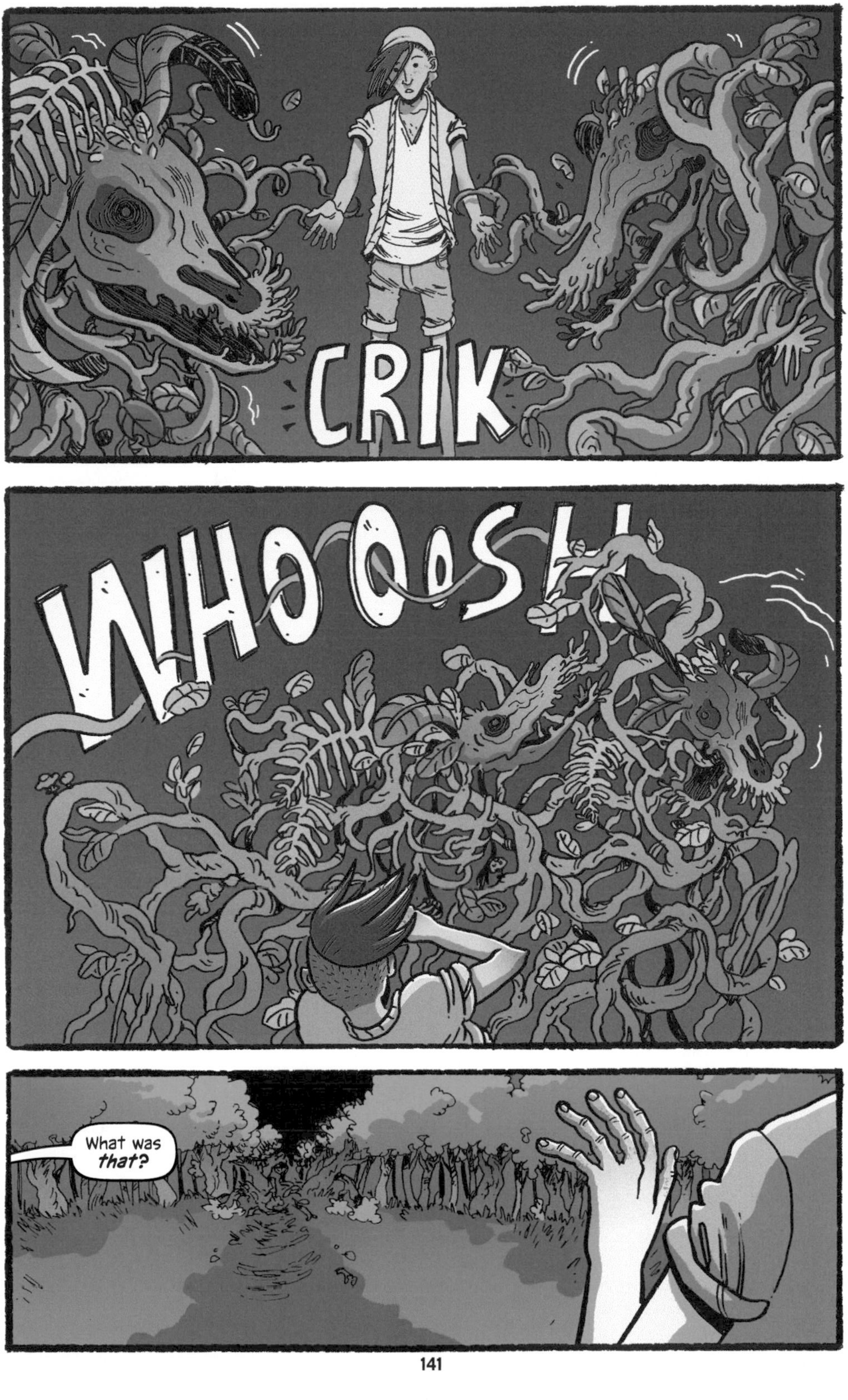
CRIK
WHOOOSH
What was *that?*

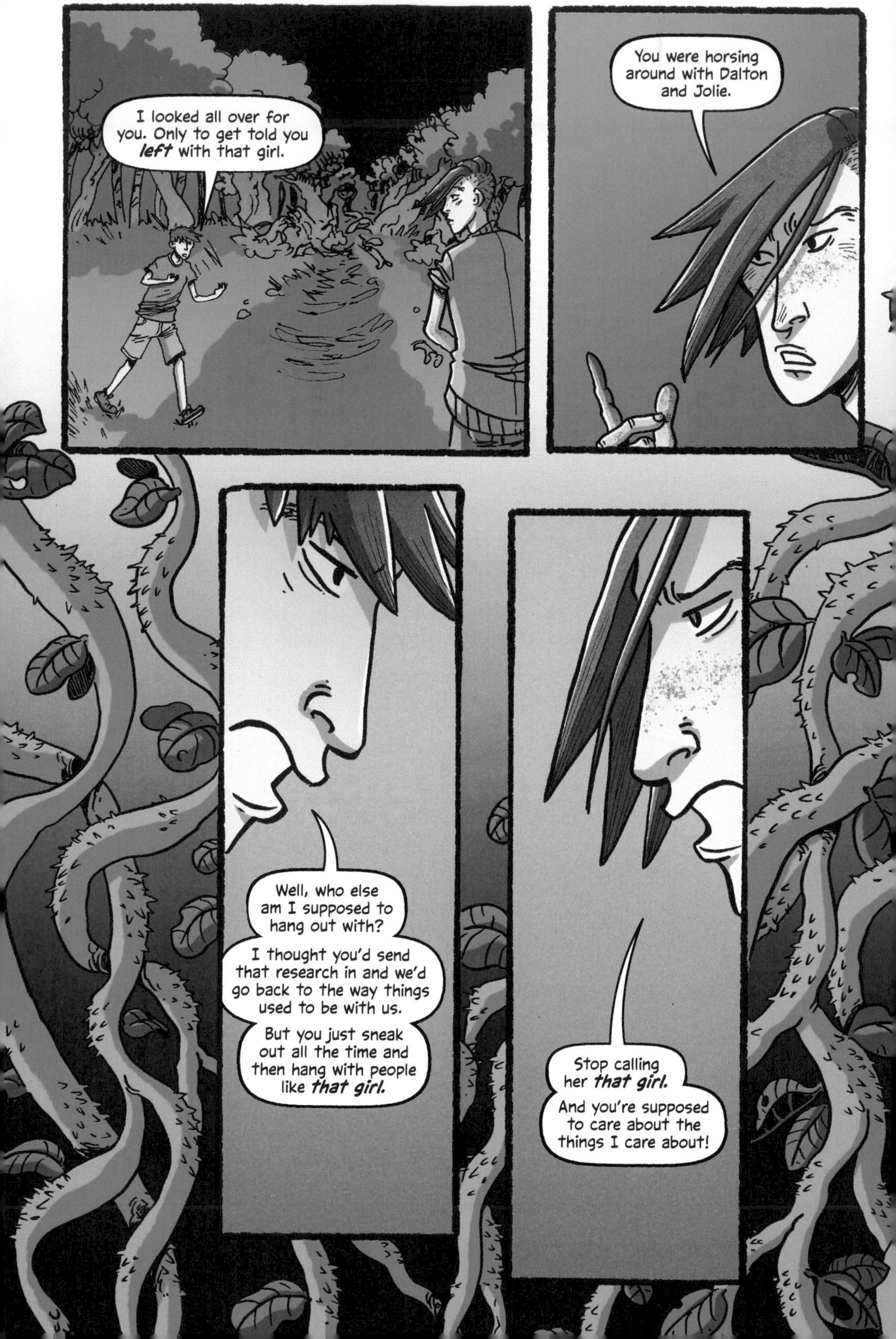
I looked all over for you. Only to get told you *left* with that girl.
You were horsing around with Dalton and Jolie.
Well, who else am I supposed to hang out with?
I thought you'd send that research in and we'd go back to the way things used to be with us.
But you just sneak out all the time and then hang with people like *that girl.*
Stop calling her *that girl.*
And you're supposed to care about the things I care about!

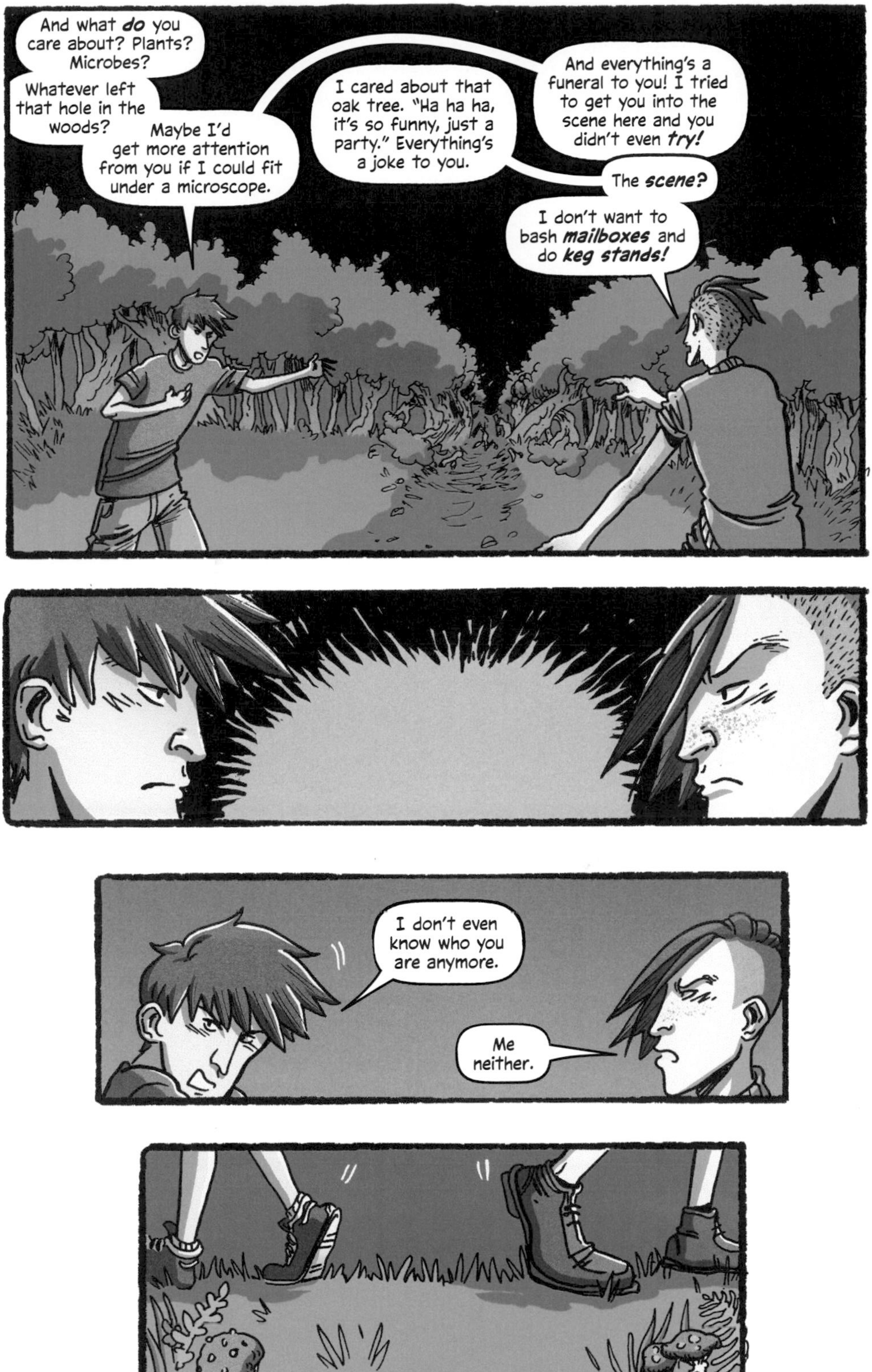
And what *do* you care about? Plants? Microbes?
Whatever left that hole in the woods?
Maybe I'd get more attention from you if I could fit under a microscope.
I cared about that oak tree. "Ha ha ha, it's so funny, just a party." Everything's a joke to you.
And everything's a funeral to you! I tried to get you into the scene here and you didn't even *try!*
The *scene?*
I don't want to bash *mailboxes* and do *keg stands!*
I don't even know who you are anymore.
Me neither.

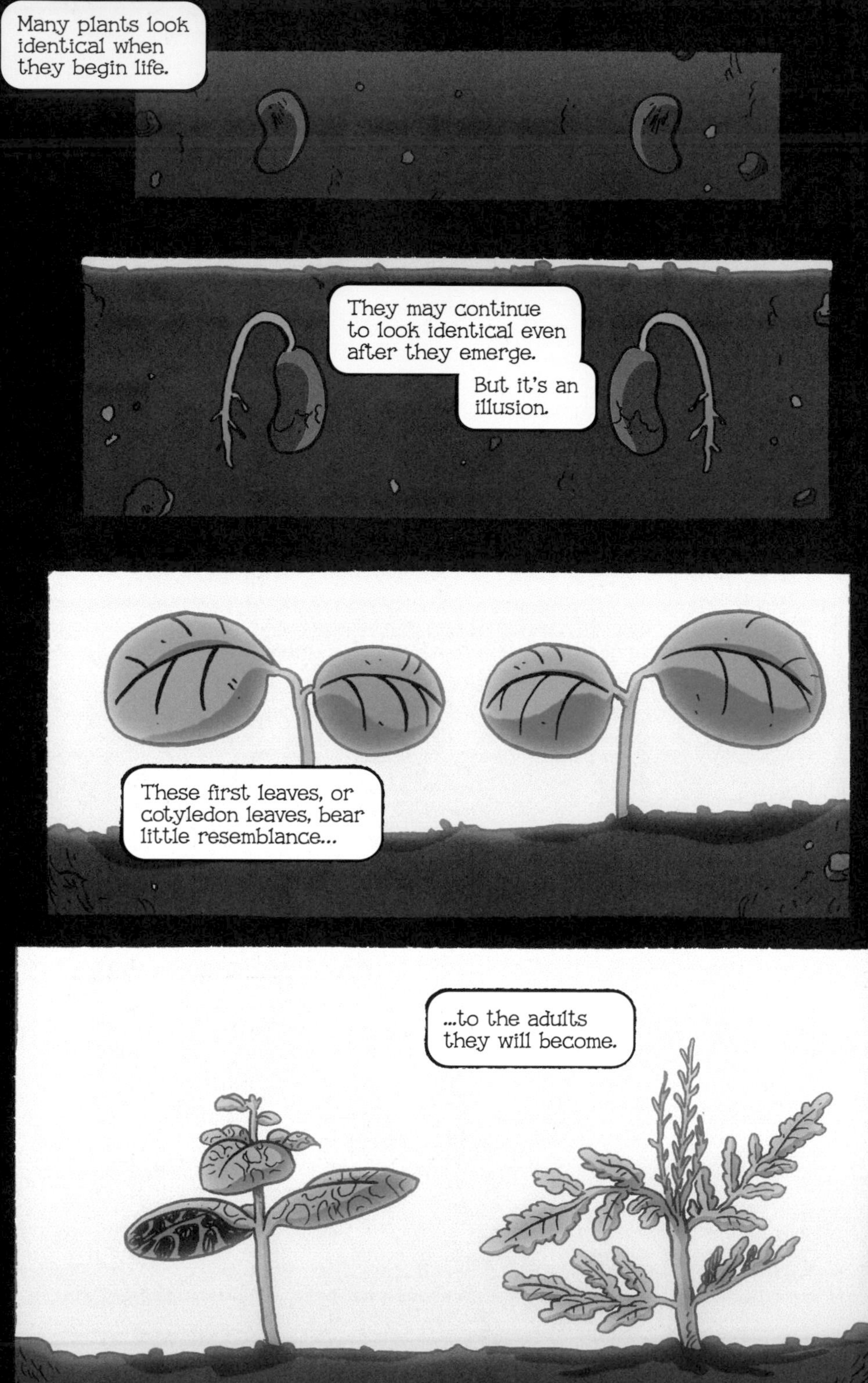

Many plants look identical when they begin life.
They may continue to look identical even after they emerge.
But it's an illusion.
These first leaves, or cotyledon leaves, bear little resemblance...
...to the adults they will become.

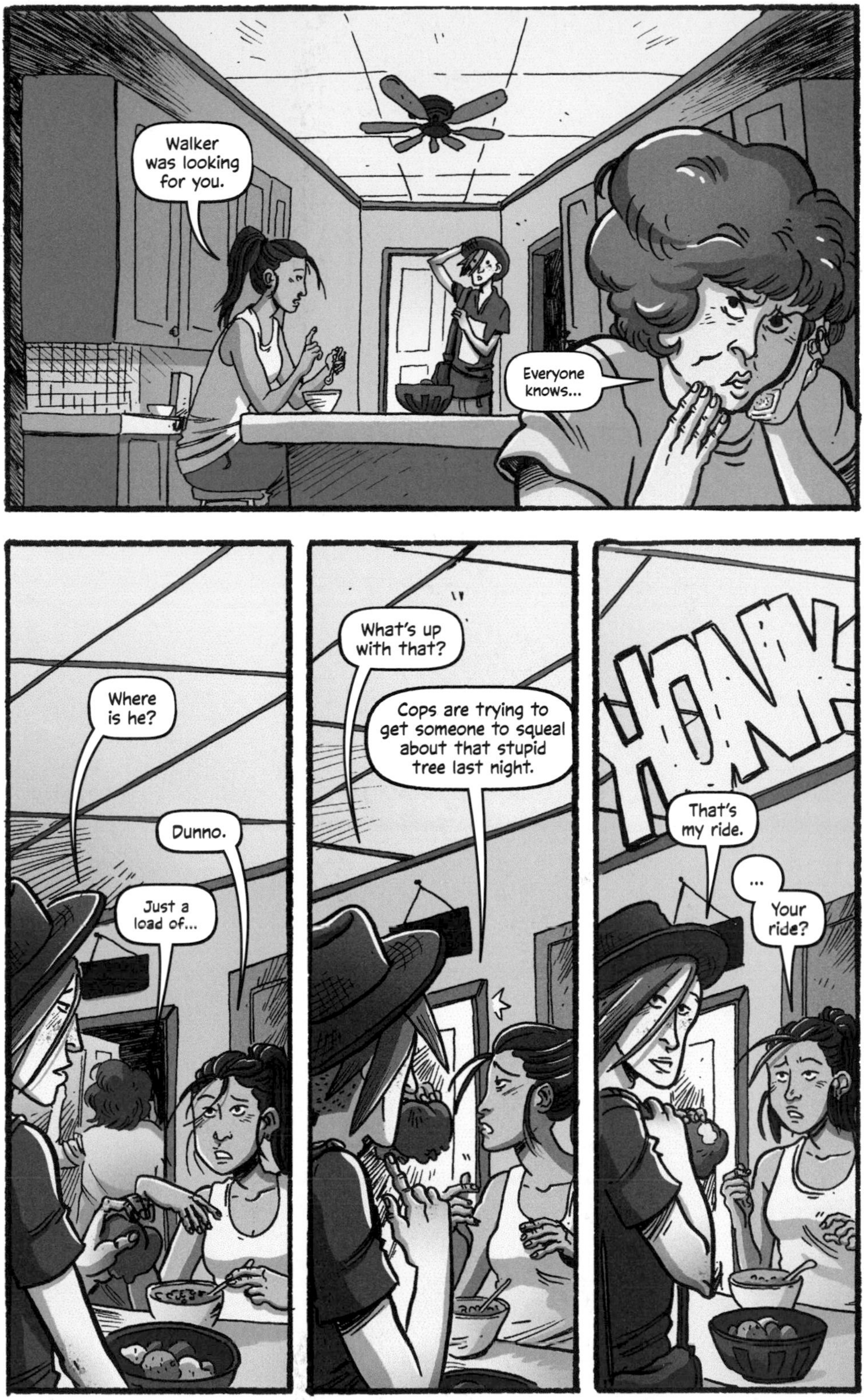
Walker was looking for you.
Everyone knows...
Where is he?
Dunno.
Just a load of...
What's up with that?
Cops are trying to get someone to squeal about that stupid tree last night.
HONK
That's my ride.
...
Your ride?

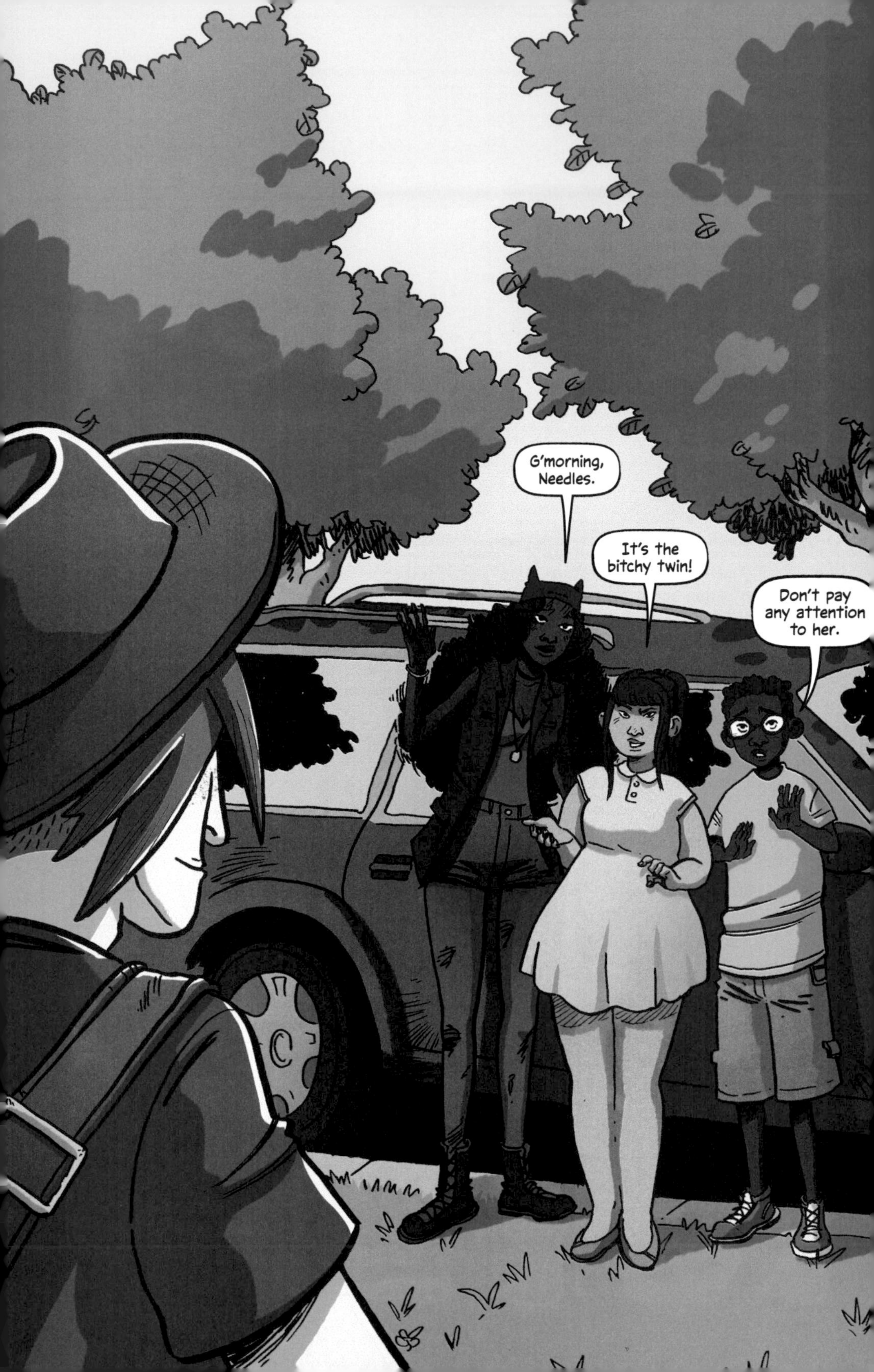
G'morning, Needles.
It's the bitchy twin!
Don't pay any attention to her.

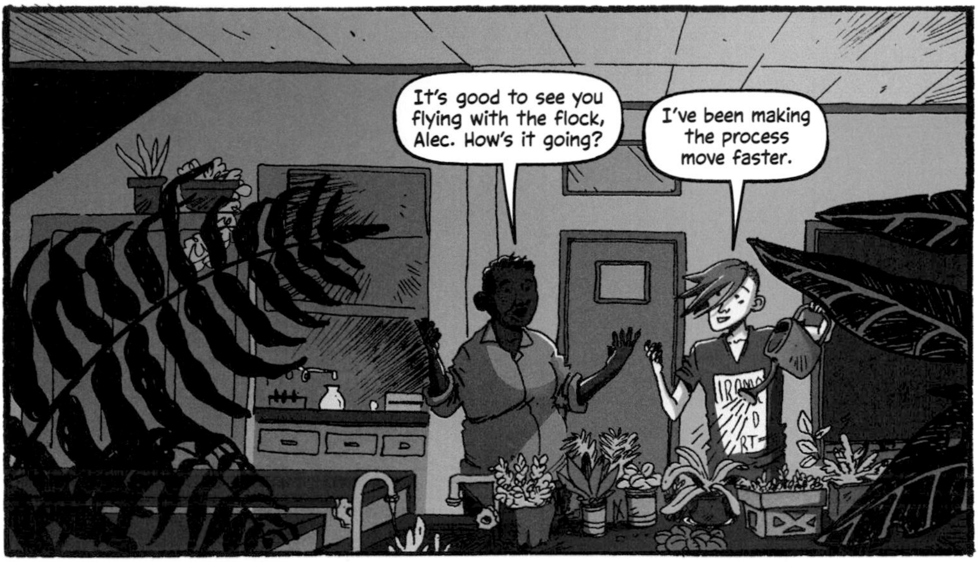
It's good to see you flying with the flock, Alec. How's it going?
I've been making the process move faster.

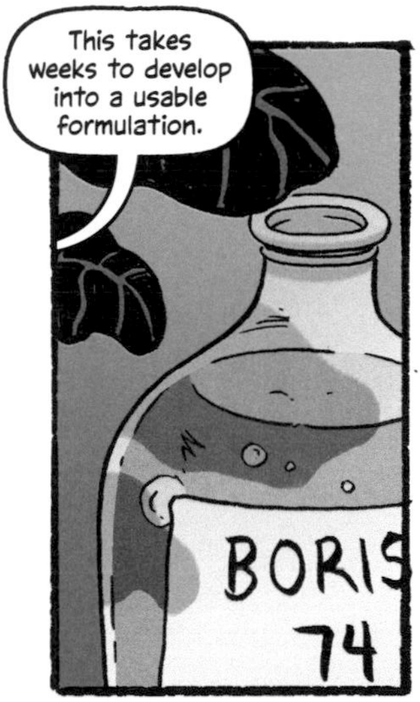
This takes weeks to develop into a usable formulation.
BORIS 74

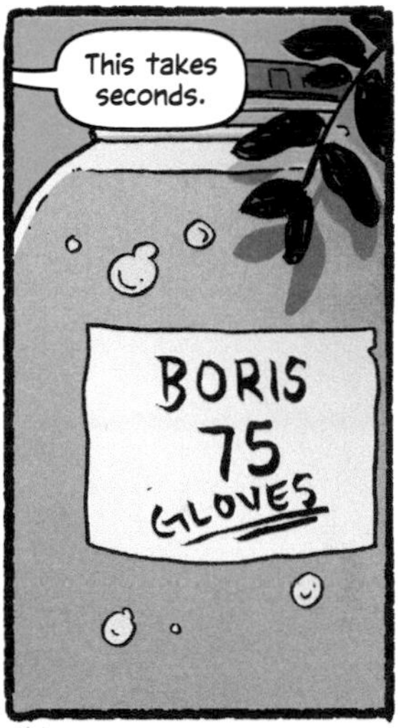
This takes seconds.
BORIS 75 GLOVES

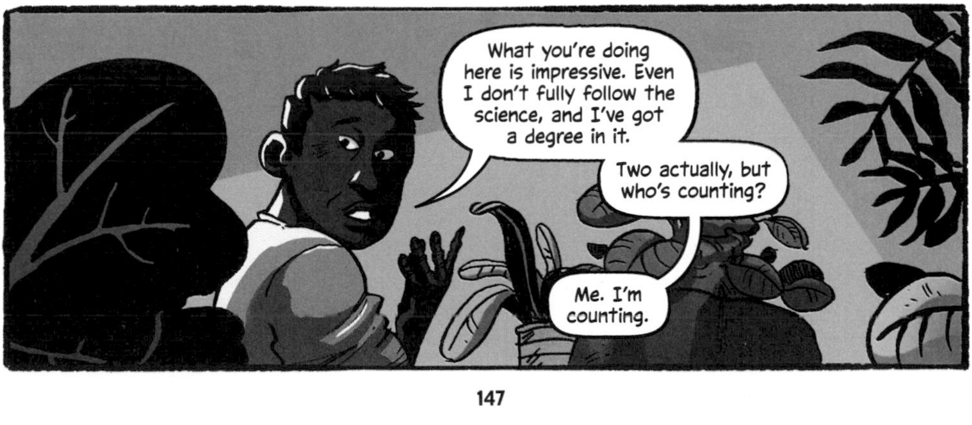
What you're doing here is impressive. Even I don't fully follow the science, and I've got a degree in it.
Two actually, but who's counting?
Me. I'm counting.

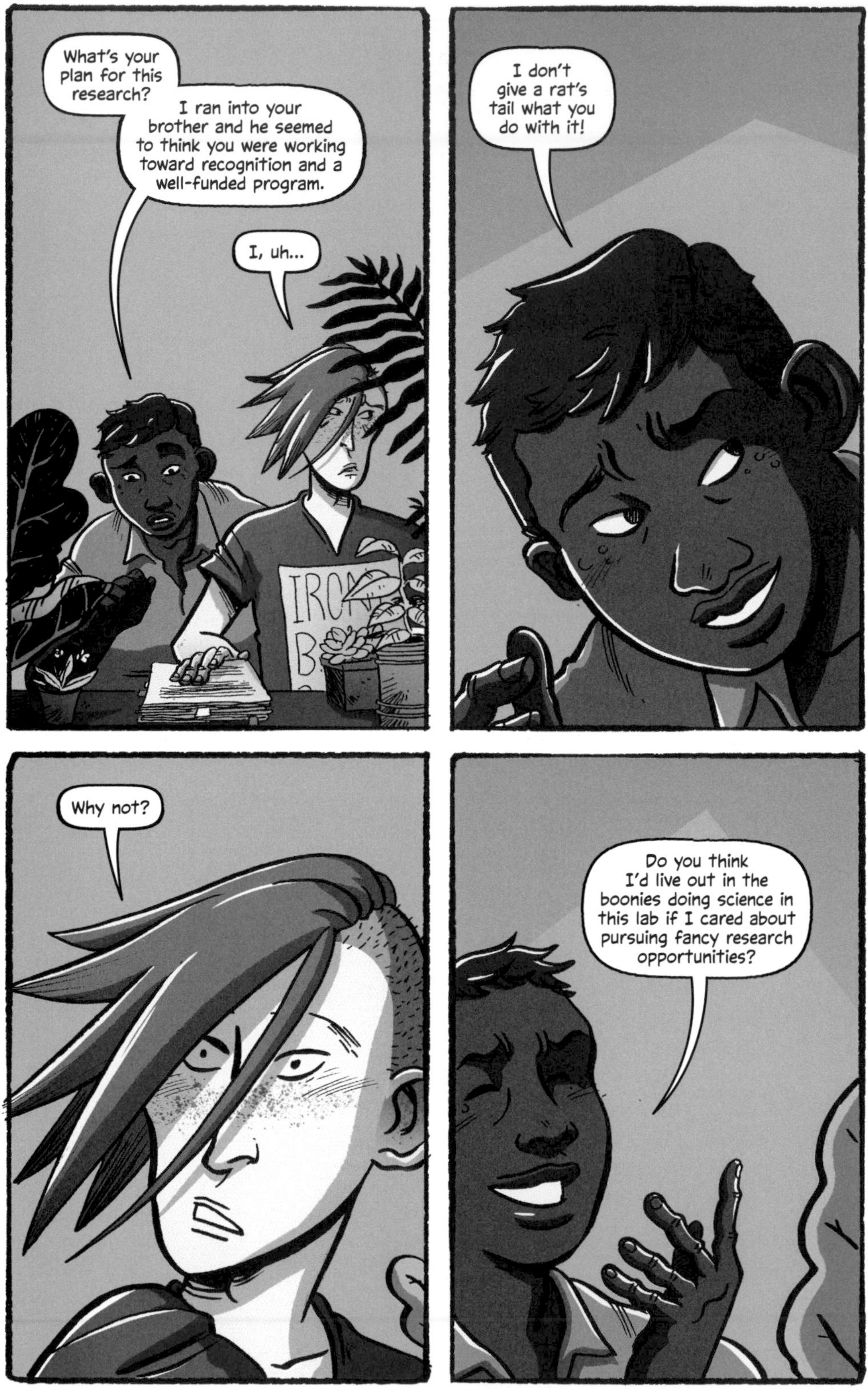
What's your plan for this research?
I ran into your brother and he seemed to think you were working toward recognition and a well-funded program.
I, uh...
IRON B
I don't give a rat's tail what you do with it!
Why not?
Do you think I'd live out in the boonies doing science in this lab if I cared about pursuing fancy research opportunities?

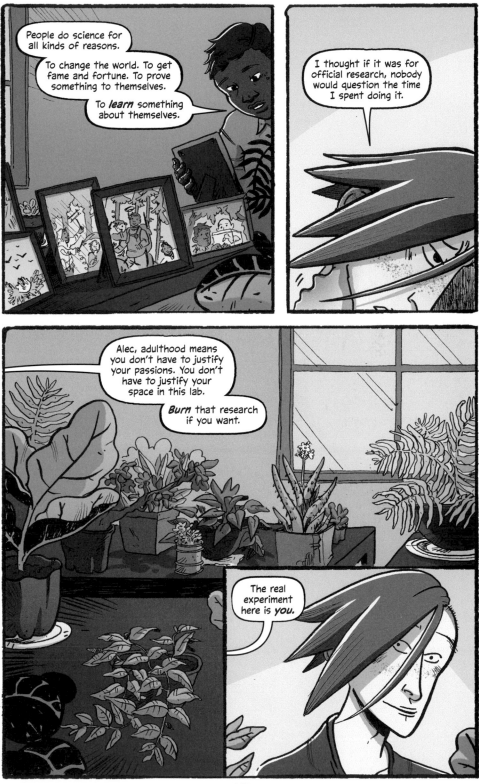

People do science for all kinds of reasons.

To change the world. To get fame and fortune. To prove something to themselves.

To *learn* something about themselves.

I thought if it was for official research, nobody would question the time I spent doing it.

Alec, adulthood means you don't have to justify your passions. You don't have to justify your space in this lab.

Burn that research if you want.

The real experiment here is *you*.

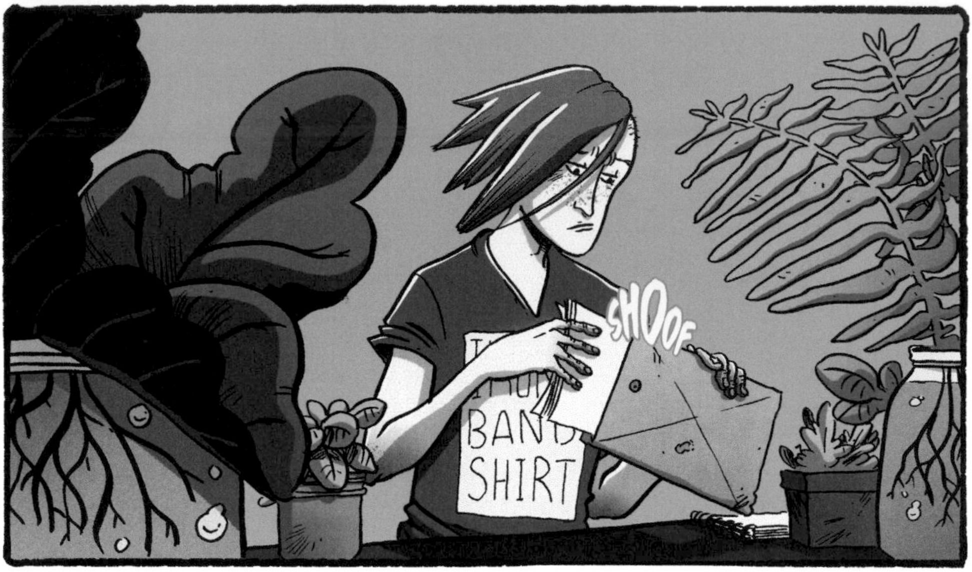
SHOOF
SHIRT

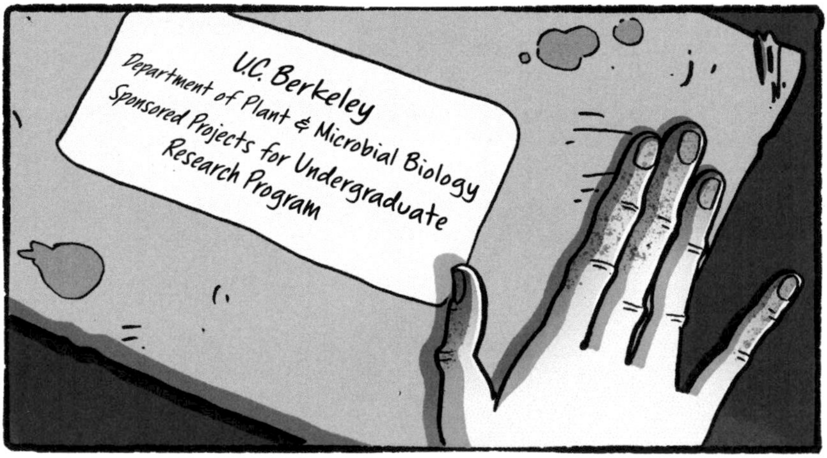
U.C. Berkeley
Department of Plant & Microbial Biology
Sponsored Projects for Undergraduate
Research Program

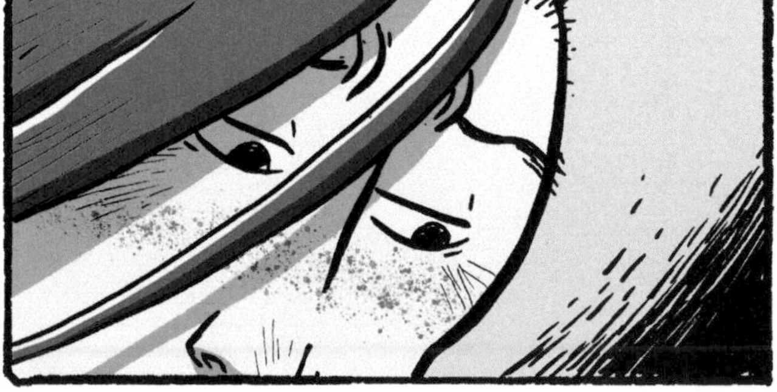

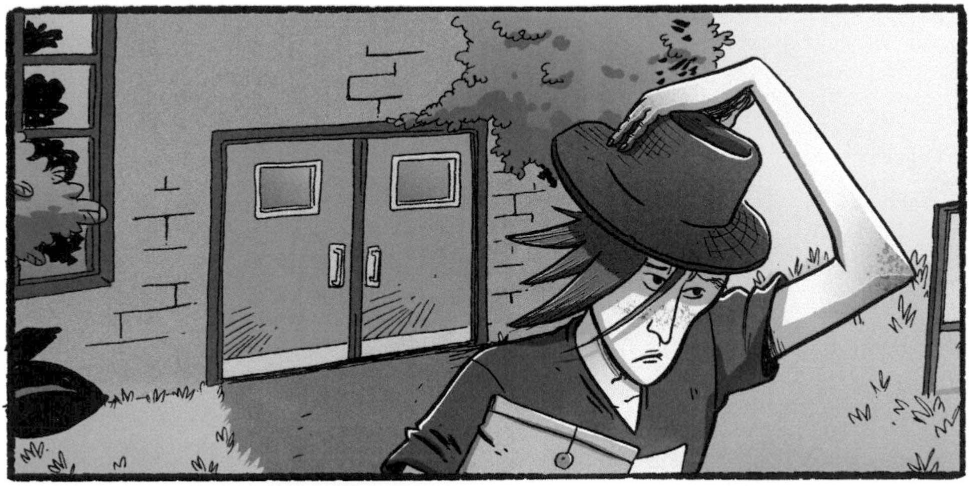

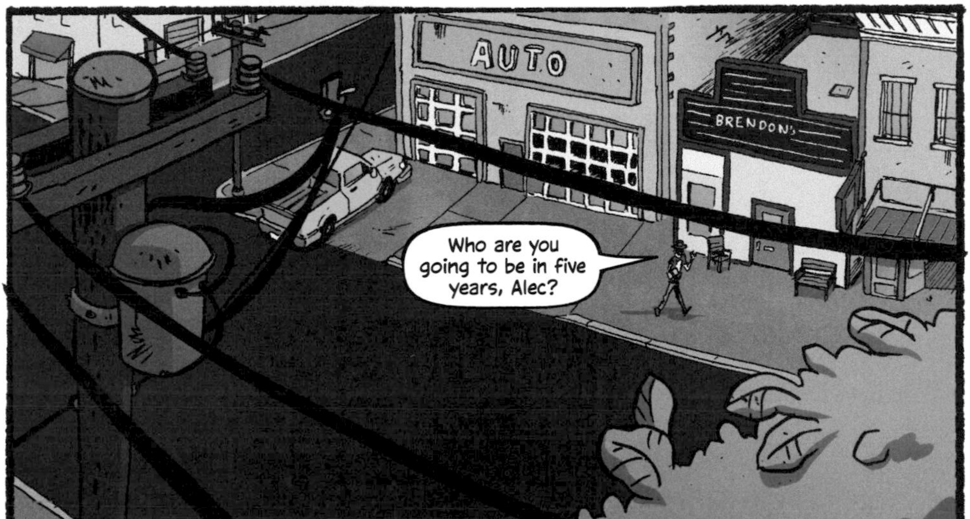
AUTO
BRENDON'S
Who are you going to be in five years, Alec?

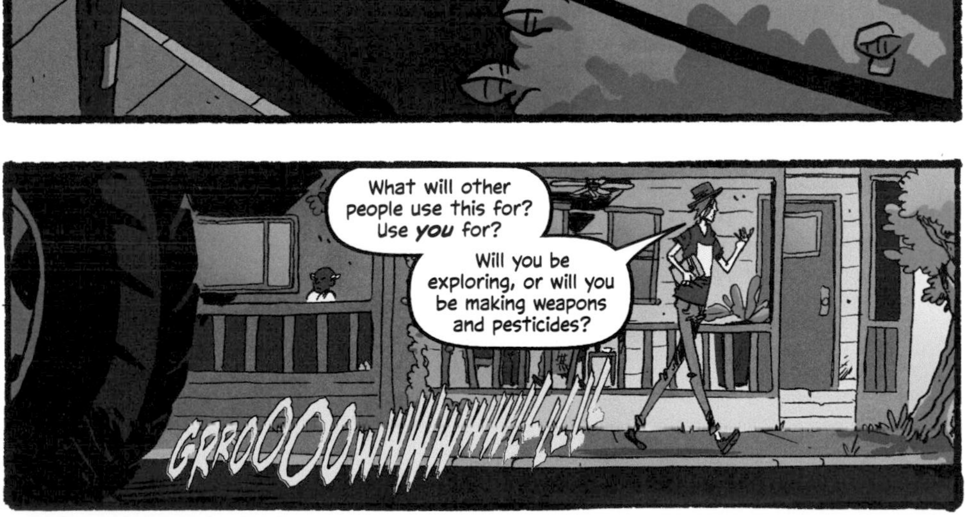
What will other people use this for? Use *you* for?
Will you be exploring, or will you be making weapons and pesticides?
GRROOOOOWHHHHHHELLLL

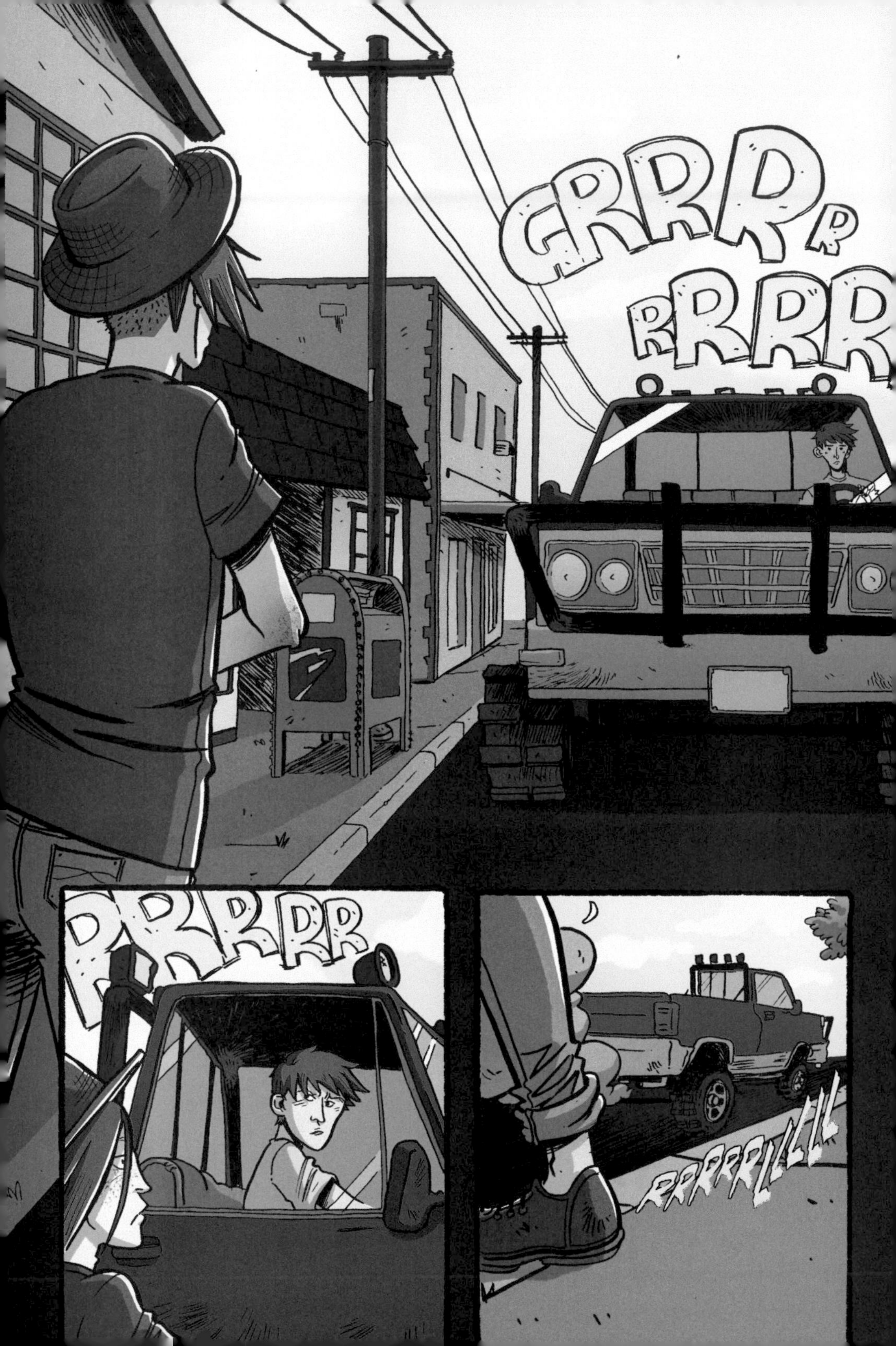
GRRRR
RRRRR
RRRRRR
RRRRRLLLL

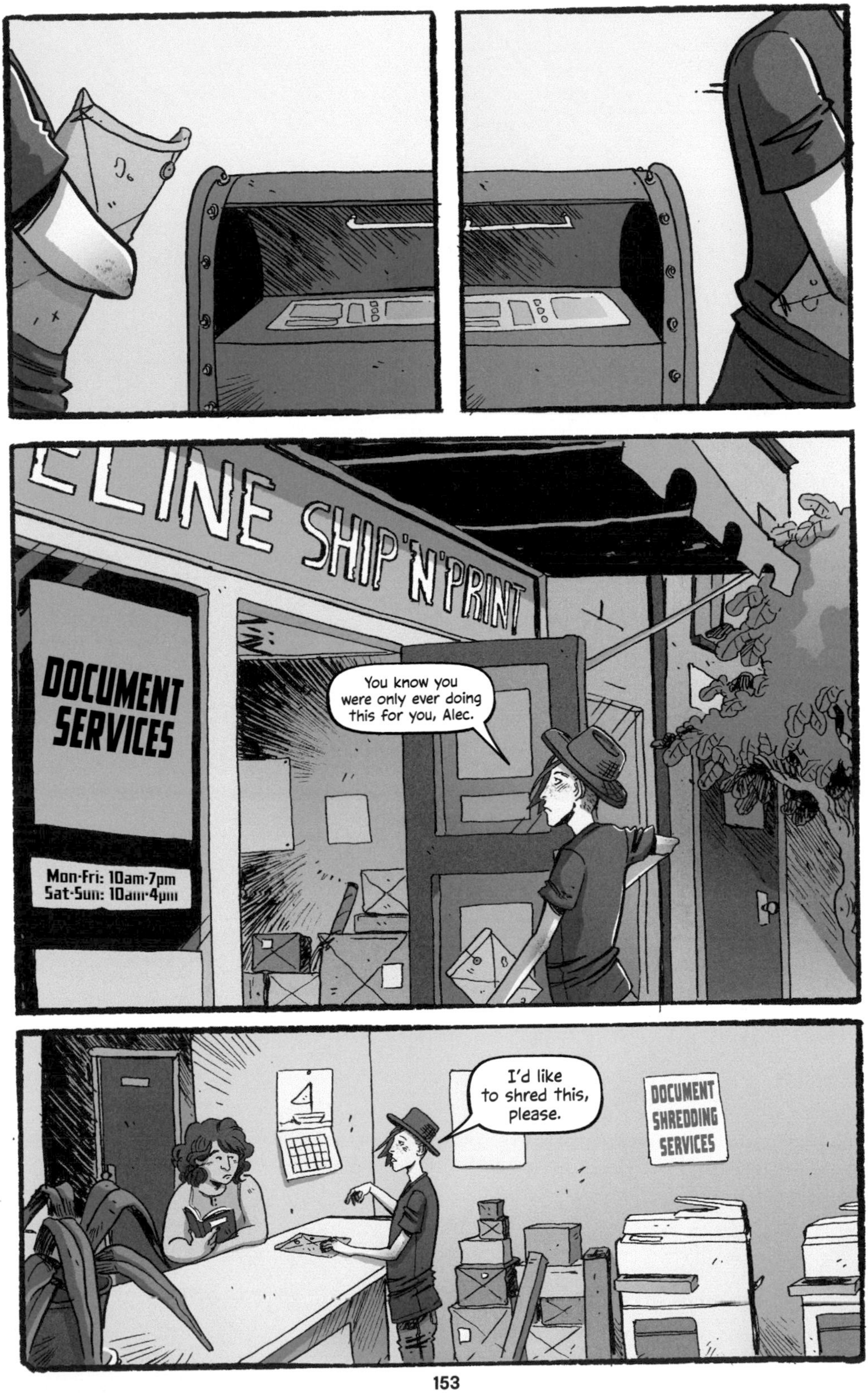
ELINE SHIP'N'PRINT
DOCUMENT SERVICES
Mon-Fri: 10am-7pm
Sat-Sun: 10am-4pm
You know you were only ever doing this for you, Alec.
DOCUMENT SHREDDING SERVICES
I'd like to shred this, please.

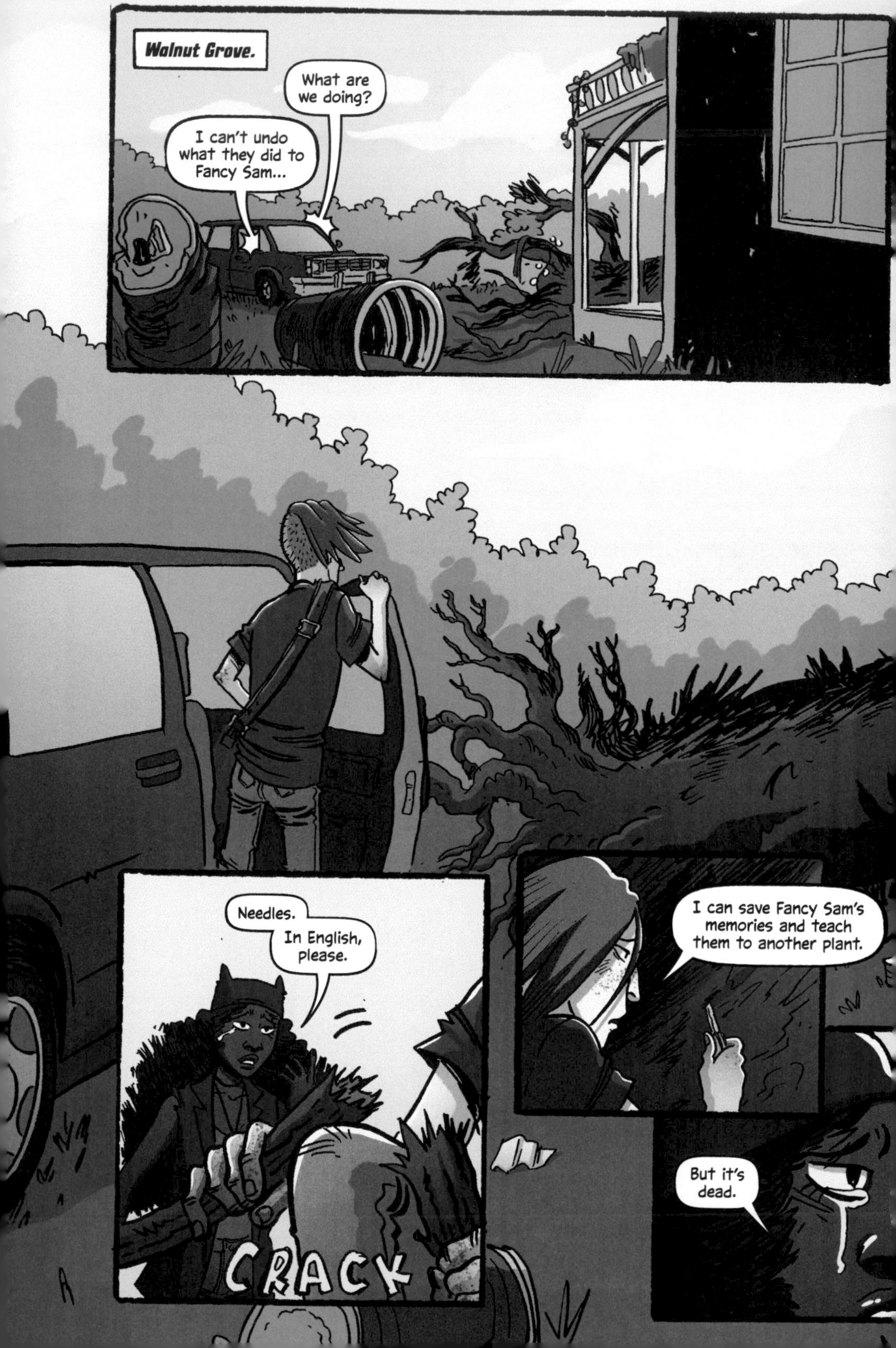
Walnut Grove.
What are we doing?
I can't undo what they did to Fancy Sam...
Needles.
In English, please.
CRACK
I can save Fancy Sam's memories and teach them to another plant.
But it's dead.

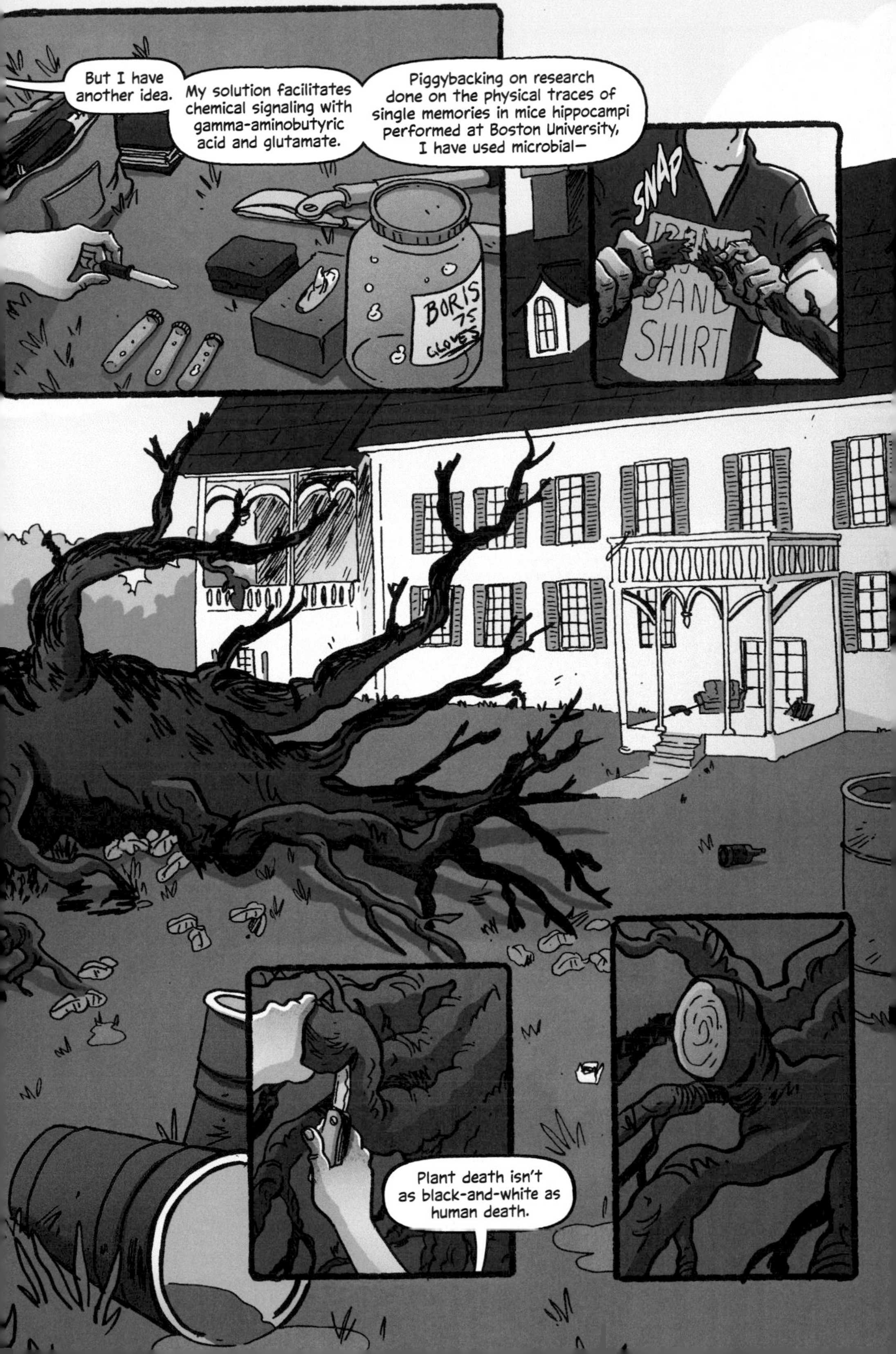
But I have another idea.
My solution facilitates chemical signaling with gamma-aminobutyric acid and glutamate.
Piggybacking on research done on the physical traces of single memories in mice hippocampi performed at Boston University, I have used microbial—
BORIS 75 GLOVES
SNAP
BAND SHIRT
Plant death isn't as black-and-white as human death.

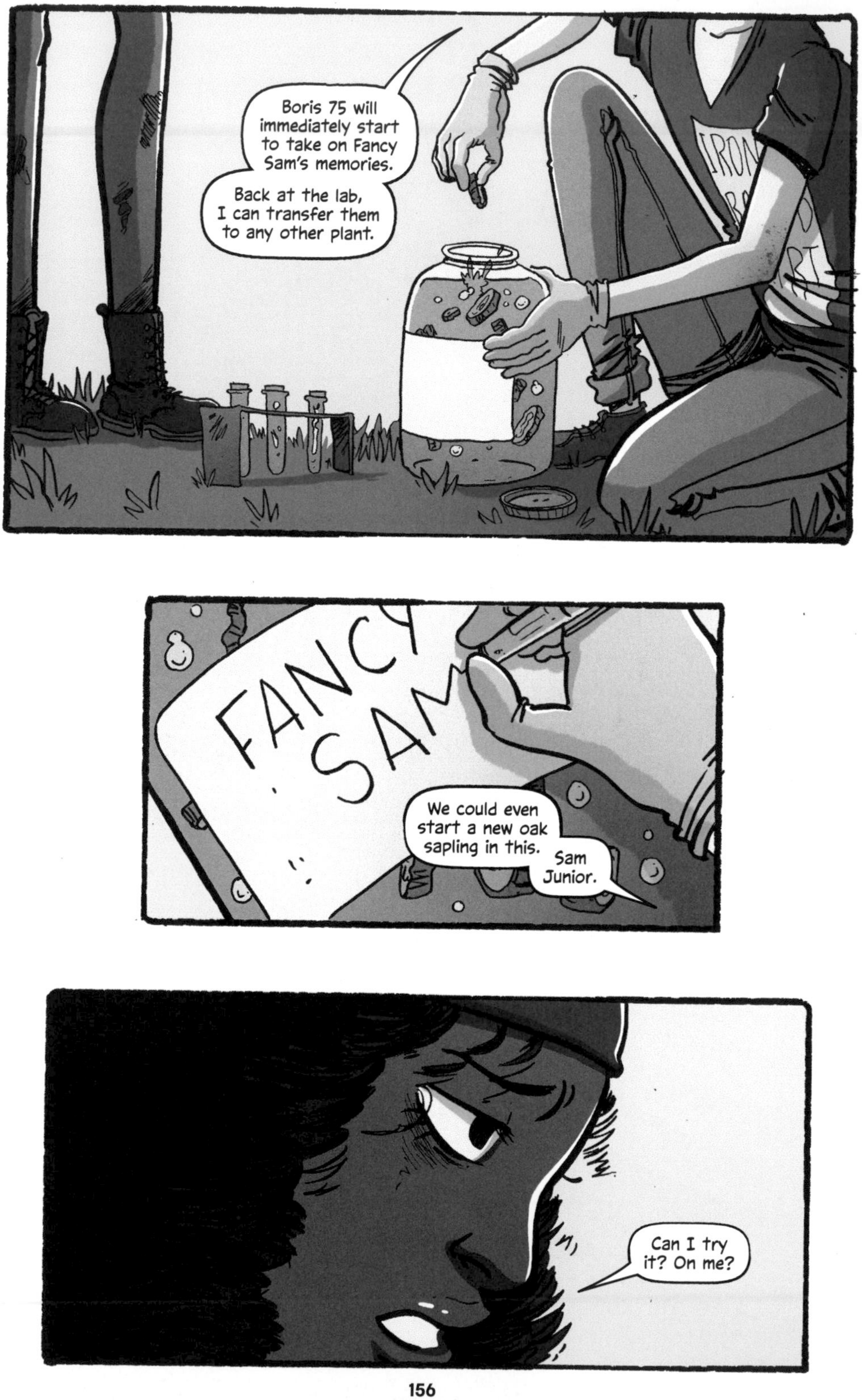

Boris 75 will immediately start to take on Fancy Sam's memories.
Back at the lab, I can transfer them to any other plant.
We could even start a new oak sapling in this.
Sam Junior.
Can I try it? On me?

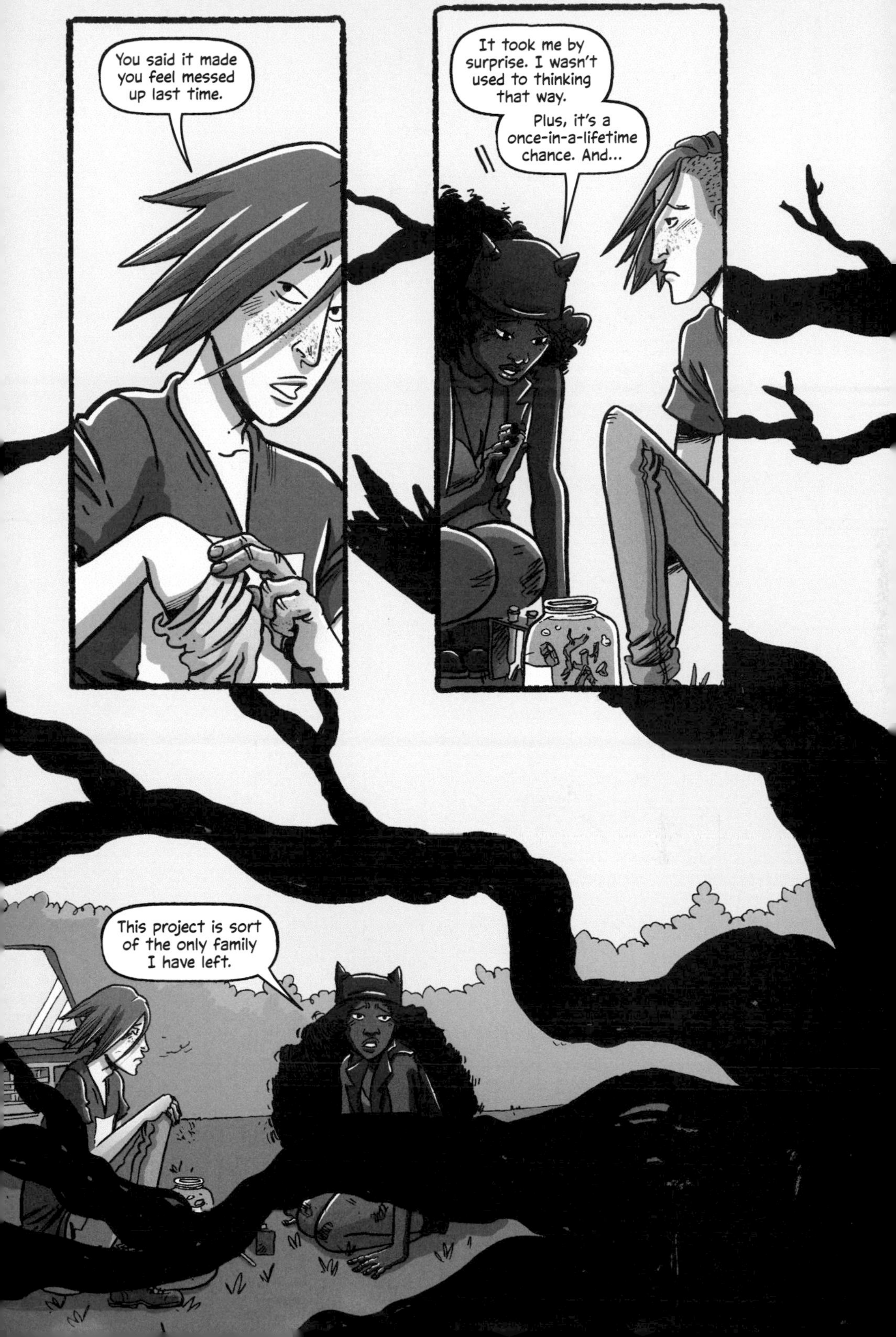
You said it made you feel messed up last time.
It took me by surprise. I wasn't used to thinking that way.
Plus, it's a once-in-a-lifetime chance. And...
This project is sort of the only family I have left.

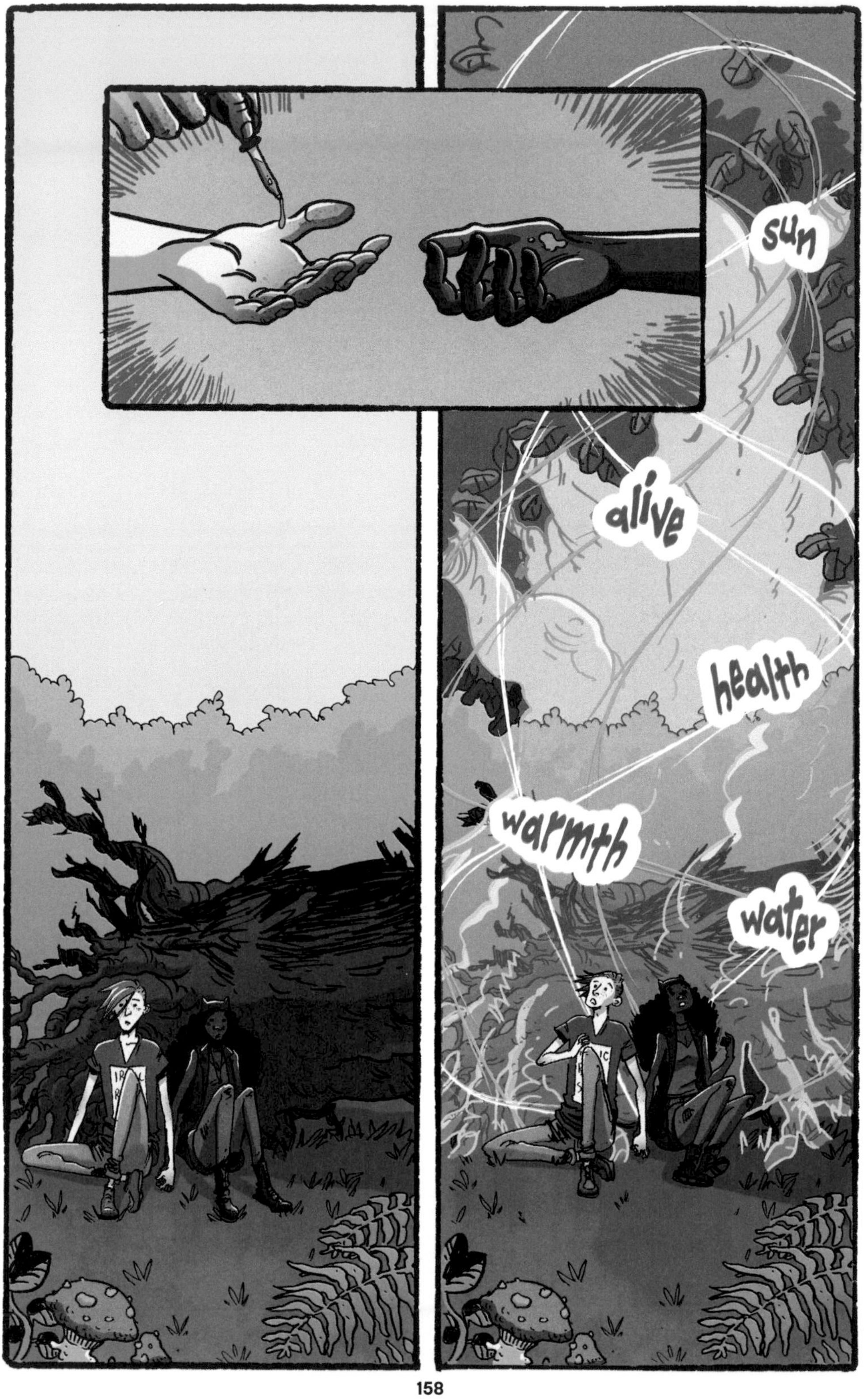
sun
alive
health
warmth
water

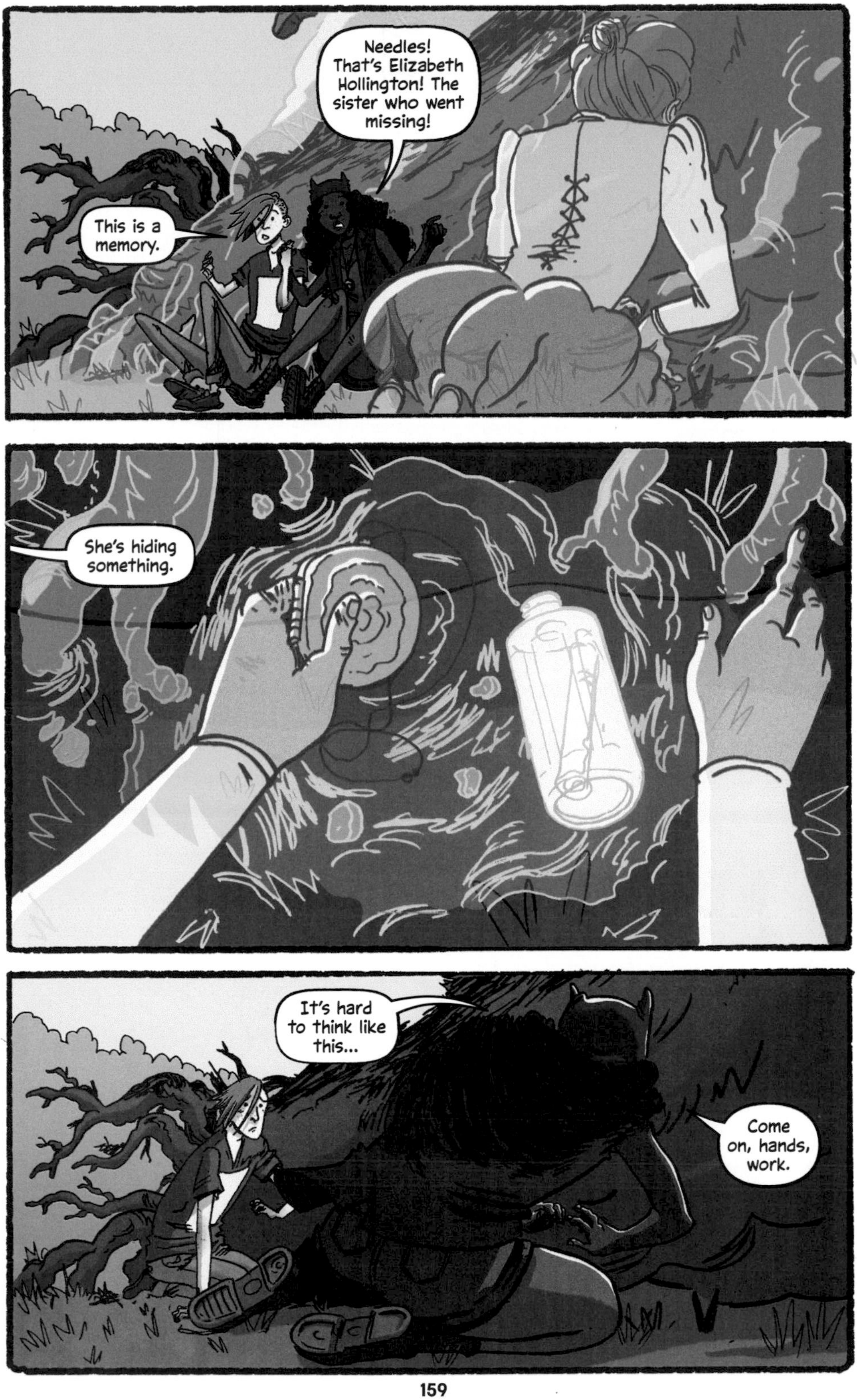
Needles! That's Elizabeth Hollington! The sister who went missing!
This is a memory.
She's hiding something.
It's hard to think like this...
Come on, hands, work.

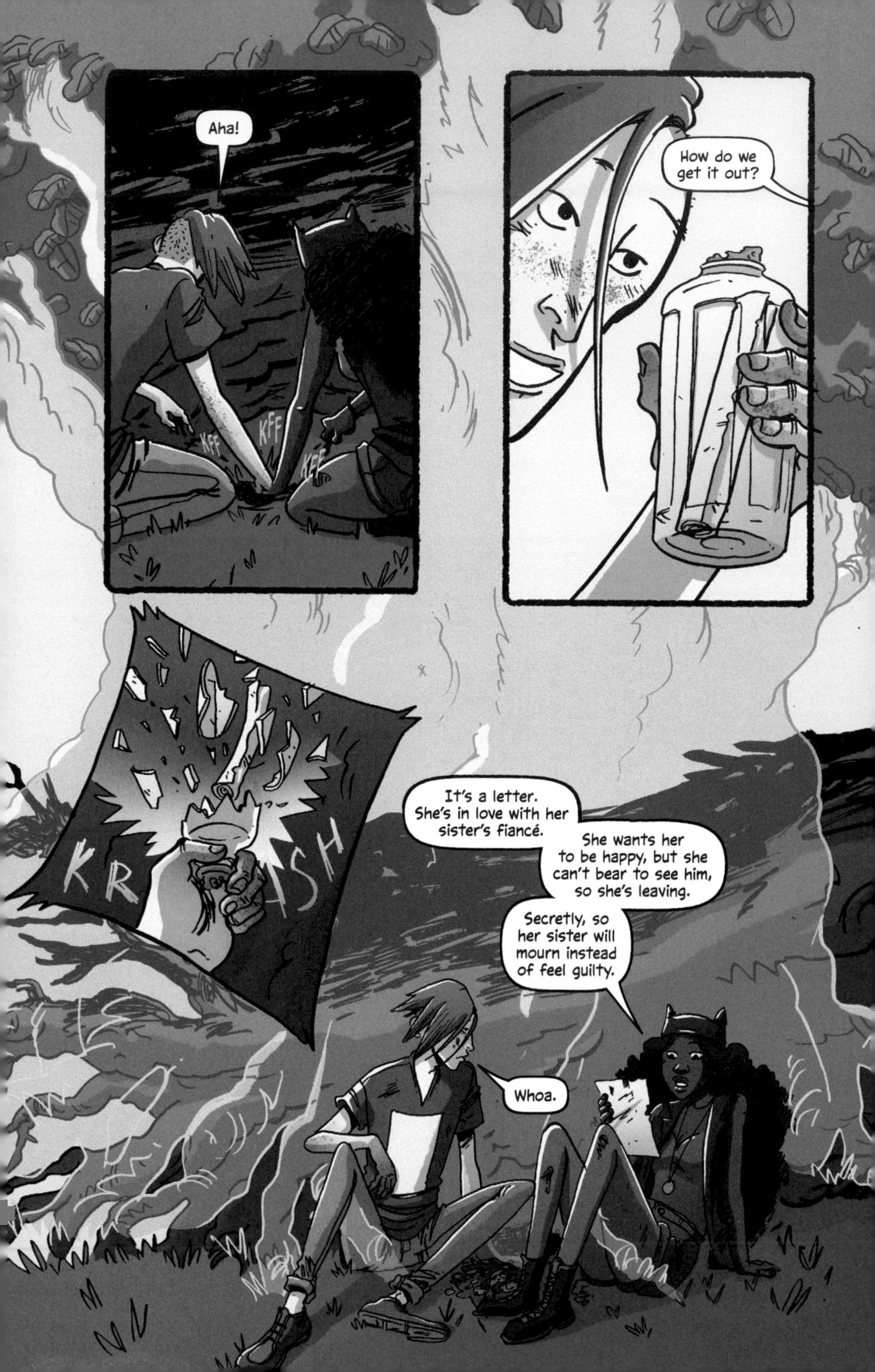
Aha!
KFF
KFF
KFF
How do we get it out?
KRASH
It's a letter. She's in love with her sister's fiancé.
She wants her to be happy, but she can't bear to see him, so she's leaving.
Secretly, so her sister will mourn instead of feel guilty.
Whoa.

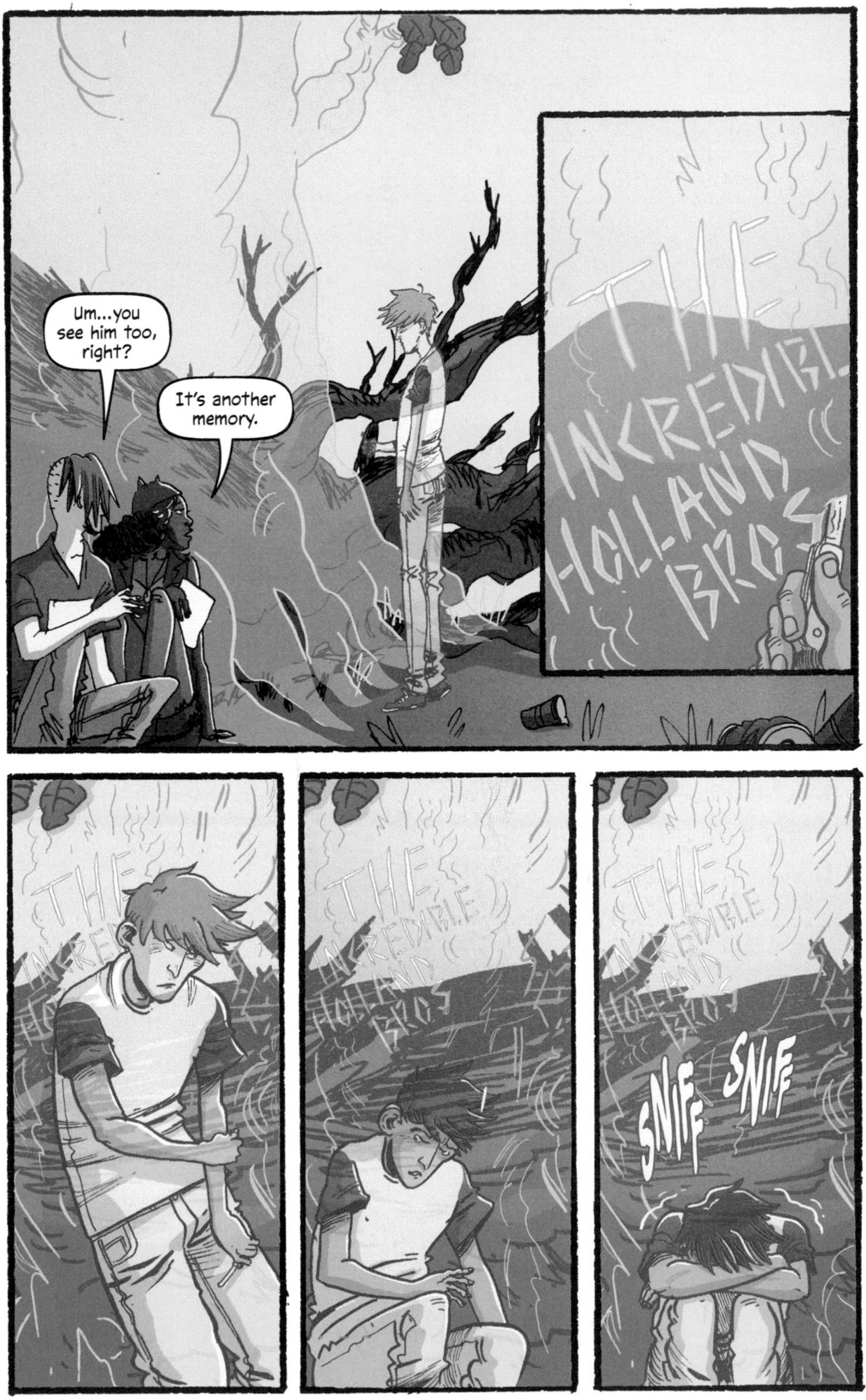
Um...you see him too, right?
It's another memory.
THE INCREDIBL HOLLAND BROS
THE INCREDIBLE HOLLAND BROS
THE INCREDIBLE HOLLAND BROS
SNIFF
SNIFF

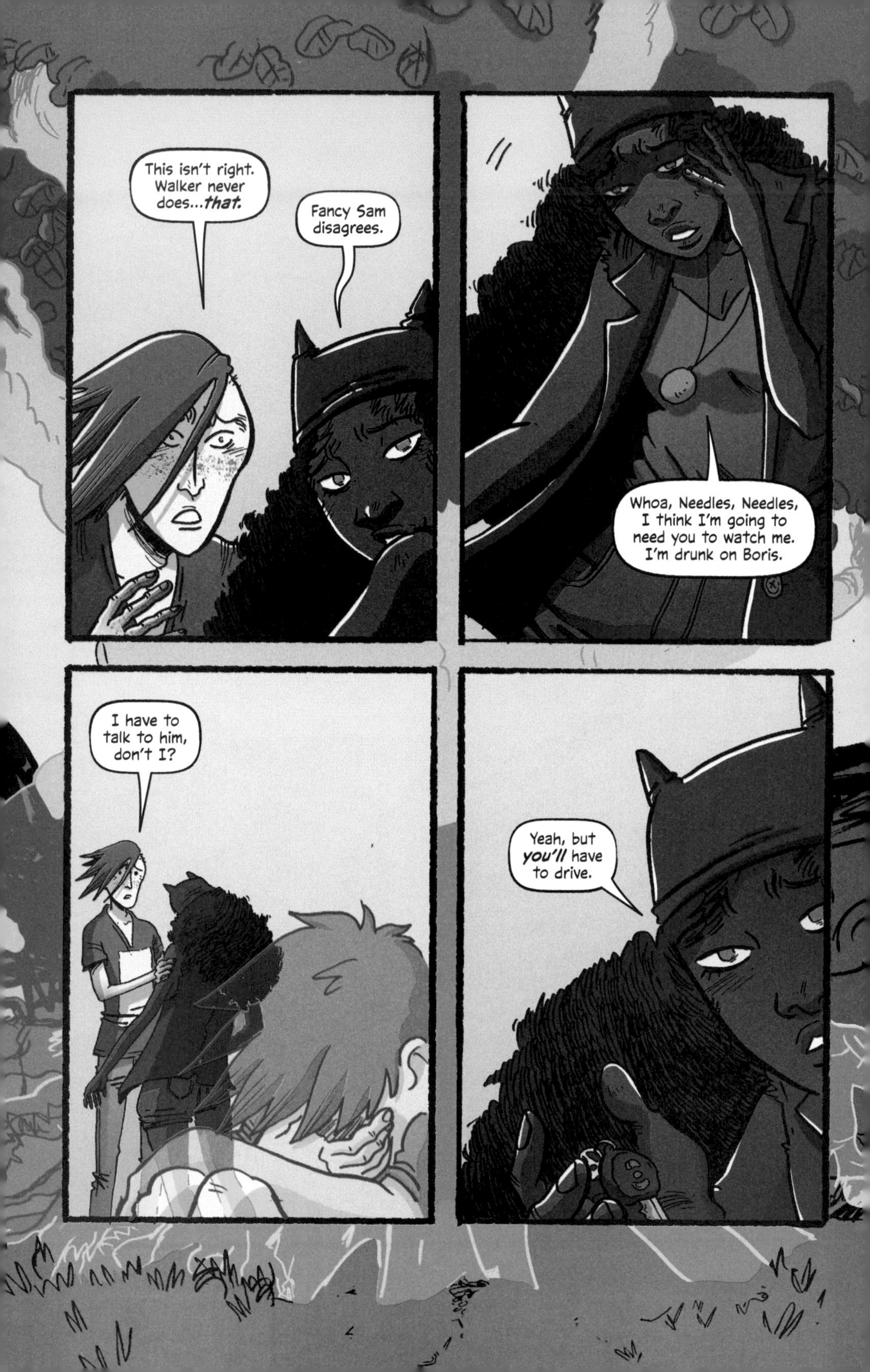
This isn't right. Walker never does...*that.*
Fancy Sam disagrees.
Whoa, Needles, Needles, I think I'm going to need you to watch me. I'm drunk on Boris.
I have to talk to him, don't I?
Yeah, but *you'll* have to drive.

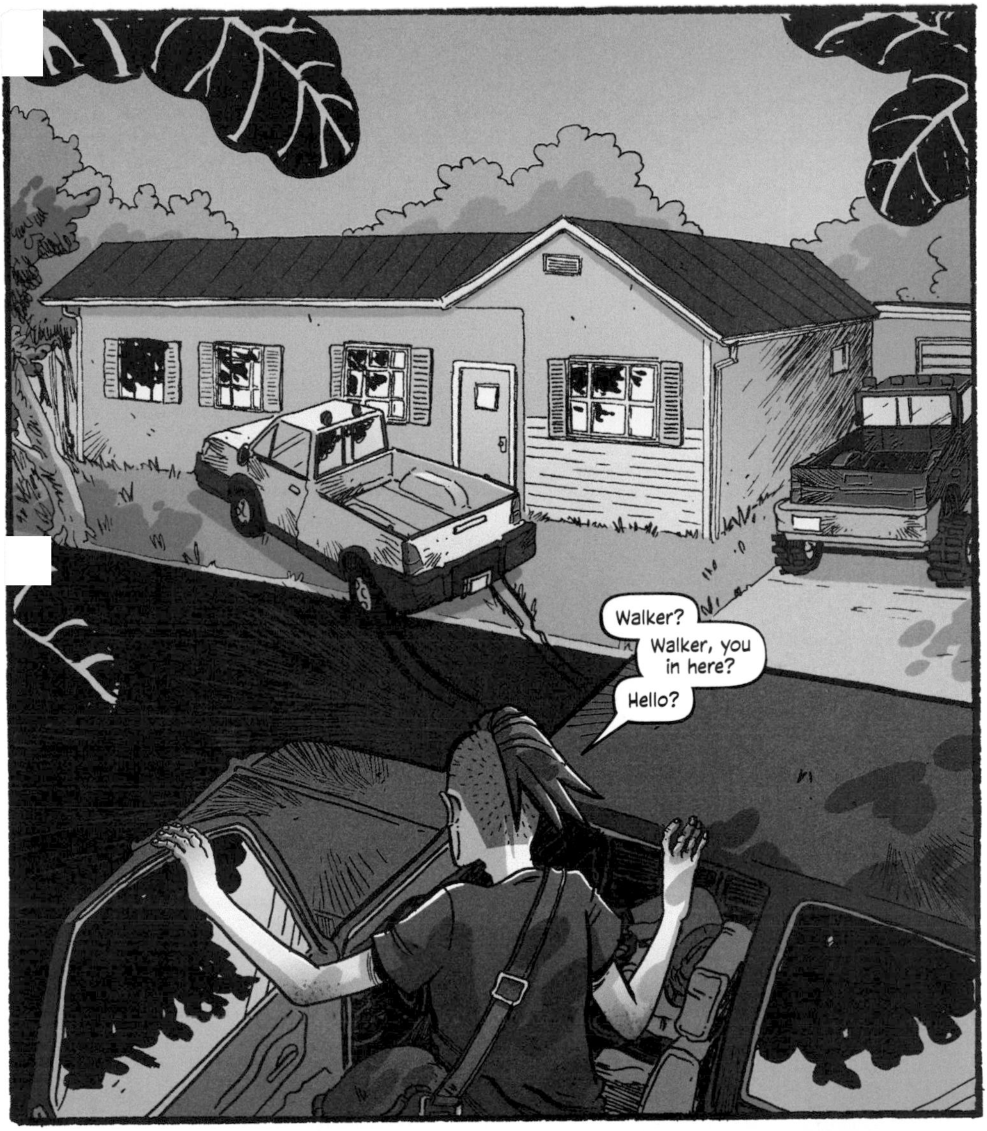
Walker?
Walker, you in here?
Hello?

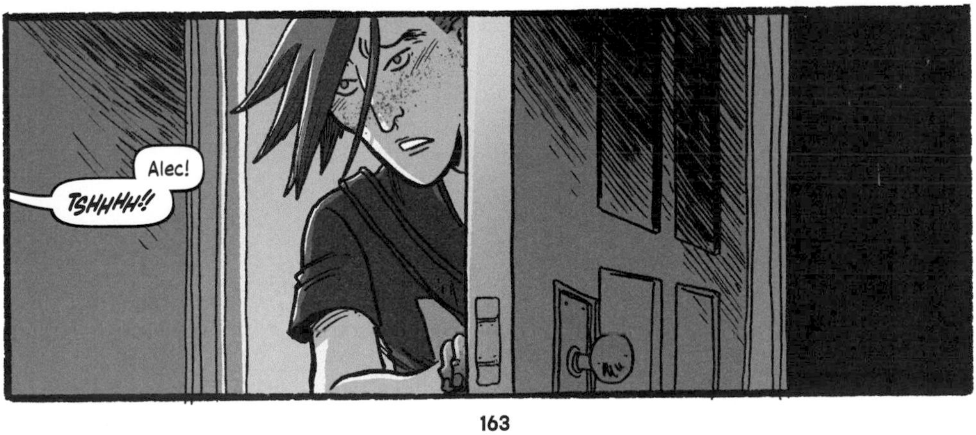
Alec!
TSHHHH!!

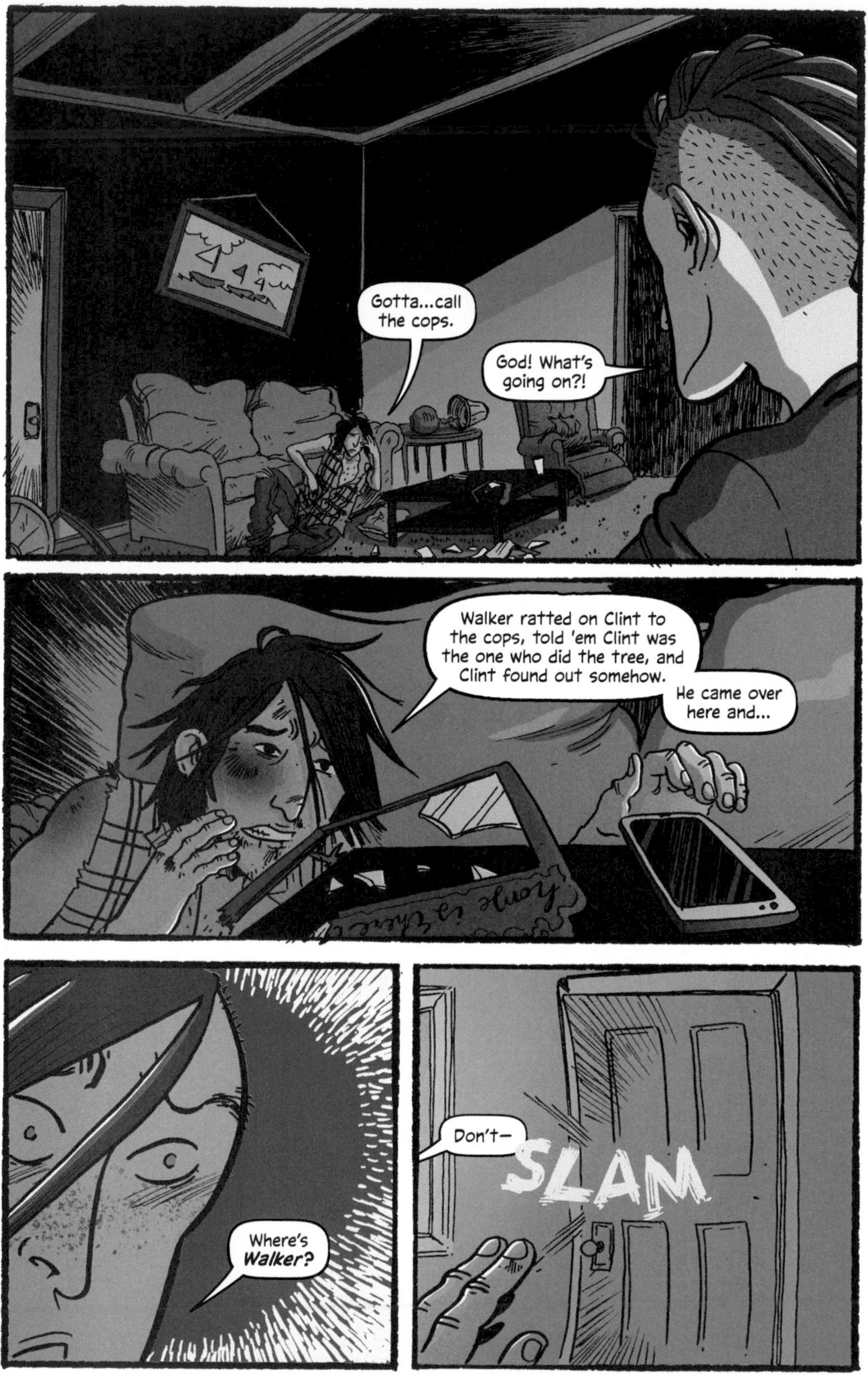
Gotta...call the cops.
God! What's going on?!
Walker ratted on Clint to the cops, told 'em Clint was the one who did the tree, and Clint found out somehow.
He came over here and...
Where's *Walker?*
Don't—
SLAM

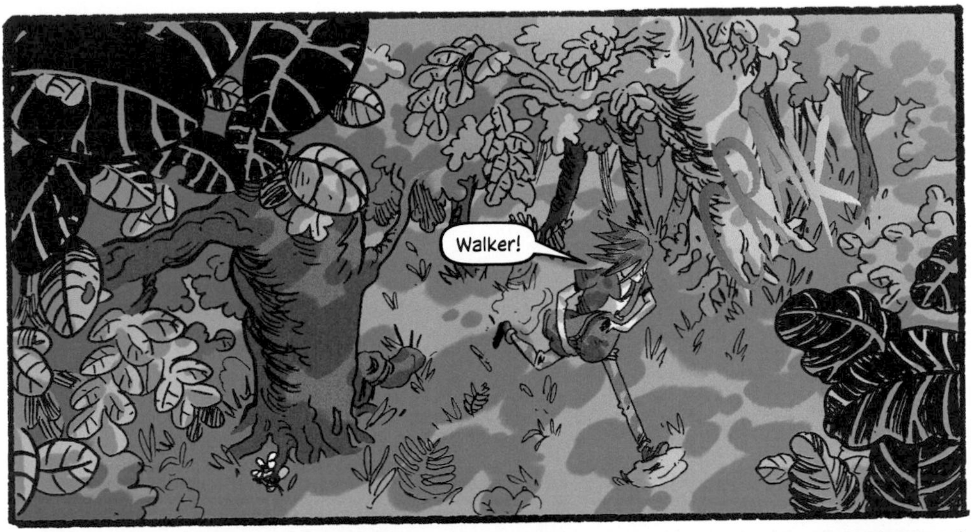
Walker!
CRAK!

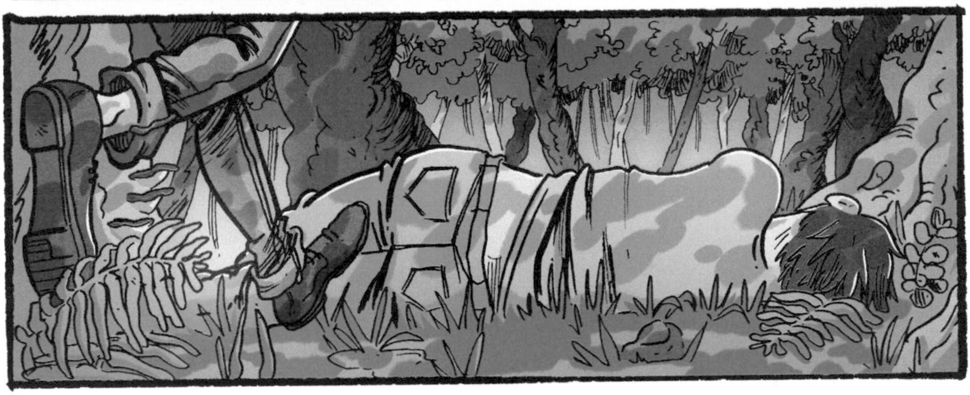

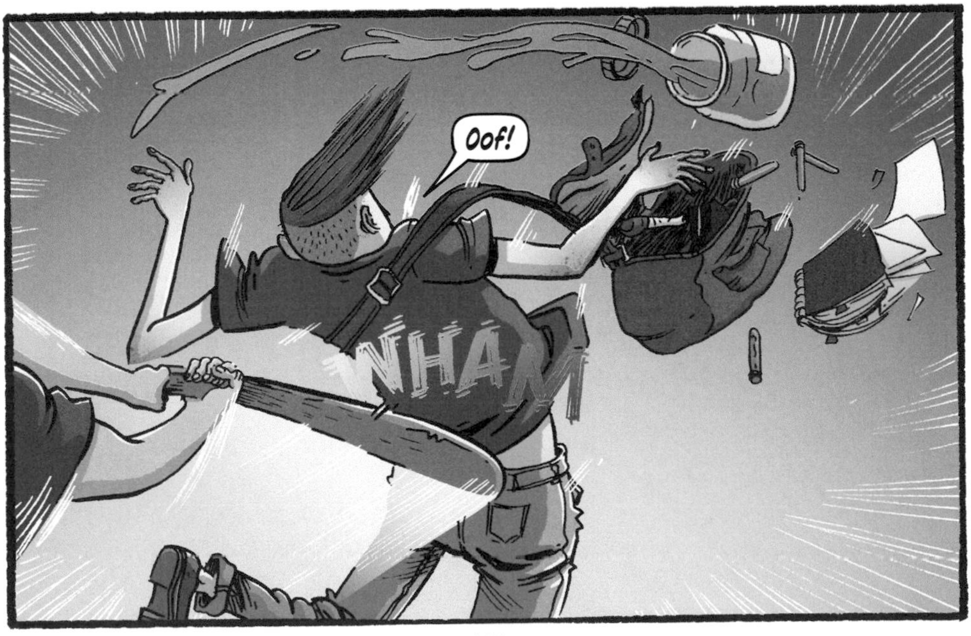
Oof!
WHAM

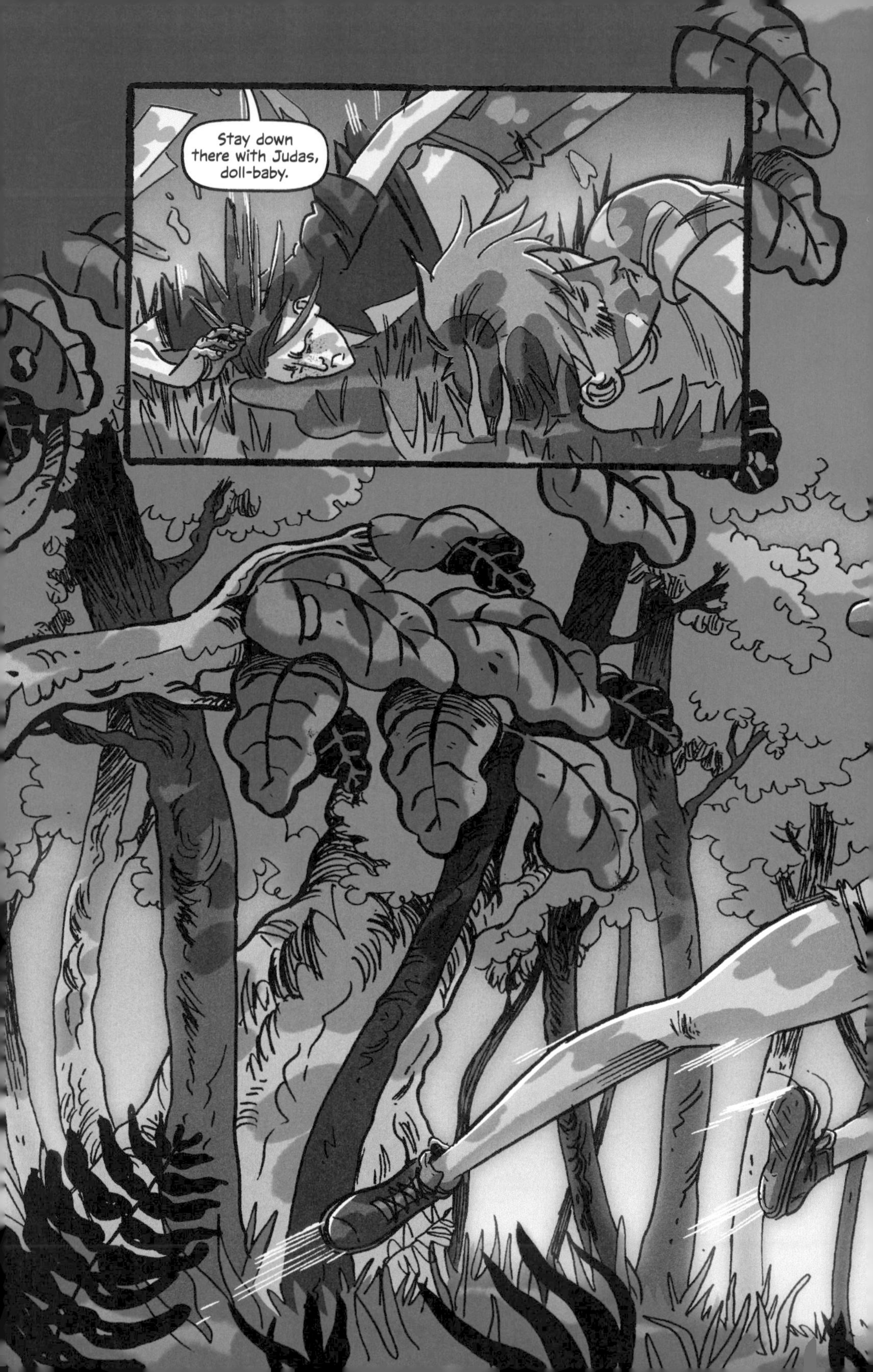
Stay down there with Judas, doll-baby.

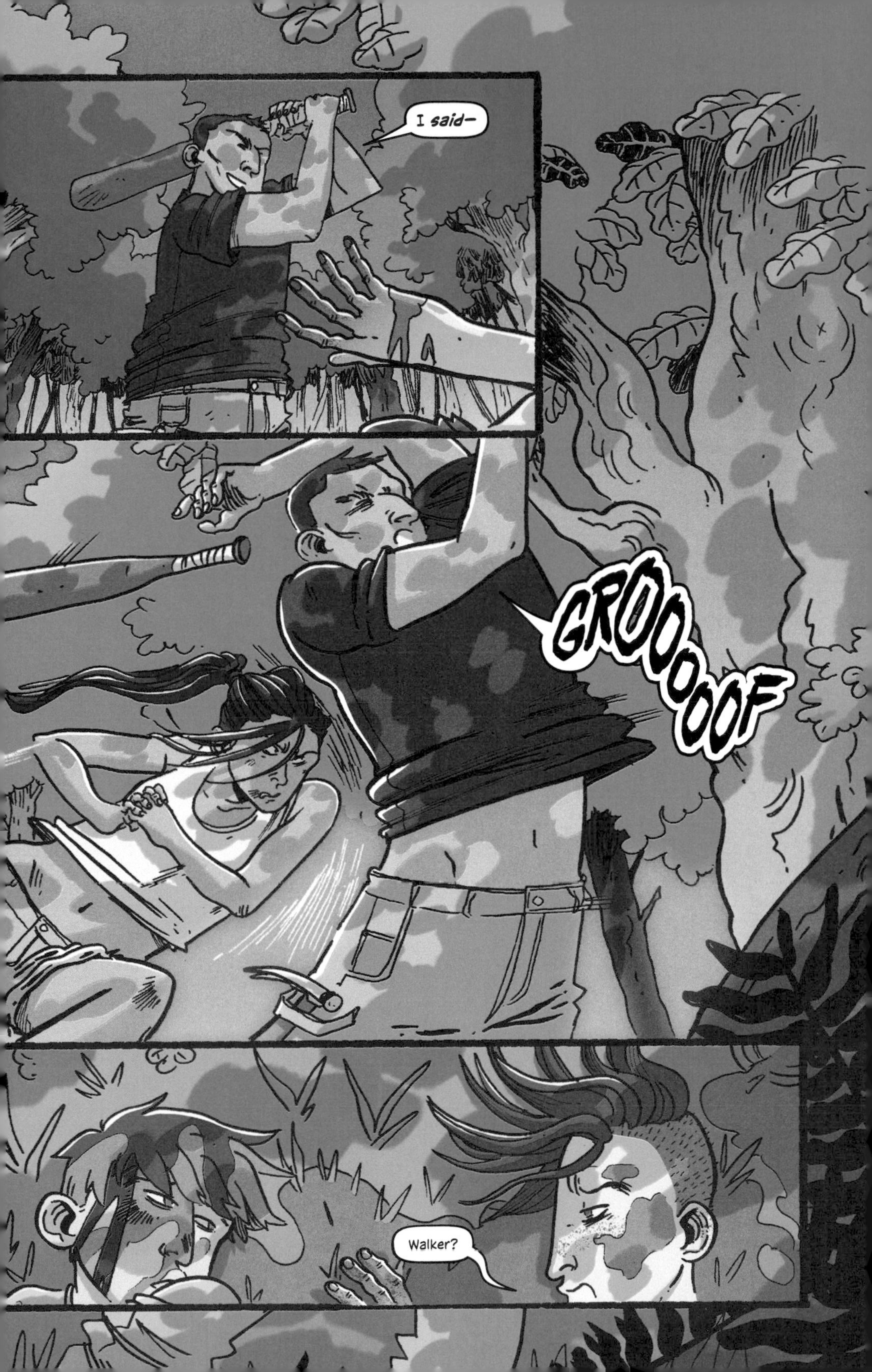
I said–
GROOOOOOF
Walker?

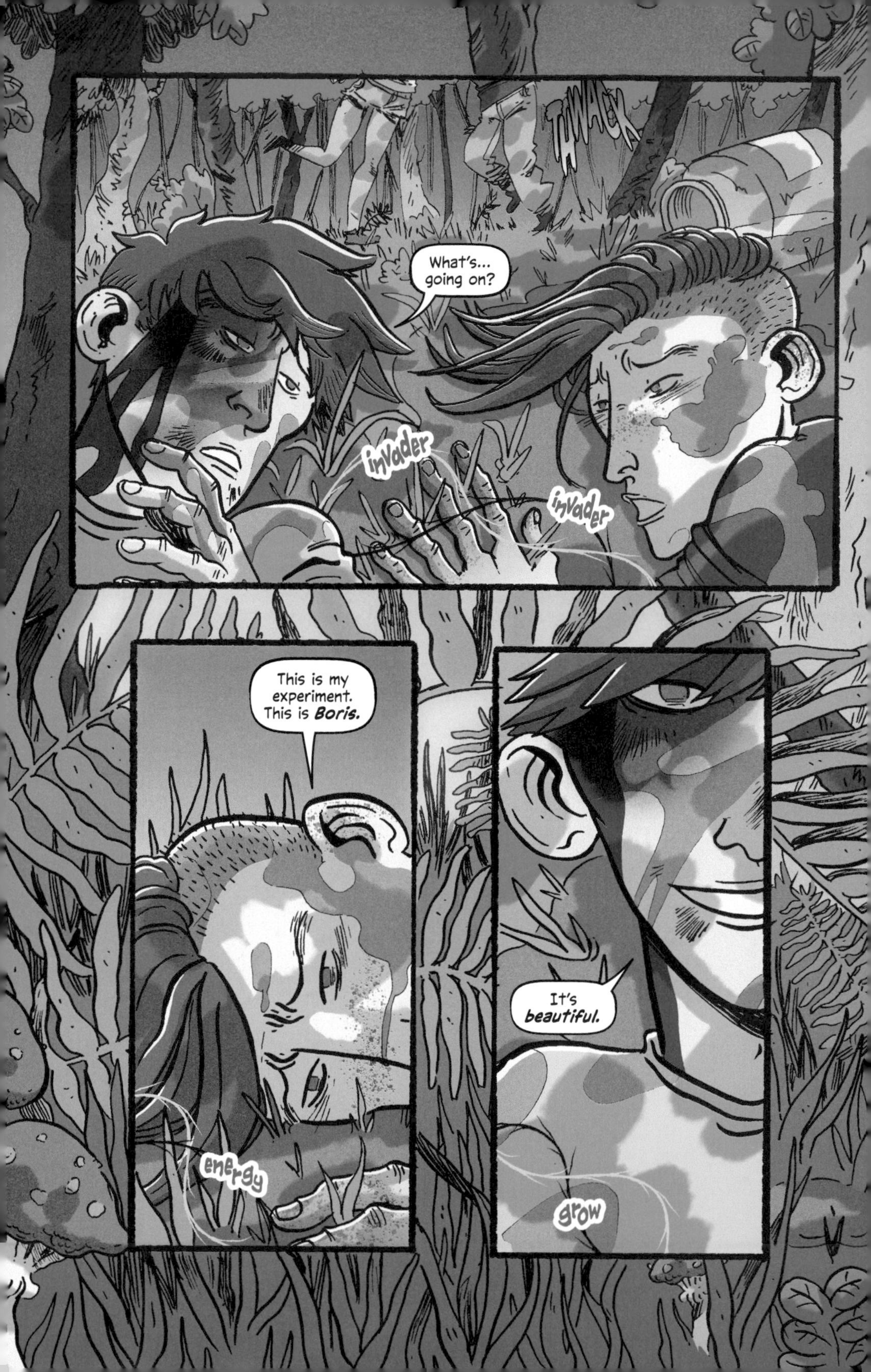
THWACK
What's... going on?
invader
invader
This is my experiment. This is *Boris.*
energy
It's *beautiful.*
grow

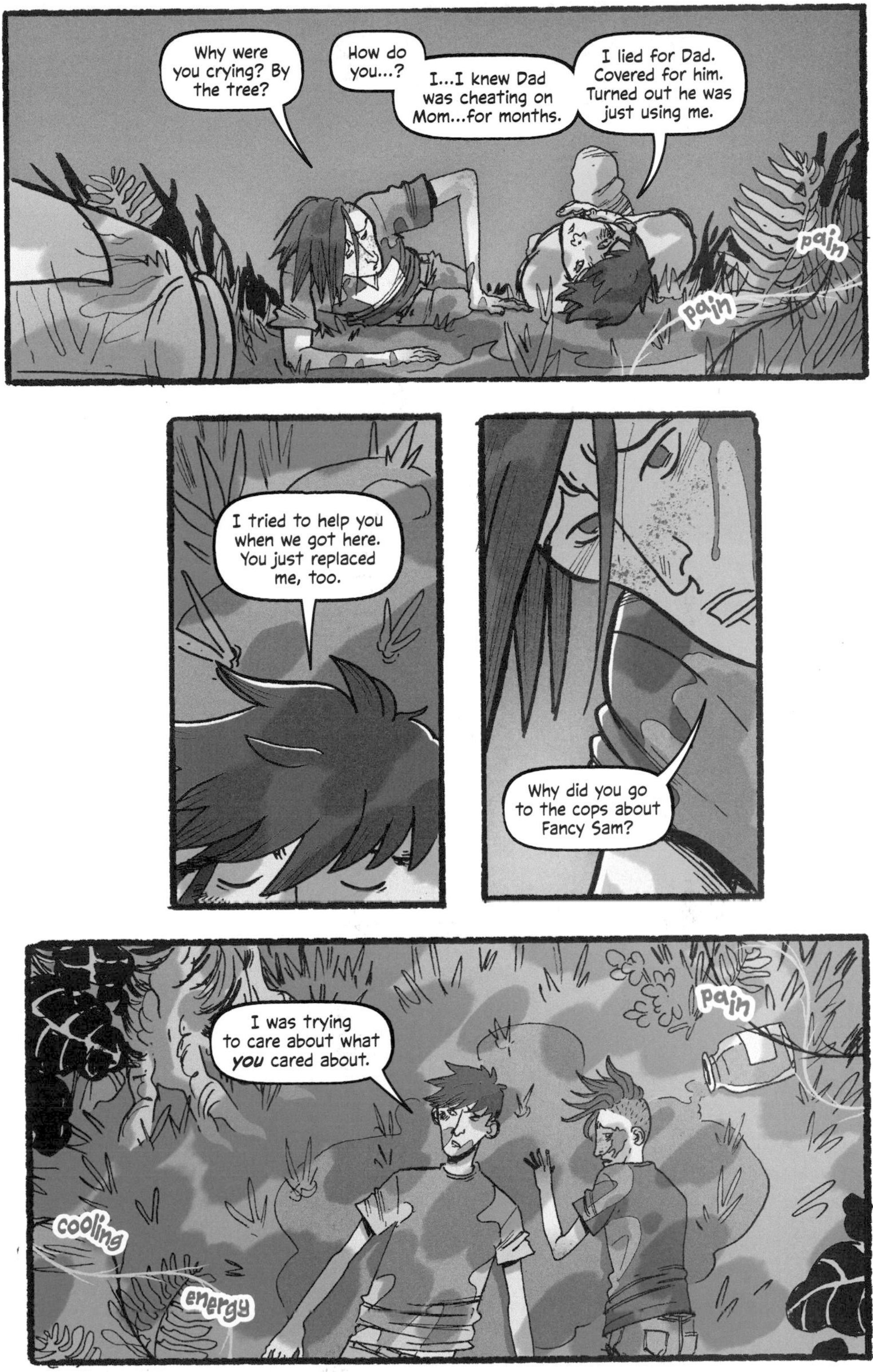
Why were you crying? By the tree?
How do you...?
I...I knew Dad was cheating on Mom...for months.
I lied for Dad. Covered for him. Turned out he was just using me.
pain
pain
I tried to help you when we got here. You just replaced me, too.
Why did you go to the cops about Fancy Sam?
I was trying to care about what *you* cared about.
pain
cooling
energy

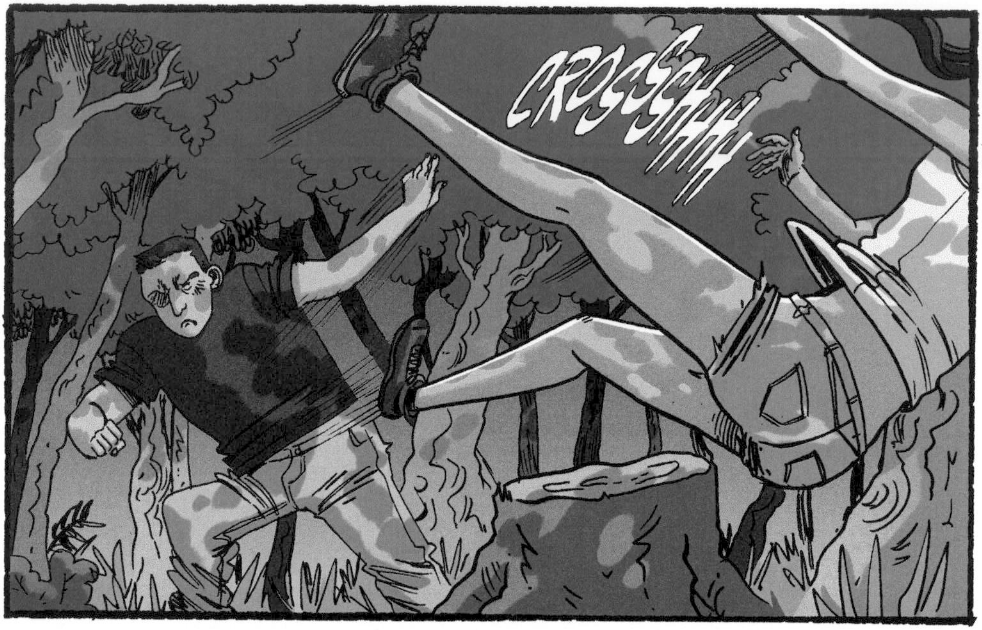
CROSSSHHH

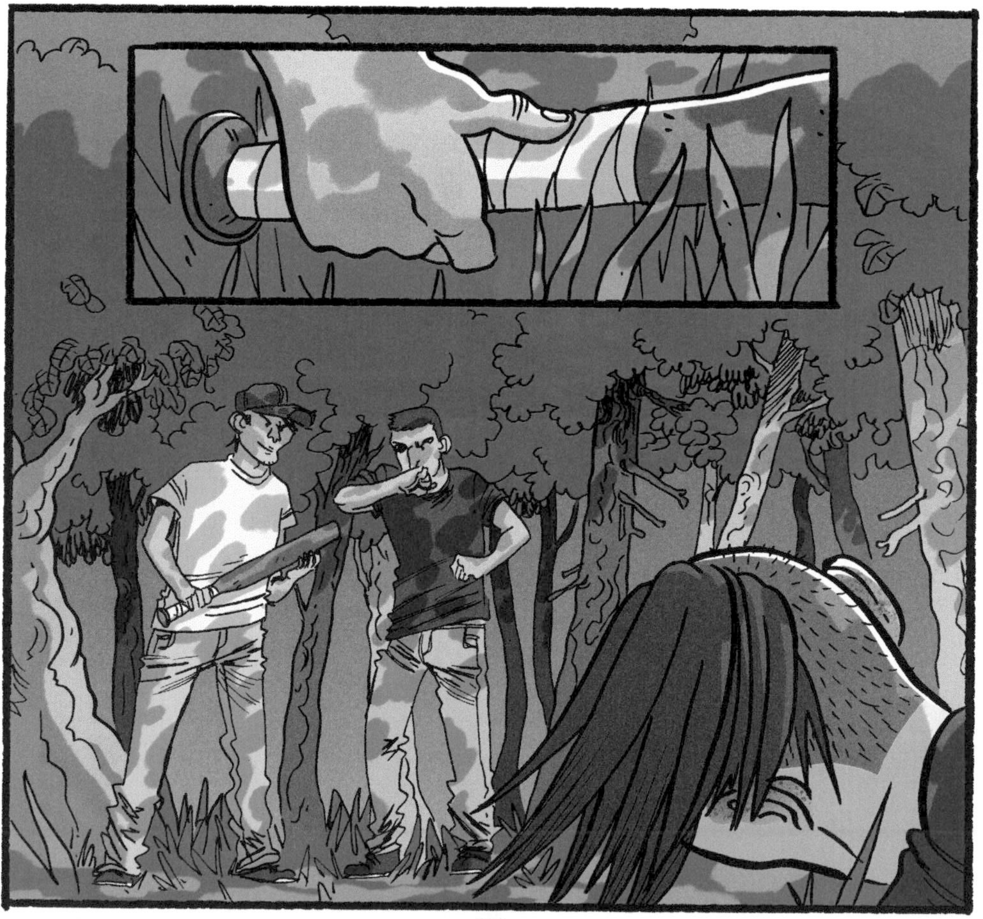

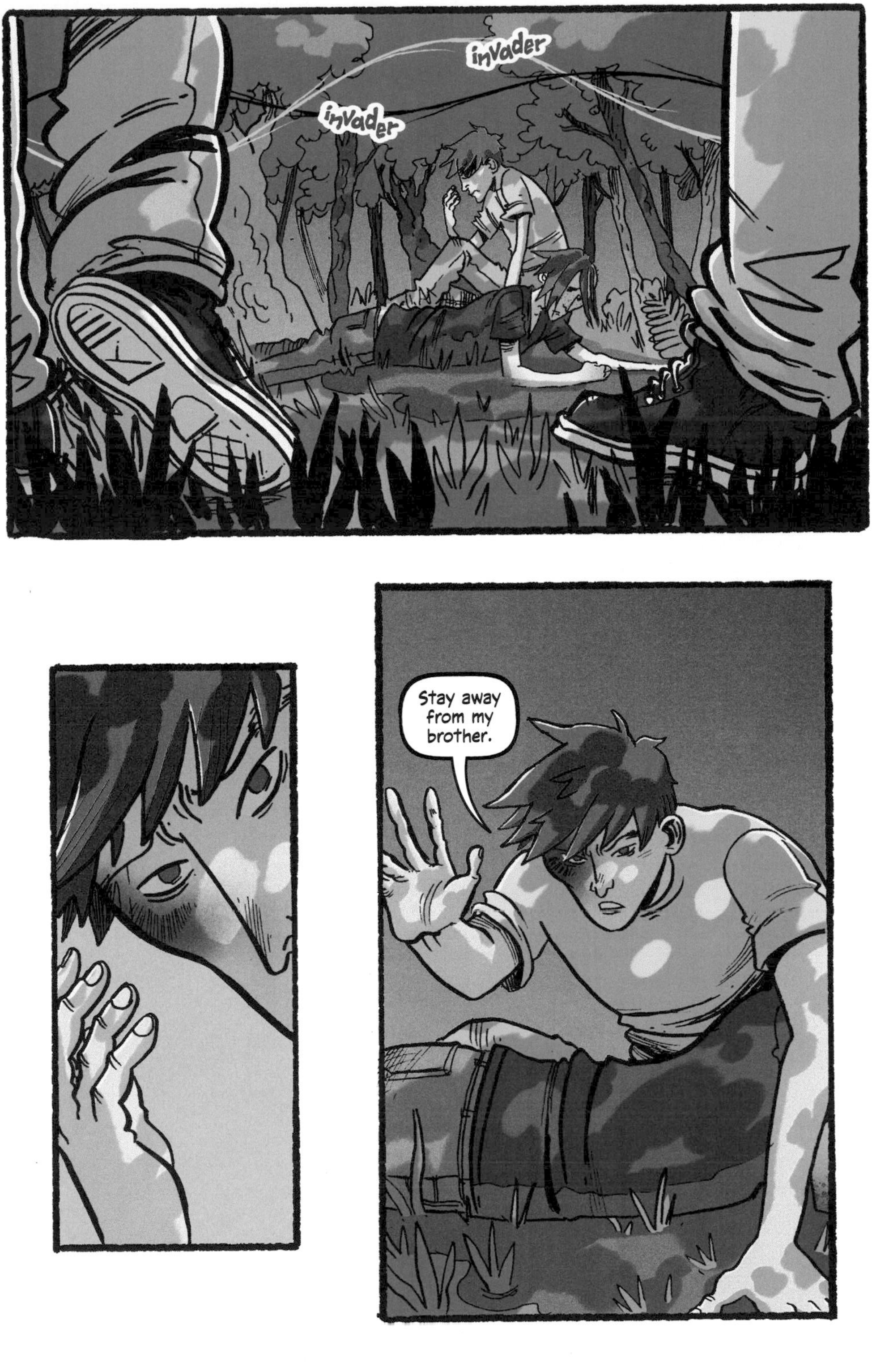
invader
invader
Stay away from my brother.

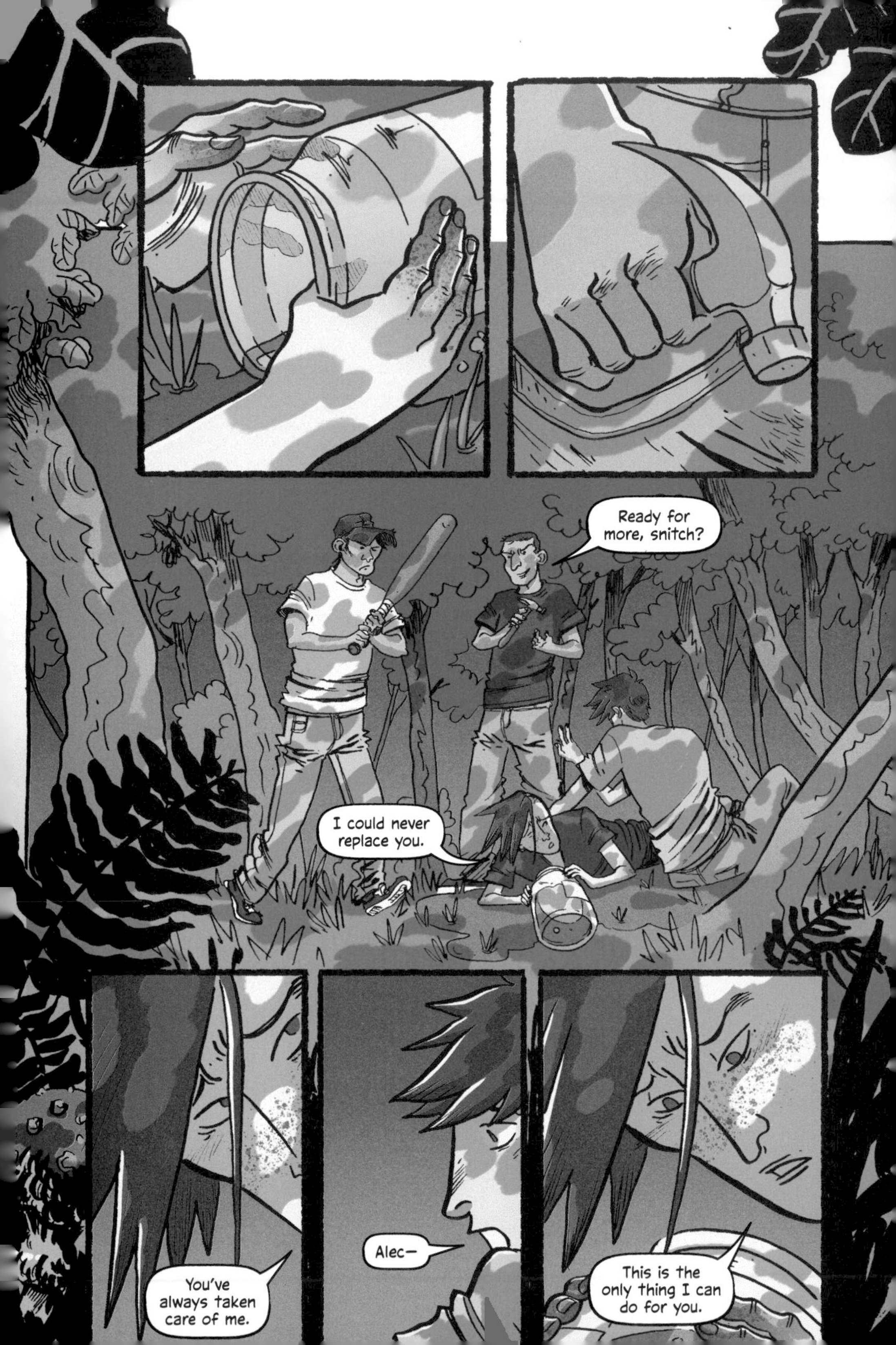
Ready for more, snitch?
I could never replace you.
You've always taken care of me.
Alec—
This is the only thing I can do for you.

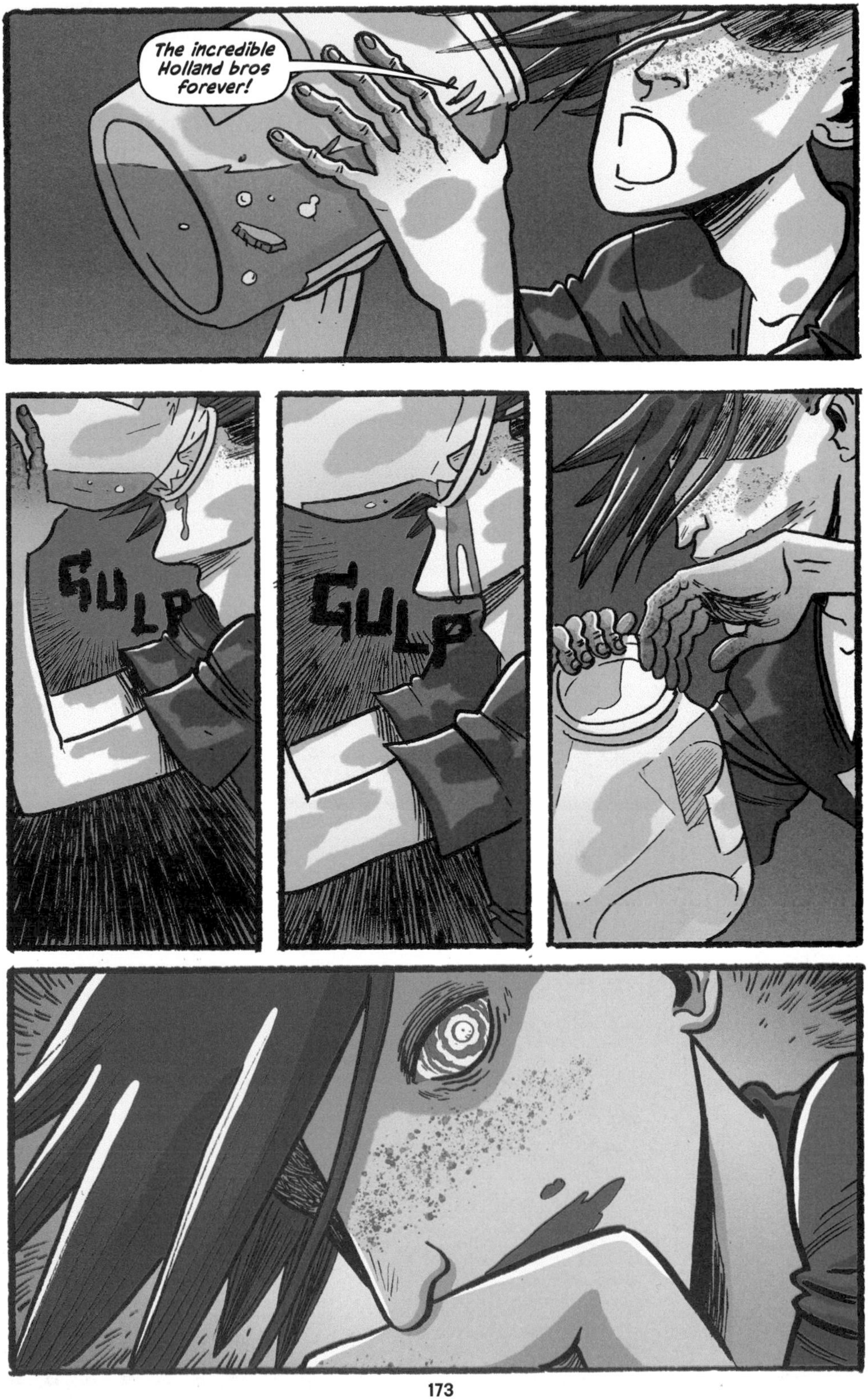
The incredible Holland bros forever!
GULP
GULP

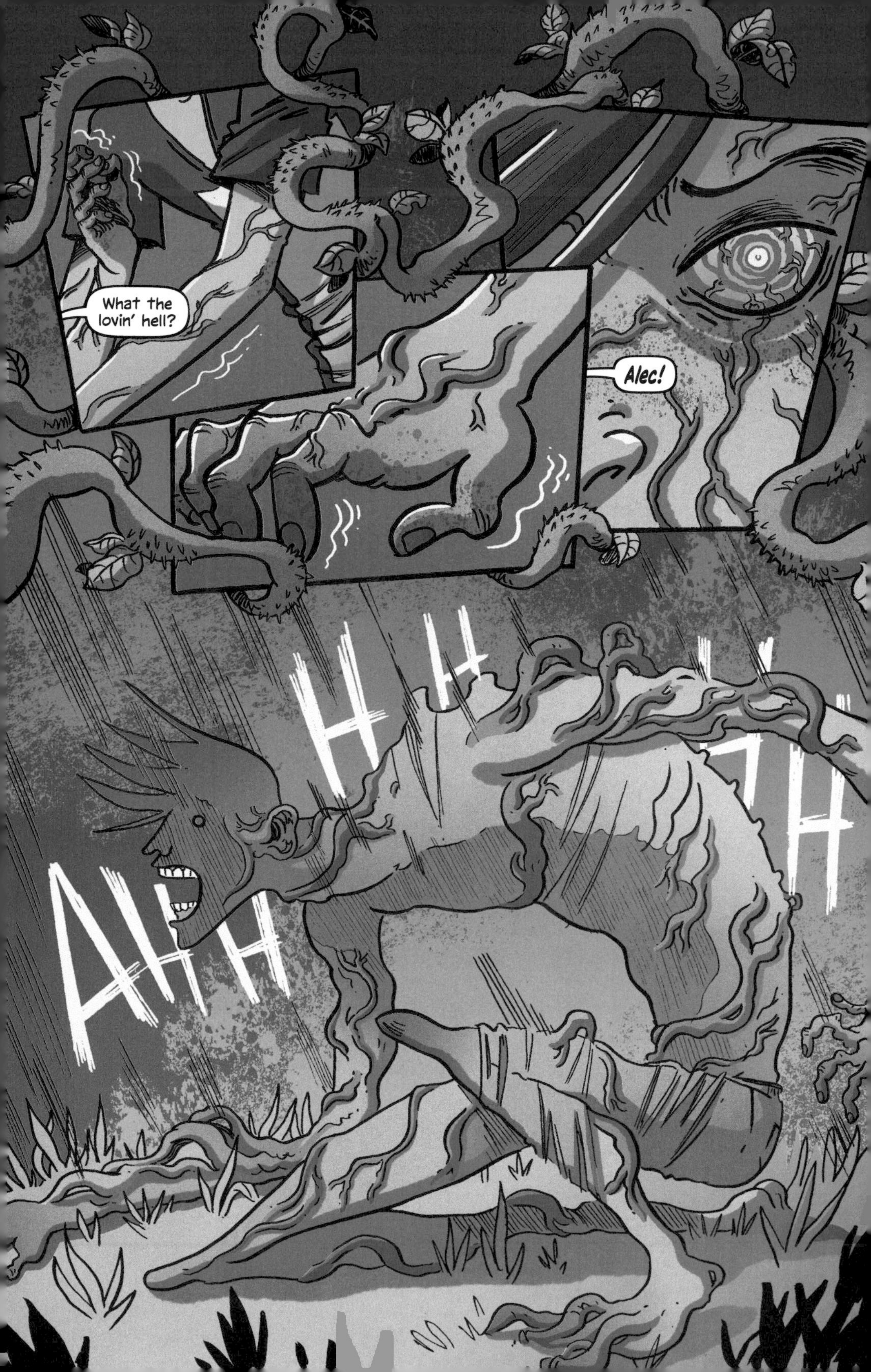
What the lovin' hell?
Alec!
AHHHHHH

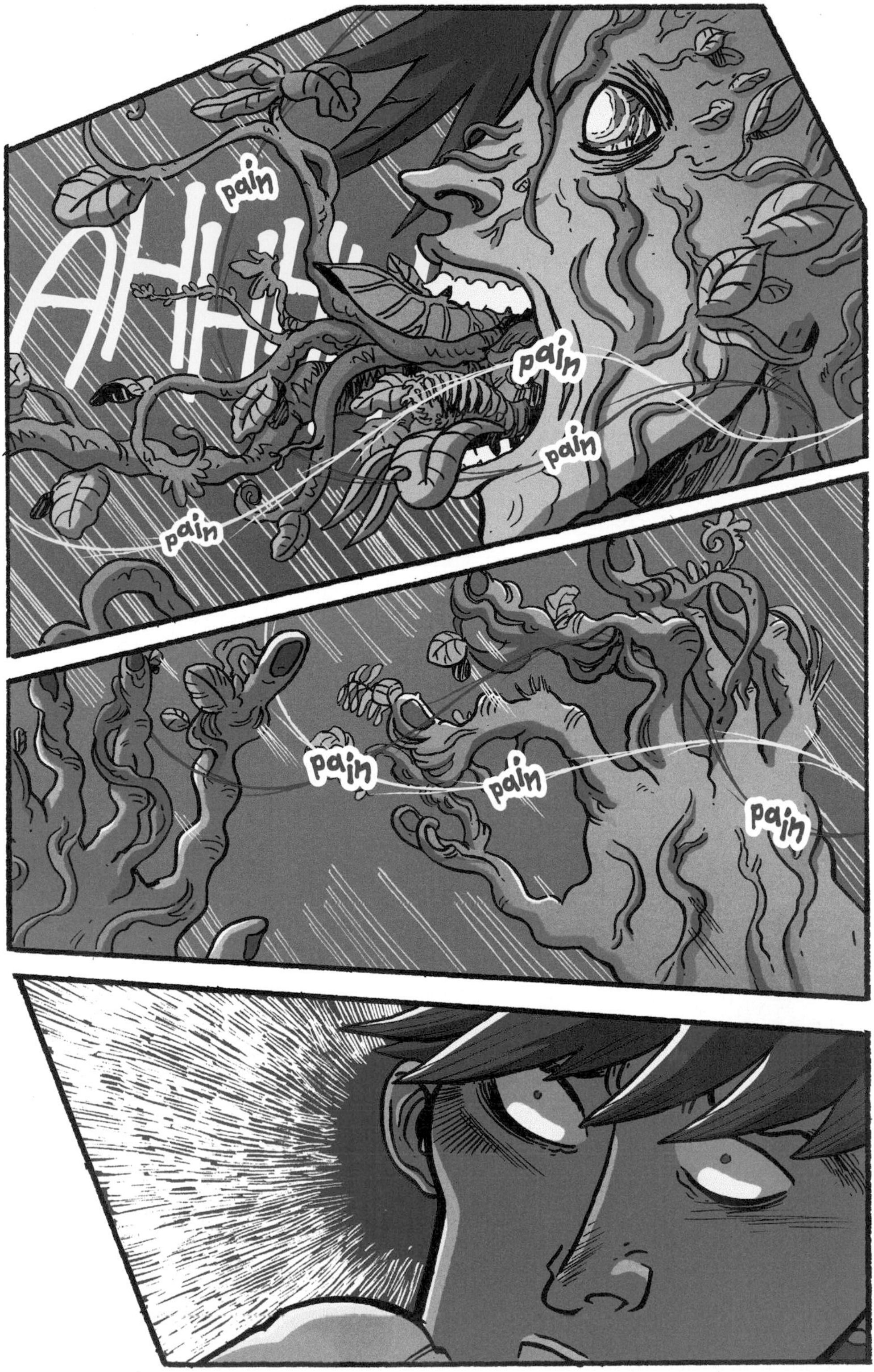
AHH!!
pain
pain
pain
pain
pain
pain
pain

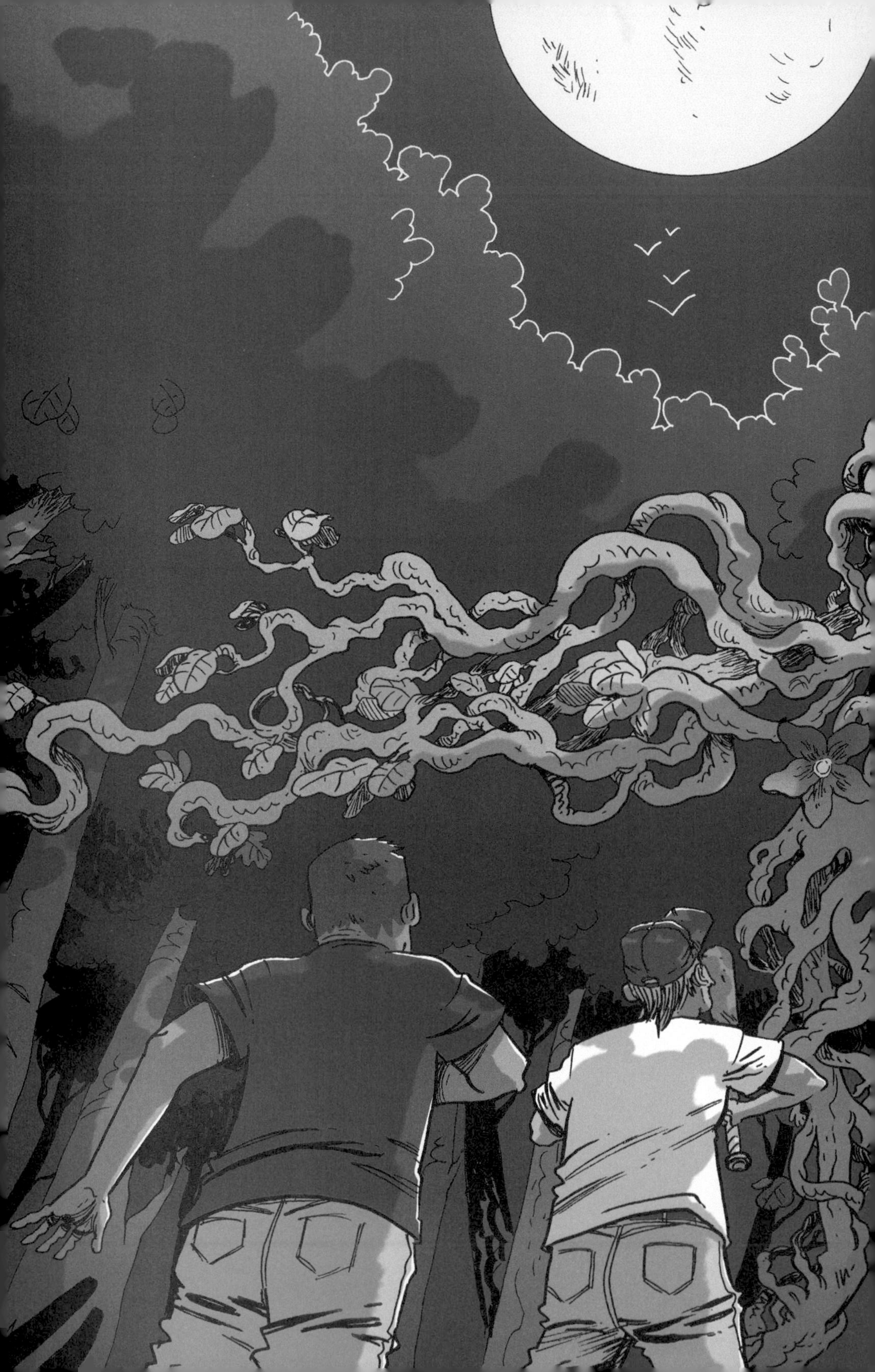

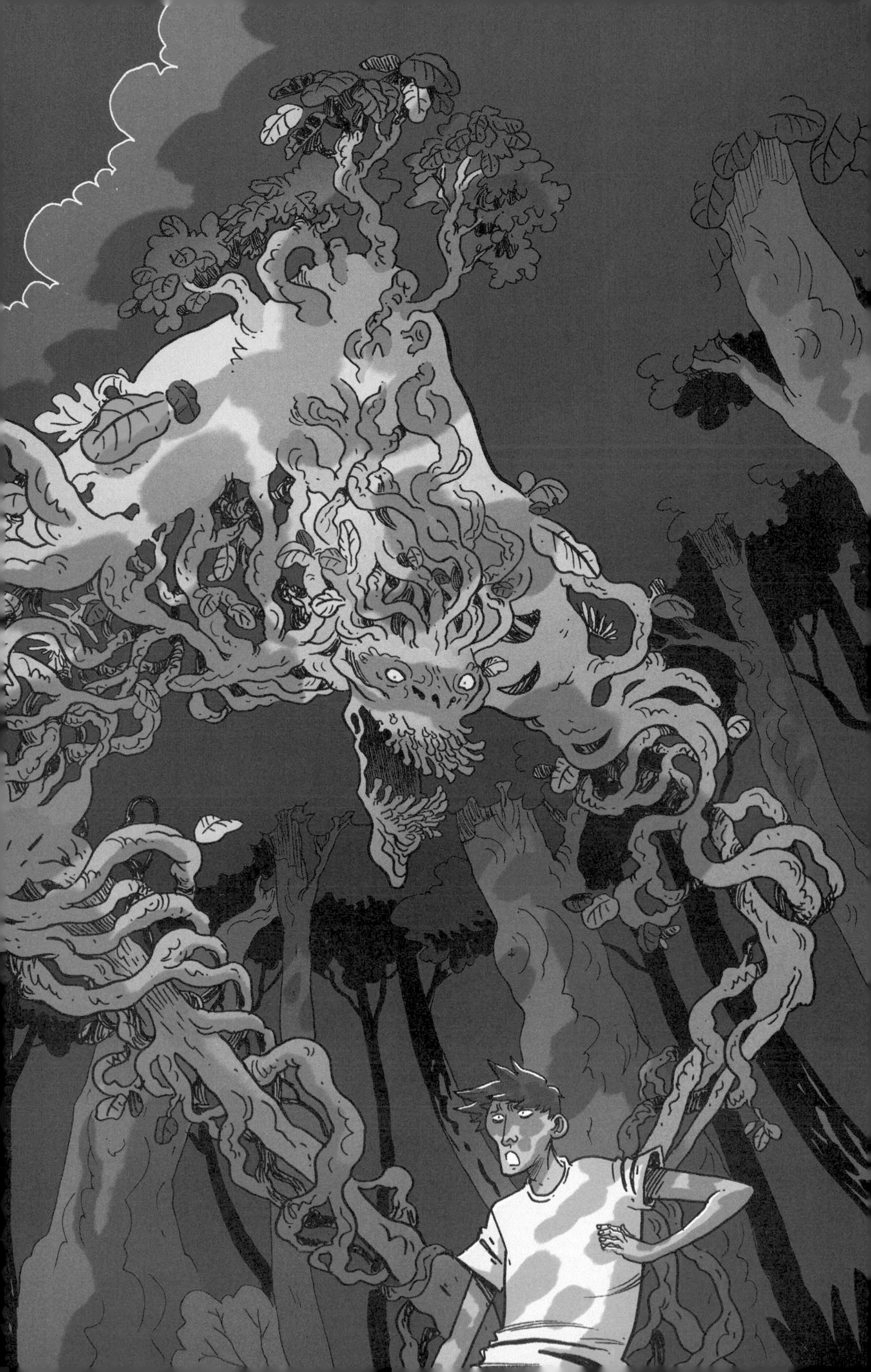

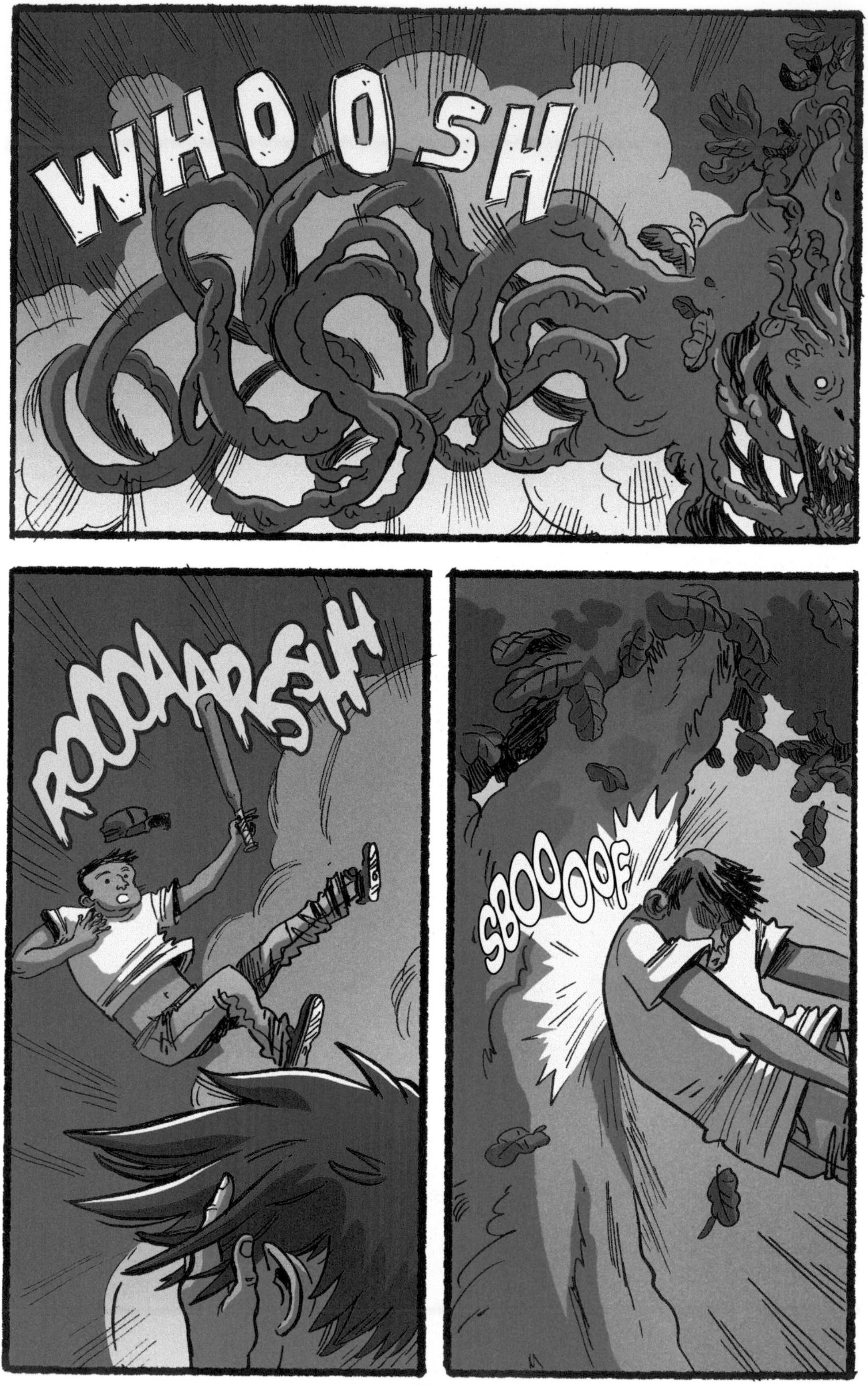
WHOOSH
ROOOAARSH
SBOOOOF

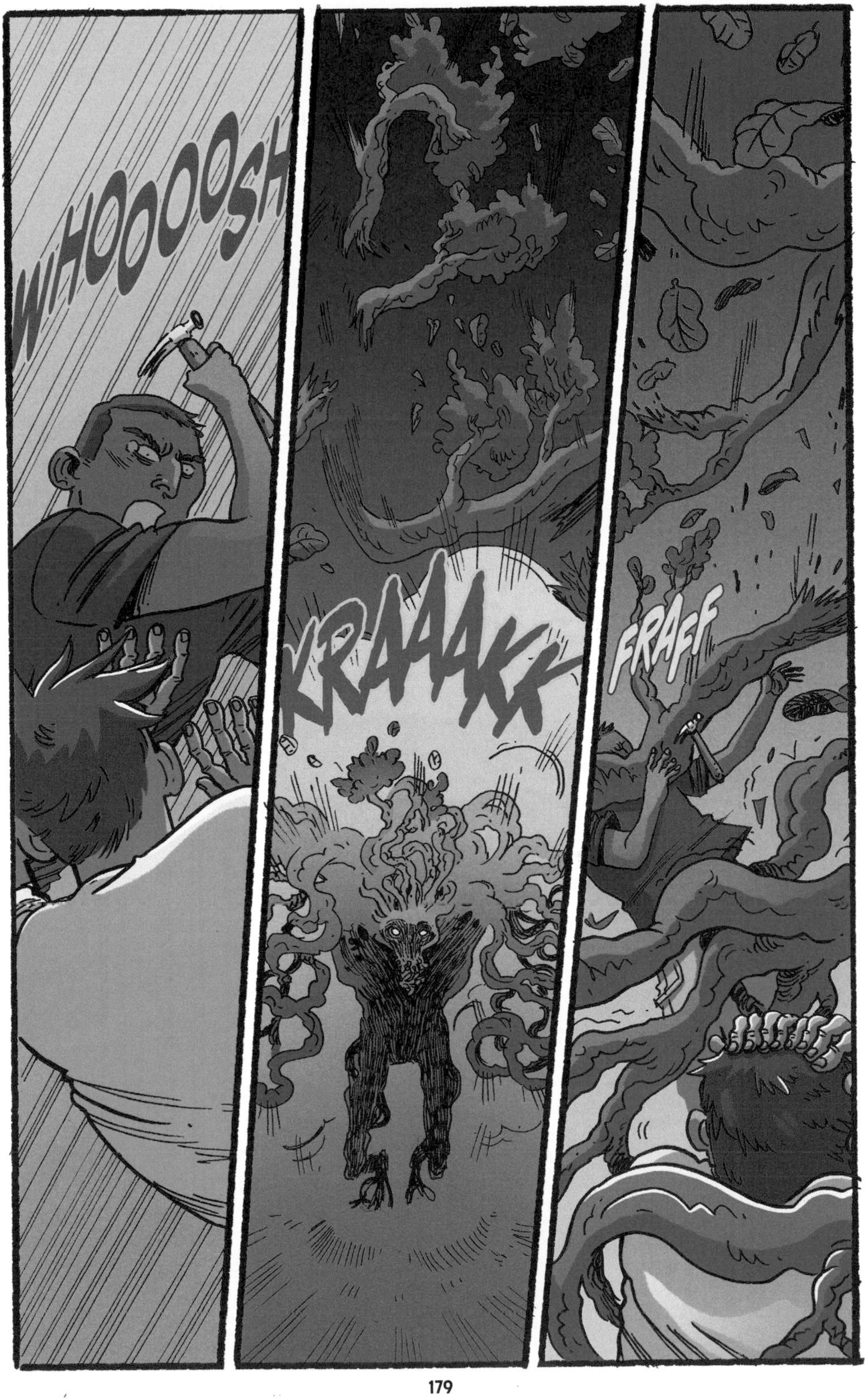
WHOOOOSH
KRAAAKK
FRAFF

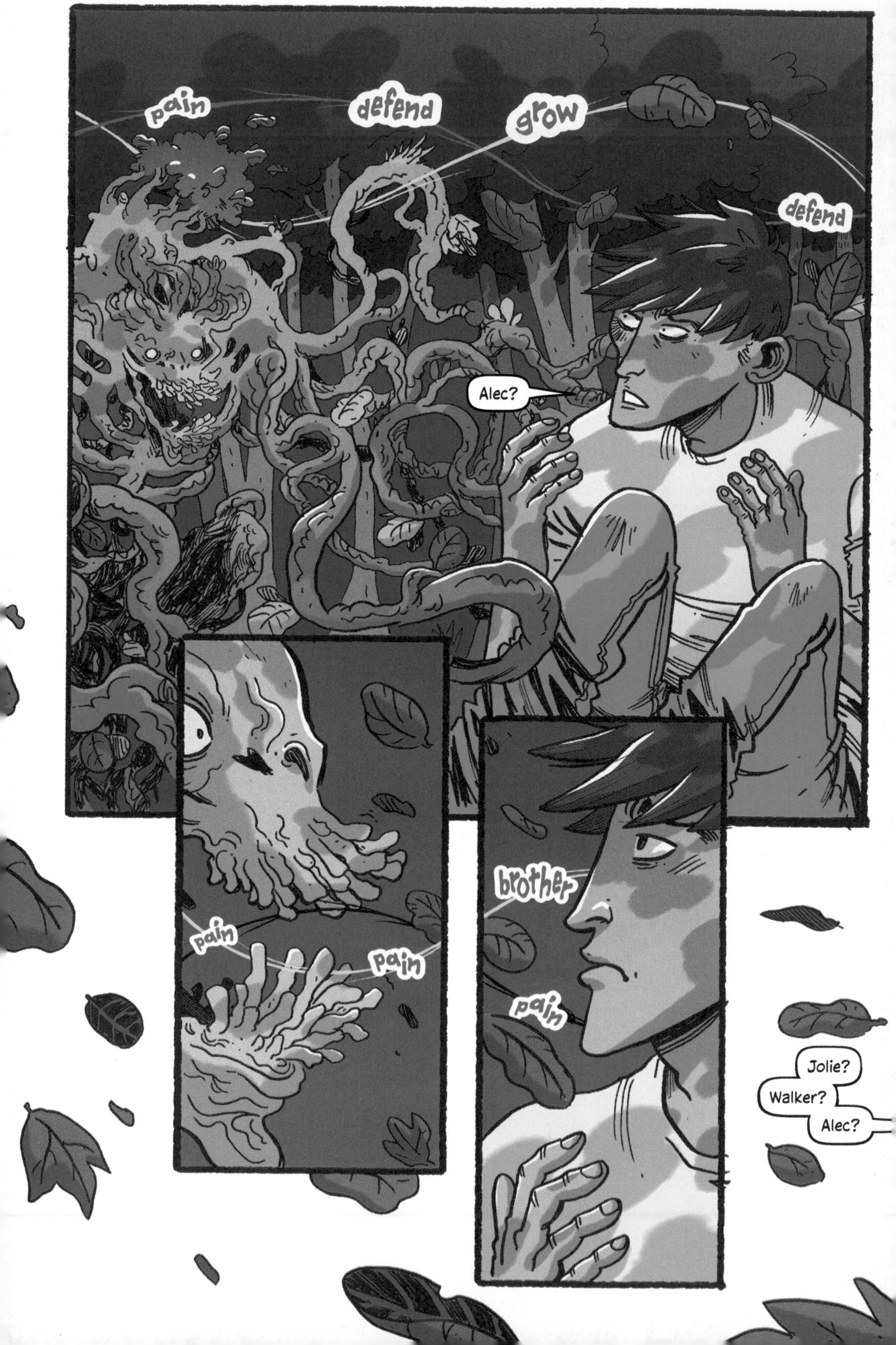
pain
defend
grow
defend
Alec?
pain
pain
brother
pain
Jolie?
Walker?
Alec?

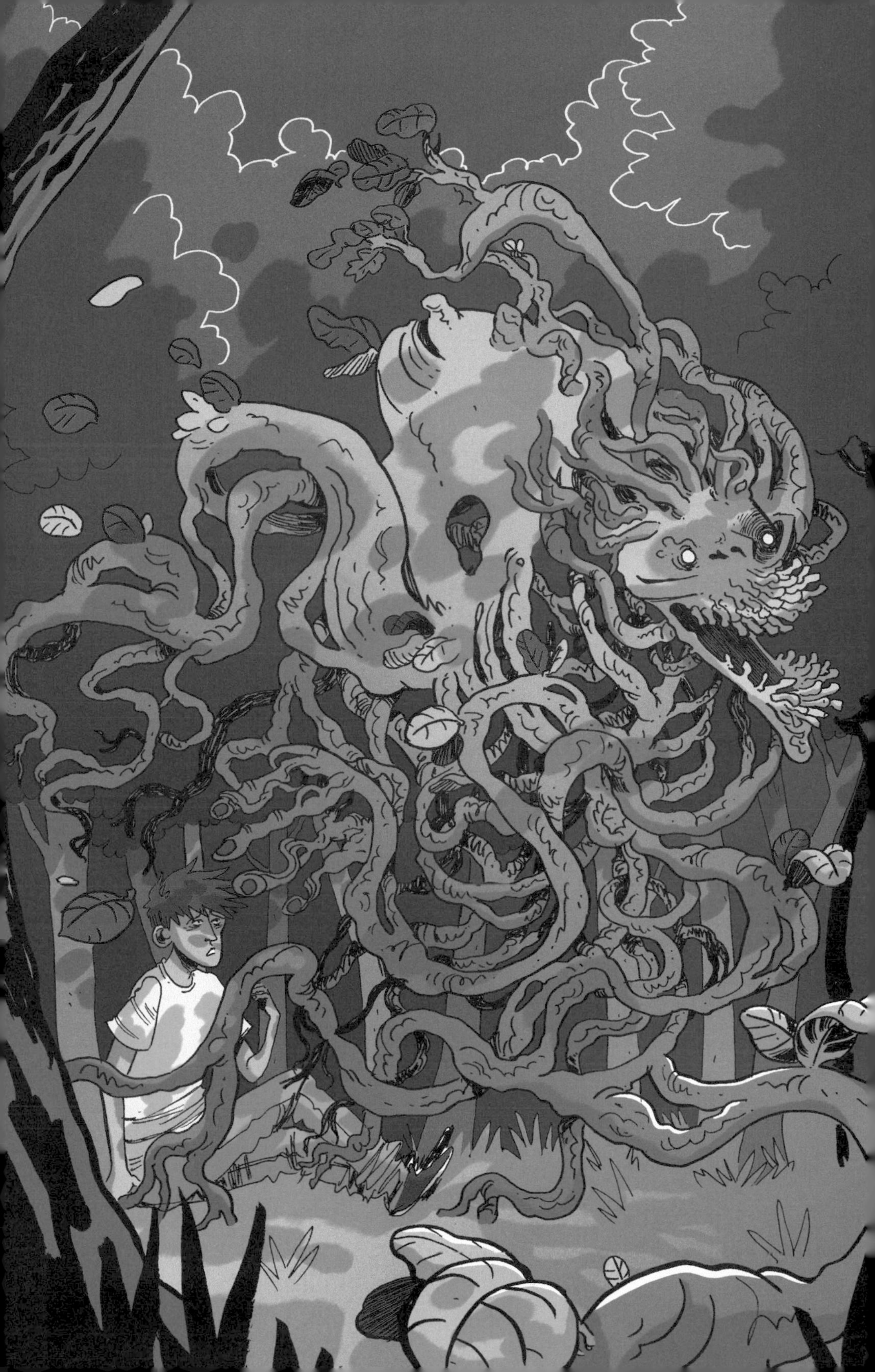

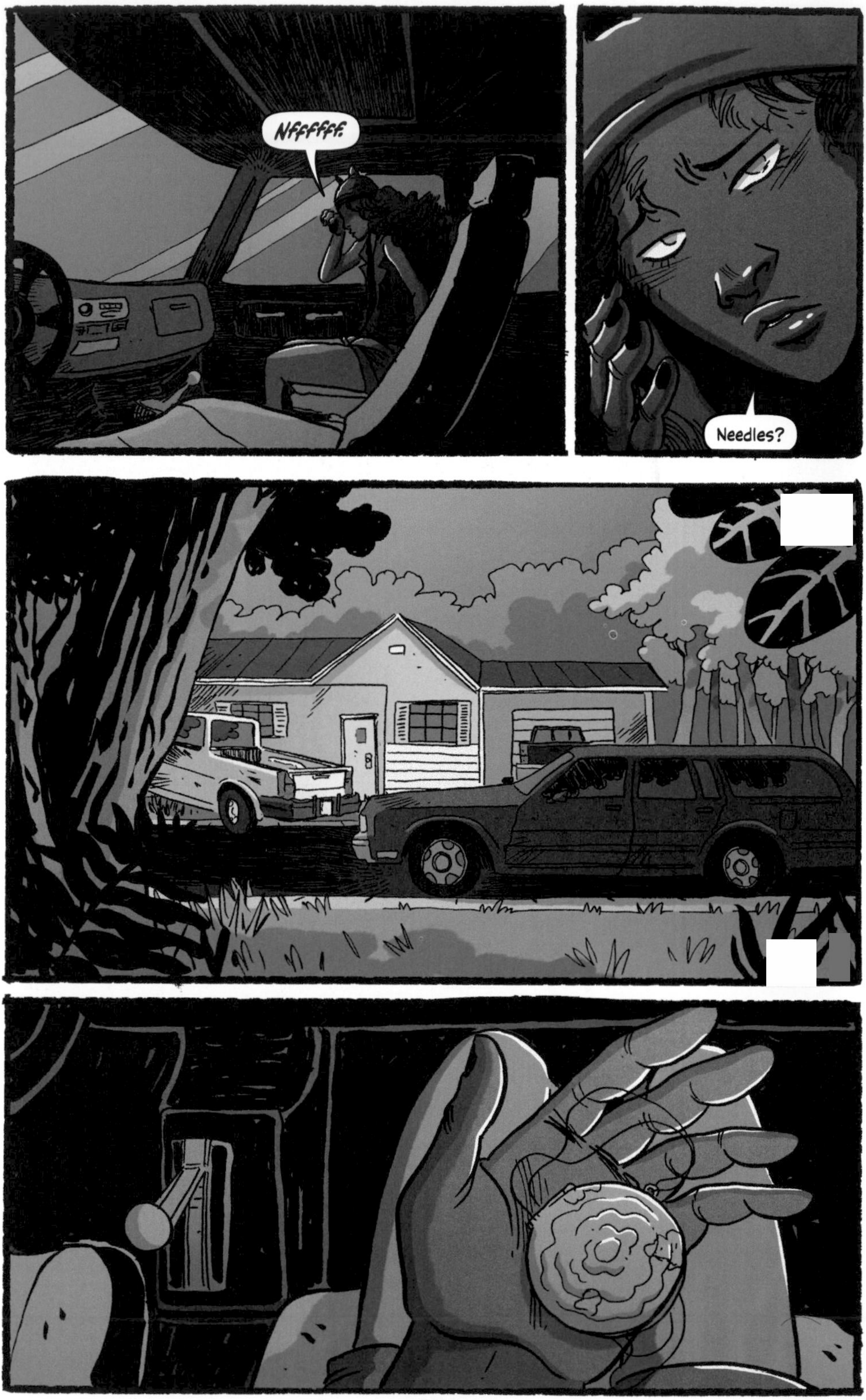
Nffffff.
Needles?

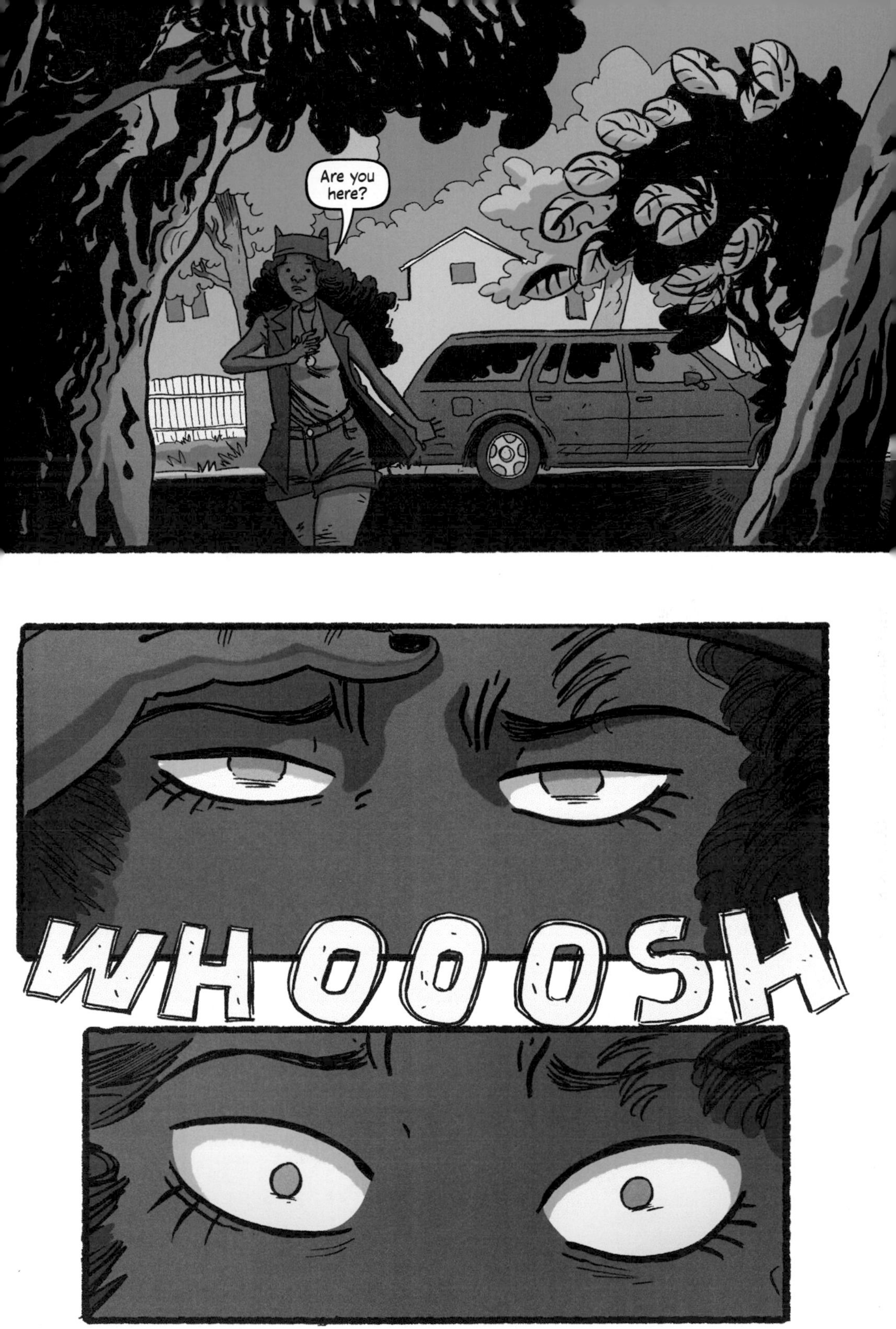
Are you here?
WHOOOSH

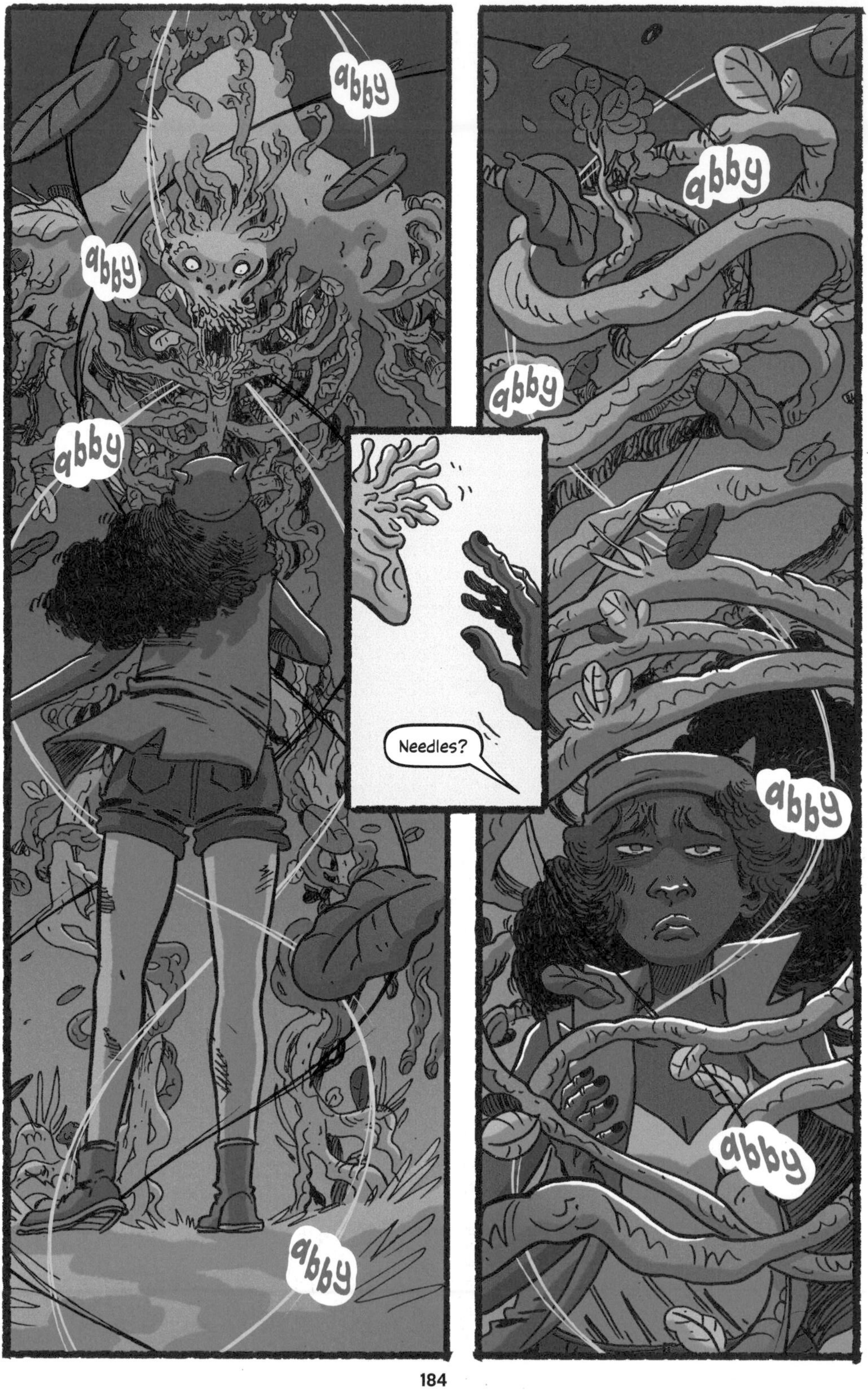
abby
abby
abby
abby
Needles?
abby
abby
abby
abby

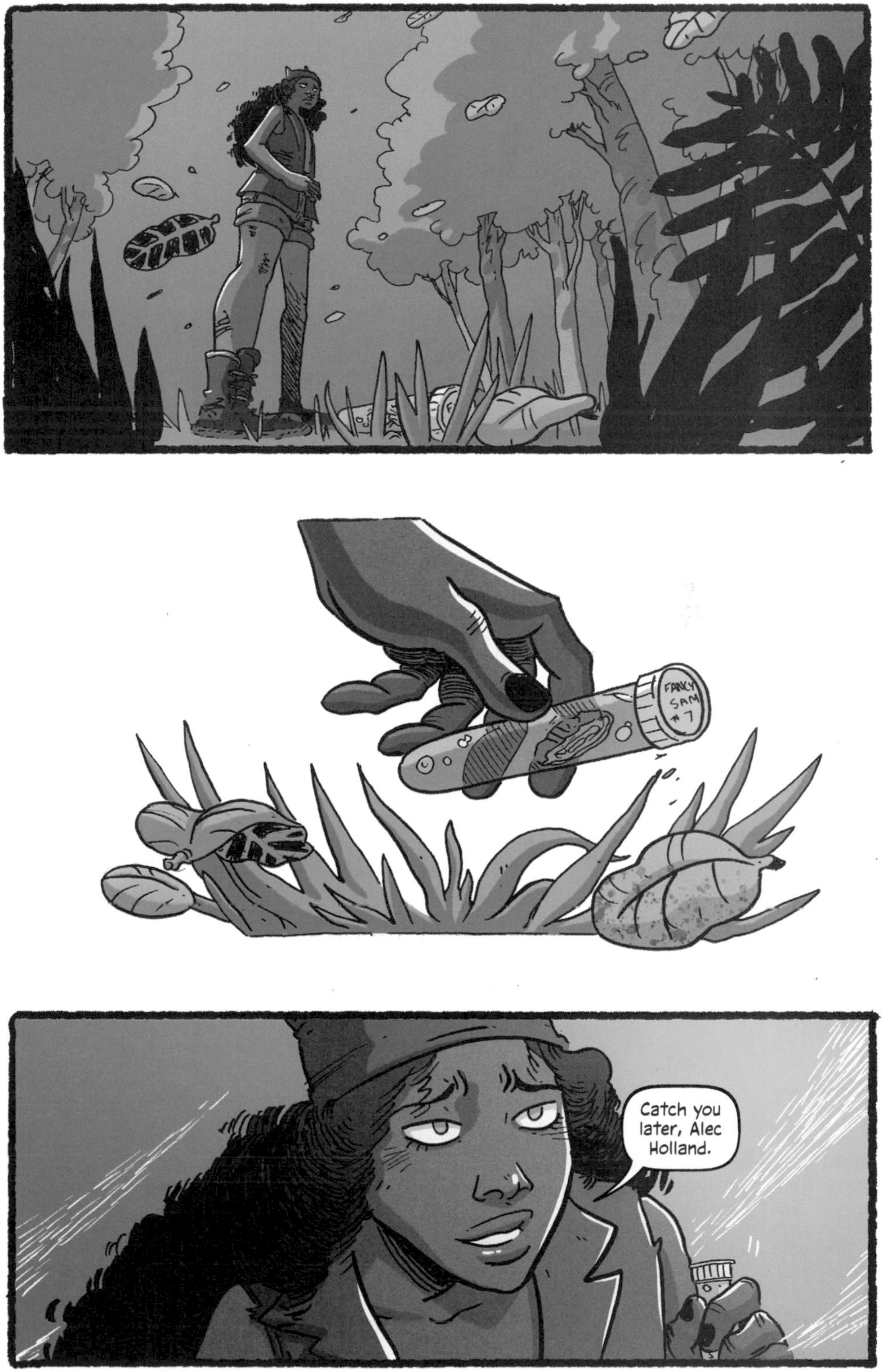
FANCY SAM #7
Catch you later, Alec Holland.

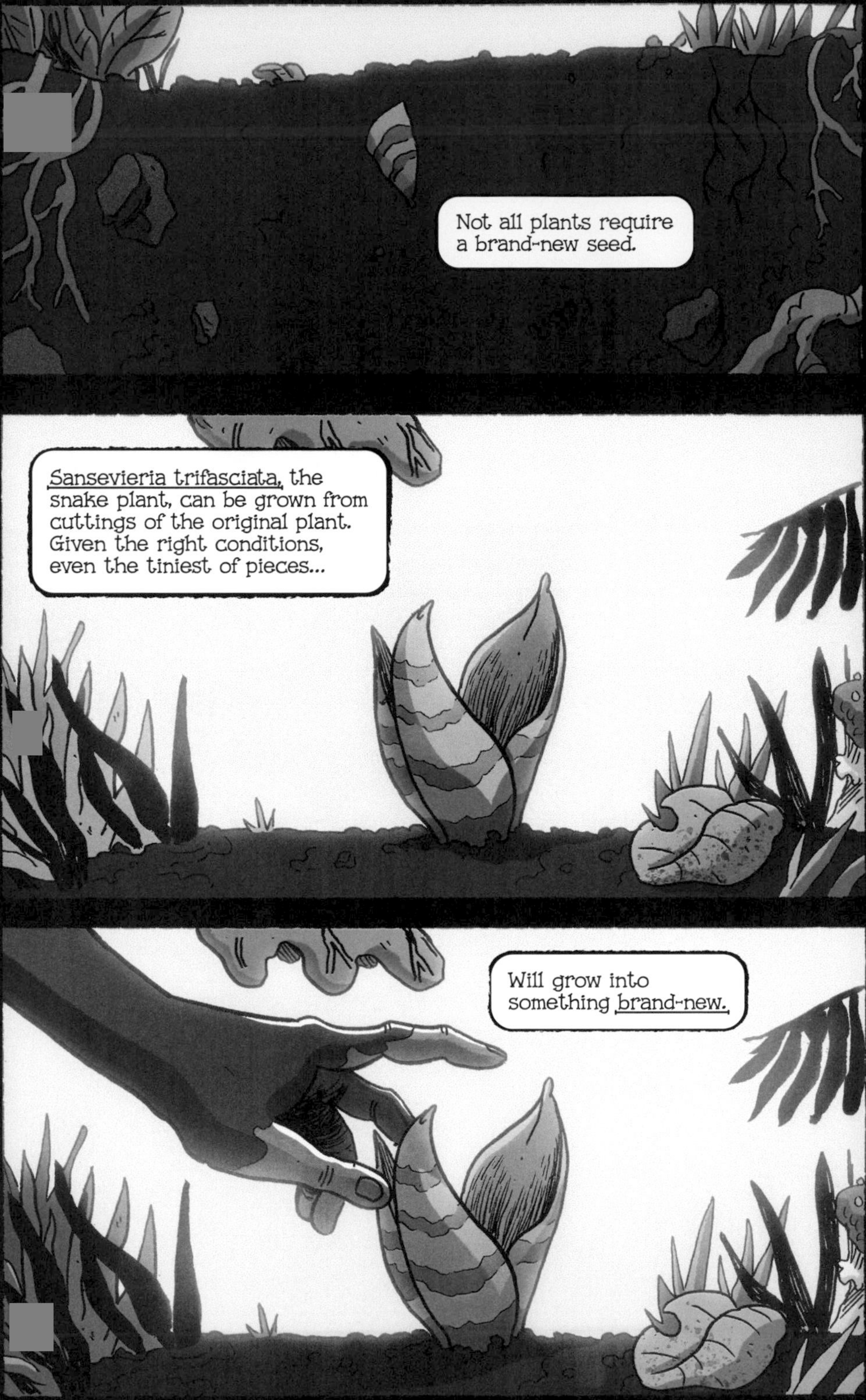
Not all plants require a brand-new seed.
Sansevieria trifasciata, the snake plant, can be grown from cuttings of the original plant. Given the right conditions, even the tiniest of pieces...
Will grow into something brand-new.

Photo by Stephen Voss.

Maggie Stiefvater is the #1 *New York Times* bestselling author of the Raven Cycle series, the Shiver trilogy, and other novels for young people and adults. She is also an artist, an auto enthusiast, and a bagpiper. She lives on a farm in the Shenandoah Valley with her husband, her two children, and an assortment of fainting goats. Find her online at www.maggiestiefvater.com.

Morgan Beem is a freelance artist and member of the Jam House collective located in Denver, Colorado. Her work is predominantly in comics and illustration. She has worked on such properties as *Adventure Time*, *Planet of the Apes*, and *Buffy the Vampire Slayer* and is the co-creator, alongside writers Justin Jordan and Nikki Ryan, of the series *The Family Trade* from Image Comics.

Photo by Lauren Assour.

Zahn is one of Krypton's elites: wealthy, privileged, a future leader. Sera is one of Krypton's soldiers: strong, dedicated, fearless. But despite society's drive to keep them apart, their paths will cross in their attempt to investigate the dangers truly threatening Krypton.

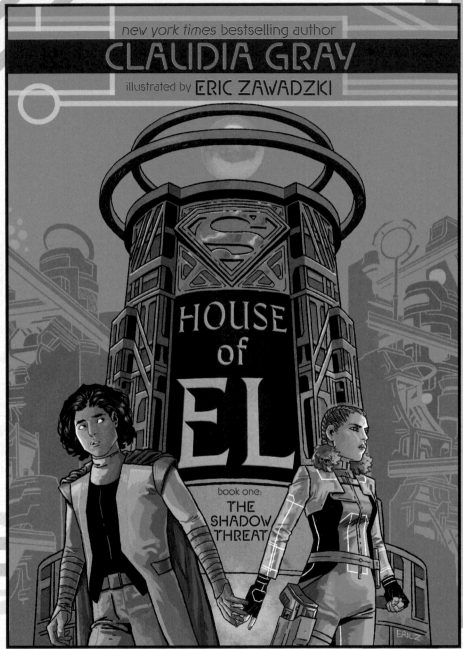

New York Times bestselling author *Claudia Gray* and illustrator *Eric Zawadzki* present a new vision of one of comics' most famous tragedies.

Keep reading for a sneak peek of *House of El Book One: The Shadow Threat!*

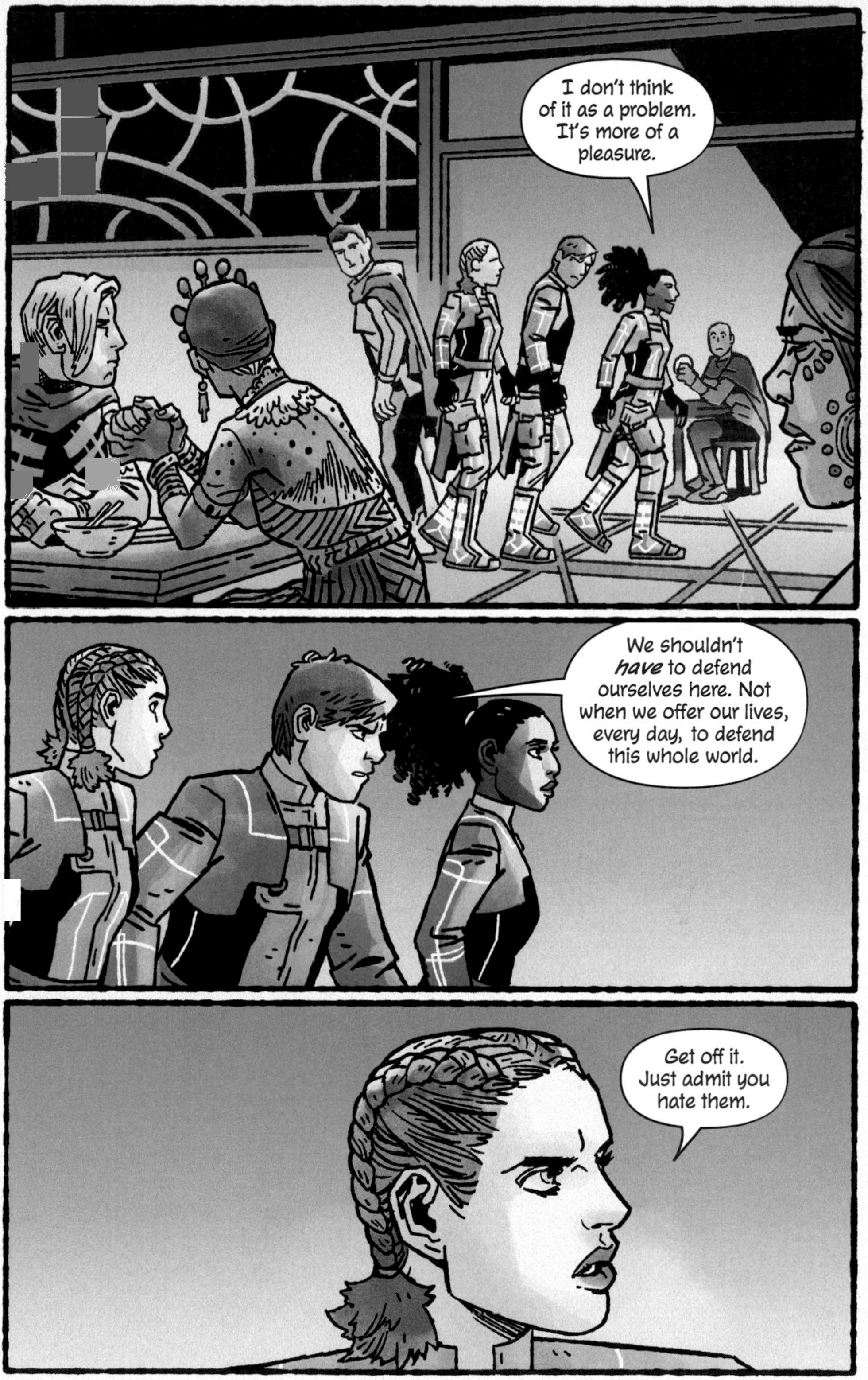
I don't think of it as a problem. It's more of a pleasure.
We shouldn't *have* to defend ourselves here. Not when we offer our lives, every day, to defend this whole world.
Get off it. Just admit you hate them.

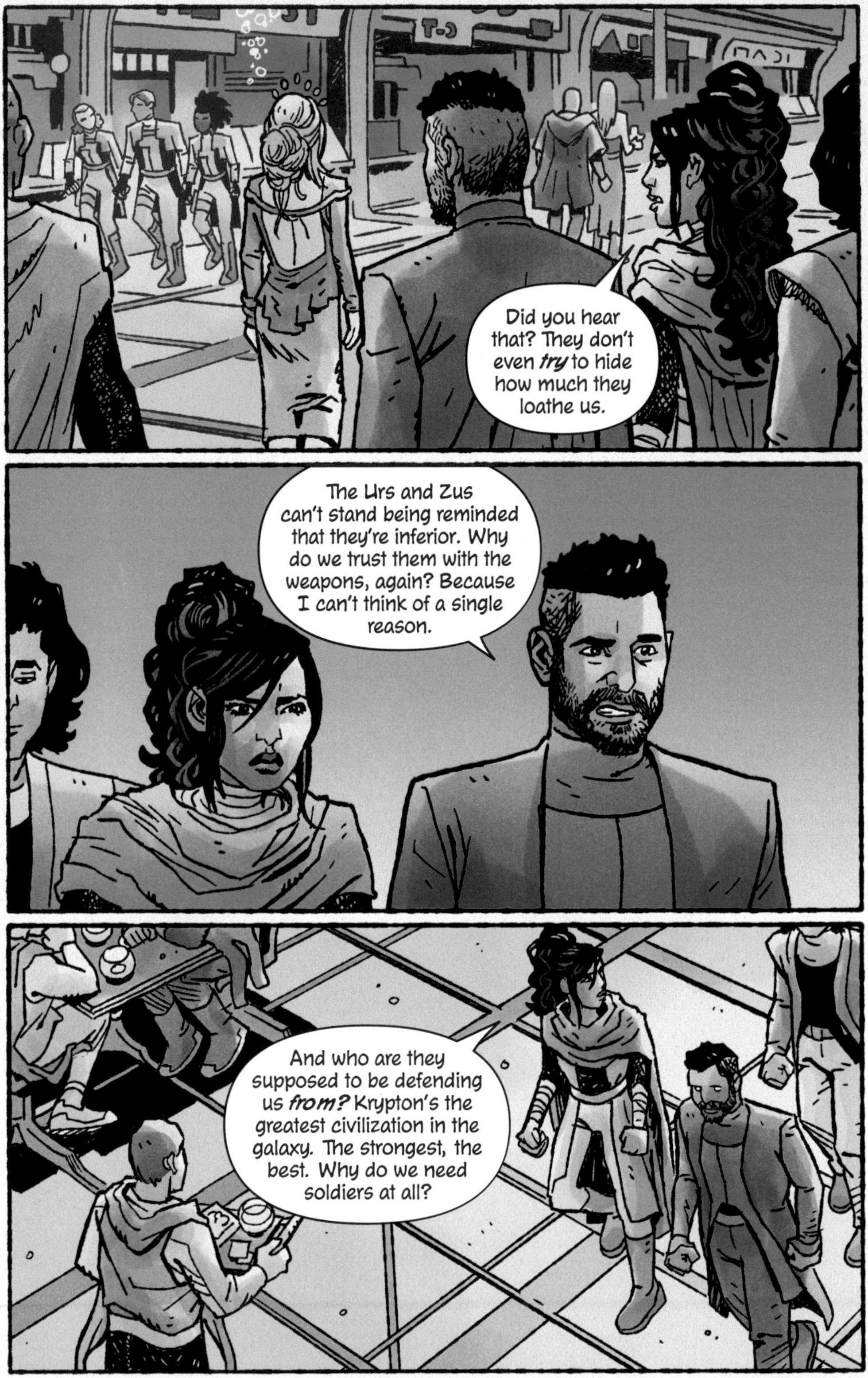

Did you hear that? They don't even *try* to hide how much they loathe us.
The Urs and Zus can't stand being reminded that they're inferior. Why do we trust them with the weapons, again? Because I can't think of a single reason.
And who are they supposed to be defending us *from?* Krypton's the greatest civilization in the galaxy. The strongest, the best. Why do we need soldiers at all?

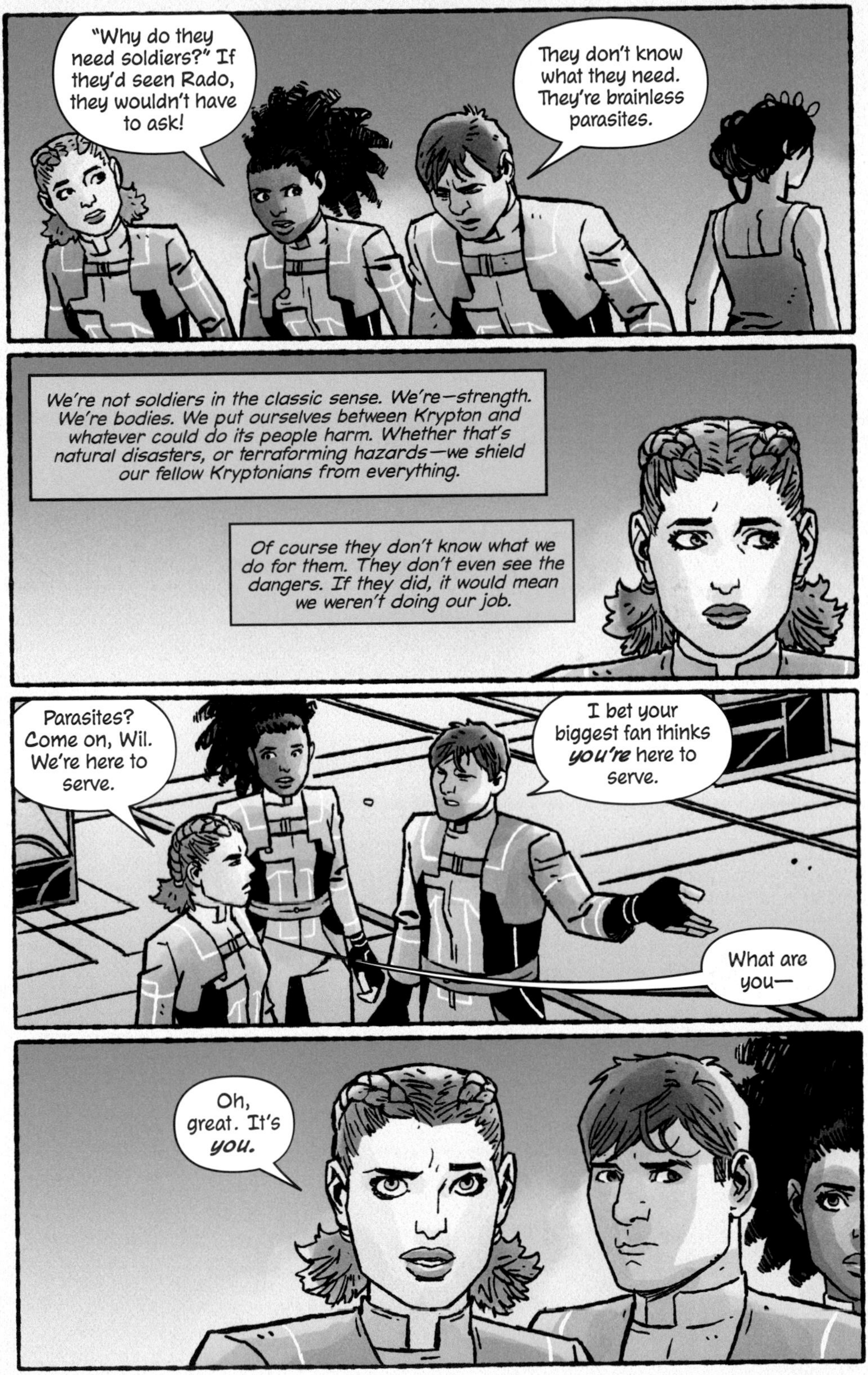
"Why do they need soldiers?" If they'd seen Rado, they wouldn't have to ask!
They don't know what they need. They're brainless parasites.
We're not soldiers in the classic sense. We're—strength. We're bodies. We put ourselves between Krypton and whatever could do its people harm. Whether that's natural disasters, or terraforming hazards—we shield our fellow Kryptonians from everything.
Of course they don't know what we do for them. They don't even see the dangers. If they did, it would mean we weren't doing our job.
Parasites? Come on, Wil. We're here to serve.
I bet your biggest fan thinks *you're* here to serve.
What are you—
Oh, great. It's *you*.

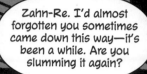
Zahn-Re. I'd almost forgotten you sometimes came down this way—it's been a while. Are you slumming it again?

This place sells the greatest vella leaves on the planet, Sera. I wouldn't call that "slumming it." Just—seeking out the best.

Not as shocking as an Ur with taste.

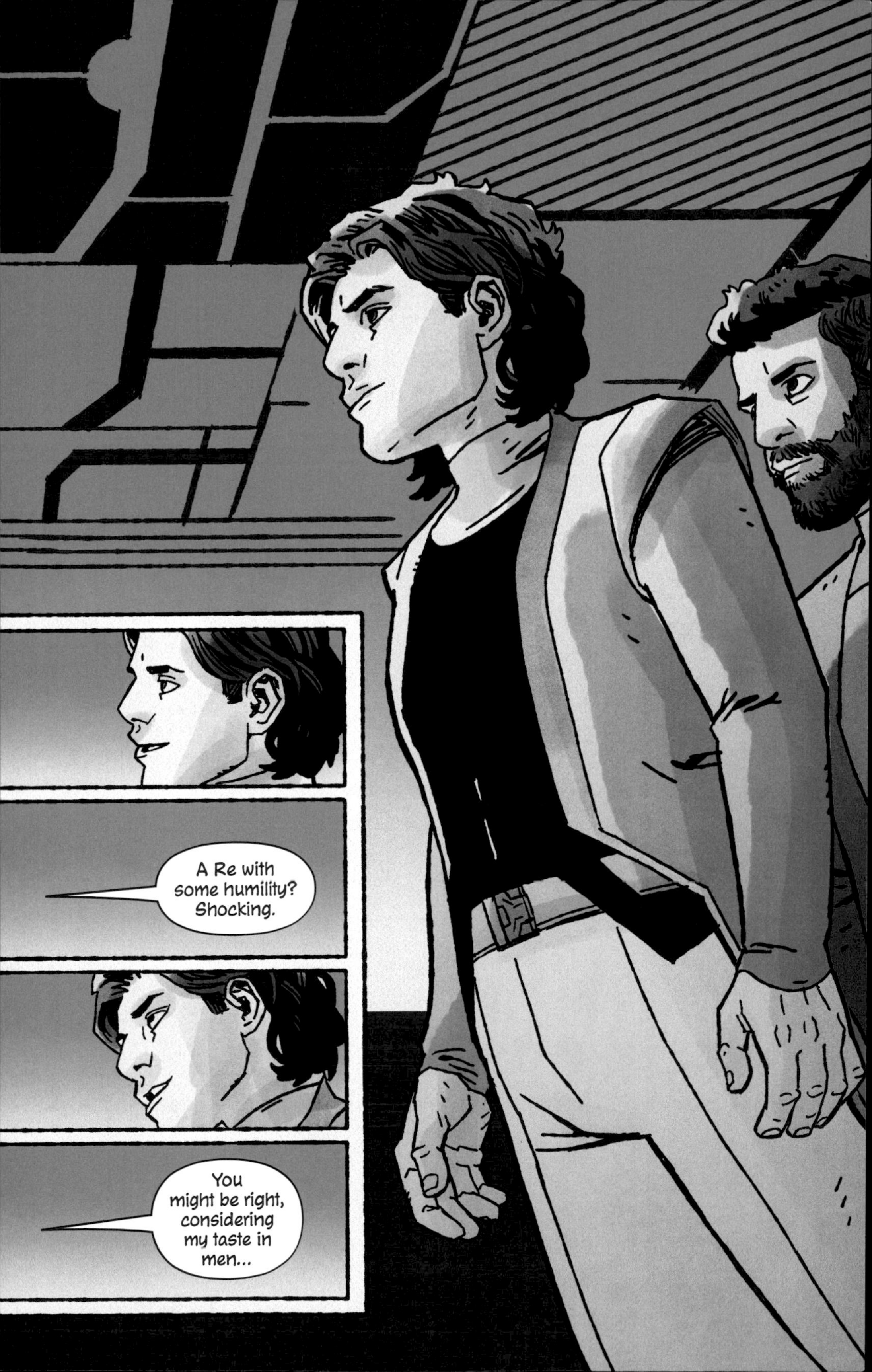
A Re with some humility? Shocking.
You might be right, considering my taste in men...

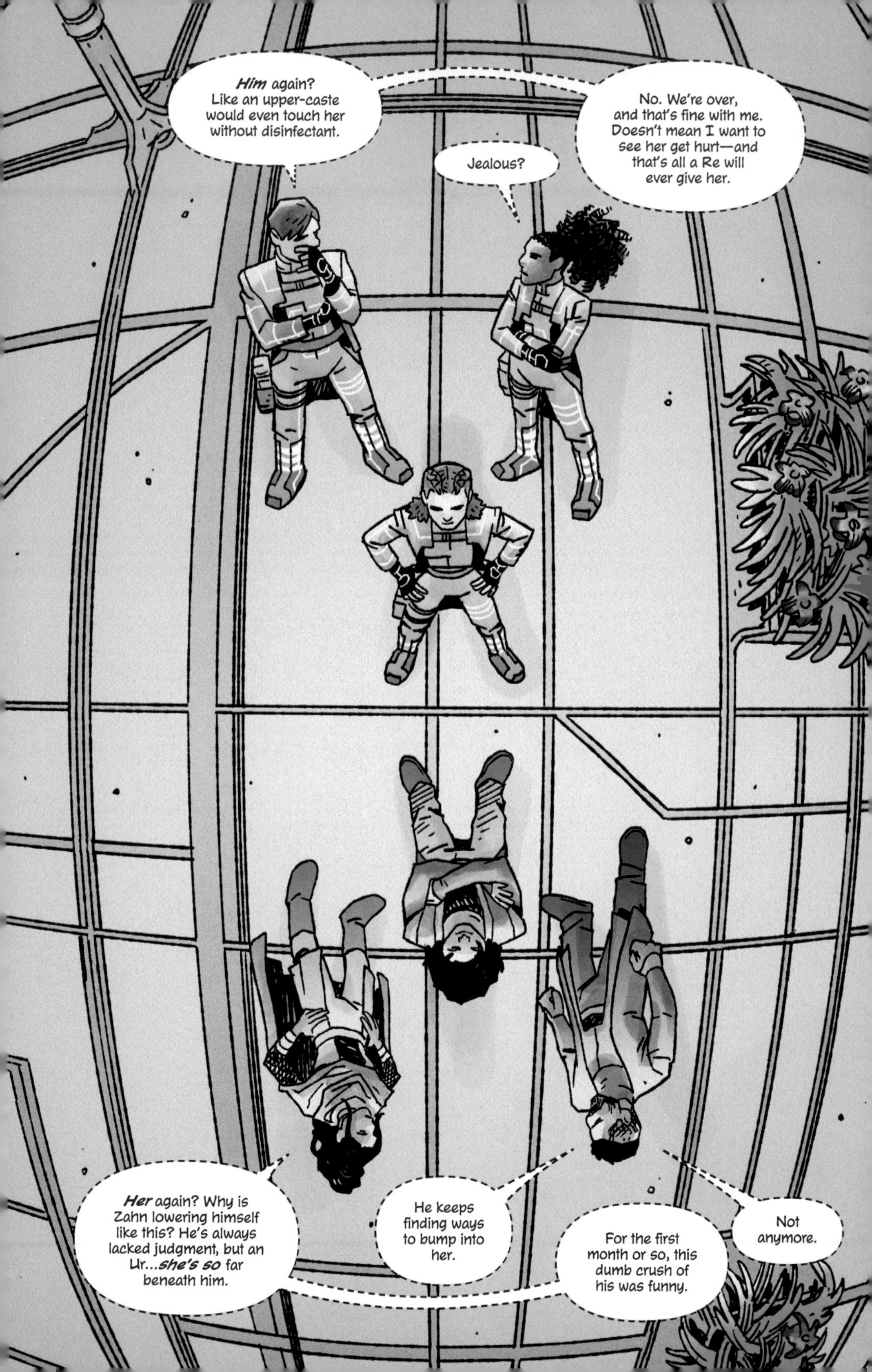
Him again? Like an upper-caste would even touch her without disinfectant.
Jealous?
No. We're over, and that's fine with me. Doesn't mean I want to see her get hurt—and that's all a Re will ever give her.
Her again? Why is Zahn lowering himself like this? He's always lacked judgment, but an Ur...*she's so* far beneath him.
He keeps finding ways to bump into her.
For the first month or so, this dumb crush of his was funny.
Not anymore.

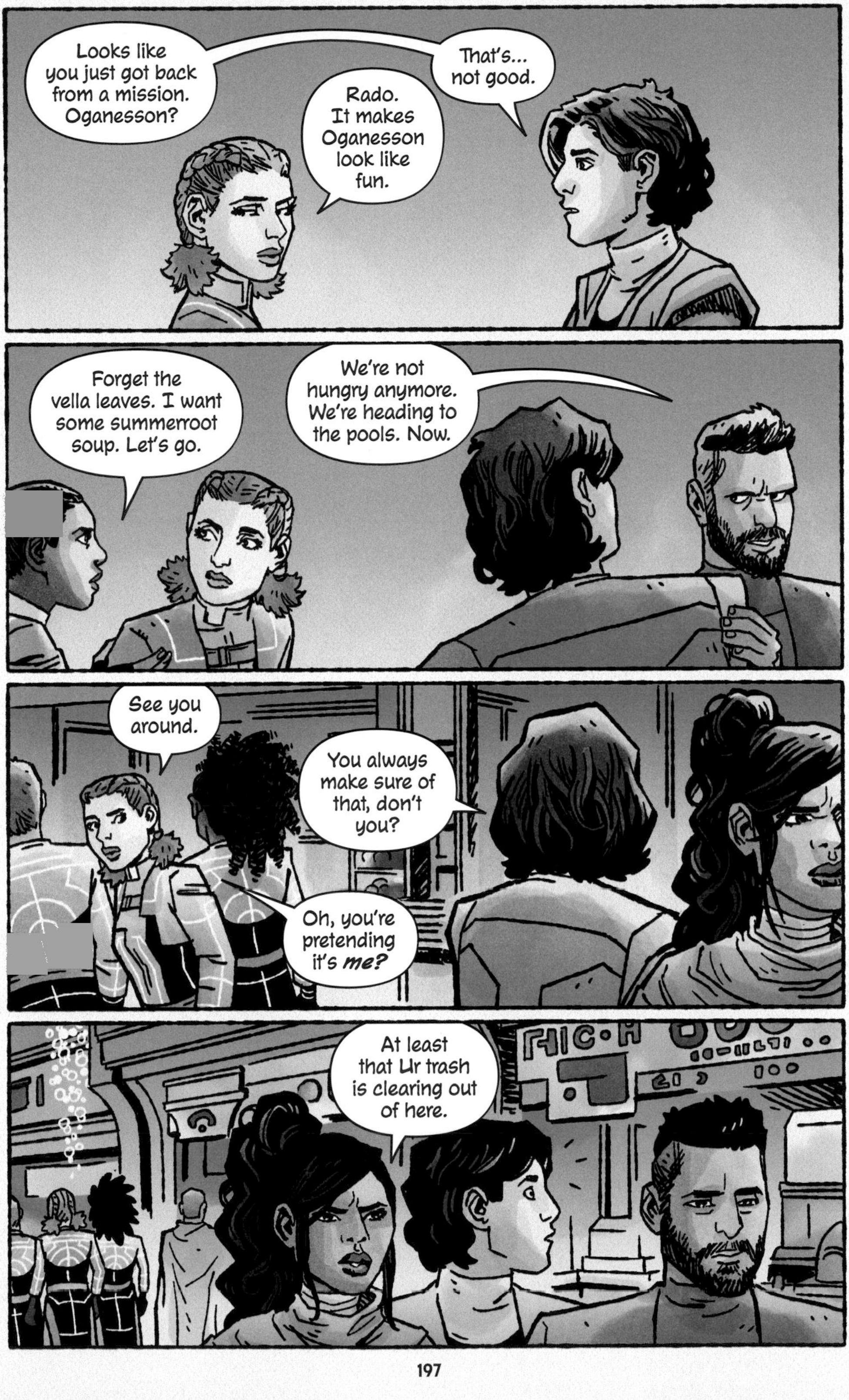

Looks like you just got back from a mission. Oganesson?
Rado. It makes Oganesson look like fun.
That's... not good.
Forget the vella leaves. I want some summerroot soup. Let's go.
We're not hungry anymore. We're heading to the pools. Now.
See you around.
You always make sure of that, don't you?
Oh, you're pretending it's *me?*
At least that Ur trash is clearing out of here.

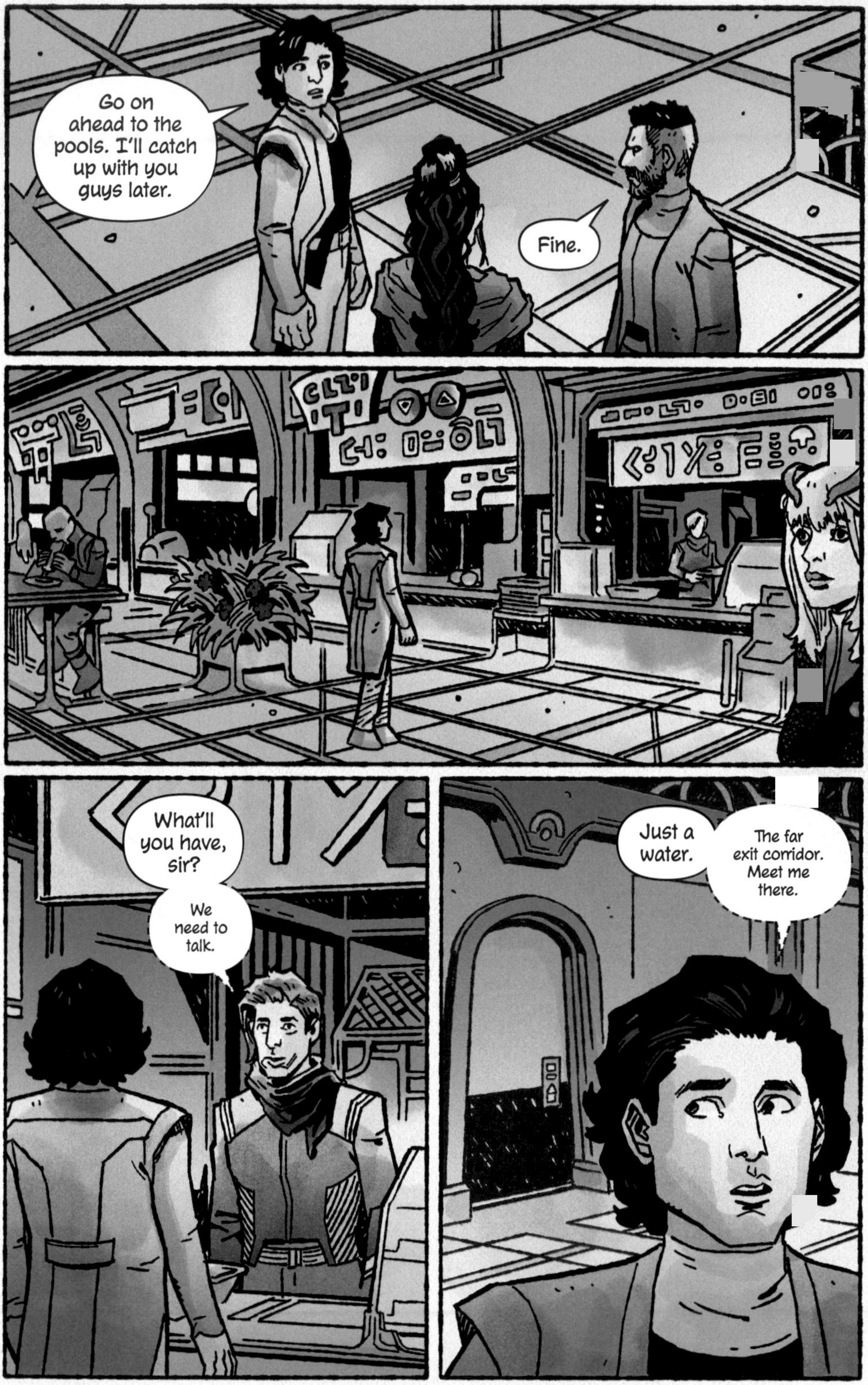
Go on ahead to the pools. I'll catch up with you guys later.
Fine.
What'll you have, sir?
We need to talk.
Just a water.
The far exit corridor. Meet me there.

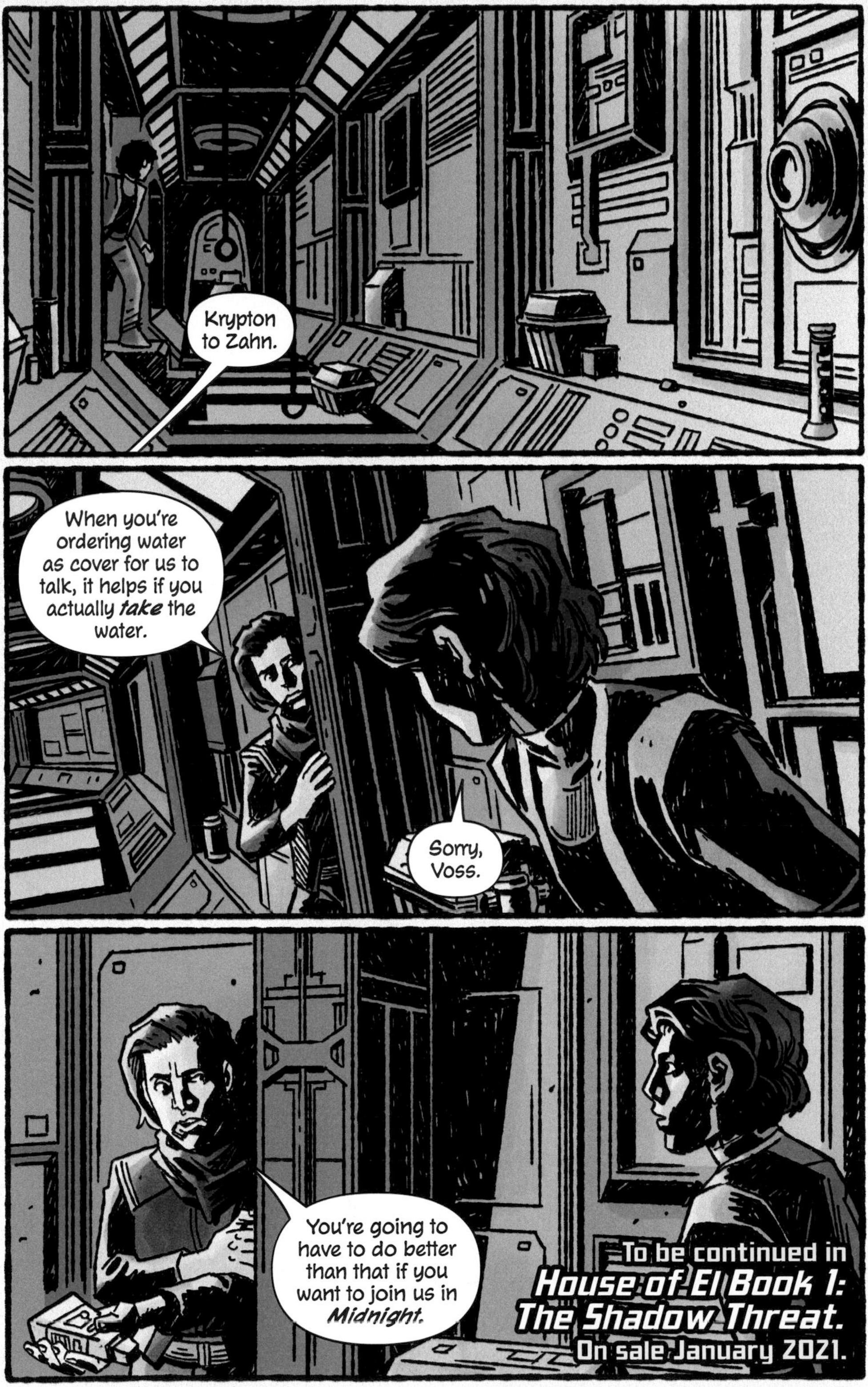
Krypton to Zahn.
When you're ordering water as cover for us to talk, it helps if you actually *take* the water.
Sorry, Voss.
You're going to have to do better than that if you want to join us in *Midnight*.
To be continued in
House of El Book 1: The Shadow Threat.
On sale January 2021.